5

CW01276330

To Judith, friend and neighbour,
with thanks for all your
encouragement over the years.

Becky

SETTLEMENT DAY

SETTLEMENT DAY

Rebecca Tinsley

HEADLINE

First published in 1994
by HEADLINE BOOK PUBLISHING

10 9 8 7 6 5 4 3 2 1

British Library Cataloguing in Publication Data

Tinsley, Rebecca
Settlement Day
I. Title
823.914 [F]

ISBN 0-7472-1243-0

Typeset by Keyboard Services, Luton, Beds

Printed and bound in Great Britain by
Mackays of Chatham PLC, Chatham, Kent

HEADLINE BOOK PUBLISHING
A division of Hodder Headline PLC
338 Euston Road
London NW1 3BH

For my grandparents
Kathleen and Eric Bryan

Prologue

June, Mount Laurel, New Jersey, USA.
Dick Zander was waiting for his Chief Executive Officer to finish a phone conversation next door. To pass the time he tapped out the melody of 'Mood Indigo' on the edge of his desk. Then he turned his leather upholstered chair to face a television screen in the mahogany cabinet in the corner of his office. It hissed white noise, like a hungry snake that wanted a video slotted into its mouth.

The office curtains had been drawn to shut out the brilliant summer sunshine currently transfiguring grey New Jersey with gleams of gold. But not even that blessing could relieve the monotony of the concrete sprawl around the Global Technologies compound. In every direction ran rows of identical modern factory units, each blank-faced box surrounded by employee car parks. Lines of cars stood glinting and baking in the sun like mosaics while their masters toiled inside the temperature-controlled atmosphere of the low-level buildings.

Perfect sailing weather – but would it last until Friday afternoon, when Zander could join his family on Long Island? In the meantime he was trapped here, playing his part as GT's Chief Financial Officer, making the money to pay for that brief glimpse of heaven at the end of every week.

Dick Zander was tall, bony and long-limbed, just the right side of fifty, with a narrow face and a year-round sailing tan. His high forehead was unlined, his blue eyes were clear, and his movements, like his mental processes, were quick and assured. He was working in shirt-sleeves, albeit Egyptian cotton ones from Jermyn Street – the same London tailor who made his dark pinstripe suits.

Max Clark walked in without so much as a knock or a word of greeting. Rotund and crumpled to the point of seediness, he moved smoothly across the mushroom-coloured carpet as if on castors. He slotted the video he was carrying into the machine, then fell back on the leather sofa which stood along one wall of Zander's office. As he reclined he wheezed like gas escaping from a balloon. His chest heaved and Zander noticed the perspiration beaded across his pale bald cranium. For a moment Clark chewed at his heavy jowls.

'Here's the latest from the Dermitron team. This is twenty-four hours after it's been sprayed. I haven't seen it yet, but the boys sounded pretty pleased.' He broke off to cough, and then waved a hand impatiently at the screen. 'The fertiliser's working like a dream, by the way. Damned plants are growing faster than ever.'

Zander pushed the Play button on the remote control and the machine clicked into life. Soon, the Chief Executive Officer and the Financial Officer of Global Technologies were watching a group of men shambling into a large greenhouse filled with vegetation. The camera's eye was positioned in one corner, but the men didn't seem conscious of it. They looked about at the foliage in bewilderment. Some had terror in their eyes. Others stood awkwardly, their ragged clothes hanging off them, quite unaware of the other men milling about the enclosed space.

'How come they're not Spics? I thought we did all this in Mexico.' Max Clark sounded puzzled and irritable.

'Don't have to any more,' Zander replied. 'Our friends are letting us have some units they've been using for drug testing – mentally ill or retards from state institutions. No relatives. Or the kind of relatives who are quietly relieved when they get a phone call saying their uncle or kid brother had an accident.'

'Makes it a lot cheaper for us, eh?' Clark said, still watching the lost-looking figures on the screen. 'I heard the Pentagon and the CIA were into this in the sixties, but I never quite believed it.' Then he chuckled.

The men wandering about in front of the camera had begun to rub their faces as if they were trying to protect their eyes. Zander checked his watch: it was two minutes since they had filed into the greenhouse. They appeared to be screaming, but as there was no sound on the film the two GT executives saw only their gaping mouths.

After three minutes, most of the men were writhing on the floor between the rows of plants, tearing at their clothing, their skin raw-looking. The flesh rapidly turned red, then almost black; the limbs flailed and the features contorted in agony. After four minutes, most of them were twitching heaps on the concrete floor. Then they were still.

Zander made a note on the pad of paper on his desk. He was without emotion, a businessman appraising the viability of a new product. He pushed the Rewind button of the video control, and looked at his boss. Clark rubbed his pudgy hands together.

'Great. They can't argue with that, eh?'

Zander nodded his agreement. Their customers would be pleased by the Dermitron test. And GT would sign another stream of contracts for something innocent-sounding like 'fertiliser'. Only their customers would know different.

Clark grinned and shifted his weight to heave himself up from the sofa. Then, puffing and flushed in the face, he hesitated.

'Hey,' he said to Zander with a hint of mischief. 'Let's see it again.'

Chapter One

2 July, the City, London

James Malpas closed the heavy pine doors of the Brodie McClean boardroom quietly behind him. He turned and began to walk along the plushly carpeted corridor, the words of the Chairman still ringing in his ears.

'Marketing is not what we do,' Sir Anthony Brook had told him with barely disguised contempt. 'Our reputation for financial prudence has always spoken for us.'

The other Brodie McClean board members had looked solemnly at the leather-bound notepads before them, leaving James to squirm. Privately they had assured their fellow director that they agreed with him wholeheartedly; the bank *did* need to promote its services in this increasingly competitive market. But those same spineless timeservers would never speak up when it mattered. The only colleague who had displayed any emotion during James's reprimand had been Charles Ravenscroft, the Chairman's preferred successor, who had found it hard to conceal his intense enjoyment.

James had left them to their pointless routine of mid-morning coffee and biscuits after the board meeting. He had more pressing matters to get on with in the Corporate Finance Department, and he knew that in his absence they would talk about him. Good, he thought as he paced along the corridor to the elevator: let them talk. Sir Anthony was stepping down at the end of the summer, and a new Chairman would be elected by the Brodie McClean board. Charles Ravenscroft was already behaving as if his victory were a foregone conclusion – but James suspected such complacency would work to his own advantage. The Corporate Finance Director knew he was the dark horse candidate, but his vociferous campaigns in the boardroom kept him right behind Charles, pulling his tail and snapping at his heels.

This morning's clash with the Chairman had been neither an isolated incident nor an unpremeditated one. At every opportunity James had raised questions about the board's decision to merge with an American bank. Charles Ravenscroft, as Head of Brodie McClean's International Operations, was in charge of negotiations between the venerable old London institution and Empire National Bank, a suitably top-drawer, long-established candidate in Manhattan. James accepted the logic of finding an overseas partner, but Charles's choice of bedmate concerned him, and he intended to sound the alarm bells as often as he could before a deal was signed.

Certainly the New York bank was highly regarded – by those who hadn't looked at its balance sheet in the last decade. From the outside, Empire National was comfortingly like its intended partner in London: a pillar of the financial community, and a bastion of sound judgement. Never mind that both banks had built their reputations in the days when only the very stupid or rash could lose money in merchant banking. Never mind that for generations its directors had backed dubious enterprises around the world without a second thought, from railway projects in Bolivia at the turn of the century, to Delorean cars.

Over the past fortnight, James had repeatedly drawn the board's attention to Empire's wobbly asset base, although his forthrightness had not been appreciated. They only had to listen to the gossip on Wall Street, he had said, or read the American business press to grasp the gravity of Empire's problems. What James really meant was that the arrogant, fuddy-duddy old fools who had clung to power at Empire for far too long had screwed up on a grand scale, and that the bank was a basket case waiting for a willing, gullible and equally incompetent suitor. Enter Brodie McClean.

The commanding heights of the bank had rejected James's analysis, but he had put down his marker, and when Empire National turned sour no one would be in any doubt who was to blame – nor who had warned them against the deal in the first place. As far as James was concerned, it was not a matter of 'if' but 'when'. He had the matter in hand already.

The thought of Charles Ravenscroft's impending derailment put a bounce into his step as he walked along the glass-walled corridor that skirted the atrium. The bank had been built in the shape of its corporate logo, a diamond. From up here, James could look down at eight decks of offices to an arrangement of fountains and trees at the bottom that had an entirely contrived appearance.

On the other side of the corridor ran beige walls adorned with the bank's collection of hideous but expensive paintings. Their modernity and cost alone justified their claim to be 'important' art. They were viewed within this institution as an investment, no more worthwhile or high-minded than funding toxic-waste incineration plants on Teeside.

In the reception area a secretary seated behind a monumental slab of dove-grey marble looked up from her word processor as she heard James's heels on the highly polished floor. He stood with his back to her, waiting for the elevator: he was tall, six foot two, and muscular. His Savile Row suit hung perfectly from his square shoulders, and its dark-blue pinstripe accentuated the length of his legs.

Suddenly he turned around, as if he had felt the receptionist's gaze on him. For a moment she was held by the steady brown eyes. They gleamed at her from beneath somewhat menacing eyebrows which met across the bridge of a long sharp nose. His dark brown hair, almost feathery in its fineness, was parted at the side, and flopped across his forehead.

A soft 'ting' announced the arrival of the elevator, and the receptionist looked down quickly. James contemplated her bowed head without interest, then stepped into the hexagonal glass cage which plunged to the sixth floor with a hushing noise.

'Anything important, Tess?' he asked briskly as he walked through his secretary's office. The horsey-looking blonde glanced up with a weary expression.

'About ten minutes ago. Sir Terence Purves, Martindale.'

The Honourable Tessa de Forrest held out a slip of paper and James took it without a word. He knew what Purves would want. Martindale, a big defence-equipment manufacturer, was one of Brodie McClean's largest corporate clients. Purves, the Managing Director, would be whingeing about the lacklustre performance of his share price, as if it was in Malpas's personal power to make it go up and down.

In the interest of keeping his client sweet, James would spare him the truth – that the market was bored by the post-Cold War defence sector *and* by Martindale, which it had labelled as a spivvy scrapmetal merchant. It had been yesterday's story. It was, in Cityspeak, 'toilet' – and everything good, and bad, about the company was 'in the price'.

James went into his own office, but he left the door open to discourage any slacking on Tessa's behalf. It was advisable for a man in his position to have a plummy, well-connected secretary, even if she did spend hours of her day arranging her social life with her idle friends.

He walked past the conference table at which he held his meetings, to a large desk in the corner. A blue and green imitation Tiffany lamp shone a gentle light on to the papers and reports which lay scattered over the shining surface. On the cream-coloured walls hung oil paintings of horses. Their virtue was age, and not much else. Directly over James's desk was a more modern painting of his own racehorse, Cleopatra.

As James sat down he reached for the phone and started to dial the Martindale number. He dreaded speaking to Purves, but it was not the Malpas way to delay anything unpleasant. Better to get it over and done with. He would tell the Managing Director that he was sending Paul Roberts, a bright new investment analyst from Brodie McClean's stockbroking wing, to see him. Legalities be damned. If anyone asked, which they wouldn't, James would claim it was a coincidence that the bank's technically separate equities operation was visiting Martindale. James would assure Purves that a solid 'buy' recommendation in a bullish Brodie McClean report would generate some positive interest amongst investors.

As he waited for the Martindale switchboard to respond, he sifted through the papers on his desk, then yelled: 'Tess, can you dig out that note on William Stone and Son plc, the one that arrived yesterday?'

A minute later Tessa, wearing a tweed suit more appropriate for a point-to-point than a City office, lolloped into James's office and handed him a report with the Brodie McClean diamond logo embossed on its cover. The Head of Corporate Finance scanned the front page until his eyes settled on the name of the author. He was waiting to be connected to Purves's secretary when he noticed Tessa waving another telephone message at him.

'I forgot. A Jim Zander rang. Some American,' she said casually, 'from Global Technologies. He said you'd met last year at the Lord Mayor's Banquet.' She looked rather doubtfully down her large nose. 'He and his wife are visiting London. That's his hotel number.' And she stalked back to her office.

James abandoned his call to Martindale and looked morosely at the name. It was typical of Tess to get it wrong – Jim instead of Dick. What did these little people matter to her, when she had an evening at Annabel's to look forward to, clutching some rampant young blue blood to her ample bosom?

At the Lord Mayor's Banquet, Zander had briefly mentioned that Global Technologies might be looking for a UK acquisition – something they could use as the cornerstone of their push into Europe – and they would need a corporate financier to advise them. James had followed up their chance meeting with a few copies of Brodie McClean research notes, but had heard nothing more. Sir Anthony Brook disapproved of costly unsolicited fishing expeditions to the United States, so that had been that. Until today.

Within thirty seconds he was speaking to the Chief Financial Officer of one of the world's largest military contractors. As they talked, James glanced through his diary and saw that he had Glyndebourne pencilled in for tomorrow. He had four tickets. The American was delighted by the idea of an evening of opera amongst Britain's great and good, and the legendary Marie Antoinette-like 'picnic' in the interval in the grounds of the fine Sussex stately home. They made it a date.

When James put down the phone he glanced out of the window, a wall of glass looking out at the Square Mile; office blocks, the Bank of England, and then mile upon mile of London, unfolding like a dirty old carpet to the distant suburbs.

Out there in Essex, amongst the rows of respectable, lower-middle-class semi-detached homes, was where James had grown up. His parents had struggled and saved to send him to a private prep school when he turned eight years old, but they had never begrudged him the sacrifice involved. It was due reward that the young James had excelled and been given glowing academic reports by his masters. Nothing should stand in the way of their clever child.

So Mrs Malpas had worked as a shop assistant, and her husband, a clerk with an insurance company, had put in even more overtime. Their gifted son had become the only boy in the street to go to a public school as a boarder; consequently they had been one of the few families in the neighbourhood who couldn't afford a new car. Only when James was safely at Bristol University (much to his parents' bewilderment and his own fury he had failed to get into Oxford) did his parents take a foreign holiday. All because James's education came first. But he tried to think about his ordinary origins and his parents as little as possible. And generally he succeeded.

Emerging from his brief reverie, he found he was grinding his teeth as the Chairman's censorious words came back to him. Whatever Sir Anthony Bloody Brook might think, James Malpas would not let a board of gutless, glorified bureaucrats stand in his way. Winning Global Technologies as a client would be an outstanding coup by anyone's standards, but he knew he would need the help of a military-equipment expert to find a suitable victim for the American predator. James was looking forward to meeting Paul Roberts, the broking operation's new defence analyst.

Then he wondered why he happened to have those much sought-after tickets to Glyndebourne, just when the American was in town.

He looked in his pocket diary, then took a pencil and wrote '*cancel parents*' on his notepad. For a moment he was puzzled by why he had been seeing them there in the first place. Then he remembered. Tomorrow he would be forty years old.

It was the third year in a row that they'd forgotten her birthday, but Charlotte Carter reminded herself that her parents led hectic lives. She loitered around her West London flat doing irrelevant chores, all the while pretending that she wasn't waiting for the postman, and making herself late to work in the process. There was always a chance that they might have mailed the card too late to reach her in time for her birthday, which was yesterday. Or so she had hoped as she filled in time dusting the leaves of her pot plants.

The postman only delivered the usual bills and timeshare offers, however, and Charlotte set off for Paddington Basin assuring herself that her parents were neither thoughtless nor unkind. They probably considered her far too grown-up to care about her twenty-eighth birthday, and like themselves, much too busy to be detained by such sentimentality.

When she finally arrived at the National News Network newsroom that morning there were no interesting financial stories around so Charlotte settled down at her desk with a sticky bun and a report on a company called William Stone & Son. It was one of hundreds of City research notes that were sent to business journalists like her by brokers looking for publicity, but this one had the virtue of being literate. It was written by an analyst called Paul Roberts from the stockbroking wing of Brodie McClean.

When she had read it for the second time she ate a chocolate bar by way of a minor celebration. The company that Roberts had profiled provided Charlotte with a good example of how British business had adapted to cuts in the military budget. Hardly a novel subject, but her programme editor wanted a piece that would be 'accessible' to the viewers. William Stone & Son plc would be part of that report.

Charlotte was struggling to concentrate on her work, however.

She had heard the Supremes singing 'Nothing But Heartaches' on the radio while she was in the bath, and it had been roaring through her head in ever-decreasing circles ever since. Combined with a slight hangover, it was rather irritating. She had stayed out late boozing with her fellow reporters last night. Their revelling had not been in honour of their colleague's birthday, though. She would never have admitted to them that she had no one to take her out on such an occasion.

Instead she had joined the regular migration from the newsroom to the wine bar after the five-thirty bulletin had been broadcast. She was doing that more and more often these days, tagging along for want of anything better to do. Her diary had been empty ever since she had wriggled out of an inappropriate friendship with a young man six months ago. He had been the last in a not-very-long line of 'mistakes' that Charlotte preferred not to think about, but often did.

How could she be such a bad judge of men, she wondered as she pretended to read an article about armoured personnel-carrier production? Was she the only woman in the world who came to her senses at the most awkward moment in a relationship? Was she alone in having those terribly embarrassing scenes where she tried to end a romance kindly but firmly, and without saying, 'I thought you were great but now I've got to know you I've realised you're a nerd'?

Charlotte wasn't looking for anything complicated, but the men she liked didn't like her. Or they turned out to be wimps or bastards, once you scraped away the obligatory interest in going to the theatre. She had decided to suspend her search until she knew what she wanted. In the meantime she would have another chocolate bar from the office vending machine, and hope rather optimistically that it didn't end up as flab or spots. Charlotte was five foot six, and well-covered – neither skinny nor fat – but occasionally, when she was feeling low, she pushed her luck by gorging mammoth quantities of chocolate.

The second delivery of newsroom post brought a pile of corporate press releases for Charlotte, none of which contained anything worth boring the viewers with this evening. There was also a Manilla envelope with nothing on the outside to identify its source. It stood out from the rest for that reason, and because it had been handwritten. Inside, she found photocopies of articles from American newspapers and business magazines. They concerned a Manhattan-based bank called Empire National, and they made rather grim reading.

There was also a photocopied bundle that had been stapled together. The cover page had a diamond logo on it, and Charlotte recognised it as Brodie McClean's. The same design had been on Paul Roberts's research note, and was familiar to any journalist who knew her way around London's financial scene. She leafed through the pages, looking for a compliment slip, or a note from whoever had sent her this interesting missive. There was none.

Charlotte pushed her shoulder-length chestnut hair behind her ears and got down to work. After ten minutes she had gleaned that these were the confidential minutes of a subcommittee of the merchant bank's main board, and they were about a merger deal with Empire National Bank. She looked back at the American articles and read them carefully. Then a smile crept across her face, and she wrinkled up her nose like a rabbit confronted with a pile of carrots.

'Bob,' she said brightly as she approached her boss. He was sitting at a desk in the other corner of the newsroom, thumbing through a tabloid newspaper. As she walked towards him, several journalists looked up from their computer news terminals and glanced at the pretty young reporter. They were not admiring their colleague's long legs but wondering if she had a juicy bit of news, and if so, would it knock their story out of the running order for this evening's bulletin.

The dishevelled programme editor sat like a buddha, with his belly pressing up against his desk. When Charlotte hovered in front of him he neither acknowledged her presence nor looked up from his paper, yet this lack of interest did not deter her. She was used to doing the hard sell to get her boss interested in any idea.

'Bob, I've learnt that Brodie McClean is about to merge with an American investment bank,' she began, hoping that she didn't sound too self-important. 'Someone on this side of the pond clearly doesn't think much of it. They've sent me some confidential minutes of a meeting, and a wodge of material from America that suggests Brodie McClean's making a big mistake.'

She knew that the word 'confidential' would do it. Bob looked up and scratched under his arm. He appeared to be chewing his cud for a moment, then he blinked – all recognisable precursors to action. Charlotte laid the photocopied articles in front of him and waited.

'All right,' he said wearily, 'get out there with a crew. I want a three-minute piece.'

Gary Smith was bored. He slouched at his desk at Brodie McClean, ignoring the Stock Exchange terminals in front of him, and flicked through *Penthouse*. Around him sat other Identikit young dealers, a new Aryan master race of moneymakers. Their uniform was cheaply fashionable but the trousers were too tight and showed the line of their underwear. The shirts also gave them away: thin white cotton-and-polyester mix, and meanly cut. And their ties were vulgar Jermyn Street imitations; the colours were too vivid, the designs too unsubtle for St James.

This new model army had open, belligerent faces, with hair clipped too short to allow any to flop on to their foreheads and thus soften the effect. The bone structure they consequently displayed so boldly betrayed their ancestral link; the knobbly turnip-faces of their East End grandfathers.

Long-established City firms like Brodie McClean owed their success to a combination of aristocrats and cunning young dealers. The yobs had moved from shifting hot merchandise on the Whitechapel Road, to the dealing rooms of the great pillars of the financial establishment. The nobs, on the other hand, were groomed for the profession from birth. They were the smooth front men who charmed the clients and presented the sophisticated corporate image, leaving the control of supply and demand in stocks to their quicker-witted social inferiors.

'Mind if I take a seat, Gary?' asked a cheerful, deep, Mancunian voice beside him. 'What's going on this afternoon?'

Gary shrugged his shoulders and ran his fingers through the blond moussed tufts of his hair with a sigh. The new analyst sat down beside him.

Brodie McClean had recruited Paul Roberts fresh from Cambridge; he was one of the grammar-school brains that had been sandwiched between the City's yobs and nobs in recent years. Paul had a broad handsome face, a mop of straight, light-brown hair and, Gary noted with approval, a less wimpish physique than the other pointy-head analysts. They were the kind of swotty creeps Gary had hated at school – the boys who had stayed on and studied, while Gary was on his way to his first BMW.

'How's my research note on William Stone and Son going down?' Paul asked pointedly, unsure if Gary was listening. Most of the investment analysts avoided contact with the salesmen, whom they regarded as simplistic and hostile to the finer points of financial analysis. In fact, they reminded them of the thugs they'd feared at school.

Paul was one of the few who walked down the long office from the monastic peace of the Research Department to the rowdy bear garden of the dealing room. Back behind the safety of their glass partition, eight bright young men and women sat silently at their desks, bent over calculators, working out financial ratios with which they evaluated one company against another. None of them had ever considered a career in industry, 'making' anything. Not enough money, and far too slow to promote clever people. Who wanted to live in Birmingham anyway?

Paul Roberts's job was to predict which military-equipment firms would give the best financial performances. He wrote in-depth 'notes' on each company, and sent them to Brodie McClean's clients with a recommendation to buy or sell the stock. Suggesting a 'hold' earned the bank no commission, and made the salesmen grumble.

Paul had not been in the Square Mile long enough to realise how rarely his notes were read. Had he known that threequarters of all the expensively-produced broking research went straight into the dustbin, he might have been less dedicated. Paul chatted to the salesmen like Gary because he wanted them to market his ideas to the clients. His analyst colleagues told him not to waste his time on the morons at the other end of the room. They couldn't read anyway.

By the same token the salesmen thought the analysts were overpaid theorists. As Gary listened to Paul talking in his intense way about some technical detail, he wondered if this brainbox could tell when a company's finance director was lying about next year's profit outlook. In Gary's book that was more important than understanding how a torpedo worked.

The salesman fiddled with his monogrammed gold bracelet as Paul told him about William Stone & Son. After five minutes the analyst drew breath and said, 'It's a good story, isn't it?'

Gary nodded absentmindedly and tapped his keyboard to get the Stone share price up on the screen. After a pause he said, 'What's going on then?'

Paul felt a stab of panic in his stomach.

'Come on, why should I stuff clients into Stone?'

'Well,' Paul started uncertainly, 'there's this ecological product which'll make them lots of money, but I promised not to talk about it till it's launched. I gave my word to David Stone, the Managing Director . . .' His words trailed off as he noticed the salesman yawn. Their eyes met.

'So what's the story?' Gary persisted.

Paul struggled to make his brain respond under fire. 'I just did a TV interview about the company,' he began, hoping he could revive the salesman's interest.

It worked. Gary turned on him with fury in his eyes. 'Why the fuck didn't you tell me that before? Christ, you're a fucking tosspot!'

Paul watched the salesman shake his head in disbelief. 'It's not going out for a few days,' he ventured. 'NNN is doing a profile on Stone.' Then, trying to put some determination in his voice: 'I'll find out when it's going to be shown, right?'

He would welcome an excuse to call the attractive reporter who had interviewed him that afternoon – Charlotte Something. The idea gave him a pleasant warm feeling, but he was distracted by

Gary snorting at the William Stone & Son share price on his terminal.

'Oh, the boys in dark glasses'll really pile into a sexy performer like that, won't they?' he sneered. 'What about the trading range?'

'I don't understand.' Paul stared at him.

'Course you don't.' Gary laughed bitterly. 'You don't get the first bloody thing about this game, do you?'

Paul studied his shoes and tried to avoid the taunting face. He sat rigid beside Gary, wondering what he was supposed to say.

'Give me something no one else in the market knows, a bit of gossip to make my clients buy a few shares in this fucking tossbag company. Heard of "price-sensitive" information, haven't you?' The salesman spat the words towards Paul, and reclined in his chair with a look of disgust on his undistinguished features.

The bewildered analyst sat up straight and thought furiously, but nothing came to mind. It didn't occur to him that Gary was suggesting they should break the insider-trading rules; that any salesman worth his Porsche was an inside trader every day of the week, and had nothing but contempt for the self-regulating City apparatus. How else did a firm of brokers drum up a sale with so much competition for so little business?

'Tell you what,' Gary said in an altogether different tone of voice. 'Fancy coming for a sharpener with me and the boys after work?'

Paul wondered if Gary was being sarcastic, but he looked friendly enough. The cloud had passed from his face. 'Great,' said Paul, not sure what a sharpener might be, but eager to be in on whatever was going on.

Charlotte was thrown forward as Steve, her cameraman, stepped on the brakes of the Peugeot Estate. She felt the seatbelt tighten and protect her from smashing through the windscreen, but her pen never left the page of the notebook in her lap. She was sketching out the script as they roared through the capital's streets, to save precious minutes when she reached the editing suite at NNN's studios.

Charles Ravenscroft would have to go in her report, even though he had neither confirmed nor denied that Brodie McClean was involved in merger talks. Evidently Ravenscroft had taken pity on her, however: when she mentioned that she intended to interview one of his colleagues about William Stone & Son, he had summoned the defence analyst immediately. Time was running out for the clock-conscious reporter, but when Paul Roberts walked into the room, she decided to delay her next appointment. She liked the look of him.

After the interview, Charlotte asked Paul if she might run him through her profit forecasts when she was putting the piece together. He readily agreed, and for a moment the reporter believed that they were looking at each other with a good measure of mutual appreciation. Later, sitting in the traffic jam on the way back to Paddington Basin, she wondered if she'd imagined it. Romantic chance encounters didn't happen to young women like her.

The mobile phone warbled, and Charlotte suppressed a groan. A call from the newsroom at this stage meant the story had been dropped because of something 'big' like a plane crash. Who would give a damn about Brodie McClean, if the network had colour pictures of bits of body scattered about a mangled airframe? It would be a 'good' story if lots of people were dead. It would be 'great' if the passengers had been white and English-speaking. And it would be 'really corking' if someone, preferably a child, had survived, and could tell the viewers what it had felt like. News values were in inverse proportion to human values.

Relief was replaced by a sinking sensation when she realised that it was Jonathan Slope, a business reporter at the BBC. Charlotte had only to think of his weasel-like face framed by never-quite-clean blond hair, his sharp features and bright beady eyes magnified by his John Lennon glasses, and she felt sick.

'Charlotte, I wondered what you were doing on the cancellation of the Jap car plant in Wales? Wouldn't want people to think you were copying me.' This was Jonathan's usual approach. He would use a 'professional' matter as an excuse, then suggest dinner in an off-hand manner, as if the idea had just occurred to him.

On the one occasion when she had accepted, Charlotte had soon realised her mistake. When they were seated at a little table in a rather too cosy Italian restaurant in Soho, he had moved conversation away from work immediately. His confiding manner, the unsubtle inquiries about whether she lived alone, and the constant refilling of her glass with the indifferent chianti, set off an alarm.

As she listened to him now, Charlotte could still see his dirty fingernails creeping across the table towards hers, like Thing, the bodyless hand in the Addams Family. When the moment of rejection had arrived, Jonathan had been without grace. Her reluctance to sleep with him somehow became her problem, not his. Why was she so cold and untactile?

Charlotte leaned her head against the window and looked out at a heap of rotting vegetables left in the gutter by a barrow. A cloud of flies was swarming around it – a fitting metaphor for herself, and the type of men she attracted. To make matters worse, 'Nothing But Heartaches' had returned for another sprint around her brain. 'Jonathan, I'm in the middle of a story,' she said finally.

There was a pause. 'I'll look forward to your weighty analysis,' he said, and rang off.

Charlotte replaced the mobile phone on the floor by her feet, thinking how typical it was of Jonathan to counter with a gibe about her intellect. Whenever she got a scoop, he suggested that she had 'used her female charms' to extract the information. Quite why he chased her was a mystery. It was on a par with that great unsolved question about the music of the Carpenters: Charlotte loathed their songs, but was word-perfect on every one. *Why?*

'I did a bit of work in Belfast last week,' the cameraman announced, as if he was recounting highlights of his holidays. As he chatted he drove fast and wild, causing people who were hovering on the edge of pedestrian crossings to skip back on to the pavement.

Charlotte, already jittery about how little time she had before the news bulletin, abandoned all hope of writing her script. 'The Falls Road bomb?' she asked, as they whined down Eastbourne Terrace.

'Yeah. Coppers wouldn't let us near, even when we told them we had to get shots for the lunchtime show. So the reporter said,

"Look, I need film, even if it's just exteriors." But they wouldn't let us in. The Chief Copper said they were still searching for something. And the reporter said, you know, "Give me a break". And the copper, he says, "Look, there was a little boy, five years old he was. And we still can't find his head".'

When the car shuddered to a halt at the NNN entrance, a rather green Charlotte gathered her belongings in her arms and ran into the lobby of the studios.

Chapter Two

From David Stone's office window he could see wheatfields stretch to the horizon. The monotony of the Cambridgeshire Fen was broken only by the occasional house, cowering under an enormous grey sky. Cereals and vegetables flourished in this rich earth, making the area the breadbasket and market garden of the nation. Which was why a Yorkshire farming family like the Stones had settled there 200 years ago.

Within two generations, the Stones had become landed gentry who employed others to till their broad acres. Their fiefdom was Westhorpe Hall, a seventeenth-century manor house, ten miles from the ancient cathedral town of Ely. The Hall was a miserable stone building with windows like mean little eyes, and a tiled roof almost green with lichen. It lay at the end of a long gravel drive, behind clumps of trees and a high wall. Although the village had sprung up to accommodate the servants and farm labourers employed at the Hall, these lesser mortals had been kept well at bay, and when they came and went, it was with much doffing of caps.

When David Stone's father William inherited the estate in the 1940s, he had taken control of a significant business – although a gentleman would never have attached such a vulgar word to the making of his livelihood. But the young William Stone was not content to spend his mornings keeping an eye on the farmworkers, and the afternoons shooting, as his own father had done.

Instead, the unconventional William had experimented to increase crop yields, had bought the latest North American machinery, and had borrowed money to expand. It was unheard-of for a squire farmer to set up a canning factory on his own land, but William ignored his more feudal Cambridgeshire peers. The neighbouring gentlemen farmers told him politely that he was mad, but they were soon paying William good money to hire his Massey-Ferguson harvesters; his cousins shook their heads and predicted disaster, but within the year they were bringing their produce to William's canning plant.

By the time David was born in the mid-fifties, his father's company had branched into other areas, more by accident than design. For years William had purchased calibrated weighing machines which were used in bundling up vegetables. When the man who owned the weighing-machine company died, William bought it – and the range expanded into increasingly sophisticated measurement products with applications in the defence sector, where engineers needed to gauge the electrical output from components. The reliable farming interests that had sustained generations of his ancestors had been transformed.

In 1979 William was called to Buckingham Palace to accept a knighthood for his services to industry. His only disappointment on that sunlit day when he strode proudly through the tall gates at the end of the Mall was that his only child , David, wasn't at his side to witness the pinnacle of his career. The young man had refused to return from Florence where he was studying art history.

In later years the old man blamed himself for never having been concerned enough by 'family things'. He had married the daughter of another Cambridgeshire landowner, not out of love, but because that was the sort of thing a chap did. William never wondered if he or Isabel were happy: he was far too busy with his company. At the age of eight, the boy had been sent to Grantchester House, the same preparatory school that he had attended. William assumed that ten years later David would join the business; he had not foreseen having a son who had no interest in farming nor in any other form of enterprise. The boy was clearly clever: his school reports were consistently excellent, as William found when he reviewed David's progress at the end of each term.

But when the eighteen-year-old announced that he had been offered a place at an Italian university, William was incoherent with rage. Agricultural college would have been quite a different matter, but he forbade his son to attend any university, let alone a foreign one. David, who benefited from a trust fund, had enough money to pay his own fees, so he simply left the country, and sent his mother a Post Office box number where he could be reached.

After his degree, David stayed on in Florence to teach at the university. He returned to Westhorpe Hall only once, to attend Isabel's funeral; his mother had died in a riding accident, thrown from a skittish horse. He and his father had had almost nothing to say to each other, and David had caught the next plane back.

Two years later, however, the world of father and son was once more disrupted. On a warm spring afternoon David had returned from a study trip to Siena to find a telegram from England: William had suffered a stroke, just before his sixty-third birthday.

David had sat in his study, a sun-tanned young man with brown eyes and gently waving brown hair, and examined the piece of paper in his hands. The happy world that he had built around himself had been destroyed in one blow. He was an only child and there was no one to cope with the changes that William's demise would demand. He flew back to England the next day.

While his father lay in hospital, David went through the family firm's accounts and was horrified by what he found. Profits were static, and no one had modernised the production lines in years. The management were glorified farmhands, his father's underlings who had simply obeyed the boss – as long as the boss was there and taking an interest.

Now the firm was unsaleable, except at a knockdown price, and that was unacceptable to David. No one would be allowed to pick up for a song what it had taken generations of his family to build. It would have alarmed him to know that exactly the same thoughts had motivated his father years before.

When William came out of hospital and got to grips with a course of physiotherapy, his determination to get better surprised his son. It was not until several months later that David realised the stroke had been quite minor. He began to suspect that he had been brought back from Italy on false pretences – but by then his father had won. David was hooked; he had given up everything and was firmly at the helm of the family business.

Since neither man could contemplate living under the same roof, a barn on the estate was converted into a home for William, with room for a nurse. The company factories lay in the fields at the back of Westhorpe Hall, discreetly hidden behind a copse planted by David's great-grandfather.

After six months, William was back on his feet, poking his head into the offices and asking why they were closing the canning operation and starting a fresh-vegetable facility. 'Canning has always done this family well,' he growled, swinging his walking stick menacingly.

The canning plant had been losing a quarter of a million pounds a year, but Stone Senior refused to listen. His methods had been fine, he insisted, even the handwritten account books, and the stock control jotted down on the back of an envelope. When David brought in computer terminals and employed a qualified accountant, William swore the firm was about to turn belly up.

Yet after two years of David's reluctant management, sales and profits had more than doubled. William was still scornful, however. 'Can't you even organise the gardeners?' he would ask, looking at the state of the flowerbeds in front of the offices. Even David's choice of wife caused weeks of cutting comments on how he was marrying beneath him.

David remembered seeing Helen at dances in Ely when he was a teenager. At sixteen she had been attractive in a dark sultry way, with a full and curvaceous figure while her classmates were flat-chested and narrow-hipped. The adolescent David was beneath her curiosity, but when he returned from Italy they met again, and this time the twenty-six-year-old Helen showed a good deal more interest.

Six months later they were married, despite William's protests – voiced only to David. Helen settled into Westhorpe Hall happily, astonished at her good fortune in marrying a wealthy man, even if he was often preoccupied and inattentive. While her first husband, an agro-chemicals salesman, had spent his spare time messing around with his car, or watching sport on television, David hid inside books she found too boring to open, let alone read.

But she was hardly going to complain about that while she had everything she wanted – a nanny to look after their baby son, clothes from Paris and Milan, jewellery from Bond Street and Fifth Avenue, and a Lotus Eclat. Even though David was always at the factory, she occupied herself by spending his money – on Cartier watches, Gucci bags, yet more shoes to add to the mountain in her dressing room. Her husband never complained. He never said anything. He just worked, and paid.

Five years after David had taken over William Stone & Son he had transformed the company, and the next and obvious step was the Unlisted Securities Market of the Stock Exchange. The flotation was well received, despite his father's scepticism, and the stock became a reliable, if unexciting holding for investors.

Once he had modernised the firm, David began the search for a proprietorial product, something unique that no one else was making. Inspiration came in the form of straw. Ever since he was a child, David had known that straw kept animals warm. He reasoned that the same basic material could keep takeaway food warm, and it would be cheaper to make than polystyrene, and more ecologically sound, too. Once he had the idea for 'Verdi', as he had christened it, David needed the technological brain to make it happen. He had found her at nearby Cambridge University, and on this wet July afternoon was on his way to check up on Sarah, who had joined the company a month before.

From the outside the lab looked like any other farm-building, but inside it was sparkling white, and spotlessly clean; a far cry from the sickly-smelling school labs of his boyhood at Grantchester House where the sinks were stained and cracked, and the shelves of bottles were covered in dust. Here there was the most up-to-date equipment, and little bowls of straw in different stages of torture.

When David walked in he found Sarah sitting on a tall lab stool, writing up her notes. She was thin and pale, like a fragile flower that has been grown in a darkened room, or in her case a chemistry lab. She wore her long blonde hair drawn back from her face in a severe bun, and a pair of gold-rimmed spectacles ledged on her rather bumpy nose. Only the husband that she had, somewhat to her own surprise, acquired ever made direct contact with those nervous eyes, but to David that was fine. He was paying Sarah for her scientific skill, not for her conversational ability.

He was reluctant to pressure Sarah for results, but today she had news for him. As he took a seat she pulled something out of a drawer in her bench. When she straightened up David could see she had a small cardboard box in her hands. She handed it to him. 'It's in there, Hamburger Container Number One,' she mumbled quietly. 'I was going to give it to you when you had a spare moment.'

Her diffidence made David smile. She must have known this would delight him, and yet she presented the first concrete evidence of her work as though it were the mouldy remains of a sandwich. The United Nations would soon be considering a world ban on styrene monomers because they were thought to be destroying the ozone layer, and to be carcinogenic. A ban would mean the end of polystyrene, and David would have the ideal alternative material ready for the fast-food industry. The timing of Verdi could not have been better.

Back in his office he sifted through the pile of telephone messages that his secretary had put on his desk. Sheila usually added a helpful remark like: '*this one isn't urgent, even though he thinks he is*'. She had been with the company for fifteen years, and could be relied to organise her boss's life efficiently.

'You're telepathic,' he told her as she followed him into his room with a cup of coffee. 'What would I do without you?' he asked.

Her chubby face broke into a smile. They were the same age, thirty-eight, but bearing three children had taken a toll on Sheila's figure and left lines around her eyes.

'Your father would like you to call him,' she said as she watered the plants on his windowsill. She waited for him to sigh, which he did. 'You know he just wants to be kept in touch with what's going on.'

David nodded silently. She was probably right, but it didn't make it any easier for him to deal with the cantankerous old man.

'The lady from NNN said she'd appreciate it if you could call her back tomorrow morning because she's working on tonight's news now.' Sheila pointed to the message. 'Charlotte Carter – you know, the reporter on the NNN news.' David looked blank. 'Oh, you must have seen her,' Sheila said, a note of exasperation in her Cambridgeshire voice.

'I wonder what she wants with us?' he asked, alarmed that some word of Verdi might have leaked out. That would be unhelpful, to say the least.

'And you're going into Ely to see Mr Jarvis in half an hour,' Sheila reminded him as she returned to her adjoining office.

'Thanks,' he muttered, and as he sipped his coffee he rehearsed what he would say to his solicitor. Beginning divorce proceedings was hardly a comfortable subject to broach.

It was not in David's nature to put the blame on Helen. He had tried to give her everything she wanted, almost as compensation for the lack of sympathy he had to offer. But the physical desire they felt for each other had subsided with time. What disturbed him was that no bond of friendship or even mutual respect survived. When their young son had died from leukaemia two years ago, nothing remained to hold them together. Some couples might have been made stronger by such an event, but Billy's death had exposed all the deficiencies in his parents' unhappy partnership.

From that terrible period onwards, neither of them had any reason to disguise their real feelings. Helen had contempt for the things David held dear – opera, antiques, walks in the country – they meant nothing to her. She wanted to be part of the local circuit of shindigs and dinner parties, whereas David loathed such 'meaningless socialising'. When they were invited to events like a Cambridgeshire Hawaiian Evening, Helen went with her own 'friends', complete with fake tan and hoolahoola skirt, while David snorted his contempt and stayed at home with a Graham Greene or Julian Barnes.

He had moved into a different bedroom twelve months earlier, and had stopped asking her .where she had been when she came home late, or who it was who telephoned so often and hung up whenever David answered. It seemed futile to carry on.

One of the notes on his desk reminded him about the Ely Cathedral Restoration Fund Dinner that evening. He would have to call Helen about it. She never remembered such 'dull bloody things'; she, the through-and-through provincial, down to her tendency to overdress, even for a trip to Sainsbury's. Or her belief that Harrods was still the top people's store. More like the top taxi drivers' store, David had scolded her.

He let the phone ring fifteen times but there was no reply. Who knew where she was, or what she was doing? He only hoped she hadn't been drinking: her bad-tempered little girl scenes were humiliating for both of them.

Then he realised he needed his father's signature on several documents. Although the old man was quite willing to have his son manage the business day to day, William Stone still presided at board meetings like an ageing Sicilian godfather. As he was passing Sheila's desk, David told her he was popping over to his father's, and would be back soon.

'Then put on a jumper or something,' she said briskly. 'It's quite chilly.' David stopped in his tracks and returned to his office for a jumper. He was wearing a light-blue button-down shirt and jeans. As he left he heard his secretary mutter, 'It's like dealing with a four-year-old child.' But there was only affection in her voice and it had a strangely cheering effect on him.

He had reached the copse when the sound of his wife's laughter made him turn around. Between the trees he saw a car parked by the Hall's back door. Getting into it was someone vaguely familiar, a man who used to work for him as a components buyer. He had sacked him for taking bribes from suppliers. For a moment David was puzzled by the man's presence at Westhorpe Hall. Then he realised why Helen hadn't answered the phone.

He broke into a run and reached the car just as the door was closing. He yanked it open and hauled the startled young man out by the throat. Helen cowered in the doorway as David pushed her visitor across the bonnet with one furious shove. But he thought better of punching his usurper, and stood back before his temper led him into worse trouble. 'Now get out of here!' he barked.

As the young man scrambled back into his car, David looked across at his flustered wife and shook his head slowly. 'Not under our roof,' he said in a voice both cold and full of pain. 'Not in the house where we raised Billy. Do what you want, if you must, but find somewhere else to do it.'

Then he turned and walked towards his father's house with as much self-possession as he could muster.

James Malpas closed the door of his black BMW and turned the key in the ignition. He savoured the first roar of the supersexed engine, then eased the machine out of its space and accelerated up the ramp of the underground car park beneath the Brodie McClean building.

He hated the congested rush-hour streets of the Square Mile, so he waited until 'the little people' had gone their way before he left the office. Every evening he went to the gymnasium in the company's fitness complex and then had a swim. It gave him a feeling of superiority that while his competitors were boring each other in City wine bars, or waiting for commuter trains that didn't materialise, he was tuning his muscles, keeping his body lean. Not for him the feeble-minded routine of drinking with the guys after hours. That was weakness. Nothing was gained.

His social life revolved around his clients, be it racing at Goodwood, the Henley Regatta, fishing in Scotland, hunting in Northamptonshire, or shooting on the North Yorkshire Moors later on in the summer. It was 'connecting' – and it all contributed to the success of James Malpas. He never refused an opportunity to make contacts with influential people.

This evening was just such an opportunity. James was heading for a drinks party in Knightsbridge where the host was another merchant banker, a director at Morton's. It was a rival firm, but it was useful to know well-placed men with whom he could exchange gossip and eventually favours, and widen his City network. It had purpose.

The rain had stopped but the empty pavements of Cheapside and High Holborn still shone dully, and the atmosphere was sticky. Within his air-conditioned car James was protected from the stink of rubbish piled outside the bug-infested sandwich bars. Nor did he notice the scattered army of Asian and West Indian women stepping down from buses, and heading for banks and insurance companies. There they would begin their second or third job of the day, cleaning up the offices of people who had long ago departed for a bottle of champagne.

As he powered down Kingsway, James savoured the tightness of his muscles, still tingling from his session in the gym. He didn't need music in the car; the adrenalin throbbing in his veins provided a stronger beat than any drums could produce.

He felt particularly in harmony with his body this evening because he had just enjoyed a special physical release, as well as the usual weightlifting and exercising. Like John F. Kennedy, he got a headache unless he had intercourse every three days. Unlike the late President, however, Malpas was not overly concerned about the sex of his conquest. It had taken him a couple of weeks to woo the boy from the bank's postroom away from the rowing machine and into the changing rooms, but he had finally succeeded.

Malpas experienced a burning sensation in his abdomen, and his legs stiffened like steel hawsers as he recalled that brief but forceful union beneath the jet of hot water in the showers. The boy had acted the helpless young thing, pawing at the side of the shower cubicle as he feigned fright, overwhelmed by his cruel and dominating conquerer. Even more alluring was the gasp when James had forced himself inside. Malpas preferred a bit of spit to lubricate his way rather than a wimpish wipe of Vaseline, and the boy had groaned and struggled as James pushed in. It had increased Malpas's enjoyment, because he had to hold him down roughly.

Most satisfactory, he thought, unaware of how banal and clichéd his fantasies were.

The BMW cruised through the underpass from Piccadilly to Knightsbridge, into the part of London he recognised as 'his'. James's mental map of the capital missed out the hell-holes around Leicester Square, Oxford Street or Tottenham Court Road: they were blanks between the City and the Royal Borough of Kensington and Chelsea.

James was also buzzing this evening because of Charlotte Carter's piece on the NNN News. Charles Ravenscroft was reputedly white with rage, stalking the corridors in search of the leaker. He had cross-questioned every member of the subcommittee, but alas he was looking in the wrong place, thought the Corporate Financier maliciously. If only Ravenscroft would learn to lock his filing cabinet, or more specifically, the cabinet of his dim Old Harrovian Personal Assistant . . .

The thought of Charles's misery amused James for the rest of the journey, but once he was at the Mortons' drinks party his mind was focused on business once more. He sipped mineral water as he surveyed the high-ceilinged salon that bubbled with talk, and was saturated with cigar smoke and perfume. Around him were self-confident men concerned with money, and their decorative women, swathed in shining materials that clung to their carefully-starved bodies. Unlike an equivalent gathering in New York they weren't necessarily talking about money, but they were thinking about it, sizing up the earning power of the other people in the room, or the value of their information, their contacts or their jewellery.

Within minutes James was in conversation with the man who ran Morton's environmental investment portfolio. They discussed how badly the bank's fund had performed, although it was no worse than other so-called 'ethical' funds. The problem, the Morton Fund Manager explained mournfully, was that consumers only switched to eco-friendly products when they were cheaper, such as lead-free petrol. Otherwise, he said, people did not connect the destruction of the ozone layer with their own lifestyles. As ever, James asked intelligent questions, and when they parted they exchanged cards, then moved on to circulate like beautifully-cut garments in an exceptionally ritzy washing machine.

The same could not be said for the back room at the Bricklayer's Arms, just off London Wall. Paul Roberts had taken up Gary's offer of a sharpener after work. That was several hours ago, and they had progressed from one wine bar to the next, a group of eight of them from the dealing room at Brodie McClean.

By nine o'clock Paul had lost his wariness of the market-makers and was enjoying their rough humour, although he found it a struggle to keep up with their phenomenal consumption of hard liquor. At university he'd been able to down eight pints of bitter a night with the best of them, but champagne, followed by serious vodka and tonics, were another matter.

As the evening progressed they moved downmarket, from the chrome and rubber spaceship-like interior of 'Coates Karaoke Bar & Restaurant', to the brown Anaglytpa walls of the Bricklayer's Arms. When they arrived the back room was already blue with smoke, and packed with shirt-sleeved young men. The sticky evening air had not cleared, and everyone abandoned the vodka regime for more refreshing pints of lager.

Kevin, the man of the moment, was holding court by the bar, surrounded by other market-makers from rival firms whom he'd got to know during his ten years in the City. He was a blond and beefy, second-generation Irishman with nothing but scorn for his father, who had spent his life taking orders from some little Hitler on a building site. Kevin earned more in a year than his old dad had in ten. He planned to be very rich by the time he was thirty. It was tiresome that the girl he had been screwing had got herself pregnant, especially as she insisted on getting married as well as living with him. But he had no intention of allowing her to stand in his way, he assured all those present at his stag party.

Kevin had undone his collar and rolled up his sleeves, revealing no neck whatsoever and white, hairless forearms the size of hams. He stood with his feet planted wide apart, and his belly overhanging his belt. The pint glass never left his hand, except when it was exchanged for a full one. The young men around him laughed at everything he said, and offered him cigarettes as he reached the end of each one that dangled from his lower lip.

At one point they were distracted by a commotion in the doorway. There was a chorus of wolf-whistles, and 'Whoo-ers!' and the crowd parted to make way for a tall blonde in high-heeled boots, wrapped in a black velvet cape. When Kevin was pointed out she advanced towards him, and another chorus of grunting approval swelled up. When the cape fell to the floor they cheered and applauded. She was wearing black stockings, black gloves, a suspender belt, and a black leather one-piece suit with a high collar and an enormous zipper down the front.

Kevin's eyes disappeared into slits as he grinned. He'd been hoping that his mates might have arranged a strip-o-gram. They chanted as the well-built creature stood in front of the groom-to-be and began to rub her crotch with a pronounced circular movement of her right hand. With her left hand she swished a riding crop and pointed it at Kevin. He watched her run her tongue over her shining ruby red lips, then put down his pint and his cigarette.

The young men formed a circle around the stripper, urging her on with growls and whoops. She pulled the zip down slowly, exposing a V-shape of flesh, but stopped at her navel. Then she knelt on the floor in front of Kevin and cracked her whip again. He obliged her by stepping forward and undoing his trousers, much to the enjoyment of his audience. The stripper rubbed her leather-clad paws against his rapidly stiffening cock, Then freed it from its confines, and to a burst of enthusiasm from the boys she came down on him.

Paul, who had a ringside position, watched wide-eyed with amazement as Kevin thrust into the delicate but willing mouth. The Irishman put his hands on his hips and looked around at his friends with triumph in his eyes as the platinum head diligently worked away at him.

'Christ,' said Gary in his ear. 'They got me a stripper for my birthday last year, but she didn't do this. Just took her clothes off.'

'All of them?' whispered Paul, not moving his eyes from the performance. 'Even her knickers?'

'Yeah. Trouble was, she had BO something terrible. The boys said to me afterwards, "What's wrong with you? You weren't even grabbing her tits." She was sticking them right in me face as well. But the smell was unbelievable.' He laughed.

By this time, Kevin had grasped the blonde head in his hands and was pushing into her urgently, with quickening gasps. The boys built up an accompanying chant of encouragement until they broke into a cheer as he groaned, then pulled himself out, and bowed.

He was basking in their applause when the blonde unzipped fully and slipped off the leather suit far enough to reveal a completely flat chest. The blonde wig came away in a flourish and the room erupted into screams of delight. The stripper, now plainly a man, blew a kiss at his victim, and swept out of the room wrapped once more in the black velvet cape. Kevin stood rooted to the spot with his flaccid equipment dripping on to his trousers.

At half-past ten David Stone parked his car to one side of Westhorpe Hall and sat for a moment, letting his thoughts clear. He had just returned from the Ely Cathedral Restoration Fund dinner – a function he had attended alone, as was so often the case. His head ached and he was longing for a drink, but he hesitated before going in: he had no idea what was waiting for him. After he had seen the solicitor earlier on, he had confronted Helen with his conclusion – that they should seek a divorce as soon as possible. In return she had given him a potted summary of his undesirability as anything but a walking chequebook. She had jumped at the chance to end their marriage, as if she was cancelling an inconvenient hair appointment. Now it was over.

David got out of the car and unlocked the front door. The house was very quiet; every chair he moved or door he opened seemed noisier than usual. He helped himself to a drink from the kitchen, then wandered from room to room, turning on the lights and sipping his wine.

When he reached Helen's bedroom he saw that the cheque he had left on her dressing table had gone. So had her clothes and her shoes – all ten thousand of them – and her vats of make-up. She had taken the money he offered her as an opening shot – £400,000 – and she had left him.

At half-past six the next morning Paul Roberts emerged from his ground-floor flat, turned left into Sternhold Avenue, and walked down the gentle incline to Balham Common. His head was throbbing and he felt queasy, as if he might throw up at any moment. Inside the hastily-donned suit he shivered and sweated alternately as he concentrated on negotiating the footpath across the broad stretch of grass.

The rain that morning was lukewarm as it ran down Paul's neck and made his collar soggy. At the newsstand he fumbled with his change, then descended into the gloomy passageways of London Regional Transport, where the full horror of his physical condition became apparent as he paced the platform. The morning air had cleared some of the steel wool out of his brain, but here, deep under the streets, he thought he might suffocate on the greasy, stuffy fumes. The strip lighting hurt his eyes and he felt dizzy. He stood still and tried to focus on the front page of *The Financial Times*, but the columns of print slid off to the left as if they were on an oiled surface. Another wave of dizziness hit him, and he realised he was still drunk.

The Brodie McClean morning meeting took place at eight in the middle of the dealing room around the main bank of desks. The analysts, who had arrived first, had been studying the papers and trade magazines for any pertinent news that might influence the market. They emerged reluctantly from their glass enclosure to face the machine-gun fire of cynicism and dismissive impatience from the salesmen and dealers.

Paul stood at the back pretending to listen to his colleagues, and marvelled at the freshness of the dealers with whom he had been drinking the previous night. Mercifully there were no company results meetings or presentations to attend today, so he planned to sit quietly behind a screen of books and engage his brain with undemanding financial calculations until it was time for him to go home to bed.

At half-past eight disaster struck: Paul was summoned upstairs to see James Malpas, the Director of Corporate Finance. Paul's boss in Broking Research had given him the message in a tone that implied that even though Malpas was in a separate part of Brodie McClean, Paul was expected to jump. It was an honour to be at the man's disposal.

Malpas had been at work since seven o'clock, but when the dazed analyst arrived the office was empty. Paul stood studying the painting of Cleopatra the horse, wondering what awful fate awaited him, and hoping he wasn't going to vomit. He had never met Malpas, let alone been upstairs to the Olympian heights of Brodie McClean. When the man himself breezed into the room, his air of 'determined executive in a hurry' overwhelmed the enfeebled twenty-four-year-old.

'So good of you to come up,' Malpas began as he sifted through the folders and files on his desk. Paul was not aware he had been given any choice in the matter. He smiled awkwardly. 'You're new, aren't you?' Malpas continued perkily. 'Take a seat . . . your note on William Stone and Son was nicely written, I thought.' He joined Paul at the conference table and fixed the analyst with his most piercing look. 'Now, it's because I liked your approach to this company,' he gestured at the Stone report, 'that I want you to study Martindale. Do you know it?'

Paul cleared his throat and struggled to find his voice. 'Well, no,' he stumbled apologetically.

'No matter. You can go there with a clear mind,' Malpas continued without letting up his steady gaze, much to Paul's discomfort. 'I'd like you to take on something important. I've arranged for you to see Sir Terence Purves, the MD of Martindale, today. I want a favourable note to tempt in a few investors, to buck up the share price. It needn't be encyclopaedic – an overview of trading activities, financial position, prospects on a three-to-five-year view, the usual kind of thing.'

Paul nodded, feeling utterly hopeless. Gone was the quiet day nursing his head. And worse than that, he would have to rush out a piece of research for this hugely important man. He would be judged on a hastily thrown together job.

'They're in Reading or Basingstoke,' James added as he got to his feet. 'Somewhere ghastly like that, so there's no problem getting there on the train. And obviously I'd like to see your draft when you have it ready.'

There wasn't the slightest hint of apology in his voice, as if he assumed that his instructions would supersede anything Paul had on his plate. Malpas turned his attention to the work on his desk, indicating that their interview was over. Paul realised he had been dismissed and backed out, wondering why he felt so foolish.

Shortly after two that afternoon, a taxi dropped Paul at the headquarters of Martindale Electronics, a functional brick rectangle on an industrial estate in Reading. Five minutes later he was sipping thin instant coffee and listening to a short man with salt-and-pepper hair tell him how stupid the British Army was. Sir Terence Purves – 'Terry' – had a bony face on which flesh hung like meat on a hook. Despite himself, Paul noticed that Purves's rubbery lips flapped around his mouth and glistened with saliva.

'Our most profitable area is spare parts,' he said, sitting up straighter in his high-backed leather chair. 'We do incredible replacement business on our frequency hopping tank radios. Reason is, the troopers use 'em as a toehold as they climb in and out of the hatch. 'Course we're the last ones going to tell the MOD they ought to make a design change to the entrance of their ruddy tank.' He roared with laughter and slapped his knee. 'Mind you,' he added when the rasping had subsided, 'they never work out how to use the equipment anyway. That's the trouble with getting someone who left school at sixteen to operate little boxes designed by a man with a PhD.'

Terry Purves was less forthcoming when it came to discussing Martindale's margins, or how volumes had held up since the end of the Cold War. Paul tried to work his way through his list of questions but the Managing Director suggested a walk around. This was a well-known ploy, a sure way to avoid unwanted inquiries.

Nothing about the size of the order books could be gleaned by watching blank-faced operatives doing brain-numbingly monotonous jobs on an assembly line. They went from one warehouse to the next, until finally they reached a vast barn where 'the pride and joy' of Martindale was being constructed.

'We've got the competition beat here,' Purves announced as he swaggered towards a pile of metal that resembled a train wreck. 'Ground to air missile telemetry,' he said with affection. 'We'll clean up the international market with this little angel.'

Only last month, Paul had been shown a similar machine at another defence company – where it had been closer to completion than this model. When he mentioned this to Purves, the businessman crossed his arms over his chest and his eyes narrowed into pouches of wrinkles. 'Maybe you can tell me how it works, then?' he snapped. Paul was alarmed by the antagonism in the man's manner, so he began his explanation gingerly.

'Instead of using a heat-seeking sensor it concentrates on a particular distinguishing movement, which in the case of a helicopter is a rotor blade. So the missile homes in on that.'

'That's the theory,' sneered the MD, 'but what happened when they demonstrated it for their customers?' Paul tried to avoid looking at the glob of mucus slithering around Purves's lower lip as he continued. 'My so-called competitors filled their assorted darkies with champagne as usual, and drove them to the fields at the back of their works to watch their wonder product in action. Then they sent up a little autogyro and they fired their missile. Well, up it went after this autogyro, then it hesitated in mid-air, and pointed its nose in a different direction. And before anyone could detonate it, it came hurtling down and destroyed an outbuilding. Arabs and other wogs not impressed. Know what happened?' Paul shook his head as was required of him, and tried not to see the spittle stringing between upper and lower lip.

'This clever bloody guidance system thought it would have a look at the extractor fan in the bogs in this outbuilding.' Purves laughed so hard he brought on another coughing spasm and to Paul's relief he wiped his mouth with a handkerchief. 'Mind you, wasn't very nice for the bloke who was in there having a crap at the time,' the MD chuckled.

An hour later Paul was on the train back to Paddington, contemplating Martindale's uncertain future. The company had made extravagant profits in the past from selling second-rate equipment to Third World dictators who would pay above the going rate for the security of remaining unidentified, but now there was a glut of Soviet hardware flooding on to the market at bargain basement prices, ruining Purves's game.

Why on earth had Malpas asked him, an analyst from the broking wing of the bank, to put together a positive assessment of Martindale? It puzzled Paul. It would have puzzled him even more had he realised that the Head of Corporate Finance was asking him to step across the legal 'Chinese Wall' between the two parts of the Brodie McClean operation, the rule that theoretically stopped a conflict of interest.

As Paul's taxi left Paddington and headed back to the City, he noticed the satellite dishes of the NNN studios and thought of the pretty reporter who had interviewed him yesterday. Charlotte Carter, her name was. This afternoon he would call her and ask her out to dinner. That would be better than analysing Sir Terence Purves's pile of garbage.

Chapter Three

'How about coffee while you wait?' asked Sheila. 'David should be here any moment.'

'Could we set up our gear in Mr Stone's office?' Charlotte suggested. 'It'd save a lot of time.'

Sheila urged them to go ahead. As Steve the cameraman lugged his paraphernalia in, he caught sight of David Stone's *Annunciation* – a fifteenth-century Italian painting of Gabriel announcing the forthcoming birth of Jesus to the Virgin Mary.

'Christ!' he exclaimed without irony. 'Gotta use that!'

With the help of the lighting man, they rearranged every piece of furniture in the room so that the painting would appear over David's shoulder when he was being interviewed. Steve and his colleagues often turned people's homes or offices upside down to achieve the right backdrop, although it never occurred to them to put the things back afterwards.

Charlotte sat on the edge of the desk, wondering what kind of businessman would run his empire out of such unlikely, modest premises. She was critically contemplating the elegant lines of her suntanned legs stretched before her, when she heard a car door slam. She looked out of the window towards an ancient Volvo Estate. A man with dark curly hair and very muddy Wellington boots was hurrying across the yard towards the office, ducking his head against the rain. He wore jeans and a baggy open-necked shirt; a farmhand, Charlotte presumed.

Then: 'Turn those lights off!' The man who had been wearing the dirty boots was standing in front of her in stockinged feet. 'God knows what damage you've done.'

He walked around her and examined the canvas, shaking his head. Charlotte immediately sprang to her feet and mumbled apologies, but an unhappy atmosphere hung over the office as they repositioned their equipment. David Stone sat at his desk, signing letters and cheques while Charlotte lurked near the door. She glanced curiously at the brown hair that curled gently down to his open collar, at the even features and furrowed brow. She had been expecting the standard issue Managing Director in grey suit, with an imposing office, the furniture chosen to emphasise the occupant's importance. Here there were no executive toys, and no semi-literate bimbo secretary. Only the admirable Sheila and the Madonna were present to keep an eye on their irascible master.

Some people could look elegant in jeans, she reflected, especially with the nice bum she had noticed despite herself while he was mourning over his painting. He was about five foot ten, she guessed. He wore a blue and white striped shirt made of a heavy cotton that almost glowed with quality: the best of the Camicezia San Marco who had kept David's measurements on their books since he had lived in Italy. She fought an impulse to touch the material and pretended to study her notes until the crew were happy with the arrangement of the furniture.

The regrettable mood of tension did not improve once they started the interview. At first, David answered all of her questions with a 'Yes,' or a 'No.' Then he became sarcastic when she explained that she needed him to expand on his theme. 'Would it be easier if you wrote me a script?' he asked. Steve the cameraman sniggered and Charlotte bit her lower lip in fury.

'Can we turn to the work you're doing on alternative packaging materials?' she persevered.

'No, we can't,' David said with feeling. 'How do you know about it? It's not public knowledge.' He leaned towards the startled reporter, eyes blazing. 'If a bigger company found out what we're up to here, they could take our idea and have it on the market in half the time it'll take us to develop it.'

Charlotte blushed. Paul Roberts, the Brodie McClean analyst, had told her about the green product, but not that it was a secret. She looked down at her hands and saw she was picking at her long-suffering fingernails. 'Perhaps we could move on to the entrepreneurial challenges at William Stone and Son, your development priorities—' she tried again, blood tingling in her cheeks.

'Ah well, I haven't been to business school, you see, so I'm lost when it comes to focused strategies. I just run a company.' David shifted impatiently in his chair, and as they glared at each other Charlotte couldn't help noticing how long and dark his eyelashes were.

Then the crew filmed David touring his factories, being noticeably more friendly with his staff than he had been with his guests. He acknowledged everyone on the shop floor by name, and knew who had just returned from holiday and where they had been. Charlotte watched him touring his site with the sure touch of a seasoned politician working a crowd.

Half an hour later the crew packed their equipment in the Peugeot, and prepared to go back to London. Charlotte, who had driven up separately after another job, waved them goodbye and started towards her own car. She was opening the door when David Stone jogged over to her from his office. She looked up at him and braced herself for another onslaught.

'I wanted to apologise for my temper,' he started uncertainly. 'I was rude, and I'm very sorry.' He smiled crookedly and glanced at his shoes in embarrassment. 'My problems are too tedious to mention, but I shouldn't have snapped at you.' He paused and forced himself to make eye contact. 'You were right to ask about my boring share performance. I'm clueless about how the City works, and I probably haven't done much to stir up any interest in the company recently. So I'm glad you're here, doing this story on us.' He rolled his eyes in mock exasperation. 'I know I didn't give you that impression. I'm just scared as hell about anyone finding out about Verdi, my green product.'

Charlotte, who had been studying his worried face, nodded her head as he finished. 'I understand, and I promise I won't mention it.'

'Thank you,' he said, and his serious manner lightened a fraction. 'Would you like a cup of tea before you go back? Are you in a hurry?'

Charlotte could have told him that she had absolutely no reason to rush back home, and that there was nothing waiting for her this evening, save a solitary trip to the Chinese Takeaway. But she accepted his offer graciously, and was locking her car door when a strange bleating startled her.

'Oh God, she's escaped!' exclaimed her host. Charlotte turned around to find a blonde, four-legged Rastafarian beside her, about to take a chew of her skirt. 'No!' said David, and grabbed the beast by one of her curled horns. She dug in her hooves, but his superior bulk decided the issue, and she was gradually pulled away. 'I'd better take her back to her paddock,' he said casually, as if he was not at that moment struggling to keep the angora goat from pushing him over. 'Shall we have tea at my house? Might be nicer than the office.'

'Yes,' said Charlotte uncertainly, and peered at the hairy mammal. No eyes were visible behind the curtain of fluff so she could not guess if its expression was malicious or benign. They walked down the drive, David still chatting to her while he dragged the goat, who reared her head indignantly.

When he had pushed her back into her field and banged the fence-post into place, he led Charlotte into Westhorpe Hall. His visitor felt as if she had entered a scene from *Hansel and Gretel*. Before her were heavy wooden doors, a high-ceilinged hall hung with tapestries and portraits of improbable mutton-faced men who looked as though they had suffered from gout, a minstrels' gallery and a long dark refectory table planted squarely before an ugly open stone fireplace. It was like a caricature of a country house, and she fully expected to see a group of tourists being guided about.

In the kitchen David offered her a seat at an enormous wooden table that stood like a ship moored in a sea of quarried tile. While he put the kettle on, Charlotte surveyed the beams from which hung strings of garlic and shallots, and wicker baskets. Gleaming copper-bottom pots and pans were suspended from hooks up the wall. She had seen regrettable attempts at this type of kitchen in Pinner or Islington, but the real thing was much more enchanting to someone as greedy as Charlotte.

'India or China?' David asked as he warmed the teapot. She gazed at him stupidly, a life of teabags having left her unaccustomed to such refinement.

'I don't mind,' she replied with an unconvincing smile. He's seen right through me, she thought as he spooned Earl Grey into the teapot. 'Looks like the domain of a keen cook,' she said brightly, fishing for a clue on Mrs Stone who did not seem to be around this afternoon.

'Well, I'm not awfully good,' David sighed as he sat down opposite her. He studied the grain of the wood between them for a moment, and pursed his lips. 'You know, I could do with your advice, I think.'

Charlotte raised her eyebrows, amazed that anyone would consult her, the Queen of the Takeaway Universe, about cooking.

'You see,' he went on,' I've concentrated on running this damned company, and sort of assumed the City aspects will take care of themselves. But it seems that profits aren't enough to keep the shareholders happy – I don't mean the people who hold a few hundred of my shares, but the pension funds and insurance companies.'

He leaned forward with his elbows on the table and his chin resting on one hand. Charlotte studied his thoughtful eyes, and wondered why they looked so sad. He had a beautiful house, a successful business, and he was probably married to a gorgeous wife, since handsome, intelligent men didn't get hitched to ugly old hags.

'You know all about the City and finance. And I'd be grateful for your advice. My merchant bank is far too busy to shepherd me along. You see, I don't buy or sell any companies, so I can't generate fees for them.'

'I don't know that I can suggest anything useful,' Charlotte began. 'I'm just a hack—'

'Nonsense,' David said with the beginnings of a smile. 'You

wouldn't have got to your position, at your tender age, without knowing what you're talking about.'

Charlotte could have told him not to be so sure, but she grinned modestly and sipped her tea. For a moment she wanted to reach across the table and stroke his hair, and a wave of lust passed through her like a shiver. Instead, she cleared her throat and struggled for something to say. 'Has your merchant bank organised a day out for the broking analysts to come and sniff over your factories?'

She watched David shake his head in horror. 'Oh God, that sounds awful. I couldn't survive a day of their questions.' He looked down at his china teacup, appalled by his own ineptitude.

Charlotte couldn't stop herself from snorting. 'You won't say that when you've met them! These people aren't capable of running a real business. I mean, surely anyone who has an entrepreneurial idea for making money is doing it for themselves, not administering a pension fund. You know, most pension funds would do better if they just divided their money between the top hundred stocks. Fund managers underperform the market all the time.'

David leaned back in his chair, revelling in the journalist's distaste for the City. 'It does make you wonder why there aren't lynch mobs stalking the streets of the Square Mile, dragging these parasites out of their Porsches, and leaving them to swing from lamp-posts,' he commented.

'City people are just like reporters in some ways. They're idle and they'll gratefully regurgitate tasty morsels about your business if you spoonfeed them. Why not start blowing your own trumpet a bit – maybe retain a public relations company?' she suggested, and saw her host wince in response. 'I know it's expensive,' she rushed on, 'but you'd be surprised what they can do to improve sentiment. Really. If Hitler had used a decent PR adviser we'd probably all be singing the "Horst Vessel" song now.'

David sighed and finished his cup of tea. 'Yes, I'm sure you're right. I'll have to learn about these things. As you might have guessed, I'm not much of a businessman.'

'Your profit figures look healthy enough to me,' Charlotte protested in surprise.

But David was shaking his head. 'You know what I mean. I'd rather read a good book, or wander around a Renaissance church.'

Charlotte nodded sympathetically, appalled that she might be forced into admitting her ignorance of such things. She employed an enigmatic smile which signified: 'I've always meant to find out about art and music, and to learn a foreign language, but I was too busy listening to Abba and reading Agatha Christie when I was younger. And now I spend every moment working.' Then she reflected on David's rather more interesting CV. 'Well, this is the perfect house for your art collection,' she said aloud, hoping she might get a tour of Westhorpe Hall.

'Have you got time for a wander around?' David asked right on cue as he got to his feet.

Charlotte was loath to admit that there was no adoring man to run home to, so she smiled and followed him along the dark wood-panelled corridor to his study. The room was book-lined, and cluttered with old paintings and furniture, like the set from a Merchant Ivory film. On David's desk was a framed photograph of a little boy who looked the spitting image of himself. Charlotte wanted to ask him about the child but he was pointing out his favourite landscape of Perugia, so she desisted. As he talked, his enthusiasm communicated itself to her, and she envied him his interest in something so unconnected with his work.

On their way out of the study, Charlotte paused by his desk. 'He really does look like you. What's his name?'

David looked away and made busy clearing-up motions with the papers on his desk. 'Billy. He died of leukaemia a couple of years ago.' He could have told her how long ago to the day, but he spared her that detail.

Charlotte had the sensation of standing on a landmine and hearing a terrific explosion that for some reason had not killed her. It would have been more merciful if it had blown her apart, she reflected. A thick silence hung like a velvet curtain between them. Charlotte tried to say she was sorry, as Americans did in movies, but it seemed such a feeble comment that she abandoned the sentence halfway through, producing an inarticulate gurgle instead.

'Oh dear, how horrible you must feel, asking me that,' he said. She could hardly bear to meet his eyes but he looked sympathetic, rather than tragic. He sighed as if to say, 'Don't worry, you were hardly to know.' But the animation had gone, and however kindly he dealt with her unfortunate question, he was obviously holding himself together. 'Come on,' he said now, with false brightness and a clap of the hands as if he were dispersing evil spirits. 'Let me bore you with a walk around the garden.'

Charlotte grinned a fragile little grin and followed him through the house. As a lifelong collector of trivial observations she had noticed that he wore no wedding ring, but she had asked enough personal questions for today.

'You will stay for dinner, won't you?' he asked her over his shoulder. 'I'd like to ask your advice on this City analyst stuff.'

In the kitchen he opened a bottle of Chardonnay, and they took their wine through to a conservatory that he modestly called a sunroom; vines crept up trellises, inside and out, and tropical plants fought for space with the wicker furniture. Charlotte looked out at the landscaped garden to fields where cows were munching. Someone had gone to a great deal of effort to break the monotony of the surrounding Fens.

Then David walked her around the estate, explaining that the original planting had been his great-grandfather's. He had built a channel to the nearest river so streams could weave though the grounds. Now it was a shady area of willow trees and ferns where little stone bridges crossed over waterways covered in lily pads. For the first time in her sophisticated metropolitan life, Charlotte grasped the point of gardening – a pastime previously dismissed as a sex substitute for the elderly. It was a revelation to see how absorbing and satisfying it could be; season after season, year after year. Such a long-term strategy bewildered a young woman who worked as if there was no tomorrow.

When they returned to the Hall, he cooked while she set the table in the sunroom. Her task completed, she stood at the open French windows, looking down the garden. The evening light cast a golden blush on the grass and bushes, and the air smelt as if every flower had released its perfume . . . Charlotte closed her eyes and listened to the silence; no cars roaring, no television blaring, no neighbour's doors slamming.

What would it be like to live here, to be married to a man like this, to bring up a child in such a lovely place? Her thoughts shocked her: then she wondered if it would drive her crazy with boredom. She had college chums who had given up madly exciting careers and retreated to the rural idyll to breed brats and grow radicchio. Was this why?

She opened her eyes and turned back to the sunroom. David stood in the doorway that led into the house. He was leaning against the doorjamb with his arms crossed. He had been watching her, for how long she didn't know. They studied each other for what seemed like minutes. She was willing him to walk across the room and kiss her, but he broke the spell. 'Could you help me serve the food, please?' The moment of lust had passed making no impression on him, evidently. Then it occurred to Charlotte that maybe she was the only one who was lusting, and maybe he had been wondering what on earth she was doing. She cringed in humiliation.

When they sat down to eat he said, 'It's a sign of greatness that Italians have designer pasta.' He speared a cylinder of rigatoni on his fork. 'You see, this is made with special ribs on the inside to hold as much sauce as possible. In Britain clever people go into advertising, but in Italy they put their energies into things that matter.'

Their conversation wandered about effortlessly and enjoyably. When Charlotte had eaten everything on her plate, and had a second helping, she thanked him for his kindness in inviting her to stay to dinner. She was most impressed with his cooking, she said.

'But I'm the one who's grateful for your company. It makes a welcome change to talk to someone about the firm who isn't my father.' He then described the elder Stone's constant interference in the business. 'I never do anything right, even when the profits go up.' David sipped his wine and shook his head. 'Of course he doesn't want to talk about *that*.'

'The things they leave unsaid are the most hurtful anyway,' Charlotte volunteered. 'My parents wanted me to be a barrister. You see, my father is a solicitor in Hertford, and my mother's a magistrate, and they'd assumed I'd go to the College of Law after university. I don't know if they've ever forgiven me for starting work on the City pages of a newspaper instead. It was as if I'd begun speaking in tongues, or drinking meths. Of course they made the right congratulatory noises when I was offered the job on NNN, but they think TV is ephemeral. At least my brother is carrying the burden of their dreams. He's in the slave-labour phase of training to be a barrister.'

It was as if there was a stranger in the room, talking with her voice, saying things she'd never admitted. David nodded in silence. We have that in common, he implied. But she was not prepared for his next remark. 'My wife left me recently – in case you were wondering why there's no one else here.' Then he laughed bitterly.

'What, er, happened?' Charlotte was torn between curiosity and the fear of crossing the borders of civility. 'If you don't mind me asking.' She was struggling to keep her pleasure in check.

'No, I volunteered the information because I wanted you to know.' He paused and ran his fingers over the pepper grinder on the table between them. Charlotte greedily consumed that last remark, hoping it meant he wanted her to know he was available. 'I don't want you to think I only asked you to stay for dinner because my wife was out somewhere. You know – lecherous middle-aged businessman in search of diversion.'

Charlotte's heart sank at his practical explanation. Then she felt ashamed for having misconstrued his words so vainly. Who are you kidding, sister, she thought.

'Coffee? You ought to have some before you drive,' he said as he stood up and gathered plates together. Charlotte carried the glasses out to the kitchen feeling that she was being dismissed, and hating herself for fantasising about winning the attentions of this man. But when he had ground the coffee beans he surprised her by answering her question.

'Once Billy was dead, Helen and I no longer had a common bond. It sounds clichéd, I know, but losing a child can expose the reasons you shouldn't be married. And as I'm sure you know, men can't bear to admit that someone else makes their wife happier than they do.'

There was no appropriate rejoinder to his candid admission so she merely sipped her espresso thoughtfully.

Then he walked her back to her car in the fading light of the summer evening, and as she opened the car door and turned to say goodbye she was sure he was going to move towards her, or touch her. But he simply told her to drive safely and backed away. By the time she had started the engine, he was gone.

Charlotte drove home wondering why she felt so angry with him. Then she remembered Paul Roberts, the analyst from Brodie McClean, and smiled to herself. He had asked her out to dinner tomorrow evening.

Chapter Four

'It's not a happy story, is it?'

James Malpas put Paul's draft note to one side, and studied the glossy cover of the Martindale annual report on the conference table before him. The analyst had been dreading this; the man with the power to make or break his career at Brodie McClean was delivering his verdict. Paul had stayed up half the night rewriting each paragraph to be optimistic without actually lying. 'But I think you've done damned well, under the circumstances,' Malpas continued after sucking his teeth.

As he was often to find when he was in Malpas's presence, Paul could think of nothing intelligent to say. He sat opposite the Director of Corporate Finance, fidgeting with a pencil and wondering what might happen next.

'I reckon just a bit more fiddling with the numbers,' James said thoughtfully, then he looked up and fixed Paul with an open-eyed, disarming gaze. 'That'll satisfy Purves.'

'I could certainly inflate the radar profits, and be a bit more lenient on the tax charge,' Paul said eagerly. 'Then I'll dig around for some angle on the trading range to keep the salesmen happy.' The young analyst was rather proud of his mastery of the trading range concept since Gary had enlightened him.

'I think we're going to work well together, Paul,' James grinned. 'What about a drink this evening, at close of play? Let's go to my club for a chat at five-thirty. That OK with you?'

As Malpas spoke he arched his eyebrows in an almost suggestive way. Paul thought the penetrating stare that accompanied it was equally peculiar, almost unsettling. But the young man's mind was fully occupied, trying to find a solution to the dilemma facing him. He had arranged to meet Charlotte Carter at seven-thirty, but he couldn't turn down Malpas's invitation. Wherever this hugely powerful man would lead, Paul would follow.

'I'm afraid I'm seeing the man himself at seven,' Malpas added. 'Purves, I mean. I'm giving him dinner tonight. But we could have one for the road, and at my club we can have a talk about your future at Brodie McClean,' he said chummily.

When Paul had been dispatched back to the Broking Department downstairs, James turned his attention to acquisitions of a more personal nature. He had decided to buy a place in the country, a rural getaway where he could entertain his most important clients.

Not that he could afford a grand spread, what with the size of the existing mortgage on his large Victorian home in Richmond. Fiona, his wife, had compiled a short list of possibilities, and James hoped that he would be able to look at her top selection this weekend.

Fiona had great plans for growing their own food, and other agrarian pursuits that had little meaning for James. He had rarely seen her so animated. When he asked where she had picked up all this knowledge, she confessed that she had always wanted to live in the country. This came as a shock to James, who couldn't recall Fiona saying such a thing during their ten years of married life. But then, he reflected, he probably wouldn't have remembered if she had talked about it. He usually had so much on his mind, and it was never her way to push her opinions.

It was obvious to anyone that he was the driving force in their partnership, the one who made the decisions, and whose career provided such a hectic and demanding life. Fiona simply followed in his wake, dutiful, obliging, uncomplaining. Were there other areas of dissatisfaction he had failed to comprehend because he was so busy forging ahead? It would be most regrettable if she ever left him; a man headed for the top of a merchant bank needed a supportive wife and a good hostess at his side. James Malpas knew how bad it would look to his peers if Fiona was to disappear.

* * *

Paul Roberts was waiting in the bank's underground car park at 5.30, and the minute he climbed into James's BMW the sales pitch began. How high was he aiming? Did he too want to have one of these? Malpas stroked the steering wheel and glanced across at his apprentice.

Paul held his breath for a moment, taken aback by the man's ability to read his mind. He nodded an emphatic 'yes' as James continued. Did he want the freedom to buy things without worrying if he had enough money in the bank? Paul laughed, and said he certainly did, at the same time wondering how the man could possibly empathise with his anxieties. It hardly seemed likely to Paul that this high-powered director had ever been short of the price of a good seat at Wimbledon. However James's next remark wrong-footed him.

'You know Paul, we have a lot in common.' He smiled knowingly at the analyst as they waited for the lights on London Wall to change. 'I'm not out of the same velvet-lined drawer as the Charles Ravenscroft mob at this bank.'

Paul nodded, dimly aware that Ravenscroft was tipped to be the next Chairman of the bank. On the one occasion he had met the man, he had seemed very nice and approachable to Paul. But from the set of Malpas's jaw he guessed that he didn't share this view.

'The reason I earn what I do is that I deserve it – just like you'll deserve it. It's brains that count, not the Old School tie or friends of Daddy's.'

Paul watched James mulling over his next sentence. He appeared to be trying to decide whether or not he could trust his passenger with a further confidence. As he steered the car into Moorgate he sighed and shook his head.

'I'm from a pretty ordinary background, Paul. My parents had to work hard so I'd have the chances the other children in our neighbourhood never got.' James paused and pursed his lips as he negotiated the intersection at the Bank of England. 'And the advantages that a dimwit like Ravenscroft takes for granted.'

Paul nodded sympathetically, but he had no idea what his driver meant, since he himself had never fought for anything except a place at the bar.

'It's all natural to Ravenscroft – how to dress, not to wear striped ties, or digital watches, or patterned socks . . . you know, that kind of thing. I had to learn the subtle little rules of the game from scratch by myself. Style's one of the things that sets the Establishment people apart from the rest, and they're still the ones who run a place like Brodie McClean. It's as if they have their own secret code. They can instantly recognise an outsider by the type of cufflinks he wears. And if you aren't carrying the right tribal symbols, you're damned for ever more,' he concluded grimly.

Paul sat to attention as they drove up Fleet Street. He was wondering how low down the pecking order he ranked for wearing shirts that buttoned at the cuffs.

'And you have to know the places to go skiing, and when the shooting season begins,' James continued with a hard edge of contempt in his voice. 'But they can always catch you out by asking if you know so-and-so, and surely your parents know the Lah-Di-Dahs, and how could you possibly *not* know the Doobry-Dunderheads?' His voice was getting louder. 'They don't care whether you can read and write, because what matters to them are the things that have nothing to do with personal ability. The sum achievement of their lives is being born into the right social position.'

By the time they had reached the Strand, Paul was feeling daunted by the thought of negotiating this complicated maze, but as they skirted the south side of Trafalgar Square his mentor's mood appeared to mellow slightly, and the young man wondered if perhaps James was going to let him in on the secret of navigating his way through the City.

'The point is that you and I have to learn their game to gain admittance to their inner sanctum, but once we're in the door we can run rings around them because we have brains, and we've been toughened up on the way there. When I was your age,' James said, turning briefly to face his passenger, 'I realised that there were basically two kinds of people in the world.'

Paul concentrated hard, praying that he was going to choose the right side of the example that would inevitably follow. His companion had set his lips in a firm lock of determination, and Paul expected the worst.

'There are the ones who stand stupidly on the right-hand side of the escalator, mouths hanging open in wonder at the world around them. Then there are the people who walk up the left-hand side. They're the ones who prefer action, rather than dawdling along, giving themselves a rest, as if they've done something with their pointless little lives that entitles them to take it easy.'

Paul blanched a bit, knowing perfectly well that he was the type who stood and stared because the adverts on the Underground were interesting, and he liked looking for attractive women as he cruised up or down. He enjoyed catching the eyes of girls going in the opposite direction, and staring at them hungrily until they glanced away in embarrassment.

'You can go as far as you want at Brodie McClean,' James said with a confidence that restored Paul's good humour. 'But you have to take advantage of all the opportunities that come your way. That's why I wanted this chat with you, away from the office. We have to decide what you're going to do.'

Paul could hardly believe his ears. James Malpas was offering him a helping hand into the big league; he was talking to him as if they were equals. The analyst's heart was palpitating by the time they pulled up in St James's.

'So it's up to you, Paul,' James said with a smile as they unfastened their seatbelts. Then he slid his hand on to his passenger's knee. Paul thought he was being patted like a dog, and he grinned nervously. He tried not to pull away but it happened automatically. James had fixed him with a peculiar stare, but when Paul twitched his leg slightly, the older man removed his hand and smiled again. 'Time for a drink,' he said brightly.

They walked up the street towards Boodle's, one of those exclusive corners of the capital that featured in gossip columns, not somewhere a grammar-school boy from Cheadle Hulme could swagger into at leisure. Paul followed James up the steps and through the grand Georgian door, hoping he appeared normal, not out-of-place and awkward, which was how he felt.

James led him through the quiet, carpeted corridors past walls hung with engravings. When they reached the smoking room they sat back in two overstuffed leather armchairs, and James ordered champagne with casual superiority. This man, who moments before had admitted his humble origins, was now as at ease as any other club member.

'Paul, tell me truthfully,' his host said when they had raised their glasses to each other, 'do you want to be one of the people who make things happen in the City?' But without waiting for a response he had shifted his position to turn himself towards his audience. Paul noticed that the friendly expression had suddenly been replaced by a sneer. 'Traders and analysts are just accessories. They run around in a panic trying to understand what someone else has made happen.'

James curled his lip slightly and leaned back in his armchair as if he was savouring its solidity. 'The real money's in bids and buyouts, advising companies, restructuring them in bad times, shrinking them in recessions, then expanding them in the good times.' The Corporate Financier gripped the armrests for emphasis.

Like a willing little puppy, Paul nodded his acquiescence. It didn't even occur to him that there might be something questionable about this; that it was merchant bankers who coaxed companies to overborrow and expand beyond their means in the first place, and that the same advisers then made a second fee for getting the industrialists out of the mess that they themselves had put them in. But it was the profitability of his work that preoccupied Malpas, not its morality.

Paul for his part was too mesmerised to be critical of the splendid portrait of life that the Mephisto-like Malpas had painted: mixing with the right people on the inside; being in the know; crafting clever deals; living in a large house in Richmond (James had told him how much his place was worth and how many of his neighbours were famous); and – this bit was Paul's private fantasy – going out with Charlotte Carter.

'Have you considered moving into the Corporate Finance Department?' James asked, and gave him a sidelong glance.

Paul tried to affect a calm demeanour, but his heart was thumping as if James had handed him the keys to Fort Knox.

'You'd have to be my man,' Malpas said bluntly, his eyes unblinking. 'Report to me alone, tell me everything you hear around the bank.'

The remark mystified Paul but he didn't give it a second thought. He wanted to be in Corporate Finance so much he would have sold his soul, if he'd known he had one. Malpas said he would do what he could to find room in the Department, then he looked at his watch and grimaced.

'I'm sorry about this, Paul, but I'm seeing Purves in fifteen minutes,' he said, drained his glass, and waited for Paul to do the same. 'Think about what I've said, won't you?'

They parted on the pavement outside Boodle's. Paul gushed his thanks and walked up towards Piccadilly, not even conscious of the direction he was taking. His head was swimming, and he hardly dared believe what Malpas had said to him.

When he reached Piccadilly he emerged from his daydream and looked around for a Tube sign. It was still early but he wanted to be on time for Charlotte. The thought of her made him even more jittery. If he could succeed with this young woman too, he reckoned he would be unbeatable.

'I think I've lost a crew.'

NNN's foreign assignments fixer spoke quietly and with sorrow rather than irritation. Maurice was used to such headaches: he organised the network's reporters, sending them to the world's trouble spots, getting visas within hours, finding translators, TV studios and satellite dishes in the middle of deserts and wars.

Charlotte looked up from her terminal and saw him running his hands through his frizzy grey hair. Then he sipped a cup of coffee and pulled a face when he realised it was cold. Charlotte got up and headed for the newsroom fridge. It was 6.30 – time for a real drink.

'What's happened?' she asked as she pushed a lager across to him and pulled the ring tab on her own can. Maurice took off his heavy bifocals, and not for the first time it occurred to the young woman that her friend looked like a thoughtful, elderly chimp.

'I've got three boys in N'Rooda, finding out if the Government's turning a blind eye to poachers breaking the ivory ban,' he explained. 'As if it's not enough that the ministers there put the famine relief cash raised by British schoolchildren straight into their personal bank accounts. Our local stringer says the militia is helping the poachers, and shooting game wardens who get in their way. Nasty business. Especially when the stringer went missing last week.'

'Charlotte, can I have a word?'

Her editor was standing at the doorway of his glass-walled office. She exchanged a split-second look of horror with Maurice, then scuttled across the newsroom to the cubbyhole in which Bob sat, surrounded by screens and empty pizza boxes.

'Shut the door, love,' he said as she popped her head into his domain. Today the little room smelt of Kentucky Fried Chicken and Bob's stale farts. She suppressed a gag, and took a seat. Five minutes later she emerged into the fresh air of the newsroom, but by then she had forgotten her aesthetic objections to her boss.

Maurice raised his eyebrows as she returned to the seat opposite him. 'Promise not to tell anyone?' she asked, her green eyes sparkling and her cheeks flushing with colour. He put his hand on his heart.

'Apparently, the powers that be on the board liked my little scoopette on Empire National Bank – you know, the leak from Brodie McClean,' she said, bouncing up and down, 'and they want me to do an in-depth feature on how the US arms industry is adapting to the end of the Cold War. No point telling Bob that every other network covered it three years ago. But it means I get a trip to the States!'

'Come on,' said Maurice, clapping his hands. He stood up briskly. 'Get your things. I'm taking a beautiful woman out to dinner to celebrate.'

'Oh Maurice,' she said, a pained expression on her face, 'I can't tonight. How about a drink? I'm sorry, I've got a dinner with a contact.' She tried to sound bored at the prospect, to hide her pleasure at going out with Paul. She didn't want Maurice to think she was abandoning him.

He shrugged his shoulders philosophically and nodded. 'OK, Princess. A drink it'll have to be.'

As Charlotte and Maurice drank fake champagne in a wine bar in Praed Street, James Malpas was asking for another bottle of mineral water at the Savoy Grill. He had only to incline his head in the waiters' direction and several appeared, eager to earn themselves a decent tip. Given their wages, the ingratiating manner was hardly surprising.

Malpas prided himself on knowing which type of entertainment best suited his different corporate clients. For Terry Purves it was the plush and expensive places where the man would believe he was mixing with the powerful élite. He was pleased by the constant attention of the staff, even if he was unsure how to hold his knife.

To a more sensitive soul than James Malpas, it would have been criminal to waste the Savoy's food on Purves, but the merchant banker had only a perfunctory interest in culinary matters. Anyhow, it was unlikely that the Martindale MD's taste buds would have registered ascorbic acid, let alone the delicate creations that arrived so prettily arranged on his plate. So a rather fine bottle of claret was sacrificed to the heathen palate of the metal-basher of Reading. James had no time for alcohol of any type, but he was shrewd enough to allow his guest to see how much he was paying for the Château Talbot. The bill would flatter Purves as much as anything would.

When a second glass of Courvoisier had been dispatched along the same route as the claret and the gin, Malpas suggested that they find a bit of distraction elsewhere. He intended the man to have the time of his life, and keep his business with Brodie McClean – and James knew just the place to take him. Malpas called a taxi and took the drunken Purves to a brothel he used for his 'valuable business contacts'. When James had delivered him into the arms of an obese woman with a pock-marked complexion and electric pink lipstick, he made an excuse about reluctantly having to get home. He preferred to leave Purves to the overpriced champagne, the disco music, and sofas covered in fake leopardskin.

James bade a hearty farewell to his guest, and left enough money with the management to take care of Purves's needs, including a taxi to Paddington Station later on. He walked back through Soho, his face aching from the effort of smiling at the man's stories and laughing at his jokes. However, Malpas was satisfied: he had diffused a potential problem. Now he and the malleable Paul Roberts would bolster up the share price a bit, and hope that kept the wretched man quiet.

As he walked, James undid his necktie and carefully rolled it up. He slipped it into his jacket pocket, retrieved a little foil envelope from his wallet, and descended a narrow flight of stairs to one of central London's more notorious 'cottages' – a public lavatory where homosexuals gathered for casual encounters. He deserved a little treat.

Kensington Place was heaving with the *jeunesse dorée* that evening. When Charlotte emerged from the revolving doors into the restaurant she was confronted by a sardine-like mêlée of black leather, dangling earrings, ruby red lipstick and dark glasses. Bright young things with spiked raven-black hair struck athletic attitudes, like extras from a squad dancing video. As Charlotte gazed around her she realised with a certain amount of relief that she was rendered invisible by her uninteresting linen suit and silk blouse.

She spotted Paul hovering at the bar, a chrome and glass construction like an Art Deco altar. He was sipping a long red drink which appeared to be tomato juice and when he caught sight of her he pointed at it and she nodded. Then she nudged her way towards him, past clutches of noisy hermaphrodites who were preoccupied with flaunting their sexuality without disclosing their sex. By the time Charlotte reached his side Paul had collared the Martian behind the bar, and a drink awaited her. She took her first thirsty gulp and felt a fire in her throat like molten lava crawling down the sides of a volcano.

'They'd call that a Serious Bloody Mary where I work,' Paul remarked with approval as he saw tears spring to her eyes. 'It's good, isn't it?'

Charlotte gasped as half a bottle of Tabasco made contact with her empty stomach. 'Great,' she whimpered. She had avoided spirits for several years, since a regrettable evening with two girlfriends and a bottle of gin. She still cringed at the memory of her virtuoso regurgitation performance on the Central Line. In the intervening years, gluttony had replaced boozing as her favourite recreational activity.

As Charlotte recovered from the assault on her oesophagus, Paul drew her attention to the mural that covered up an entire wall of the restaurant. It was a modern pastel event with *Déjeuner sur l'Eau* as its approximate theme. He was pleased with himself for choosing Kensington Place. It was buzzing with sophisticated cosmopolitan types who radiated arrogance the way that only Londoners do. They baffled him, but he hoped it impressed Charlotte.

'It's ages since I last came here,' she shouted above the chattering and laughter. Mercifully there was no canned music but the bare walls and floor conspired to create an echo chamber which intensified the drawled exclamations of the inmates.

'Oh.' Paul tried to keep the disappointment from his voice. 'D'you know this area, then?'

'I work down the road – Paddington Basin, behind the station. One of those converted warehouses that are *de rigueur* for satellite TV network studios. And I live in Gloucester Road.' Charlotte looked at his open face and clear eyes, and noticed the absence of any reaction. 'So how did you end up in the City?' she asked, loathing such banal conversation, and pondering how she could get him on to something more interesting. 'What else did you think of doing?' She sounded like a reporter searching for the real story.

'When I went to college I thought I'd be a physicist. I even did two years of a PhD. But then I got an approach from Brodie McClean, through some contact they had with my college. And the money was better than I could get in the defence industry.'

Charlotte grinned at him, thinking what lovely, even teeth he had, and admiring the healthy glow of his complexion. She wondered what he was like without any clothes on. After twenty-five minutes of fighting to stay upright in the crush around the bar, and exchanging unoriginal remarks about the state of the City, they were given a table. It was by the window looking out at the antique shops of Kensington Church Street, and a collection of black plastic rubbish bags that had been dumped at the bus stop.

The menu appeared to have been written by a spider with a square-nibbed quill. Charlotte, who was bored by the very concept of a main course, ordered two starters; a pan-fried *foie gras* on a buckwheat and sweetcorn pancake, and then a dozen oysters. Paul went for a smoked fish ensemble, followed by chicken in tarragon sauce. He had never known anyone order precisely what they wanted, and disregard the usual routine, as Charlotte had just done. The waitress didn't even question the reporter's anarchic decision. Paul had always thought there was some sort of rule about complying with what the menu indicated you should do. Why else would they set out a first course followed by a second course?

In his respectable middle-class youth in Cheshire, going out to eat had been a rare event, to celebrate a special occasion. His mother would invariably be intimidated by the waiter, and his father would be too chummy. He still found it a bit peculiar that people in London popped out for a meal with indifference. They must know some secret source of money he had never found.

Charlotte watched him studying the wine list. 'Oh, I don't know,' he sighed. 'It's all the same to me. How about, er, Muscadet?' he suggested, picking something he had heard of. He was surprised when his guest winced.

'Mind if I have a look?' she asked, and plucked the wine list out of his hands before he could answer.

''Fraid I don't know much about wine,' he apologised rather feebly.

Charlotte glanced up at his ingenuous expression. 'Neither do I,' she said tersely, and looked back at the wine list, 'but I do know it's a crime to waste money on some overpriced French muck when you can have something with flavour from the New World.'

Paul had no idea what she was talking about, but she spoke with such authority and feeling that she must be right.

'What do you fancy?' she asked him, as her eyes passed down the list. 'A Chardonnay, a Sauvignon Blanc, a Pinot Blanc – maybe a Semillon?'

'Is it OK if we have white?' he replied.

Charlotte searched his handsome face and thought how refreshing it was to be with someone whose every sentence did not of necessity involve some nugget of bullshit.

'I'd love to do a documentary on the Great French Rip-Off,' she said, as she leaned forward to make herself heard. 'You know, how they've conned us into believing they're the most civilised race on earth; that their wine and food is the best; that their art and music and literature and fashion is superior, and that the only cultural movies come out of France.'

Paul looked blank.

'Do you know what I mean?' she continued in an encouraging tone, hoping he might venture an opinion. When he didn't react she tried a more extreme position. 'The French are just white Arabs.' Still no spark of understanding. 'The food is better in Belgium, the Italians dominate the world of design, the South Americans are churning out fantastic books, and we don't do too badly either. Those smelly Frogs just cash in on the image, they trade on pretentiousness.'

'I get the impression you don't like the French. Did something horrible happen to you there?' he asked in a jolly tone.

'No.' She looked surprised.

'You seem pretty steamed up about them,' he said with a chuckle.

For a moment she was confused, then angry. She wanted to bang her fist on the table protesting that she wasn't steamed up at all. But she exercised masterful self-control and explained that she simply had views.

'I'll bet you have strong opinions on things . . .' she said, but the suggestion was met by a vacant expression, '. . . like the companies you follow?' she added somewhat desperately, feeling thoroughly steamed up by now. How could she coax him to contribute a bit more to their conversation?

He shrugged his shoulders in a good-natured way. 'No, I'm pretty laid back. I sort of let the world go by, and if it doesn't bother me then I don't bother it.'

'So what *are* you interested in, Paul? You know, what's important to you?' she asked. Charlotte Carter, wound up tighter than a spring, was the last person to understand the manifesto of the easy-come, easy-go.

'Love cricket, and rugby,' he said, finishing off his Bloody Mary. 'I flop in front of the telly and enjoy just about any sport.'

Charlotte experienced a terrible sinking sensation. She was at a loss to say anything intelligent on a group of activities she considered the world's most pointless, but her inquiry did at least have some effect. Finally Paul seemed to open up, and he told her about his enthusiasm for different sports until their food arrived. It had been artistically arranged on black hexagonal plates, and Charlotte was transported to paradise with the first delicate mouthful of *foie gras*. 'This is damned good,' she groaned with pleasure. 'How's yours?'

'Yeah – lovely. Wine's good too. Well-chosen.' He lifted his glass to her. 'I can see I'll have to learn a bit about the arts of gracious living. I'm a real bachelor the way I live. Couldn't cook an egg.'

'Oh, come on now. I bet you're being modest,' she crooned, carefully registering the fact that he was not living with a woman. Charlotte found it a bit infuriating that her companion did not appear to possess a real interest in anything apart from sport and military equipment, but he was very attractive to gaze at across a dinner table, and with half a bottle of the Sonoma Valley's best in her stomach, his naïvety seemed a positive advantage over her past suitors.

The previous year there had been a young man who had seduced her with wonderful food. For several weeks they had eaten their way around the most marvellous restaurants London had to offer, sharing the phenomenal cost fifty-fifty. But as soon as Charlotte had surrendered to his charms, she discovered that he regarded eating as a form of conspicuous consumption. At home he drank orange squash and gorged on cheap gristly hamburgers from the deep freeze. Unless he held a dinner party when he could flaunt his expertise to his friends, he was indifferent to Charlotte's favourite pastime. 'Every time I open a new menu,' she used to say, 'it's like starting a new love affair.' But she had definitely got it wrong on this one. He had passed his sell-by date, and she had departed, doubting her judgement.

Charlotte had the normal quota of unresolved conflicts left over from childhood, and humiliations from adolescence to deal with. But her choice in men continued to trouble her. The rival TV reporter and ultra-creep Jonathan Slope pestered her, while more desirable men in her profession would not give her a second glance. What disturbed her most was that men who were as ambitious as her, and might therefore make good boyfriends and eventually husbands, actively loathed her. They seemed to be looking for women who would be dedicated and uncritical cheerleaders, not equals. It went some way to explaining why her love-life to date had been disastrous.

They were well into their second bottle of the Californian nectar when Charlotte asked Paul what he made of David Stone.

'Oh, he's a good businessman, all right,' Paul said between gulps of wine. 'And did you know he doesn't have a chauffeur? He drives himself around in this old Volvo, which is a bit odd considering how rich he must be. And he wears jeans.' Paul looked mystified by the man's eccentricity.

'That's how toffs behave, I suppose,' Charlotte said with a worldly shrug. 'They don't need to prove themselves, so they don't flaunt their money. They think new cars or designer clothes are a wee bit vulgar.' She saw the incomprehension on her companion's face. 'And the other giveaway is that posh people use plain English. They don't try to professionalise their jobs, or raise their social standing by using over-complicated expressions to describe what they do or are. I mean, where other people say "purchase" and "request", they say "buy" and "ask".'

'I don't think he likes City people,' Paul mused as he recalled how reluctant Stone had been to divulge any details of his R and D work. Only when Paul had promised not to breathe a word of it had David shown him around the labs. The analyst hadn't really broken his word on that, he reckoned. Well, he hadn't put it in print anyway.

Twenty minutes later they were standing on the pavement waiting for the little yellow light of a free cab for Charlotte. Paul mentioned how strange it would be to see himself on television for the first time, and in a flash of half-drunken lust, Charlotte asked him if he wanted to come around to her flat to watch the programme together on Sunday evening. He accepted eagerly and saw her into a cab. Then she vanished into the traffic heading towards South Kensington, while he walked up to Notting Hill Gate to get a Tube home. He was feeling remarkably contented with the evening, and himself.

David Stone was locking up Westhorpe Hall for the night. Apart from the usual creakings of an old building and the ticking of the grandfather clock in the hall, the house was silent. On his way up to bed he was thinking how silly it was for one person to live in such a huge place. But it was only when he turned out the light and lay on his back in the dark that he realised the full impact of Helen's decision. She was gone. His son had gone. Now he was alone. At least he had his business, the reluctant entrepreneur thought, and nearly choked on the irony. He cursed his father and turned over.

Chapter Five

Charles Ravenscroft bore all the hallmarks of an Old Etonian: effortless charm, a vagueness about detail, the need to have complicated things explained more than once, and an air of authority not often challenged. He was in his mid-forties and stood just under six foot tall. His hair was straight and blond, not too short, and swept back from his high forehead. The scion of a family of bankers, he dressed as his father had, in unassertive but well-tailored suits of excellent material, not cut to reflect the current trend, but to flatter his broad shoulders and non-existent hips.

Charles was the head of Brodie McClean's international arm. His department arranged loans to foreign companies and governments, and managed the funds of overseas clients who wanted to invest in the UK but preferred a local to organise it for them. Less happily, Charles was also up to his neck in negotiations with Empire National Bank in New York, which entailed phone calls at all hours, since Americans seemed unaware of the time difference between the two countries.

When he had received a curt message to attend a meeting about Martindale in James Malpas's office 'immediately', he had been mildly irritated by the assumption that he could drop everything at the Corporate Financier's request. Charles's department had pushed their overseas clients into Martindale in the days when it had been a racy stock-market performer. Several Arab governments were still significant shareholders, but Charles hardly thought it was his duty to attend some briefing on the company.

He and Paul Roberts had barely taken their seats around the conference table when James launched into a staccato summary of the situation. Paul was producing a detailed note on the company and it was time to pump up the price a bit, he explained.

'Why doesn't Martindale do a tour of the City institutions to drum up interest?' asked Ravenscroft, and then without waiting for a reply he added, 'Or get what's-his-name to give his investors a spin in a Tornado, or something. That usually thrills them to bits.'

Malpas bristled and avoided the languid blue eyes while he explained that their friend Purves did not inspire confidence. There would be as little investor contact as possible. It was some minutes before the Old Etonian grasped that the once-mighty electronics firm was hovering on the edge of a financial abyss. Ravenscroft pulled a censorious face.

'Perhaps I should be telling my chaps to start shifting out of Martindale and into something else in the sector. Any good ideas?' he asked Paul innocently.

Charles was evidently unmoved by the possibility that Martindale could take its business to a rival merchant bank if Purves found out that Brodie McClean's overseas clients were selling his shares. It would be Malpas's job to explain it to the board.

'You're the Martindale expert, are you?' Ravenscroft asked Paul mildly. 'What do you make of things? Would you really hang on to the shares if you were a holder?'

Charles noticed the look of stark terror on the young analyst's face, and the quick glance at Malpas before he replied. What he didn't see was the fury his question had caused the Corporate Financier. Who gave a damn about shareholders, thought James. The fee was what mattered.

Paul cleared his throat, and glanced down at his notes. 'There's enough work to keep the production lines busy. And these kind of volumes mean big margins. Martindale's still in some very attractive niche markets. Really the shares are at the bottom of their trading range, and begging to be bought at this level.'

'Precisely,' said Malpas fiercely. He was so tense he was one jump ahead of a fit. James liked his instructions to be carried out quickly, and without argument. He did not need advice from Charles Ravenscroft, who was famous for the length of his lunches and the size of his expense account.

'So when's this note going out?' Ravenscroft sounded unhappy, but resigned, and Paul realised the man had probably given in through boredom.

'Monday morning,' he replied.

Ravenscroft glanced at his watch and got to his feet with a brief smile. He could not bear dealing with men like Malpas who became so utterly wound up about one little deal.

James scowled at his retreating back. He would have liked to tear the man's arm off and ram it down his throat. Meanwhile Charles wafted back to the upper regions of carpet and silence with a pleasing Debussy melody going through his head, and not much else.

'You handled that well,' James commented simply when the Old Etonian had left. 'What's your mother's name? She's still around, I hope?'

'Irene. She lives in Cheadle Hume.' Paul was a little bit thrown by this sudden interest in his personal life. Then as he sat at the conference table, watching Malpas silhouetted against the window, making a call, he heard a dealing account being opened for Mrs Irene Roberts. Mrs Roberts was placing an order to buy 5000 shares in a stock he'd never heard of. Malpas covered the mouthpiece and hissed at Paul to write down her address.

Two minutes later Malpas was sitting opposite him again, his eyes twinkling. 'You had better warn your mother that a settlement note'll be arriving. That share will have performed by settlement day, so you won't have to pay for them before you sell them. With any luck, she'll be getting a nice cheque.'

Malpas hesitated as Paul's eyebrows knitted together. 'Settlement day is ten days after shares are purchased. If your shares have gone down then you have to pay up, but if your investments are performing then the money flows your way. It's the moment of reckoning – the final judgement.'

Paul's jaw hung open as Malpas explained that he dealt with the firm of brokers in Bristol that he had just called so regularly that they would take his word for it that Mrs Irene Roberts could cover the cost of the purchases. Paul was thrilled at the prospect of explaining to his mother how damned clever he had been, and giving her a share of the spoils. But more, much more, he felt profound delight that he was finally accepted in the gang of people who really knew what was happening in the City.

'So,' James said cosily, 'let's talk strategy. We need to tell investors in the defence sector why they should be shifting their weight of holdings into Martindale.'

Paul looked doubtful, but James anticipated his reservations. 'That's the point of creative accounting,' he explained gently. 'Take a positive view of Martindale's prospects, and be a bit bear-ish about one of their competitors – doesn't matter who. Second—' he said, and paused for Paul to catch up with his instructions.

'Draw up a list of bull points for the salesmen to use to persuade their clients to go for more Martindale.'

Malpas was getting into his stride. This was what he loved about his job – the fight, the campaign to win over the investors, the tactics and the persuasion. The words flowed as if he had done it all before, which of course he had. After half an hour's dictation the master sat back in his chair, rubbing his hands. Paul knew when he was being dismissed and headed for the door.

'I'd like to see the final draft as soon as you can,' James called after the analyst.

'And Paul,' he added quietly, 'don't use an office phone to call your mother, will you? Remember, they're taped down in your department.' He smiled briefly, and turned back to his papers.

Dick Zander pulled a rectangle of plastic from his pocket and waved it over the sensor beside the door. The red light clicked to green, and he pushed through the double doors into the Fertiliser Division Research Facility. The Chief Financial Officer of GT knew these corridors well enough to have no problem in finding the rooms he wanted. He felt an almost fatherly interest in the development work in the department, and he visited this area of the GT site often. The sums involved in Dermitron were huge, both the capital invested, and the potential returns: this little darling would have whatever it needed to help it graduate from prototype to production.

When he arrived at the Dermitron laboratory he was pleased to see the five team members hard at work. 'Bruce!' he said in a cheerful drawl. 'I've got something for you.'

The man he had hailed looked up from his terminal screen with a slightly startled smile. 'How's it going, Dick? Good trip?'

Zander eased himself into the empty chair beside the lean, sandy-haired man in his late thirties. 'Well, I'm still in the phase of jet lag where you feel like you've been hit by a truck, but it was a pretty good vacation.' He slid a gramophone record in a battered cover on to the lab bench between them. 'And I found this for you in London.'

Carretta's sharp features contorted into a broad toothy grin. 'Jesus, you are some kind of hero,' he said admiringly as he picked up the record with careful, loving hands. 'Miles Davis, 1964. Where the hell did you find it?'

'Hours of happy hunting through second-hand record shops and stalls in London,' Zander said, as he stretched his long legs out in front of him. 'You should see the haul I've brought back. But the minute I found this, I knew who'd want it.'

Carretta shook his head in wonder and examined the record cover as if it were a religious relic. 'This is incredible. What do I owe you?'

'Not a thing. Just turn Dermitron in on time,' Zander said with a wink. 'How's it going?'

The head of the Dermitron team grimaced slightly. 'Can we talk? I'll just put this in my office.'

A moment later they were both out in the corridor, walking slowly side by side, hands in pockets. 'Nancy have a good time?' Carretta asked for something to say until they were out of earshot of his colleagues.

Zander snorted. 'The trade deficit'll take a hammering this month: she bought every woollen sweater Marks and Spencer had in stock, so that's the Christmas presents dealt with. And an investment banker took us to Glyndebourne Opera. Nancy loved every minute of it. She adores that stuff, as you know, and it's impossible to get tickets unless you're with a member, so she had a helluva of a good time.'

'I always knew investment bankers must have some use,' Carretta commented with a shrug.

'Max is still keen on finding a British company to buy so we can get into Europe – and the Middle East, of course. The British have been sucking those people's peckers for so long that they've got some solid contacts there. Discreet, too.'

'So we're looking for a British company?' Carretta mused.

Zander nodded. 'But quietly, yeah? Don't let that go too far.' Then, as they pushed through another set of double doors that marked the end of the Fertiliser Division corridors: 'So what's the problem?' he asked in an altogether less conversational tone.

'One of the guys is shaky,' Carretta told him, like a thoughtful schoolmaster worrying about a promising but errant pupil. 'I'm concerned about his commitment to the project. It's just off-the-cuff remarks at this stage, but I think it's serious, and I want to do something about it now.'

'Who are we talking about?' Zander asked as they paused by a drinking fountain.

'Raul Gutierez, the Mexican guy from LA – remember? He's falling apart.' Carretta bent over for a slurp of water and wiped his mouth with the back of his hand. 'Very unhappy about his work.'

'What's happened – has he got religion or something? Not another Born Again Christian, surely?' Zander asked with a cold laugh.

'No, that was a different one.'

'The bearded guy?'

'Yeah, but he's gone. No problems with him.'

'You sure? He hasn't turned into Albert Schweitzer?' Zander asked with an impatient jangle of the coins in his pocket.

'No, really Dick,' Carretta said with a placating and nervous smile. 'Nothing to be concerned about with that one. He's gone off to Washington to the Right to Life crowd.'

Zander pulled a face, as if he wasn't convinced by Carretta's explanation. 'We're keeping an eye on him though, aren't we?' he asked pointedly.

'Yup. Relax,' Carretta responded a little too quickly. 'This guy is more of a problem. It isn't religion with him. His kid brother was shot in a mugging a couple of months ago. Some drug addict killed him, and Raul is preoccupied by it. I'm worried he's going to start spreading disaffection.'

'Has he seen anybody about it?' Zander's voice had lost all trace of its usual good humour. 'How far has this got?'

'Don't worry. It's just throwaway remarks at this stage, but I think we should act immediately.'

'We haven't got a whole lot of choice,' Zander responded, and set his jaw in a Clint Eastwood scowl for a moment. 'Does your department want to deal with this?'

Carretta stopped in his tracks and the colour drained from his already gaunt cheeks. 'What about Security?' he asked with a wobble in his voice.

'Nope,' his superior replied with pursed lips. 'Let's keep this as localised as possible.' Then he paused and took note of the terror in Carretta's eyes. 'You got a problem with this? Can I still count on your commitment to the programme?'

'A hundred per cent, Dick,' his subordinate chipped in with terrified enthusiasm. His upper lip had become moist, and he blinked under the steady glare of his boss.

Then a smile crept across Zander's face. 'How's Bruce Junior doing, by the way? Still giving 'em hell in the Little League?'

When Charlotte reluctantly crawled out of bed at ten o'clock on Sunday morning, she found a treat awaiting her in the kitchen. She dipped her spoon into the little plastic tub of aubergine pâté and took a chew of cold lamb kebab. It was good, but not wonderful. She wiped her mouth with a paper towel and surveyed the remains of the takeaway on her kitchen table. Here was the empirical evidence that cold Lebanese food for breakfast simply could not compete with the remains of an Indian meal.

Prawn dansak, coagulated and mixed with lumpy rice; cold bhindi bhajis; the butter chicken that just couldn't be finished when it had been brought home after work . . . now *there* were the makings of an excellent breakfast. Charlotte realised how dull and conventional it was to concede it, but the Lebanese had tasted better hot, when she had fetched it from the place around the corner the previous evening. She gathered up the containers with regret and put them in the bin. They had died magnificently.

Charlotte's flat was the home of a devoted journalist and career woman. It was neat because she paid a Portuguese girl to come in twice a week to clean, wash and iron. And it was tastefully furnished because she had raided her parents' house in Hertfordshire. But there were no traces of its occupant. Charlotte spent very little time here, but when she unexpectedly got an evening to herself she didn't feel particularly comfortable within these magnolia-painted walls. Even with the television on, or a compact disc playing, the place had the impersonal, empty tension of a hotel room.

The bedroom was a mere dormitory, not a sanctuary from the rest of the world where she could retreat for comfort. Here there had been no great moments to cherish, and even the Klimt posters on the walls were made bland and unerotic by their neutral surroundings. The only personality in the room was Alfred the Rabbit who had slept in her bed since she was six. Apart from his benign presence, the flat knew it was being used at a functional level, and gave nothing in return.

When Charlotte examined her face in the bathroom mirror that morning, she saw that her tan was in need of a top-up: a healthy complexion was advantageous on the small screen. Her flat was at the top of an Edwardian house that had been renovated up to affluent young persons' standards in the 1980s and she had only to climb one flight of stairs to be out in the full glare of the sun. She settled down on a beach towel and tried to occupy her mind with something interesting that did not involve childish fantasies about how successful she might become; or paranoid seethings about what a failure she would be, and how everyone would enjoy watching her falter.

Then she remembered her dream from the previous night. She had been sitting in the back seat of her father's car with her brother, and her parents were in the front. She had kept asking them where they were taking her. Her mother had pretended not to hear, and her father had concentrated on the road with grim determination. Her brother stared out of the window, uninterested. Finally her mother had said they were taking her to the vet, who was going to put her down.

It distressed her when she uncovered these mountains of rubbish piled in dark corners of her brain. Her parents were ideal, Charlotte told herself firmly, as if she was trying to win an argument. They did not interfere in her private life, for instance: their legal work gave them a large enough slice of other people's rapes, divorces and murders to satisfy their curiosity about the human condition. Indeed, they might have been disappointed by their offspring's very occasional flings, had they known about them. That was how she herself felt – disappointed.

What about Paul Roberts? Was she going to start something with him this evening – unadventurous, unpromiscuous Charlotte? She shifted her position on the roof to stay in the full blast of the sun and considered the possibility. Wasn't he too laid back for her? But perhaps he could teach her how to relax and get more out of the simple things in life; things like taking it easy and being mellow?

Fuck the simple things in life, she thought in a frantic wave of anger. My existence is pointless enough when I run about like a maniac, keeping too busy to confront the irrelevance of my ceaseless activity. Isn't it even more futile and self-indulgent to yawn along in a nirvana-like state, without even the diversion of getting terribly annoyed about the Catholic Church, or people mistreating animals?

Then she realised that she was lying there with fists clenched and teeth grinding, and she laughed out loud at herself. At that moment there was a clink of porcelain from the adjoining roof where someone from the neighbouring building was having breakfast. They had gone quiet, perhaps concerned that an escaped psychopath was hiding next door, cackling and muttering behind the chimneys. A blushing Charlotte gathered up her belongings and returned to her flat to begin battle in the kitchen.

Three-quarters of an hour after Paul had arrived, they were naked and writhing about on Charlotte's bed. His jeans and T-shirt lay in a tangled heap on the floor with her white cotton dress. An empty bottle of Edna Valley Chardonnay stood in her kitchen, awaiting its final journey to the bottle bank. He had brought the wine with him as a contribution towards dinner. It was exactly what they had drunk at Kensington Place, and Charlotte would later reflect on that gesture as symptomatic of Paul's character and lack of originality.

But right now, with a good portion of the bottle in her stomach, she was diverted by his athletic body and his broad shoulders, rather than those other, more subtle, failings. Paul might not have known his way around an opera libretto or a wine list, but an active social life at college had given him no such reticence with sex. He took her confidently and firmly, pushing her down on the bed, and spreading himself on top of her, holding her arms away, and kissing her neck and breasts eagerly. There was no question of Charlotte playing an active part such as rolling on top of him; he was in complete control and he explored her with an energy she found exciting. He said nothing, no murmured affection or confessions of longing. It almost frightened her when he separated her legs and tried to force himself inside.

'Ah,' she gasped as she wriggled away. 'Aren't we forgetting something?' She leant on one elbow, and pushed the hair out of her face. Then she smiled when he looked bemused. 'Did you bring one?' she asked gently. He shook his head, and she had to push him off her so she could reach the drawer of her bedside table.

'Oh,' he said flatly as she handed him the little foil envelope and kissed his moist forehead. A few seconds later he was back on top of her, and he had slipped into her, but with less urgency than before.

Charlotte hoped her intervention hadn't cooled him down. Then she felt a tremor of ecstasy as he began to push, and she ran her hands along the ridges of muscle on either side of his back. He pounded into her faster and harder, panting and then groaning, as she tried desperately to hold him close enough to get some pleasure herself. But he would not be slowed down, and she realised he was completely unaware of how far from orgasm she was.

When he had come he lay with his head buried in her hair, and she heard him sigh with contentment. It was, she thought, the nearest she had ever come to identifying with a cow mounted by a randy, insistent bull. She waited for him to ask her how it was for her, to apologise for losing control of himself, overwhelmed by his solitary orgasm, to say something, anything. But he stretched and smiled, then asked if she had any tissues.

For a moment her cheeks burned with indignation, then she was filled with sadness, and a feeling of inadequacy. While he was in the bathroom she lay on her stomach wondering what was wrong with her. Orgasms were wonderful, she thought wistfully. It was just sex that was such a drag. Coming was like eating an artichoke: all that effort for the good little bit at the end. Why did it have to be so difficult? Why couldn't she get there as effortlessly as everyone else on the planet obviously did?

Why had Paul made no effort, beyond the perfunctory bite on the nipples that constituted foreplay? Was she so odd, to need the encouragement of a tongue or a finger to get her machinery working, she thought, and she looked miserably at the early evening sunshine coming through her curtains.

Then Charlotte wondered if she was frigid – whatever that meant. It made her restless and irritable so she got up and pulled the bed straight. She felt her vagina burp, and waited for the glob of semen to roll down the inside of her thigh. Then she remembered the condom, and his surprise at her request that he use one.

When Paul reappeared, looking fresh and cheerful, she pushed these lingering concerns to the back of her mind and headed for the bathroom. While she took a quick shower he dressed, opened a second bottle of wine and turned on the television, ready for the NNN *Business Programme*.

'What did you think?' he asked her cautiously when the show was over.

'Of you, on the TV?'

'Yes,' he said, sounding a bit ashamed of having asked.

Charlotte put the plates on the table and tried not to smile. The sexual conquerer was once more the gauche and diffident young man. She pulled the casserole dish out of the oven; a whiff of garlic, cheese and olive oil drifted up into her nostrils, and she shivered with excitement. She preferred a good meal to a screw any day. An orgasm is an orgasm, but a plate of pasta is a damned fine meal.

She served the wedges of molten food and assured him he was a television natural. Then she sat down opposite him and looked him straight in the eyes for the first time since they had got out of the bed. 'And what did you think?' she asked.

'What do you mean?'

'My report,' she said with a smile. 'Did it tell the viewers what they should know about William Stone and Son?'

He chewed a mouthful of pasta thoughtfully then nodded his head. 'It was good, though you weren't hard enough on Stone about his share price under-performance. This is wonderful,' he broke off to say, flashing a broad grin at her. 'Did you make it yourself?'

'Yes. But what do you mean about Stone? Isn't it the kind of company we need more of in Britain – with quality products, good design, and research and development – even if he won't talk to me about it on TV.' She rolled her eyes heavenward.

Paul looked at her face across the table and thought how beautiful she was. He had never been to bed with such a lovely woman before, and he intended to make sure it became a habit with this one. He could hardly believe his luck.

A quarter to nine on a Monday morning was late for James Malpas, but for Sir Terence Purves the phone call from his merchant banker was frenetic crack-of-dawn activity. Malpas was checking that his client had received a copy of Paul Roberts's note on Martindale in the post that morning. Purves had indeed looked at it, although he had not got around to reading it yet.

'It's an excellent piece of research, and it should generate quite a bit of interest amongst new investors,' Malpas said prissily. As

Purves listened he thought the tension in James's voice was like a rubber band being stretched.

'Well, it hasn't done anything yet,' complained the self-made man. 'Share price is still at a turd of a level.'

'It's only a matter of time,' Malpas continued glibly. 'Give the investors a chance to absorb it and they'll soon be piling in.' The merchant banker paused significantly. 'Of course, we could help the share price on its way, Terry . . . and you could make a bit of money at the same time.'

'What do you mean?'

'Get the Martindale staff pension fund to buy some Martindale shares, then when they go up you'll be turning a profit for your own benefit.'

'Oh Christ, how much's this going to cost me?' the businessman grumbled. Neither he nor his merchant banker were overly concerned that the manoeuvre was against the law unless Martindale's shareholders agreed.

'You'll find that you don't have to buy many shares to have an effect,' Malpas commented archly. 'There's very little activity in the market at the moment, summer holidays and all that, so any movement is exaggerated.'

'Yeah, well you make sure I'm not bankrupting meself. It's not the bloody point of the game, is it?' Purves snarled.

'You're absolutely right, of course,' Malpas was quick to agree, although he was gritting his teeth at the man's stupidity. Purves was a true 'graduate of the University of Life', with all the arrogance that usually accompanied that qualification.

When he had got Purves off the phone James sat quietly for a moment, reflecting that he had dealt with his client calmly and firmly. Merchant bankers, like politicians, never concede the possibility of defeat. Yet Malpas knew there was a degree of downside if he failed to bolster up the Martindale price. His department would get a fee whatever happened, but his reputation could be damaged by anything other than total success. Reputation was what brought in business, but in a recession you couldn't be too fussy about the business you took in.

These were not happy times for Brodie McClean: the broking wing was losing much more money than had been budgeted. It was not that they had done particularly badly, Malpas had to admit; there were simply too many competitors out there. James's progress within the bank would be greatly helped if his department didn't add to the collective grief this year.

Malpas turned back to the task at hand. He would buy as much Martindale as possible – quietly, of course. He would stick the stock in two offshore nominee accounts, Cleopatra and Marlborough, but not enough to get his activities noticed, or to cross the five per cent point when he would have to declare his holdings to the Stock Exchange. Later he could sell the stock at a profit, he hoped, and no one would ever know about it. James thought of himself as a cat burglar, stealthy, silent, and leaving no paw-prints anywhere. Shame that his skills were being wasted on salvaging a dog like Terry Purves.

How much better to be engineering elegant, imaginative deals for GT, he thought mournfully. If only he could identify a suitable candidate for the American giant. He stared balefully at Paul's Martindale note, which lay on his desk. Then James had an idea.

Downstairs in the Brodie McClean dealing room, Paul Roberts was hovering over the sales desk, urging Gary and his cavemen to market the Martindale note more aggressively. So far the publication had had little impact on the depressed Martindale share price, and Paul dreaded to think of James's reaction. This was the young man's opportunity to get into the big time: it was his bad luck that he was being asked to make a third-rate relic of the eighties look attractive to recession-burned investors in the nineties.

As the day wore on, Paul worked his way down a list of the biggest insurance companies, talking their fund managers through his research, one bull point at a time. But his phone calls were like spitting in the wind. By four o'clock the analyst had run out of arms to twist, and he was back at his desk in the research department, wondering how on earth he could explain his failure to Malpas. When Gary swaggered up to him, hands in pockets, and smirk on face, Paul expected more bad news, but he was to be pleasantly surprised.

'We've found a home for some excess stock that was clogging up the market,' Gary announced with a cocky toss of his head. 'Mopped it up into one of my client's underweight funds, so the price'll firm up now.'

'Which client?' Paul asked. He could barely stop himself from springing to his feet and hugging Gary.

The salesman shrugged. 'Reckon you owe me a bottle of sherbert. Fancy one at close of play?'

'So who is this special client?' Paul repeated two hours later when he returned from the bar in Coates with another bottle of champagne. He squeezed in beside Gary Smith, and refilled the glasses of the other five Brodie McClean employees who were still in there drinking. Even at eight o'clock, Coates was packed with young men guzzling 'sherbert' as if the recession had never hit the stock market.

Screens suspended from the ceiling displayed the latest prices in New York where the exchange was still open. But more heads were turned towards the other screens where music videos flickered and blared out across the flying-saucer-shaped room. The tables and chairs were made of a dull black metal covered in rubber, and the bar was all chrome tubing and blunt angles. It was as if the bridge of the *Star Ship Enterprise* had been adapted for a lunatic asylum where the inmates had to be protected from doing themselves damage.

'Now, you gotta promise not to pass this on, mate,' Gary said quietly, 'but my client . . . well, let's just say 'e really owes me one, so whenever I get in a tight corner, or we're landed with a shit-line o' stock, old Gordon comes to the rescue.'

'But why?' Paul asked with a furrowed brow. 'It must lose his fund lots of money every time he does what he did today.'

Gary saw their companions were discussing the English cricket team's latest disgraceful performance so he leaned closer to the flushed and perspiring Paul. 'Now, you promise not to breathe a word of this, 'cos 'e'd kill me.'

Paul shook his head vigorously. 'I won't tell anyone.'

'Well, I was Gordon's alibi in court, see. I got up in the witness box and told everyone that it couldn't 'ave been Gordon what done whatever it was, 'cos we was together at the time. Easy. Gordon gets off, but 'e owes me a bit of a favour, doesn't 'e?'

'I suppose he does,' Paul said thoughtfully, and refilled their glasses. They rejoined the cricket conversation but then Paul suddenly remembered the time. 'Shit!' he said, grabbing his jacket and standing up to go. 'I've got to find a taxi. I'm supposed to be meeting someone.' He looked flustered as his friends teased him about rushing off to some bird. Then Gary said he might as well go too.

Out in Moorgate it was still light, and a rosy pink cloud hung over the deserted streets. Paul looked around hopelessly; there were no cabs anywhere. Gary was still chatting away at his side. 'Come on, you're better off with the Central Line' he remarked, seeing Paul's panic. 'It's OK,' he added comfortingly. 'She'll wait for you. Birds always do.'

'Yeah' Paul said without confidence.

As they jogged down Moorgate, Paul thought about Gordon again. His mind was muddled with champagne and he was gasping to catch his breath, but he managed to ask Gary what offence this Gordon had been charged with.

'Someone murdered 'is wife,' Gary puffed as they dashed down the steps to the Underground. 'Someone killed Gordon's wife, and it ended up being 'im what was charged.'

'Really? Bloody hell, that's incredible. Murder . . .' Paul said in pissed astonishment as they got on the escalator down into the bowels of the earth. A gust of warm, sweaty air blew up from the train platform, carrying the stale odour of the recent rush hour with it.

'No wonder he's grateful,' Paul marvelled as they stepped off at the bottom, and loitered between the platforms waiting to see whether an east- or westbound train got in first.

'Yeah,' Gary laughed, ''specially as I was nowhere near the geezer that night.'

A dull roaring noise announced the imminent arrival of Paul's tube.

'But you said you testified that you were with Gordon. That you were his alibi . . .' Paul shouted above the clanking of the train as it pulled in.

'Yeah,' Gary sniggered, pushing Paul towards the open doors of the westbound carriage. 'Wouldn't 'ave been much of a fucking favour otherwise, would it? See ya tomorrow, mate!'

Paul slumped into a seat and watched Gary disappear on to the other platform, his jacket thrown jauntily over his shoulder. There was no time to think about Gary's 'favour' now because the young analyst needed to concentrate on inventing an excuse to give Charlotte. He was already late, and he was also bursting for a pee. As the train hurtled towards Tottenham Court Road he wondered if he would be able to run to the wine bar quicker if he emptied his bladder first. Or should he concentrate on minimising his lateness by missing the pee and dashing through Soho, trying to locate this wine bar that he had never even been to before?

Paul heaved himself to his feet as the train lurched into Tottenham Court Road Station, and the pressure on his bladder became so unbearable that his previous calculations were rendered redundant. The priority was peeing. He stumbled about the circular concourse at the top of the escalator, searching for the welcoming sign with the little stick man, but all he found were unmanned 'passenger information' kiosks, and piles of rubbish.

With a whimper he gave up and tried to climb the stairs to Oxford Street without rupturing his abdomen. When he reached the top he gazed about like some unfortunate alien beamed down from a more civilised planet. He was unfamiliar with this part of town, even when he was sober. Now he was confronted by a distressing cabaret of cow-faced Eurobackpackers chewing McDonalds, and throwing the wrappers on to the pavement. Bagwomen sat in doorways, displaying skinny blistered limbs and wrinkled brown breasts. Menacing young men with knobbly shaven heads and tattoos paced by, looking for trouble.

Just don't make eye contact, Paul told himself as he steered through the crush. Then, for what seemed like an eternity, he wandered about Soho asking directions to Dean Street. When he finally tumbled into the wine bar, he barely noticed the coolness of Charlotte's welcome, such was his desperation to relieve himself. He blurted out an apology and rushed towards the lavatories.

When he returned and slipped on to the bench beside Charlotte he felt at peace with the world. He could walk again without fear of damaging his insides, and she had poured him a glass of white wine, so it seemed that she hadn't noticed he was slightly rat-arsed. When he looked at her properly she seemed more lovely than ever; tanned, and poised.

'So, how was your day?' she asked with a thin sort of smile Paul had not seen before.

He made a facial expression that fully conveyed his exhaustion. Then in a rather pompous tone he explained that he'd been ramping up the Martindale share price. And that he'd soon be working directly for James Malpas, the Director of Corporate Finance, he added reverently. He was pleased when Charlotte wanted to hear more about his prospects in Corporate Finance. And as a business journalist he reckoned Charlotte would appreciate how clever it was to stuff institutions into Martindale.

'Yes, your note landed on my desk today. You wrote glowingly about Martindale, but I thought it was a lousy company. Aren't they in financial trouble – you know, debt?' she asked.

'They've made a real mess of it,' he said dismissively. 'Anyway, that's not our problem. We're there to keep the share price up. That's our duty to our client,' he added with casual expertise. 'Anyway, you're not averse to pushing people's share prices up, are you? Seen what your profile did to David Stone's little company?'

Charlotte nodded, although she didn't think her TV package was quite the same as twisting the truth in a broking note designed to ramp the price. She had tried to present a balanced picture of David Stone's company. For a moment she felt a pang of disappointment that he had not called her to say, 'Well done,' or, 'Thank you,' or even, 'Why didn't you mention so-and-so?' But her thoughts were interrupted by Paul's latest revelation.

'I reckon Stone's an ideal candidate for a bid,' he was saying in a lecturing tone. 'You could do a brilliant job splitting his operation up, and turning each part into a profit centre. It's a wonder someone doesn't come along and swoop on him while his share price is this low. I'm going to put together a note for James suggesting just that.'

'How do you reckon David Stone would react to that?' Charlotte asked simply.

'Well, that's his problem, isn't it?' he shrugged. 'Law of the jungle and all that.' He stroked her hand, which was lying on the table, tensed up into a fist.

'Ah, the law of the jungle. I feel a touch of the efficient market theory coming on,' she said, as if she were a Chinese cadre reciting the thoughts of Chairman Mao. But from the curious expression on Paul's face it was clear that her sarcasm had passed him by. 'A bit of good, old-fashioned asset stripping?' she enlarged, and extracted her hand from beneath his. Through the haze of well-being, Paul detected a critical note in her voice.

'It's the way of the world,' he said affably. 'Dead wood's got to be weeded out. The weak are prey to the strong. It's only healthy.'

'So William Stone and Son is dead wood, is it? That's odd, you know, because when you wrote about that company you seemed pretty impressed.'

Paul shrugged once more and drained his wine glass. He could feel the unpleasant tightening in his bladder once again, and feared he would have to take another trip to the lavatory. He wondered why Charlotte was watching him so carefully, as if she was appraising him from a distance, and it puzzled him that her mood could have changed so quickly. He was getting to his feet when she picked up her handbag, and gripped it firmly under one arm like a sergeant-major's baton. She rose rather more steadily than he had, and frowned as he fumbled to support himself against a chair. He was now quite keen to use the urinal again, but the severe set of her mouth and the hostility in her eyes stopped him in his tracks.

'What is it? Did you have a bad day at work or something?' he asked, and prayed that her answer would be a brief one.

'I think we're wasting our time, Paul. I'm going home.'

'Hang on.' He gestured towards the back of the wine bar. 'I'll be with you in a moment.'

She sighed and shook her head with a swift, irritable movement. 'Paul, you don't understand. I'm not interested in carrying on with this evening. I'm utterly appalled.'

His bladder had begun to throb, and heat prickled across his forehead like a tidal wave of sweat. She sounded very annoyed: perhaps she had guessed that he'd had a few after all, even though he'd carried it off quite well up to now. He held up his index finger and asked her to bear with him for just a minute. 'I don't know what you're on about, but I must get to the loo, . . .' he said, hopping on the spot.

'I'll tell you what I'm on about,' she hissed. 'I'm on about your underdeveloped sense of morality. You can't just pump David Stone for everything there is to know about his company, then get someone to bid for him. It's loathsome, and you know it.'

'Oh, bloody hell!' he wailed. 'I'll talk about it in a second. I've really gotto—'

'Get on with it then, but don't expect me to be here when you return. I despise your behaviour. It's horrible to treat people like that,' she growled through clenched teeth.

'Charlotte, don't get so steamed up. Just hang on a moment before you storm off in a state . . .' he begged her as he edged towards the back of the bar, and that desirable little tiled room.

'Don't tell me I'm *getting steamed up!*' she snarled, her arms rigid by her sides. She turned on her heel and swept out of the bar and into Dean Street.

Paul jiggled up and down and tried to decide whether to go after her or pee. Then he realised he might die if he did not use the loo immediately. He scuttled into the urinal, undoing his zip even before he was at the trough. As he felt that delicious release he considered Charlotte's behaviour. She must have been cross about him turning up late and a bit tipsy, he thought with a snigger. He could make up with her tomorrow, when she was less annoyed, he concluded, shaking himself free of drops.

He collected his jacket from the empty table where they had been sitting a moment ago, and wandered out into the balmy London evening, wondering when he might take her home to Cheshire to meet his parents.

Chapter Six

Raul Gutierez was well-known for the long hours he put in. He might have his doubts about the product he was developing, but he was still conscientious about his responsibilities. The other reason he stayed after hours at the research lab was that his wife Kathy also worked late, and he saw no point in hanging around an empty house, waiting for her to return. As it was he was usually the first one to get home, and he generally made dinner for them both. It seemed only fair since Kathy's job was more emotionally and physically demanding than his: she was in charge of a local shelter for homeless people, and the scale and difficulty of her work had grown at an alarming rate in the last few years. Before the recession most of her clients had been mainly drunks, a few junkies and Vietnam Vets. Now she had whole families to feed, clothe, and save from the inevitable slide into despair and crime.

Some men might have resented the time Kathy put in at the shelter, but Raul was proud of his wife and her devotion to her duties. One of them had to do something socially useful, he reasoned, and it certainly wasn't him. This occupation had not been his first choice after he got his master's degree at CalTec, but that was the way it had turned out. Now he was trapped at GT by the need to pay the mortgage, and the shortage of alternative jobs in his particular branch of industrial chemistry.

Raul, a rotund and bushy-haired twenty-seven-year-old Los Angeleno, considered himself lucky to have such a well-paid job. He wasn't so idealistic that he would throw his career away for the sake of his principles. Anyway, he and Kathy wanted children, and that meant one of them had to earn a reasonable salary to support their family.

At a quarter to seven Raul was debating whether to quit for the evening, or plough through another scientific journal article. He could take the publication home, but he wouldn't concentrate on it if he knew there was something mindlessly diverting on TV. Better to read it with a fresh mind tomorrow, he thought, and marked his page with a ruler.

He was packing his rucksacks when he heard the outer door of the lab open and close, and the key in the lock turn with a metallic click. The cleaner had already been around, so Raul was surprised by the interruption. He put down his bag and poked his head around the corner into the adjoining lab. For a moment he wondered if someone from a fancy-dress party had wandered into the research department by mistake. A man looking like an astronaut in full spacewalking kit was walking slowly and deliberately across the room towards him.

Raul peered into the visor and grinned. 'Bruce, is that you?' he asked in disbelief. 'What are you doing here?'

The astronaut wearing the head-to-toe protective clothing did not return the grin. Nor did he stop until he was two feet away from the dark-eyed, olive-skinned chemist.

'Why are you dressed up like that?' Raul asked with a laugh. But the bemused smile left his face when the astronaut raised his right arm and took aim. He was holding a simple pump-action sprayer, the kind used by gardeners to water plants.

Raul automatically took a step back but the liquid from the sprayer had soaked his face and the upper part of his chest. He shouted and grabbed for his eyes, but it was too late. They stung as if they were on fire, and he felt a sharp pain in his windpipe. The shock made him stagger against the wall, and slump down on to the floor. He coughed and choked, but every breath was like swallowing acid. He couldn't make a noise, let alone get to his feet again. It was as if someone was rubbing sandpaper into his eyes and mouth, and banging an iron bar against his head. He blinked and blinked, but the pain in his eyes got worse, and the clouds in front of him became dark. Then he felt a sharp, prickly shiver go through his head like a wave, and he lost consciousness.

The astronaut looked down at Raul's twitching body, and waited until it had stopped moving. Then he pulled the inert corpse across the floor to the window, which he opened. He returned to the work-bench and laid a chair on its side on the floor. Then on the bench above it he arranged a selection of bottles of liquid that he had pulled from his spacesuit pocket. Some were on their sides, as if they had been knocked over.

Next he turned on the terminal and logged into the Dermitron team's secure files. He brought a page of chemical formulae on to the screen, and squeezed his spray at a patch of the bench counter around the computer. Finally he unscrewed the top of a bottle that was empty, and left it on its side in a small puddle of the liquid. With the window open all night the potency would be gone by morning, when people arrived for work. He would be the first person in anyway, and he would raise the alarm to show there had been an industrial accident. Then they could seal the room until it had been cleansed, and made safe once again. It would be obvious to everyone what had happened to poor Raul.

Few Brodie McClean directors enjoyed easy access to the Chairman of the bank. Even board members made formal appointments to speak to the great man, rather than drop into Sir Anthony's office in the certain knowledge that they would be welcome for a chat. But for Charles Ravenscroft the Chairman's door was always open, as was the drinks cabinet. Perhaps the warmth of Brook's manner had cooled ever so slightly since the leak of the Empire National Bank negotiations; perhaps he did not offer Charles quite as many insights into the confidential matters in his in-tray; but the two were still relaxed and frank with each other. The younger man had no reason to doubt that he was still Brook's chosen successor as Chairman of the board.

It was because of this chumminess that Charles did not think twice about raising his concerns about James Malpas with Sir Anthony when he popped into his office for a glass of sherry before lunch, on the last Monday in July. Their shared background meant that they could dispense with oblique references to their fellow board members or bank affairs.

'There's been some grumbling round the building about Corporate Finance's latest pantomime,' Charles said while the Chairman was pouring him a chilled Tio Pepe from the minibar. 'They put out a ludicrously optimistic note about Martindale, and stuffed all and sundry into the bloody stock on the back of their recommendation. Now I'm hearing rumours round the market that Martindale could show a loss when it reports its half-year figures next month.'

Charles paused and hoped the Chairman would meet his gaze, but the older man occupied himself with the dispensing of sherry. Ravenscroft wondered if he had understood anything he had just said. Then Brook grunted and handed him his glass.

'You know you can't go snooping around Malpas's department, Charles,' he said in a weary voice. 'I dare say Martindale *is* a shady company, run by a little tyke, but until those interim profit figures are released we have no grounds to chastise Corporate Finance.' He sat down heavily behind his desk and looked exhausted from the effort of pouring the drinks. 'Malpas has been keeping large portions of this bank afloat with the results he produces, year after year. So let's just give him time to sort out the Martindale situation.'

'But it doesn't look good for us.' Ravenscroft's voice sounded unusually hard and angry. 'And more to the point, this charade could cost us dear – not to mention our wretched clients. Martindale's plummeted since the note was published.'

Brook gazed at the carpet as he concentrated on this distressing analysis. To make him feel more uncomfortable, his International Director completed the picture.

'People in this building are saying he's been using those bloody nominee accounts of his to try to keep the share price up. Oh I know it's just gossip, and we have no way of knowing what James is actually up to, since his department is as tight as a bear's bum, but just for the sake of argument, say he *has* been buying Martindale.

What happens when he dumps his shares on the market? He'll make a bloody great loss – that's what he'll have to handle, a possible shortfall on his profits this year. I tell you,' Charles said angrily, 'James had better come up with something brilliant to dig himself out of *this* particular hole.'

Ravenscroft stood by the window and watched the Chairman wearily rubbing his eyes. His retirement at the end of the summer couldn't come a day too soon as far as Sir Anthony was concerned. He intended to bow out after signing the deal with Empire National Bank; that would be his swan song. He no longer had the enthusiasm to plunge into the minutiae of inter-departmental warfare. He would leave all that to the willing Charles Ravenscroft, his successor. He couldn't foresee any stumbling blocks that would prevent Charles from stepping smoothly into his shoes – and that, at least, was a comfort to him.

Beside *'Anthony Brook'* Malpas wrote the initials *C.R.*. He put the same letters by the name *'Charles Ravenscroft'*. When he came to the bank's financial man he penned his own initials. If there was a vote tomorrow, he concluded, it would be a close-run thing; Ravenscroft had the chairmanship, but only just. The stewardess offered him a glass of champagne which he refused. His mind was racing ahead to what favours he would have to deliver to clinch the support of the main board directors.

Paul Roberts was sitting quietly beside him, studying the Global Technologies' annual report. He was disappointed to see his boss turn down the champagne, but he followed suit. He had been looking forward to the perks of travelling Blow Job Class; finally he was one of the princes of the global expense account village. Then he realised that his boss was deep in his work, and he felt obliged to concentrate on the purpose of their journey.

As with most Malpas projects, the trip to America was shrouded in mystery. It was only when they had met at the airport that Malpas had handed him the GT file and revealed that they would be trying to win the giant US defence contractor as a corporate client. The dumbfounded Paul was advised to study the company, and be ready with suggestions for GT's expansion into the British and Continental military markets through acquisition.

Paul was baffled by the need for the MI6-style secrecy, but he received his work without question. Malpas's mood had become increasingly sour since the less-than-successful Martindale share ramp. That was hardly surprising, even though there had been no adverse publicity about it. Charlotte had been right about the laziness of journalists when she had told him there weren't many Woodwards and Bernsteins in the Square Mile, he reflected.

Paul was working in an office adjoining Malpas's these days. As promised, he was the Head of Corporate Finance's right-hand man. His pay had doubled, but so had his hours, or so it seemed. He would have had little opportunity to see Charlotte now, even if she had wanted to be with him, he thought bitterly. He turned his attention once more to the Global Technologies statistics.

Back in London, at the National News Network studios, Charlotte sat at her terminal scanning the wires services for something interesting for tonight's news. The only stories that had broken by lunchtime, however, were both from the United States, where the day was just beginning. There was a report from Washington DC on the forthcoming congressional debate on the President's new war on drugs. The Administration wanted to pay for the destruction of drug crops in narcotics-producing countries, and to provide seed and manpower to plant new commodity crops for local farmers. The money was supposed to come out of their overseas aid budget, and this was causing controversy, as was the whole programme. However, the journalist who had filed the wires report predicted that the President's initiative would win the vital vote.

This dispatch was followed by one from the United Nations in New York. Informed sources had indicated that Britain would be joining America and several other industrialised countries in rejecting a move to ban styrene monomers, a substance used in polystyrene packaging, which was thought to be destroying the ozone layer.

Neither report lingered in Charlotte's brain for more than a nanosecond; then they were sent the way of interviews with football stars and items on health scares – the mental rubbish bin. It was obvious that township violence in South Africa would dominate this evening's NNN News. Never mind that it wasn't a new or particularly strong story; never mind that worse violations of human rights happened in Tibet and East Timor every day. Reporters in Britain believed that South Africa illustrated the world at its worst, and the viewers must be told so, even though they weren't interested. The handy thing about reporting events in Soweto was that the good guys were conveniently painted black. It made it much easier for journalists to comprehend than civil war in Bosnia or the Sahel.

The monotony of the morning's news made Charlotte's mind wander: like an uncontrollable dog it was best kept on a short lead. Her thoughts had settled on Paul, and the return to her solitary life as ambitious media woman. She was glad that she had chucked him, she decided sensibly. But Paul would not be metaphorically shrugged off so easily.

To convince herself that she had done the right thing, she imagined the monotonous routine; Saturday night with cans of beer in front of the telly, watching Paul watching The Match; meeting his friends – nice blokes who discussed the relative merits of cars – in slightly seedy pubs; merry conversation before and during the vindaloo at the local curry house. Then his humourless sex-by-numbers. Inevitably there would have been earnest sessions with his sweet and lovely Mum, cosy little chats over the washing up. She would gaze at Charlotte with liquid eyes and watch her face for a response to the hints about 'settling down' and 'starting a family', never put so bluntly as 'marriage and children', naturally. Charlotte squirmed in embarrassment and got up to hunt down a chocolate bar.

When she returned to her desk she found that the second post had arrived, and in among the tedious press releases on new innovations in banking there was a letter postmarked Ely, Cambridgeshire. Inside was a card with a painting of Venus by Botticelli. Within was a brief, handwritten message: *Dear Charlotte, I enjoyed your profile of our company, and I've been acting on your valued advice. I've got my merchant bank to arrange a series of City lunches for me to meet my investors. Would it be too much of an imposition to tap your brain once more before I face them? I know you are terribly busy, but can I propose dinner? Please call me. Yours ever, David Stone.*

A pleasant fizzing palpitation of the heart brought a blush to her cheeks as she re-read the card, and she struggled to keep the Cheshire Cat grin under control. Then she reached for the telephone.

Paul wanted to go out and see New York City when they arrived, but James insisted on dinner at the hotel, then went to his room to work. Paul was left to his own devices so he wandered around Manhattan, but had no idea where he was. When he returned to the hotel he saw James, dressed in a black motorbike jacket, slipping into a cab. His boss didn't notice Paul, and the bemused younger man had no intention of saying hello. He went to his room and entertained himself, flicking through the multiplicity of television channels.

While Paul marvelled at game shows where contestants won the equivalent of the gross national product of Guatemala for answering questions even a ten-year-old could have coped with, Malpas was trying to catch the eye of a short blond boy. He reckoned the slender, muscle-bound creature he was watching couldn't be more than sixteen. They were standing at the bar of a Greenwich Village club called The Mineshaft. James had been giving the boy meaningful stares, but the blond had been camping it up with his friends further down the bar. His taunting, offhand attitude irritated James so much that he was determined to get him. It was the worst kind of teasing, and the more he watched the blond flaunt himself, the more James became obsessed by his quest.

Eventually the boy allowed his big blue eyes to settle on his admirer. He sidled up, and the older man bought him a drink. After a perfunctory conversation they retreated into a room with black walls and dim lighting. There were several other couples there, sprawled on mattresses on the floor, but the noise of the disco music drowned out all other sounds. In one corner, slings hung suspended from the ceiling, where men sat and spread their legs, rather like a gynaecologist's couch with stirrups. Underneath them their partners would crouch, shirt-sleeves rolled up, and ready to insert their fists. But fist-fucking was not to James's taste, as he made clear to Blue Eyes. Nor was he interested in watching him defecate on to the floor, which was another popular form of supposedly erotic behaviour here. Vibrating 'butt plugs' and 'enema masters' had no allure for him, either.

James made sure that the boy understood there was to be no rough stuff; he didn't want any marks left on his body. Many of the men at The Mineshaft dressed in a manner that made it clear to potential conquests that they yearned for a bit of bruising and pain. To prove it they wore 'cock rings', leather collars studded with metal to increase the sensation during penetration; or steel rivets through their nipples for no obvious reason. They also sported harnesses of black leather under their jacket and trousers, as other people wear vests and boxer shorts. Leather was universally thought to be both sexually stimulating and practical because unpleasant messes could so easily be wiped off.

James and the blond with the beautiful cheekbones went in search of an unpopulated corner in the black room. The boy's semen tasted of raspberries, and he offered to sell James the powder that produced this desirable effect. When it came to James's turn the older man reached into his jacket for a condom, but this provoked a bad-tempered response from the handsome young creature.

'Oh no, you don't!' the boy spat. 'If you want me, you take me as I am.' But before James could ask what he was talking about, Blue Eyes sat up and was reaching for his shirt. 'I don't know how you can believe all that shit,' he remarked testily.

James grabbed his hand to stop him doing up his buttons. He wasn't about to let this little Adonis disappear so easily. 'What do you mean?' he asked.

'It's a heterosexual plot, the HIV thing,' the boy explained fiercely. 'It's a means of control to stop us expressing ourselves.'

James had never been part of the 'us' to which the angry young man referred. In fact, he would have denied he was 'gay' – a word he loathed almost as much as he hated the fairy politics being espoused by his captivating partner. He scorned Queer solidarity in all its manifestations, and felt only contempt for the limp-wristed queens who shouted it from the roof-tops. James just followed his physical instincts, and shunned categorisation.

As he listened to the fury of the pretty boy beside him, his only thought was to calm him down and carry on with what they had been doing. James assumed he had insulted the boy by inferring that he was infected, so he stroked his suntanned chest and coaxed him back on to the mattress. When the boy eventually obliged, he had unscrewed the bottom of the silver bullet that hung around his neck and offered it to James. The Englishman willingly sniffed the amyl nitrite deep into his lungs and passed the bullet back. When the rush hit him, James was beyond restraint.

The following morning he rose early for a vigorous swim in the hotel pool, and by eight o'clock he and Paul were on the New Jersey Turnpike, headed south. Paul looked out of the window and thought of the Simon and Garfunkel line about counting the cars on the New Jersey Turnpike. The reality was disappointing. Mount Laurel itself was a six-lane freeway of a town, lined by Dunkin Donuts, waterbed showrooms, and funeral homes that looked like municipal lavatories.

The GT compound was more familiar territory, resembling every industrial park at home. As soon as they had taken their seats around Dick Zander's conference table, Malpas got to the point, saying he believed he had a candidate worthy of consideration. Paul's ears pricked up at this news. He'd thought they were here to discuss generalities with the Americans, and he felt increasingly uncomfortable as his boss continued.

'Its share price is bombed out,' Malpas explained. Paul had a nasty feeling he knew what was coming next, and he tried to keep the look of horror from his face. 'Investor confidence is low because of years of mismanagement, but the core business of Martindale could make a good fit for you.' Malpas gestured towards Paul, who flinched involuntarily as if someone had poked a stick at his eyes.

'Paul Roberts here knows the company inside out. He can explain how Martindale would give you a manufacturing capability in the UK, a sales force with strong credibility in the most promising countries who are establishing or modernising defence forces, and of course a launch pad for your push into Europe.'

Zander picked up a pencil. 'Let's talk money, shall we, James – *before* we get Paul to run through the whole thing.'

The Chief Financial Officer smiled briefly at the analyst who had broken into a cold sweat. Malpas leaned forward with his hands folded neatly on the table, and addressed the American's question with a cool authority that concealed his nerves.

'I think Martindale would cost GT the equivalent of two billion dollars in cash, but you don't have to lay out a penny. Not with desirable stock like yours,' he added quickly. 'Martindale shareholders would be pleased to take your paper instead of the stuff they hold. In reality it would be a partial bid to get enough stock to have effective control.'

'So if the investors are so reluctant to hold Martindale,' Zander asked mildly, 'why should GT want to take it on?'

'Paul?' said Malpas, handing on the question like a perfect rugby pass.

'Argh,' the analyst squeaked, but James was deliberately looking down at his notes. Paul cleared his throat and grinned stupidly at Zander. 'Martindale,' he began slowly, 'has suffered from unwise expansion at a time when domestic defence markets were drying up, and the management lacked the wit to diversify or upgrade. There are several component parts of Martindale that could be sold off quite profitably.'

Zander grinned as the young man smoothtalked his bank into earning a fee from the dismemberment of the wretched Martindale. Fees for mergers and acquisitions; fees for divestiture; fees for lending money, Zander thought in jaded amusement. At least the foreman in a meat-packing factory doesn't pretend he's finding creative solutions; he says he's overseeing people packing meat. When would these mediocrities find a proper occupation, the American wondered.

Paul fished two copies of his recent Martindale note out of his briefcase, having just remembered they were there, more by luck than good judgement. 'I go through each production facility,' he explained. 'The capacity, the—' He stopped abruptly as Zander plucked both copies from his hand.

'Mind if I take these?' the American said as he stood up. 'I'll let the CEO see this. He's going to join us later, but I'd like him to run his eyes over this first.'

When Zander had left the room, Malpas turned to his colleague with a tense smile on his face. Paul was about to ask why he had been thrown in at the deep end, but James was one step ahead of him, as usual.

'Well done, Paul. Very nicely handled,' he purred. 'That was most impressive.' And Malpas grinned at his prodigy's shaken expression.

'I thought our first duty was to our client,' Paul countered. 'That's what you told me before. This is against the rules, isn't it?' he scowled.

James rolled his eyes in irritation. 'The rules, Paul, are there to frustrate creative people. Playing by the rules is just an excuse that dullards use to justify their failure and lack of imagination. Look, I was afraid if I told you about it you'd try to dissuade me, or would refuse to come here. But you did brilliantly,' he said heartily, and poured out more flattery. Paul's anger subsided. Then he began to feel quite pleased with himself.

'This has to be the one, you know Paul,' James confided. 'All over Wall Street there are blue chip investment banks working on bid ideas for Zander and Clark: that's what we're up against. I worked on Wall Street in the mid-eighties when the bank bought a brokerage there. Everyone in London was doing it at the time, nurturing fantasies of building a global network, because London's time zone is halfway between America and Japan. Of course, using the same logic Accra was also a candidate, but no one had thought of that,' he sneered.

'But you know, the six months I spent there really exploded some myths. For instance, the men who power-dressed, and shuttled about in limousines talking into two mobile phones at once, were not always worthy of the Gordon Gecko image. They spent days on their calculations, to be fair, but their conclusions were less useful than those of a British accountant working out sums on the back of an envelope. The difference was style and presentation, and this is where the Americans win hands down.' Malpas paused for breath and flicked a speck of lint from his sleeve.

'The ones I knew were preoccupied by who was taking the most expensive skiing trip to Aspen,' he went on. 'And they used this crypto-military language around the office, especially the ones who hadn't served in Vietnam, but pretended they had. These same men were afraid to take the subway home from work. Of course, the ones who'd actually been to Vietnam stayed quiet.' Malpas stared out of the window as if he was in a trance. 'Extraordinary that a whole nation can be traumatised by the death of less than sixty thousand troops, a mere morning's losses at the Somme.'

'Max's just coming now,' said Zander as he stuck his head around the door, and they stood up to shake hands with the Chief Executive Officer of GT.

Max Clark grunted a monosyllabic greeting and eased himself into the chair at the head of the table. He stank of cigars, and beads of perspiration dotted his cranium like condensation. 'OK,' he mumbled to his money man.

'Paul, what would you do with Martindale's capacity?' asked Zander.

They were on to one of Paul's favourite areas now – the future of the European defence hardware industry. He was confident on this subject, and for the next twenty minutes he took Zander and Clarke through the arguments for smart defensive weapons, rather than heavyweight offensive equipment.

'How about destroyers and carriers?' interrupted Zander.

Paul shook his head. He doubted that many nations could invest such huge sums of money in relatively unmanoeuvrable, inflexible platforms; and they were exposed to attack and easily spotted, Paul added.

'Kid's right,' said Clark, waving his cigar at Paul. 'Navy's fucked.'

When they got to money the discussion was back in Malpas's court. Paul had no way of telling what impact their sales pitch was making until the bluff Chief Executive held up his chubby hands and all conversation stopped.

'OK. Enough horseshit. This fits most of the things we been looking for. This is good,' he pronounced in his guttural growl. 'But how come you know so much about their finances, eh?' he asked and squinted at Malpas as if they were communicating across a foggy room.

'They're our clients.'

Clark nearly fell off his chair laughing. He dusted the cigar ash off his trousers and shook his head with amusement. 'I like these sons of bitches,' he said to Zander. 'Let's do business.'

It was arranged that Paul would stay on for two days in Mount Laurel to go over every aspect of the GT organisation, and meet the technical people who would need to know the A to Z of Martindale. He would write the first draft of the necessary documents and liaise with Brodie McClean in London by fax and phone.

Malpas returned to England the same day to set the wheels in motion, but before he got back on the Turnpike to New York, he phoned a financial journalist from *Business Week International* in Manhattan, and they arranged to meet at the airport for a drink before James's plane departed. He had known the reporter from his days on Wall Street, and the hack was keen to swap gossip on Empire National Bank.

Six hours later, Malpas took his seat in the Upper Class section of the Virgin jumbo and anxiously re-checked his share calculations. As soon as he could, he would start selling the Martindale stock in his Marlborough and Cleopatra offshore nominee accounts to push the price down. Then he would go short of Martindale in the options market, further depressing the share, and making it attractive for his American clients. Then, just before GT bid, he would buy it back, and make a whopping big profit for his department.

He might be able to solve several unpleasant problems with one deft move. But it would be a balancing act, and GT might pull out at any point until the zero hour of the bid. That was a gamble he would have to take. What had stunned him was how easy it had been so far. He was also looking forward to the next edition of *Business Week International*, he thought with a shiver of glee.

Chapter Seven

On Tuesday evening, Charlotte hoped that she looked appropriately nonchalant as she swept past the absurdly dressed flunky who held open the door. But once inside the Ritz her performance faltered. She peered down the gilded corridor and blinked away the clouds of smoke and perfume. As far as she could see, glamorous women were tilting their heads very slightly to inspect the person who had just entered. They sat at little circular tables, sipping drinks with studied elegance, and occasionally catching sight of themselves in the huge mirrors that lined the walls. Every one of them had shiny blonde hair that had been scraped back into a perfect bun, as if by some cosmetic vacuum cleaner. After appraising Charlotte they resumed their chatter, satisfied that the new arrival was of no threat or interest.

The television reporter had come straight from the studio, and felt foolishly out of place in her simple pastel-green silk dress, without shoulder pads, bejewelled belts or high heels. She walked past the circular tables, hoping she was invisible to the critical scanners on either side.

Charlotte eventually spotted David Stone when she was only five feet away from him, She did a double take as he stood up, smiled, and held out his hand. Before she had time to recover from his appearance he had kissed her cheek. Her critical faculties were knocked out by a wave of lust that left her tingling, and speechless. She eased herself into the chair beside him and gazed at him admiringly as he poured her a glass of champagne and asked how her day had been. She gurgled something incoherent and wondered if she was blushing or drooling.

Although she had not imagined that he would turn up in Wellingtons and jeans, she was hardly prepared for the 'International Businessman of Substance' look. He was wearing a dark grey suit, perfectly tailored, and the most beautiful silk tie she had ever seen. Charlotte had to stop her hand from reaching out to stroke him. Instead she sipped the Tattinger and cleared her throat.

'This is lovely,' she said, 'champagne after a day spent struggling to make the money supply figures sound interesting.' The bubbles fizzed in her already enfeebled brain and induced another gush of passion.

'Thanks for meeting me,' David said warmly. 'I hate asking you to sacrifice an evening to give me your advice.'

Charlotte could have assured him that she would have met him in the middle of the Gobi Desert if he had asked her to. And what's more, she would have crawled naked along a road of razor blades to get there. Instead she asked him about his merchant bank, Weinbergs.

'I spent this afternoon there. We're having some lunches so these fund managers can quiz me about where I want to take the company.' He stopped and sighed as he tore the cover of his *Economist* absentmindedly. 'I can't compete against these gurus who know hundreds of companies inside out. I'll come across as a buffoon – you know, a country bumpkin.'

Charlotte leaned forward, trying to catch his pensive eyes. 'David, these people get their kicks from membership of the Institute of Actuaries! They didn't go into accountancy because they were frightened of the pace,' she added, becoming more expansive as she sipped the Tattinger.

Then she tossed her head and her green eyes flashed wickedly. 'Let me tell you about a couple of hugely important City fund managers. They were lunching at a broking firm I know – just a sociable get-to-know-you-occasion, two brokers from the firm and two senior fund managers. Anyway, their guests had drunk three bottles of wine before they'd finished eating. So the brokers ordered up some more from the cellars and the lunch party carried on in a jolly sort of way, brokers hardly touching the booze, clients getting merry . . .

'By three-thirty they'd made their way through a bottle of vintage Taylors, too,' she continued. 'The stockbrokers, ever-polite and willing to please, rang down to the cellar and had another bottle of port fetched up to keep their guests happy, listened to their boring stories, stuck to the Perrier.

'Well, by *five* o'clock the brokers hinted that maybe it was time everyone returned to work. They said it in a jovial sort of way, but the senior fund manager got ugly and demanded more port. The brokers reluctantly refused, so the fund manager picked up the phone and called another firm of brokers down the road, and he offered them two thousand pounds' worth of commission on a deal if they would deliver a bottle of vintage port to the dining rooms of their rivals immediately. Which they did.'

'Splendid,' David laughed.

But Charlotte hadn't finished yet. She held up her finger and took another sip of Tattinger. 'There's a nasty event every year called the Analysts' Dinner. It happens at one of the big Park Lane hotels. Every broking analyst takes a client, and pays for them to eat and drink and smash the place up and go on afterwards to night-clubs and whorehouses. And this goes on from six in the evening until any point the next day.'

David screwed up his nose in distaste and refilled Charlotte's glass. 'Perhaps I should save myself the expense of paying Weinbergs their extortionate fees. How about if I hire the Manoir aux Quat' Saisons for the evening, and let my biggest shareholders trash the place?'

Charlotte giggled, then saw a little cloud pass across David's face. If he had been a cat he might have twitched his tail, or turned away quickly to wash a paw vigorously. 'The advertising man that Weinbergs've saddled me with suggests that we do a promotional video for shareholders,' he said noncommittally.

'I see,' said Charlotte. David studied her cool expression. 'Great idea – *if* you use Pinewood. Have you got fifty thousand pounds to throw at it? I'm sorry, perhaps I shouldn't be so negative.' Charlotte shifted in her chair as she imagined the tinky-tinky pop music on the soundtrack, the slightly out-of-focus shots of the production process, the staff looking deeply embarrassed. 'No,' she decided. 'I've seen so many company videos, and they're chronic, humiliating, and unintentionally funny.'

'Oh.' David looked deflated by her swift and dismissive analysis.

'It's better to do a good annual report,' she told him. 'We may not be a post-literate society like the States yet, but remember the intellectual limits of your audience.' Her scepticism had made David gloomy, and she wanted to hold his hand to encourage him, to make him laugh again.

'How about *my* intellectual limits?' he muttered disdainfully.

'I don't understand why you denigrate yourself so much,' Charlotte said in mock desperation. 'You're a combination of Getty and Aristotle, compared to most of the management this lot will have encountered.'

'Whereas you never undersell yourself, I suppose,' David said with a mischievous smile. 'Sorry, that was a bit personal.' He looked down at his glass as Charlotte's jaw sagged. 'I'm sorry,' he repeated. She could have told him that if he had asked her to sit on his face it wouldn't have been personal enough for her liking, but she flashed her most cheekbone-enhancing grin instead.

'How about something to eat?' he suggested. 'I've booked a table at Le Caprice. I hope that's OK.' He slipped the battered *Economist* into his document case.

Charlotte's stomach and eyes were united in their adoration of her host. As they walked past the hard-faced Eurotrash at their circular tables she noticed their greedy glances with satisfaction.

It was a warm sunny evening, and as they emerged from the Arlington Street exit of the Ritz she took David's arm. A slightly more sober Charlotte would never have dared, but it seemed the most natural thing in the world to do. As they walked down the sloping street towards Le Caprice, the bells at St James's tolled seven o'clock, and she thought her heart might burst with happiness, strolling along by his side. He would stop and take her in his arms and kiss her. It would happen any moment now!

But it didn't. 'Your profile of the company was a great help,' he remarked. 'Thank you.' He glanced towards her as they walked. Charlotte thought he had squeezed her arm which was wrapped around his. She squeezed back.

They passed into the noisy restaurant and were seated by the window of the airy white room. Charlotte was distracted by the menu for a moment, and gorged her mind on the agonising choices confronting her: grilled monkfish, or fricassée of chicken in some divine-sounding sauce. Then she noticed that David was leaning towards her in a manner that presaged an important announcement. She felt the butterfly sensation inside once more.

'What do merchant banks actually *do*?' he asked.

She tried to hide her sour reaction to this anticlimactic and straightforward question. He really had invited her out to dinner to ask her such penetrating things. There was no ulterior motive, and the gibbering longing was entirely on her side. Why did her first genuine experience of love have to be of the unreturned variety? Would she ever see him again after this evening, or was she fated to admire him from afar? What a tragic role, she thought as she waded into her reply like an enthusiastic teacher.

By a quarter to nine they had eaten and talked their way through three courses. David apologised for having to abandon her in central London, and made some disparaging remarks about the hopelessness of the train services back to Cambridge as he signalled for the bill.

Charlotte fought the feeling of misery as they left the restaurant and wandered back up to Piccadilly discussing leveraged buyouts. This time, she noticed, he was carrying his document case under the arm nearest to her, so there was no chance for her to slip her arm through his. He saw her into a cab with a most noncommittal kiss on the cheek, and a shower of gratitude for her words of wisdom. She rode back to Gloucester Road contemplating the hopelessness of unrequited love.

As David Stone's train chugged back to Cambridge that evening he was unaware that his company was the subject of a strategy meeting at the Global Technologies' headquarters in Mount Laurel, New Jersey.

Dick Zander's hastily formed takeover team was supposed to be plotting GT's assault on Martindale, so Paul Roberts was surprised when Zander asked him about William Stone & Son, and in particular its Verdi product. As Paul's eyes narrowed in confusion, the American explained that when the analyst had handed him his original notes on Martindale, he had inadvertently included the notes from his visit to Cambridgeshire. In the course of his reading, Zander had come across Paul's handwritten pages on Stone's Verdi product. Now GT's Chief Financial Officer was talking about bidding for William Stone & Son.

'Do you mean instead of Martindale?' Paul asked cautiously.

Zander grinned at the question, knowing precisely what was going through the young banker's mind: much smaller takeover target, much smaller fee for arranging it. 'No, Paul. Martindale *and* William Stone and Son. What's the problem with that?' he remarked amiably.

Paul looked relieved and sat back in his chair. 'It's a great idea,' he said with genuine admiration. 'I've thought Stone is ripe for takeover ever since I visited it. Beautiful little niche businesses. But I didn't think you'd be interested because it's so tiny.'

'True,' Zander said with a thoughtful nod of the head. 'But imagine what we can do with Stone's technology.' He sipped his mineral water and smiled pleasantly at the analyst. 'Son, it was an act of Fate that those notes of yours were mixed up in the Martindale files.' He held out his hands in benediction like an indulgent pope. 'Can't look a gift-horse in the mouth, eh?'

Paul returned his grin, and relished the prospect of telling Malpas they'd be earning an even bigger fee. But that would be *after* he had instructed his mother to buy some shares in William Stone & Son plc.

On Wednesday evening, James Malpas was sitting in his study in Richmond, surrounded by shelves of first edition books. He had never read them, but they were valuable and looked impressive. He took a piece of paper from his desk drawer and smoothed it out. It was his list of Brodie McClean board members and their voting intentions, and this evening he was able to put his initials beside the name of the director in charge of Unit Trusts.

Malpas smirked as he did so, thinking how easy it had been to win that vote: an innocent aside over lunch. He had imparted the information as if he was sharing a burden with a friend. Any investor with half a brain would ditch the Martindale shares now and pick them up after the dreadful half-year figures that were on their way. The Unit Trust boss had nodded sagely.

James slipped the list back into the drawer, well pleased with the erosion of the Ravenscroft power base. The *Business Week International* article had certainly helped the process: a sea of blood had washed through the bank as a consequence. It was as if Joseph McCarthy himself was stalking the corridors, denouncing people and making accusations, but the Ravenscroft mob lacked the wit to detect who had planted the story. They suspected Empire National Bank had leaked the details because Brodie McClean had come out of the article looking foolish, as if the Americans were taking them for a ride. Charles Ravenscroft had initiated a bad-tempered showdown with the CEO of Empire National, and the merger idea was now virtually dead. This brought a glow of satisfaction to James's otherwise worried expression.

The cause of his concern this evening was Fiona. He realised he was not particularly sensitive to his wife's feelings: so much was left unsaid, and he had always been far too busy to decode her signals. She did not force her opinion on him or pressurise him, James reflected gratefully. Those were qualities that made her a perfect social match and hostess: she never contradicted him, and she was skilled at getting people to talk about themselves, while avoiding any revelations of her own.

James had recognised these characteristics in her ten years ago, when they had met at an exhibition opening in a Bond Street gallery. Fiona was training as a picture restorer, and when they had been introduced James had spotted a quiet reserve and a discretion that appealed to him. He had also appreciated that her height, five foot eleven, made her shy. Her pale face had a good bone structure, but she had fought a life-long battle against looking too thin. This didn't worry James, who detested fat people. She wore her blonde hair straight and shoulder-length, but most often it was pulled into a simple pony tail. The minute he had seen her he had known that she was entirely appropriate, and within six months they were married.

Fiona Carmichael was from an upper-middle-class Scottish family who had provided her with a comfortable allowance to give her the freedom to pursue her artistic career. James had learned about manners, dress and charm through her example. By listening to her he had stopped saying 'pardon', 'lounge' and 'toilet', and now referred to sitting rooms and lavatories, and said he was sorry when he had not heard what was being said to him. She was an asset to him in every way, and he had never begrudged her the fact that she was unable to bear him a son and heir.

The Director of Brodie McClean's Managed Funds Department and his wife were joining them tonight. This was one of a series of dinners that James had arranged to sound out his fellow board directors on whether they were supporting his bid for the chairmanship. A social setting gave the financier an excellent opportunity to persuade and impress, or so he imagined.

James found his wife in the dining room of their Victorian house, laying the table, and checking the wine glasses for smudges or flecks of linen. As usual there was nothing to fault; he knew the food would be excellent, and she was wearing a charming long flowery skirt and silk blouse. In three minutes he had bullied her into telling him why she was so subdued.

She had received a phone call from Mrs Collins, the old woman who owned the farmhouse in Hampshire that they were planning to buy. James hovered at the head of the dining table, fearing that he knew what was coming, and wondering how he could explain it to his rather naïve wife.

'I was a bit surprised when Mrs Collins told me that we'd withdrawn the offer,' she began hesitantly, and tried to avoid James's eyes. 'She was upset, naturally, and I couldn't help her.'

'It's just a technicality,' James responded cheerfully. 'I'm making them a more reasonable offer. The estate agent obviously hasn't explained it to Mrs Collins properly.'

Fiona studied the flower arrangement in the centre of the table and frowned. 'Mr and Mrs Collins are committed to buying a bungalow in Budleigh Salterton,' she said simply. 'They've signed the contract, and now they're in an unpleasant position. And they can't work on the assumption that someone else will come along and buy the farmhouse.'

James sighed. 'For goodness' sake, Fiona.' She seemed preoccupied with rearranging her flowers, so he raised his voice. 'I'm going to make them another offer tomorrow, when they've had time to think about it. This will concentrate their minds a bit.'

He had withdrawn his offer that morning, hoping to force them to accept a lower figure. He knew that the old couple had signed the contract on their wretched bungalow because the witless estate agent had told him so. James saw that this put him in a position of power, and he intended to exercise his advantage. He had every intention of coming back with a lower offer in a couple of days, but he hadn't counted on the chummy Mrs Collins leaning on Fiona.

'They're going to get quite enough money out of us for a very comfortable retirement,' he sniffed. 'I don't see why you've decided to be a social worker on their behalf, my dear.'

She nodded her head, as if everything he had said made sense. 'I'm sorry,' she whispered, and went into the kitchen.

For a moment her husband stood gazing at her flower arrangement, and gripping the chair back in irritation. He would have to find a better moment to explain to her that their bank manager wasn't prepared to give them a big enough loan, so he had had to get the price down. Clearly, now was not the right time. James followed her out to the kitchen with the intention of uncorking the wine before their guests arrived.

Halfway through lunch the following day, David realised why the young men seated around the table glanced down at their laps so often. It wasn't their napkins they were scrutinising, but Extel cards that gave them a potted history of William Stone & Son. The ten fund managers consuming Weinbergs's overcooked lamb and roast potatoes represented a good proportion of David's major shareholders, and he had turned up expecting a tough grilling from the sharpest brains in the Square Mile. But as far as he could see they were more interested in the shapely buttocks of the waitress refilling their wine glasses.

Whenever silence fell on the assembled company, which it often did, David would volunteer information on some aspect of his firm's work. But as he surveyed his audience he realised that they felt no obligation to converse. They were gauche, ill-mannered and even rude – as if they regarded their very attendance at the trough as a personal favour to David. And they were unapologetic about knowing nothing of his products or his profits, not even where he was based.

This insolence surprised David. He hadn't expected his investors to be spotty mathematicians with a shadow of fine hair on their upper lips. He was not to know that no fund manager had been interested in lunch with an insignificant little firm like his: they had sent their graduate trainees instead. The latter scuttled back to their offices at two-thirty, and David headed for Liverpool Street Station, wondering why on earth he had bothered in the first place.

Over in Mount Laurel, Bruce Carretta was knocking gently on Dick Zander's office door. 'Here's the Art Blakey CD I mentioned,' he said when the Chief Financial Officer looked up from his papers.

'Great, come on in,' Zander said expansively. 'Park your butt for a moment, why don't you? And close the door.'

Carretta did as he was told and handed his superior the CD. Zander grinned and smacked his lips as he examined it. 'Great, great. This is classic stuff – the best. I'll tape it tonight and let you have it back tomorrow.'

'No hurry, boss,' Carretta crooned. 'Just savour it.' He paused, and tried to choose his words carefully. 'Bit of a problem with Kathy Gutierez.' Zander looked up from the CD cover and his eyes narrowed. 'One of the guys' wives met her at the mall yesterday,' Carretta explained. 'She was saying some strange things, apparently. Doesn't seem to accept the circumstances surrounding Raul's death. You know – she's suspicious. Thinks it was more than an accident.'

Zander's mouth had disappeared into a hard line. 'This is more than the distraught widow scenario, is it?' He sat back in his armchair and noted Carretta's unease. 'Reckon Raul was sharing his reservations about the project with her?'

'Seems so. They were pretty close,' Carretta remarked, then his lip curled downwards as if he had eaten something bitter. 'And she's a real bleeding heart liberal shit-disturber. Persistent, too.'

'Is she going to cause problems? I mean, how much does she know, and who can she take her story to?'

'Like I said, she's an activist type. She's always sounding off in the local rag about the iniquities of this or that government cutback. She has friends in the press, which is why I'm concerned, Dick. I wouldn't bother you with this otherwise.' And Carretta gave an apologetic shrug.

'No, I appreciate that,' Zander said thoughtfully, and tapped his index fingers against the CD cover. 'Another accident would look fishy,' he added at length. 'Statistically unlikely.'

Carretta nodded. 'Yeah, I've been giving it some thought. Maybe we should consider the environment she works in – you know, that Skid Row hostel on the other side of town.'

Zander looked blank for a moment, as if he was searching his memory banks. Then he recalled the earnest and rather pretty Kathy Gutierez, and her appeals for donations to her homeless refuge. He'd met her at the annual staff barbecue, and her face was familiar on the local TV station news. In fact GT had given her a few thousand dollars from time to time. 'Yup, I know the place you mean. Full of psychos and junkies. It's a dangerous part of town for a young woman to hang out alone.'

Carretta hesitated for a moment and watched the agonisingly sincere expression on his boss's face become a grin. 'There's a lot of it about,' he agreed with a concerned shake of the head. 'Drive-by shootings, innocent bystanders killed in gang-warfare battles, deranged teenagers roaming the streets with assault rifles.'

Zander looked at the CD in his hands again. ''Specially in that part of town, Bruce. It's the truly American way to die. Statistically more likely than cancer or Aids or car accidents these days. Particularly if you're mixing it with the dispossessed.' He yawned and rubbed his eyes. 'What a fucking country.'

Chapter Eight

'You've got hold of the wrong end of the stick on Martindale, you know.' Jonathan Slope looked at her slyly from behind his John Lennon glasses. 'It's just a crappy company, like this one.' He inclined his head towards the platform where the chairman of one of Martindale's rivals was announcing dreadful profit figures. 'There's no grand plot behind the price fall, and you've gone right out on a limb with your vendetta against Brodie McClean. You should be careful . . .'

Charlotte shushed him and pretended to concentrate on the press conference.

'Defence has had a difficult few years,' the chairman was concluding in a suitably mournful tone. He might as well have said, 'The nightmare continues for arms manufacturers – it's high time for a war with a Third World country.'

Jonathan Slope was clearly amused by her dogged insistence that someone was running a deliberate bear operation against Martindale. In her last TV package she had gone as far as suggesting that the company's own merchant bank, Brodie McClean, knew more than they were letting on.

'Stop pretending you're on to the Watergate of the Square Mile,' Jonathan said with an air of authority that Charlotte found belittling, 'and just smile prettily at the camera.' He slipped his arm around the back of her chair. 'Why not let me write your scripts for you? We'd make a good team.'

He was trying to look down her blouse so she leaned away from him and did up the top button. But her fingers fumbled, and she heard him laugh. 'Charlotte Carter – all nipples and bones. When are you going to stop being a little girl and let me take you to bed?'

'And when are you going to clean your fingernails or change your socks?' she hissed back, but Jonathan affected not to hear her.

'I've got a friend at work who's doing research for the *Mastermind* prog.,' he said, switching tack. 'You'd be amazed at the subjects these cretins want to answer questions on.' He sniggered. 'Motorway routes going anywhere in the UK but beginning in Letchworth, for instance. Or hip replacements. Or "cooking for one",' he said with a snarl of contempt.

Charlotte made no comment, but the more she considered it, the sadder it seemed that people were experts on cooking for one. For some moments she thought about unnamed but numerous individuals who led miserable lonely lives. Just yesterday she had passed a lamp post with a hand-written note on it, appealing for anyone who had seen a certain dog to contact the phone number given. There had been a photo of the pet, and Charlotte had kept thinking about how unlikely it was that the dog was still alive, and how dreadful the owner must feel. Maybe the latter was an old person who depended on the dog for companionship. Worse and worse.

This line of thought brought her unwillingly but inevitably to wondering how terrible it would be to be old and blind, or alone, or poor. Or worse still, to be blind, old, alone *and* poor. Then she recalled reading a news wire the week before about some children in the East End of London who had stoned an old man's guide dog to death, just for the fun of it. And there was that recent court case in which four little boys had admitted torturing a cat to death by hurling it repeatedly off a balcony until they broke all its bones.

By this time, Charlotte was hovering on the edge of tears of anguish on behalf of the animals, and rage against the brutality of human beings. To take her mind off the subject she glanced around the room, recognising fellow journalists who gathered for every results briefing, presumably for the free wine at the end, rather than the information they gleaned. Her attention was arrested by a familiar head in the second row. Paul Roberts might have been elevated to the commanding heights of the Malpas regime but he still had to keep an eye on events in the defence sector. When he, too, turned to examine the rest of the audience, their eyes met. Charlotte ducked her head and pretended to be scribbling on her notepad.

The company chairman continued to read his text like a Communist Party apparatchik announcing fictitious steel output statistics. Could Charlotte hide behind her camera crew and sidle out of the room without Paul seeing her? Caught between a rock and a hard place, she thought as she eased away from the grubby tweed jacket of Jonathan Slope. Charlotte suspected he would be the type who described an erection as 'a surprise' and plonk her hand on his crotch. Desired by the smelly and the inadequate, she reflected bitterly, but not by David Stone. She shut her eyes and recited her most positive mantra: *tomorrow is another restaurant; tomorrow is another restaurant . . .*

Wrong about David. Wrong about Martindale, too? Her inquiries had revealed that Paul's boss James Malpas was behind the downward pressure on the price. Why, she couldn't imagine, considering Sir Terence Purves was his client. But where could she get hard facts? Her eyes fixed once more on Paul's light-brown head a few rows in front.

After ten minutes, a mood of ill-feeling settled upon the room: the journalists had decided it was time to hit the buffet. The Chairman started to thank everyone for attending but he was drowned out by the scraping of chairs. Charlotte bobbed up, keen to avoid Jonathan. She pointed the crew at the rush of reporters who had stampeded for the vol-au-vents and Chablis, then she sat down, pretended she was reading over her notes, and waited for Paul to approach her.

That afternoon, as Paul headed back to Brodie McClean, he congratulated himself on putting business before pleasure when he had encountered Charlotte. He would have liked to ask her out for a drink that evening, but he knew he couldn't escape from the mountain of GT work waiting back at his desk. And he also had the feeling it was too early to exploit their renewed friendship.

Instead he had talked to her in a friendly, dispassionate manner, letting none of his irritation show at all those unanswered phone calls. Nevertheless he had been alarmed by her questions about Martindale. Her market sources were undoubtedly good, he reflected, but he had diverted her away from her quarry by telling her to watch out for William Stone & Son. From the bright light in her eyes he could tell he had pressed her journalistic scoop button.

It mattered little, because William Stone & Son was small fry, and she would never guess who was stalking it. If it kept her nose out of Martindale, Paul's life would be much easier. Sadly, this wasn't a victory to be shared with James, who would probably overreact at the prospect of a reporter sniffing around William Stone & Son. He wouldn't appreciate the subtlety of Paul's deflecting manoeuvre.

Paul leaned back against the leather seat of the taxi and shut his eyes. When the GT bids were announced, and he had more time, he would begin his careful assault on Charlotte's beautiful edifice once more.

'This is terribly short notice, but would you like dinner tonight?'

Charlotte's throat went dry and she counted to three before she accepted. He probably wouldn't be fooled by her pretence of consulting her empty diary, but dignity prevented her from yelling, 'Yes, yes, yes!' down the phone line to Cambridgeshire.

By the time the news bulletin was over at six o'clock she was gibbering with anticipation. She had to stop herself skipping to the reception area, where she found David reading *The Financial Times*. He threw it to one side when she appeared, and got to his feet, smiling.

They made their way through the rush-hour pedestrians and into a tapas bar where they secured a bottle of white Rioja and found a table. Then she explained what she had hinted at on the phone, when she had rung him up earlier in the day. His shares were roaring up for a reason: someone expected his company to be bid for. The flurry of activity in the options market indicated the same thing.

'Of course, it's just gossip – and anyway, there are a few tricks you could try,' Charlotte said in an upbeat, encouraging manner. 'A "Crown Jewels lock-up", for instance: you float off the bit of the company you reckon a bidder wants most, and that makes your firm less attractive.' David hardly raised his eyes from the wine glass in front of him. 'Or else you bid for something bigger than you are,' she continued. 'Take on a staggering amount of debt. Or spend every penny in your balance sheet. That'd scare them off.'

She tried to catch David's eyes, but he was gazing despondently into the flame of the candle between them. 'It's better than losing your company,' she added with a coaxing smile.

'So you reckon I might lose?' He sounded as if he couldn't quite believe it.

Charlotte cursed herself for her bluntness, and tried to choose her words more carefully. At the same time she wanted to impress on David that he had to act. 'Don't give up,' she said cheerfully.

'Astonishing that twenty fund managers can decide the fate of much bigger companies than mine,' he began, as if he had not heard her. Charlotte watched him pick at the candlewax on the bottle. Then his eyes settled on hers for a moment. 'I've been wanting to call you up, but I couldn't think of a good excuse, and you would have thought I was chasing you, and told me to go to hell.'

'Oh no, don't be silly,' she said casually, suppressing an urge to throw herself at his feet.

'If I were a pretty and successful young media star, I wouldn't want to be chased by a middle-aged farmer whose wife had deserted him.' He laughed without humour.

'That flatters me, and denigrates you,' she mumbled.

'Well, here comes the next personal question. Do you live with someone? I mean, do you have a boyfriend?'

'No.' She looked up in surprise and searched his eyes.

'Am I crazy to pursue you? Or shall we be friends, and you can find it amusing to be admired by an older man.'

'*I think we should go back to my flat right now and fuck each other's brains out*,' she could have panted, but she smiled demurely instead and said, 'You're not crazy.'

Five minutes later they were in a taxi heading for Gloucester

Road. He made no move towards her in the cab, nor in the hallway of her flat when she had closed the door. No fumbled grasping. No passionate kiss. No grab at the buttons of her blouse. She led him into her kitchen wondering if mature men outgrow frantic impetuousness. David talked to her all the time, uncorked the bottle while she started a bath, and when she returned he commended her taste in wine. Then he wandered away and looked at her library of novels without remark – an ominous sign, she thought. He winced when he examined her CDs.

'I do have some classical music somewhere,' she said defensively.

'The Four Seasons?' he murmured as he peered at a book about the chemicals industry.

'How did you know?' she asked crossly. 'I suppose you don't like rock music.'

'That's unfair. I listen to Crosby, Stills, Nash and Young. Together and separately.' Then, seeing the incomprehension on her face: 'Before your time. Do you actually read these tomes? You must be very good at concentrating on dull things.'

'Why are you being horrible?' she asked petulantly. He turned around and took the glass of wine she was offering him.

'Because I'm nervous; this isn't just manly reticence. I'm out of practice, and I can't think what I'm supposed to do that won't frighten you off. So,' he said, walking around her and towards the bathroom, 'I shall lie in the bath and avoid making the mistakes I'm bound to make.'

A few minutes later he called to her through the open door: 'Why don't you bring the bottle in and refill my glass?'

Charlotte went to the kitchen and pulled the Monopole from the fridge, wondering what on earth would happen this evening, or ever. But once she was sitting on the lavatory lid, drinking and talking to him, the tension dispersed and she took a few surreptitious looks at his body. His chest was smooth and hairless, trim, but not muscle-bound. The legs were long with a light covering of brown hair, not ape-like. The rest seemed to be in acceptable shape.

'What time are we eating?' she asked him heartily.

'You are the woman for me, Charlotte. Food really matters to you if it's uppermost in your mind at a moment like this. We don't have to be there until eight-thirty.'

He hoisted himself out of the bath, and Charlotte leapt up and rushed off to the airing cupboard for a towel. She watched him wrap it around himself. But before she had time to contemplate the embarrassment of undressing in front of him, he had his arms around her and the towel had dropped to the floor.

'You have no idea how much I've thought about doing this to you,' he laughed between kisses. Then he led her into the sitting room and pushed her gently on to the floor.

'Oh yes, I have every idea,' she purred as he knelt beside her and undid her blouse.

'What a beautiful woman you are,' he remarked as he stroked her skin, then kissed her breasts softly. He removed her clothes until she was wearing only her white silk French knickers, which he approved of a great deal. He lay down beside her, and rubbed his finger very lightly up and down along the flimsy silk between her legs. His hand moved rhythmically and steadily, and he watched the excitement on her face become ecstasy as she gripped his shoulders and writhed around on the floor. When she came her whole body shook, and she clung to him until the last tremor had faded.

'That was amazing, wonderful, incredible,' she said through hazy eyes. Then she pushed him on to his back and sat astride him with her hands on his chest. 'You're even better than I imagined you'd be.'

'High praise indeed.' He reached up and stroked her leg.

'I want you so bloody much,' she whispered, and leaned forward until she was lying on top of him.

'And I want you too,' he said between kisses. 'But we ought to get some of those disgusting things. I suppose we can amuse ourselves in some harmless way in the meantime.'

Charlotte smiled. 'There're some in my bedroom,' she volunteered cheerfully, and disentangled herself from his embrace.

'Silly me,' he said flatly. 'Answer something first.' He held her tightly. 'Tell me how you know someone's planning to bid for me. Who told you?'

'David, I want you, right now. Can't we talk about that later?' she asked. But when she tried to get up he rolled on top of her, and kissed her neck. She felt him throbbing hard against her thigh, and knew how good it would be to have him making love to her. 'Please,' she whimpered.

'You get nothing until you tell me how you discovered such interesting inside information about my shares,' he whispered in her ear.

'Right. That settles it,' she laughed and wrapped her legs around his. 'I was chummy with the analyst who wrote the note on your company. Do you remember him?' He nodded and stroked her hair. 'Paul's the one who suggested your company was ideal for a bid. He's in Brodie McClean's Corporate Finance department now.'

'I'll never show one of those shits round my factories again. Or tell them everything I'm doing – half of it off the record, I might add,' he said, and wondered if Verdi was now common knowledge.

'Last week I met him at a City presentation, and he told me your company would be in play,' Charlotte continued.

'Really? Why did he do that?' David loosened his grip on Charlotte and sat up.

She pouted and tried to pull him close again, but he resisted. 'I don't know,' she said, bored by the subject.

'Are you sleeping with him?' he asked her, his voice rising. 'Is that why you have condoms lying around the place? Or did he think you'd sleep with him if he gave you a useful bit of gossip?'

'No. What are you talking about?' She shook her head and tried to make light of his concern.

'You aren't very good at lying, Charlotte,' he said, getting to his feet, every sign of excitement fading fast. 'Are you leading him along, or are you sleeping with him?'

Charlotte was startled by this sudden change of mood, and she sat up and pulled her legs together. She felt very naked and cold all of a sudden. Before she knew what was happening, David had gone to the bathroom and fetched his clothes.

'I knew I shouldn't be such an ass to think I could handle this,' he muttered to himself when he returned with his shirt and boxer shorts on.

'I'm *not* sleeping with him,' she said dismissively. 'Anyway, it would be a stupid woman these days who didn't keep a supply of condoms. You should be grateful I'm so careful,' she snapped at him as she watched him do up his trousers. 'Your side of the bargain can never be relied upon to think of such boring details.'

He looked at her coldly but she noticed his hands were shaking. 'Oh come on, David,' She got to her feet and tried to put her arms around him, but he pushed her away gently but firmly.

'No. You aren't going to play around with me. Pick on someone your own age. I'm far too old to get used and discarded. I'm not looking for that, Charlotte, so try some other poor fool, like your stockbroker friend.'

'Why are you treating me like this?' she gasped as he went towards the hall.

'I've humiliated myself enough,' he declared and shut the door behind him.

She heard him running down the stairs to the street. Then she stumbled to the sofa. How long she sat there, she didn't know. Finally, a shiver shook her out of her melancholy and she got up to switch on lights and collect her clothes from the floor where they had fallen. They looked like the evidence of some crime that had occurred – an incident between two strangers; no one she knew.

Charlotte pulled on her dressing gown and let the water out of the bath, barely capable of understanding what had happened this evening. A terrible pain roared in her head and she trailed into her bedroom, not even conscious of where she was going. Then, as she remembered rolling around the floor with him, she sank on to the bed as though her spine could no longer keep her upright.

With one insensitive comment, one thoughtless indiscretion, she had surpassed her own record for destroying great opportunities. Why couldn't she have lied about getting the tip-off from Paul? Why hadn't she realised how bad it sounded? Why did she have to open her big mouth?

Charlotte curled up in her bed with Alfred the Rabbit, and buried her head in the pillow, trying to suffocate the memory. But there was also indignation swelling up inside her. What was that performance about her having the condoms handy? Had his wife's unfaithfulness left him with a textbook full of unresolved psychological problems? This would be the last time she let her wayward heart out by itself. It wasn't old enough to cross the street without getting run over.

She closed her eyes and the tears squeezed out. For the first time in as long as she could recall, Charlotte Carter didn't feel in the least bit hungry.

Chapter Nine

As David Stone was travelling back to Cambridge in a foul mood, his company was once more the subject of discussion in Mount Laurel, New Jersey, where it was still afternoon. Dick Zander was sitting opposite his CEO Max Clark who, he noticed, was smelling particularly strongly of sweat today.

'I still think the best way to deal with the situation is simply to buy the company – just bid for it at the same time as we're going for Martindale. That way, no one will make a big fuss about it,' he advised his boss.

But Clark was not convinced. Zander checked his exasperation with a diplomatic shrug of the shoulders. It was Clark's way to opt for the most underhand and thuggish strategy; always his first instinct to go in with flame-throwers at the ready.

'Frankly, Max, David Stone's company isn't expensive. It'll cost us about what we pay for our directors' annual country club fees. It's peanuts, and a bid won't attract the negative publicity that your strategy will involve.'

Clark screwed up his nose. 'I don't know. Seems like a lot of hassle – and you're sure about this polystyrene thing?' he asked doubtfully.

Zander nodded and crossed his arms defiantly, or as defiantly as he dared in the presence of the master. When Clark sighed and reached for another cigar, Zander knew he had won the argument.

'All right,' the CEO conceded. 'We bid for the little fucker.'

It was ten to midnight when Kathy Gutierez pulled the door of the hostel closed behind her and began to walk towards her car which was parked down the street. It had been a long evening, what with fights between grumpy old drunks who were trying to steal each other's favourite beds, and the arrival of confused, distressed addicts.

Kathy was leaving the shelter in the hands of her night-worker – a dedicated but inexperienced young man who was straight out of college. He would get the idea with time, but right now he was far too indulgent of the more cunning drunks. Kathy had tried to explain that they were seasoned survivors, and didn't need his attention: the ones to watch out for were the young women who arrived on their doorstep with babes in arms, and stories of rejection, abuse and worse. The priority was to give them some sense of security and hope, Kathy had insisted.

It was a chilly evening for August, and she pulled the bulky woollen sweater around her as she walked down the silent, empty street. Her jeans were still stained with the vomit that a drunk had deposited on her earlier in the evening; she hadn't had time to do any more than sponge the mess off. There were more pressing priorities than her sartorial elegance, or even combing her long brown hair, for that matter. Since Raul had gone there seemed little point in making an effort; her clients would hardly notice if she turned up with a shaven head.

The one virtue of her work was that it kept her so busy she had no time to mourn. When she was alone she simply slept away her exhaustion, and tried to remember to eat. Otherwise she kept her mind occupied. Tonight her head was throbbing with such a skull-crushing ache that she was barely conscious of where she was going. She padded along the sidewalk to the spot where she always left her Honda Civic, hardly registering the familiar surroundings.

Kathy never noticed the approach of the car in the road behind her, and she didn't turn to see who had pulled up at the kerb. She was too preoccupied to hear its idling motor, or the hum of the electric window opening. And she hardly felt the impact of the bullets that tore into her back in a deafening burst of noise. She was almost dead by the time she crumpled on to the sidewalk. Almost. She belched blood for about two minutes, then she died. By then the car with the electric windows had squealed off down the street, and was gone. There were two other drive-by shootings in New Jersey that evening, so her death didn't even make the state-wide headlines the next day.

James!' bellowed Tessa de Forrest. '*James!* For God's sake, pick up the phone. It's that man at Martindale.'

Malpas had been expecting this call for some days. Better to get it over with now, he thought as he lifted the receiver. 'Hello, Terry,' purred the merchant banker. 'I hope life is treating you well?'

His caller did not share his cheerful disposition. 'Have you seen the state of my share price? What the hell's happening?'

'Well,' said Malpas in a more sombre tone when he had registered his client's irritation, 'the whole market's weak at the moment.'

He heard Purves curse in exasperation and waited for the expected tirade, but what followed surprised him. 'There's some reporter pestering me with lots of snoopy bloody questions like – did I know my merchant bank's selling my shares? That kind of thing,' he ranted. 'Now what the fuck is up?'

The smug expression had left Malpas's face. 'Who is he? What's his name?' he demanded.

'It's a she – Charlotte Carter,' said Purves with hatred. 'Little bitch comes on all nice and cute, then sticks an assegai up yer arse.'

James knew exactly which journalist his client meant. Carter had been helpful to him in the past, although she didn't realise it. 'I'll look into that immediately,' he replied smoothly.

'That's not the bloody point,' Purves whined. 'What's she found?'

Malpas hunched himself over the telephone and spoke calmly. 'She's just a hack at a loose end searching for a story, Terry. They resort to stupid things like this during late August. It's the silly season. Take no notice.'

'Does she know something I don't?' the man fretted. 'It'd explain the share price, wouldn't it,' he rasped belligerently.

'I'm sorry you take that view, Terry,' Malpas said evenly. His tone was calculated to drive Purves berserk, which it did. James heard the businessman wheeze as he drew in a lungful of breath.

'Is that the best you can do? Christ-all-bloody-mighty!'

Malpas wrote '*NNN*' beside Charlotte's name, and then opened his internal phone directory with one hand while holding the receiver to his ear with the other.

'I tell you what,' Purves shrieked. 'I'm going to find myself a merchant banker who's a bit more awake – that's what I'm going to do!'

'I'm sorry to hear you say that, Terry,' Malpas interjected at random, then checked his diary to make sure he was free to nip upstairs to see the Chairman. There was silence at the Reading end of the call, then a barrage of noise exploded in his ear.

'*Sorry?* You're going to be fucking sorry!' Purves wailed.

'Shit!' Tessa shouted in the adjoining office, her exclamation accompanied by the noise of breaking glass. She had destroyed another coffee-making machine: generations of blue blood and military valour defeated by a simple household gadget. Malpas struggled to suppress a laugh. He put his hand over the phone but a snort escaped, and winged its way to Martindale's head office.

'Right!' Purves barked. 'That's it, you're fired. You and your fucking tin-pot bank are fired.' And the line went dead.

Malpas heard a second, terrible crashing in the next office, then the outer door was slammed violently shut. That would be the last of Tessa for today.

He dialled Sir Anthony Brook's office, and was told that the Chairman could see him immediately if it was necessary. Malpas slipped on his jacket and headed for the lifts. He was not unduly concerned at the prospect of the older man's anger at Purves's decision. He had worked out a credible explanation on his way back from GT in New Jersey.

A well-bred knight like Sir Anthony was bemused that due to some terrible mistaken idealism that could be blamed on Macmillan's malevolent influence, Purves had ended up with the same title as he had. Malpas reckoned he was starting with that advantage in trying to explain why he wanted Brodie McClean to resign from the Martindale account.

In the event he was right; Brook was relieved to hear that their association with the proletarian Purves was to be terminated, especially when Malpas explained his suspicion that Martindale had been using its pension fund to buy its own shares, without its shareholders' authorisation. There was potential negative publicity in the pipeline, he told the worthy Chairman. This had the desired effect, coming as it did so soon after the appalling press coverage they had been getting over the collapse of the deal with Empire National Bank. Brook seemed pathetically grateful to James for volunteering to drop Purves. Could he issue a press release that afternoon? James asked.

When they had agreed on a form of wording, Sir Anthony glanced at his watch and offered James a drink. As they moved from his desk to more comfortable armchairs, Brook asked him for his views on how Brodie McClean could be downsized. The Broking Department was still losing thousands of pounds a month, and the Chairman wondered how much longer he should be prepared to give the operation before the plug was pulled.

As Malpas argued for the termination of the Equities Section and for large-scale redundancies throughout the bank, Brook appraised this fellow about whom Ravenscroft was so irrational. It seemed a shame that Charlie was so consumed by jealousy. It gave him second thoughts about the International Director's judgement.

It was a quarter to ten that same night before Paul emerged from Brodie McClean and climbed into a passing cab. He sank back in the seat and shut his stinging eyes. He was working longer hours than his boss these days. Consequently there was never any milk or fresh food in his flat, and he was going home to an empty refrigerator. If his mother knew he was surviving on sandwiches gobbled at his desk she would do her nut. It would be impossible to explain that there was no room for domestic details in his day. Mrs Roberts wouldn't believe that his employer expected him to work all the hours he wasn't asleep.

Thinking of her reminded him that they needed to sort out their complicated share-dealings, and he reached for his mobile phone. It puzzled her that their conversations were nocturnal, and conducted while her son was rattling though London's empty streets in a taxi, although he had explained that personal calls from the office were discouraged.

Paul hoped his mother would pick up the phone. He disliked having to justify the lateness of his communications to his father, who was inflexible in his view of 'what a man did for a job', and when people worked. Mr Roberts disapproved of 'that stocks and shares game' his son had 'got himself messed up in'. He thought the City of London was a legalised haven for criminals, and couldn't understand why Paul had gone there when he could have landed a perfectly good job in industry.

Paul tried to sound cheerful when his mother answered, but Mrs Roberts detected the exhaustion in his voice and gave him the third degree about the hours he kept.

'I'm not out living it up of an evening, Mum,' he said a bit testily. 'I'm working on a special project at the bank, and if it goes OK I'll get more promotion. I'm doing very well here, you know.' It seemed to have escaped his parents' notice that their son was rapidly climbing up the Brodie McClean pole.

'Paul,' his mother said quietly, 'a piece of paper's arrived from your stockbroker people.' She hesitated. 'It says I've got ten thousand pounds in my account. It's not a mistake, is it? Your father doesn't like what you're doing, Paul.'

'Dad doesn't know the first thing about the stock market, so just tell him to mind his own business,' her son snapped. 'It's my money, not his, and any profit we make is going to be split between you and me.'

'For goodness' sake, Paul – why are you in such a temper? Dad's just worried.'

Mr Roberts worked in local government, reaching the dizzy heights of Assistant Chief Executive of a district council in Cheshire. He had often lectured Paul on the worthlessness and greed of banks who pushed bits of paper about and made millions of pounds, without adding any value, or helping British industry. And he had warned his son that it was immoral for him to be making so much money for 'so little effort'. It was bound to end in tears, he said gleefully.

When Paul had finished talking to his mother he looked out of the taxi window at the darkened streets. It was the old man's double standards that angered him. His father was a past master at milking 'the system' for every last penny of expenses. He knew all the fiddles, put in a claim for each cup of tea he bought while going about his business, Paul reflected bitterly. If his father worked for a multinational it would have been just the same: Roberts Senior would be one of the middle managers who knew the company car policy inside out, and wasted his firm's money on status symbols, while contributing nothing to profitability. Occasionally Paul spotted such 'executives' in first-class train compartments, staring blankly into space, cosseted by an air of self-satisfaction. If anyone had suggested that their company sent them first-class so they could get on with some work, they would have been gobsmacked. Paul had overheard them on their mobile phones, discussing how many spuds they wanted for dinner. They'd never 'worked' in their lives; not like Paul worked.

Such were his uncharacteristically acidic thoughts as his taxi swept past pubs and restaurants disgorging happy, carefree people. Paul wondered when he would next have a chance to go out and forget GT. Not that he had anyone to take out for an evening. The memory of all those futile messages he had left at NNN, asking Charlotte to call him, put him in an even darker mood. So much for renewing their friendship.

Then he considered his next move, and his spirits rallied. Tomorrow morning he would dash out to a public phone to place an order with his broker. He was going to pick up options to buy Martindale. That would get him some nice furniture for his flat. He bade the taxi driver good night and turned the key in the front door.

Chapter Ten

'You're losing weight.' It was a Monday late in August, and David Stone's secretary was appraising him critically.

Sheila felt for the flab under David's chin. 'Gone,' she remarked with disapproval. 'I shall find it difficult to work for a thin boss. Please try to eat a bit more.' He nodded obediently, but she knew that her words would go unheeded.

'Now, Charlotte Carter just called,' Sheila resumed in a businesslike voice, 'and she's asked if we can send her an up-to-date share register. She wants to look at who's buying our stock. Are you OK, David?' His expression was strained.

'Fine. I'll write a note to go with it,' he said, tugging the share register out of her hands.

When Sheila had left his office, David searched through his desk drawer for some appropriate notepaper, and in his travels came across a pale-green business card, which he pulled into the light. It read: *Hon. Nicholas Durridge. GreenBack Investments*. This was an environmental investment group based in St Albans, and Nick had told him all about it at the Grantchester House school reunion two months ago. David laid the card by the phone, intending to invite him to dinner that night. A gossip with the effervescent second son of a viscount might just raise his spirits, he thought bitterly.

Then he found the notepaper and wrote a polite apology to Charlotte for having caused the unpleasant scene at her flat. He left it at that, because he suspected that he wasn't up to any relationships, and that he would end up with burnt fingers. Then he put it in an envelope with the share register and asked Sheila to post them to the NNN Studios.

Next, he rang Nick. His longstanding friendship with Durridge dispensed with the need for any opening small talk. David told his old schoolchum why his share price had been rising, and that he feared he was being stalked. He had no idea by whom – but he assumed they were asset-strippers.

The fate of Verdi, his polystyrene replacement material, was of particular interest to Durridge, who spent his days finding funds for ecologically-sound commercial proposals.

'Look, I've got an idea,' Nick boomed down the phone in his plummy baritone. 'You must search through your annual reports, David, and every single press statement,' he instructed. 'This is absolutely *vital*. I want you to make sure you've never publicly mentioned Verdi. Then we'll discuss it over dinner.'

'I'll do as you say.' David paused as he remembered how stupid he had been to trust the young stockbroker, and to show him around the labs. Now he had two reasons to wring the bastard's neck.

'Yes, yes,' Charlotte said with strained politeness. 'I understand you can't say it on the record.'

She crossed another investment institution off her list, then slouched back on the sofa. This was how Charlotte spent her days off now – working from home. It was Tuesday, 27 August: she had telephoned twenty major holders of Martindale stock and from each she got the same grumbles about the share price. No one was surprised that Purves had sacked Brodie McClean. What *was* curious was the lack of embarrassment at the bank's headquarters. The salesmen were apologetic, but there wasn't a squeak of remorse from Corporate Finance. Charlotte's problem was lack of proof: any TV report that laid blame at the Brodie McClean doorstep wouldn't make it out of the editing suite.

She sat on her sofa, fiddling with the silver butterfly fastener at the back of one of her earrings, and wondering what to do for the rest of the day. It was too late for a shopping expedition, and she wasn't in the mood to try on shoes or skirts: it would only make her wish she had something to dress-up for. Her social life revolved around going out after work with a gang of reporters and producers at NNN. So much for the glamour profession image. She didn't know anyone who lay in a Jacuzzi drinking expensive champagne, yet that was how media people behaved in novels. A pint of lager and a packet of crisps were more the norm at NNN.

She checked her watch and grabbed her handbag. She would pop into the studio under the pretence of digging out the files on US arms-makers. Then she could begin the background work for her trip to the States – and if anyone happened to be leading a mob to the cinema or the pub, she'd tag along. A minute later she was in Gloucester Road waving down a taxi.

Maurice was distracted from his struggle with the fax machine in the far corner of the newsroom. He looked around the office for the source of the noise. The news was on air, and he had assumed everyone else was in the director's gallery. Then he spotted Charlotte with her back to him, bent over her desk. He terminated his futile attempts to fax Moscow and stood quietly for a moment.

Charlotte had also assumed that she was alone in the newsroom, and she was crying quite openly over David's letter. Maurice coughed, just to let her know he was there. She reached for her handkerchief and shielded her eyes as he walked up to her. 'It's only me, Charlotte,' he said softly.

She buried her head in her hands. 'Oh . . .' she groaned. 'Oh, Maurice . . .' The words were muffled by the handkerchief.

'Do you want to tell me?' he asked. 'Or would you rather I went away? I'll understand.'

She shook her head and sniffed. 'No, don't go away.

'Do you mind hearing this rubbish?' she asked him twenty minutes later, as they sat in the corner of a quiet wine bar.

'My dear girl,' he said softly, 'it isn't rubbish to have your heart broken.' Maurice crossed his thin, frail legs and sipped his spritzer. 'So this was the one, was he?'

'The nearest there's been,' she whispered. 'Yes.' She bit her tongue to stop the tears. Maurice reached for her hand and squeezed it.

'I don't think he sounds as if he's worth a rare prize like you. Forget him, Princess,' Maurice chided, 'or it'll drive you crazy.

Throw away that letter, or you'll read something into it that isn't there. Now, you save your love for someone less messed up.' Then he rubbed his grey whiskered chin. 'Mind you, I might have got a bit annoyed with you if I'd thought you were only after my share register.' He chuckled and squeezed her hand again. 'How about some dinner – at our favourite Chinese restaurant?'

After they had demolished enormous quantities of food and wine Charlotte returned to the office 'to collect a few things', as she explained to Maurice. When he wasn't looking, she retrieved David's letter from the wastepaper basket and put it in her handbag. Then she picked up the share register for a little light reading, and went home to bed. She sat up until midnight, sipping herbal tea and crosschecking new Stone shareholders against an old list.

As her head cleared of alcohol, Charlotte realised that something quite unusual had been happening recently. Someone or something called Cleopatra had acquired 4.9 per cent of Stone, as had another investor called Marlborough. A quick glance through old shareholders' lists showed that they hadn't held the stock before. Puzzling, she thought, and shut off the light.

She turned on to her back and tried to empty her brain of speculation about Stone the company. Instead, Stone the man came into her head. Before she could stop her wayward mind she was back on the floor with David, kissing him, holding him, lying beneath him and wrapping her legs around him. She could almost imagine him screwing her. She tried to coax herself along with her finger, but there was no activity between her legs. Ain't nothing like the real thing, she thought bitterly, and squeezed her eyes shut.

When James Malpas arrived back in Richmond that night, he found his wife in her studio at the bottom of their garden. As he walked towards the brick outbuilding he saw her through the window, her blonde head bent over a pile of books, and a pool of light from an Anglepoise lamp shining on to her drawing board. Fiona looked happy and self-contained, working there by herself, late into the night.

In the past he had thought that his wife was like a refrigerator, and only he caused the light to come on when he opened the door. Now James was not so confident that she was simply a moon orbiting his sun. He was pleased that she was dedicating herself to her plans for their prospective country home, but it annoyed him that she never asked him how his work was going, even though she knew he was on the verge of the biggest takeover of his career – and the battle for the chairmanship of the bank. Such was his workload, and the number of late nights he was putting in, that he hadn't even fucked her since his return from America – not that the absence of physical contact seemed to concern his cool Fiona.

When he pushed open the studio door, she lifted her head from the horticultural books to acknowledge his presence with a brief smile. He planted himself before her desk with his hands in his pockets and jiggled up and down on the balls of his feet – always a sign that he wanted an audience. Then he launched straight in on a subject that was guaranteed to grab her attention.

'I'm going to call the bank about a loan,' he began brightly. 'Then we can push ahead with buying the farmhouse.'

His wife's eyes blinked at him for a moment, then her gaze returned to the neat sketch of a vegetable patch that she was planning for a house that was not yet theirs. 'Are they going to be difficult about it, do you think?' she asked cautiously. 'The cost of the building work might come as a surprise to them, on top of the purchase price.'

James responded with a puff of irritation. He was exhausted from the last-minute work on the GT bid, even though Paul Roberts had handled most of the detail. 'No, they'll see we're making a good investment.' He paced across the studio to an easel where an oil painting of a flower arrangement stood unfinished. 'Well, I'm going to bed now,' he said pleasantly. 'Are you coming?' He smiled at her bowed head, but she did not look up from her sketch.

'Oh,' she said at length, 'would you mind if I just finish this?'

For a moment he glared at her, but she evidently had nothing more to say to him, so he left her alone. When he had gone, Fiona Malpas allowed herself a small, brave smile. Soon she would be moving her possessions into the farmhouse in Hampshire – once they had bought it – and she would immediately begin divorce proceedings. Then never again would she have to tolerate the tedium of life in Richmond: the dinner parties with hours of sterile, self-important talk; the awful bank functions where the board members' vicious and empty-headed wives sized up each other's outfits; never more would she hover about the house like a ghost or a servant waiting for her lord and master to return from the City at some improbable hour.

And never more would she receive tearful, pathetic, anonymous phone calls from one of the tormented young men James used and then dumped cruelly, having as much concern for them as he did for his stools once he had flushed the lavatory.

Never again . . . once she had persuaded James to buy the farmhouse.

'I hope this makes sense to you,' said Sheila as she walked into her boss's office the following day, 'because it's as clear as a Peruvian bus timetable to me.' She passed the note to David. 'Charlotte Carter just called. Apparently we've got to issue a 212 Notice on these shareholders, Marlborough Investments and Cleopatra Holdings.'

Then she noticed that the colour had drained from David's face. 'Is this bad news?' she asked.

'She didn't want a word with me, to, er, explain this?' He handed the note back to Sheila.

'She said she didn't want to waste your time. Sensible girl. If everyone took that attitude we might get more done, mightn't we?'

'Yes,' he said fiercely. 'I've had enough of these media people.' He pretended to concentrate on his work.

Sheila stood by his side, looking down at his dark wavy curls. 'This media person is helping us find out who's so keen to have our shares, my lad,' she commented dryly, and then retreated to her office, whistling under her breath.

So, David thought when he was alone, Charlotte had had the chance to respond to his note, and she had avoided him. Was she still seeing that analyst? David tried to recall what he looked like; taller than he was, athletic build, good-looking in a sporty way that wouldn't stand the test of time. The bulging muscles would give way to fat, and he would get a horrible bald patch at the crown of his head, like a monk. Was Charlotte still sleeping with him? What were they like together, he wondered. Did he take her in the shower, and do those energetic things that David had lost the will for, years ago? Maybe he had screwed her last night . . .

'David, you were supposed to sign that letter, not rip it into shreds!' He snapped out of his daydream, and found his secretary watching him with exasperation. 'What in God's name is wrong?' she asked. He had methodically torn the piece of paper in front of him into long strips.

'Sorry,' he faltered. 'I can't imagine what was going through my head.'

'Neither can I,' she muttered. 'I'll print out another copy, and if you destroy it again you'll be given a Number One Spanking.' She waggled a finger at him. 'You get more like your father every day.'

At the NNN studios, Charlotte Carter was studying her stock-exchange terminal. The William Stone & Son share price was continuing to rise, and so were the options. Then there were Marlborough and Cleopatra, the mysterious twosome on the Stone share register. The amount of stock they'd purchased between them made the options-market dealings look insignificant. But how long would it take to get their true identity in response to the 212 Notice? Weeks, maybe even months. Many companies had the most primitive share registration arrangements, revolving around an elderly lady in the back room of an obscure bank in mid-Wales.

Solid proof that both share-buying vehicles led back to Brodie McClean would only come when the 212 Notice forced Cleopatra and Marlborough to divulge their true paternity. There lay her problem. She ate a Mars bar and flicked through the glossy William Stone & Son annual report absentmindedly. When she came to a picture of David she stopped, all thoughts of 212 Notices gone. Instead there was lust and pain, in equal proportions. She would never see him again. Never even talk to him. The Mars bar lay heavy on her stomach.

She was getting nowhere on either Stone or Martindale stories, and her boss wasn't interested in guesswork, or snide little references to Brodie McClean. NNN was unpopular enough with the bank after their scoop on its troubled merger talks, so Charlotte was to lay off them. After all, the network might one day need their help to finance a franchise deal for them. A great example of the independence and integrity of commercial news organisations, she thought sourly.

The only bright spot on the horizon was her forthcoming trip to America, where she was doing a special on the defence industry. It was one way to leave the memory of David behind her.

Maybe she should make a new start in her career, Charlotte pondered as she scanned her notes on Pentagon expenditure on non-hazardous footwear. Find a job as the US correspondent for a British network, perhaps? Easier said than done, though: journalists across London were slitting each other's throats for an opportunity to report from Brussels, let alone Washington. Charlotte did not rate her chances against them. In the meantime, how about a bag of liquorice allsorts? If a woman had not food, what had she?

'Gawd David, this is good. Is there any more?' The Honourable Nicholas Durridge pointed his fork at the plate. 'Be a crime to let it go to waste.'

Nick grinned like a satisfied whale, and wiped his forehead with a handkerchief as if the effort had exhausted him. The thirty-eight-year-old Durridge, blond hair thinning and oyster-eyes bulging, was not so different from the chubby boy with whom David used to share his tuck. A glance at his friend's waistline confirmed that sweets, or their adult equivalent, were still a significant feature of his diet.

When David returned from the kitchen with the food, he set a new bottle on the table. If Nick had noticed that his host was sinking a lot of wine, he made no comment: he was too busy explaining his idea. David was to start a new company just for Verdi, and employ any staff who were interested. He must sack them, and then re-hire them. That way, if someone *did* bid for William Stone & Son, they would get a calibrated weighing machine and conventional packaging company, just as the company had been described in its prospectus when it was floated on the Stock Exchange. If no predator emerged then nothing was lost, and David would have made more sense of his business structure. By separating the Verdi product out, he was making it a profit centre, and giving it its own funding.

Nick would organise a private offering of shares in this new company, seeking long-term investors who knew that the rewards would not be immediate. Then David's product could capture the market when the UN decided to save the ozone layer, rather than discuss it.

When Durridge had finished his second helping he sat back with a flush of contentment on his ruddy face. The buttons of his Viyella shirt strained to hold his belly in. David studied the bleary blue eyes with affection. Nick was becoming a caricature of a corpulent eighteenth-century squire, he reflected. It would complete the picture if he wore a velvet frockcoat around his barrel-like chest, and a tricorn clamped on his head.

'It's good of you to help me like this . . .' David began, but even through the fog of alcohol he suspected that whatever else he said would sound sentimental. His words petered out.

'So what happened with this woman?' Nick said bluntly. When David had explained about Charlotte his friend curled his lip in disgust. 'Have you become a member of the moral majority? How do you imagine she felt when you grabbed your knickers and fled?' Under this verbal assault David sank back in his chair and sipped his wine.

'Why don't you give it another go,' Nick urged, 'after you've begged her forgiveness, of course.' They exchanged frowns. 'What have you got to lose?' he said with a flourish, and added sternly, 'You may get hurt, but it's better than feeling nothing whatsoever.'

David looked away, but his friend, who enjoyed a soapbox, would not leave him alone.

'Is this woman – what's her name—?'

'Charlotte,' David replied weakly, and pretended to be examining the toes of his shoes.

'Is Charlotte anything like Helen? Is it purely lust, or can you actually have a conversation with this one? Is she pretty?' Nick probed, but before David could respond he went on, 'Of course she is. Then you must have children. It is the duty of pretty, middle-class people to populate the world with intelligent, well-mannered and attractive children.' He spoke loftily. The fact that he himself had renounced women for men made no difference to these sentiments.

'Whatever happened to your socialist egalitarianism?' David scoffed.

'The older I get,' Nick began, savouring the chance to climb on another soapbax, 'the more I value trees and dolphins rather than the smelly masses.' He waved his hand grandly like a philosopher handing out intellectual gems. 'Let them chant their mantras about getting where they did without poetry or paintings cluttering up their dull brains.' He shook his jowls and chins in mock outrage. 'No, no. The continued existence of the toucan is really much more worthwhile.' Then, almost in contradiction he said gently, 'You must have another child, David. It's up to you to fight back.'

'But what if our children grow up to despise everything we care about?' David countered. 'What if they drop out of school, and beat up Pakistanis, or torture rabbits?'

'No child of mine would dare,' said Nick stoutly, and peered at David down his nose. 'Of course the British aren't quite as open-minded about letting faggots adopt children as the Americans are, so it's academic for Mark and me . . .' He sounded bewildered. 'I suppose we could move to some ghastly inner-London slum where the social workers would let us adopt a baby just so they could boast about it. Look,' he said, rushing on, 'you must throw yourself at this young woman, and see what happens . . . and try not to drink so much. It'll damage your complexion.'

Having handed out this advice Nick hauled himself to his feet, declaring it was time he headed home, and they walked out to

Nick's car discussing the Verdi project. Before he climbed into his Mercedes, the bear-like Nick hugged David and praised his host's cooking once more. Then he was gone, and David was alone once more in his silent, empty house. His brain was awash with wine so he left the kitchen looking as if it had been shifted to Beirut. Instead he stumbled up to bed, and went to sleep imagining painful ways of killing Paul Roberts.

James Malpas had spent the evening at a barbecue at the home of a fellow director. He would not normally have relished the occasion, but tonight, with the election campaign hotting up, he had loved every minute of it. He had canvassed one colleague after another as they sipped Pimms in the Rickmansworth garden, and from his soundings it seemed the tide of opinion on the board had turned his way. If appearances counted for anything, the Ravenscroft entourage were looking sick about the Empire National Bank mess. It had been worth attending the party, even if the food was ghastly and the directors' wives were silly. Thankfully, Fiona had discreetly detached them whenever they had got in the way of his conversations with their husbands.

Later on, when they had returned to Richmond, his wife had timidly asked when he would make a new offer for the farmhouse in Hampshire. They had stood in the kitchen, like generals facing each other across a battlefield of terracotta tiles, and James had told her that there were bureaucratic delays. It was preferable to admitting that he had yet to persuade the bank to lend him the money. In truth his bank manager was already concerned about James's rising expenditure; the monthly payments on his Range Rover, the cost of stabling Cleopatra, his various club membership fees. On top of that was the mortgage on their Richmond home.

Fiona had sipped her generous scotch and water, and shaken her head sadly; everything about her behaviour was uncharacteristic – the doubts and the drink. James went to bed and wrestled with the sheets for twenty minutes, wondering when she would consent to let him have sex with her. When he had signed the contract for the farmhouse, perhaps? Then realising the futility of his anger he directed his thoughts toward a more creative goal: the forthcoming GT bid for Martindale. Every aspect of the operation had been double-checked, but Malpas was a perfectionist; he lived for the detail, not just the headline-grabbing thrill of surprising the City with a dawn raid.

He was also a shrewd judge of how to motivate his underlings. An hour before the bid was announced to the Stock Exchange, he would call together his salesmen in the dealing room and give them his 'march towards the sound of gunfire' speech. Like any effective performer, James was quite aware of the impact his melodramatic rallying cry had on his troops, and he delivered his last-minute instructions to full dramatic effect, like Noël Coward addressing his crew in *In Which We Serve*.

He lay there, constructing his speech and savouring the internally-sourced cocaine high that the exercise produced. But not once did he consider the other firm for which GT was bidding – the relatively small and insignificant William Stone & Son. Thankfully Paul was taking care of it, although Malpas had never fully understood why Dick Zander and Max Clark wanted the Cambridgeshire business in the first place. He was not to know that, as far as his clients were concerned, David Stone's company had become far more important than Martindale.

Chapter Eleven

On Monday, 2 September Charlotte took a flight from Florida that got her to Washington DC by five o'clock on a humid, sultry afternoon. She was tanned and rested after a weekend at the Boca Raton Resort & Club, just as her editor, Bob, had suggested. But even the plates of giant shrimp on offer there had failed to expunge David Stone from her mind.

She checked into the Phoenix Hotel in the centre of Washington, and took a shower to rinse away the stickiness of the day. While she was dressing she wondered how hard it would be to find a job in New York; the friend she was about to meet could give her some useful advice, she thought as she brushed her hair.

She found Scott Burns nursing half a pint of Guinness in a corner of the Phoenix bar. The place had been fitted out to resemble someone's idea of a Dublin pub; sawdust on the floors, little wooden tables, and stout on tap. When he saw her, Scott leapt to his feet and threw his arms around her like an affectionate pet snake. He was stocky, as the locals would say, with dark hair that appeared to defy gravity by sprouting up and back from his pale forehead like a brush. They had met last year, when the thirty-year-old reporter was stationed in London with ABC. He had returned to the States with his English wife to become a Washington correspondent.

He and Charlotte launched into conversation as if one of them had just returned from the bar with another round, and as with most members of their profession they began with unflattering gossip about former colleagues in London. Then Scott filled her in on the latest Washington backstabbing, involving a bribery scandal that was ruining the careers of several Democrat politicians. But after a couple of drinks they got down to the purpose of Charlotte's trip.

'The most important person for you to interview is Senator Marc Sandal on the Armed Services Committee,' Scott told her. 'Good grasp of the subject, but no friend of the arms industry. His favourite line is that since 1947 the US Army alone has received enough federal dollars to rebuild every man-made object in America, from popcorn-popping machines to airports.'

Charlotte scribbled down Sandal's name, and took a mental note of Scott's warning that the senator would do anything for publicity.

'I hope you don't mind,' Scott went on, 'but I've fixed for us to have supper with a defence analyst friend of mine this evening. He's one of the best, a former Pentagon man himself – you know, military turned Wall Street – very plugged in to what's happening. Ed Stanfield, Dought McMurchy, Wall Street. He's in town tonight, and I thought the three of us should get together. Is that OK?'

'Wonderful,' she replied with gratitude. 'I need all the help I can get.' They drained their drinks and wandered out into the steamy Washington evening to find a cab to Georgetown.

The first thing Charlotte noticed about Ed Stanfield was the nervy way he stood at the bar of the restaurant, looking around with startled eyes. There was a rather attractive menace about the man, a nuclear power station's worth of electricity, packed into a sombre Wall Street suit. He had a broad flat face, reddened by booze or exercise, Charlotte imagined. His hair too was red, but the eyes were so captivating that the fiery setting became unremarkable. They were pale blue and they seemed to stand out on stalks. If she had to guess his age, she would put him in his early forties.

'Charlotte,' he proclaimed as he shook her hand with both of his. 'This is splendid. My God, Scott, what a wondrous creature.' He stared at her and hung on to her hand with his shaky grip.

When they were seated they had Cajun cocktails, which tasted like pure tequila with a bit of black pepper ground into them. While Charlotte was gagging on her drink the stockbroker advised her to see a Colonel Vagg at the Pentagon, a big wheel in defence procurement. Then over several Cajun cocktails Ed Stanfield gave her a rundown on the state of play.

'The Stealth Bomber programme: makes me proud to be an American. Would have cost less to build it out of solid gold. Wings freeze up, too. Pentagon boys got mad as hell when they found their top-secret F117A on the counters of department stores because some toy manufacturer had gotten hold of the design.'

He paused and stared at Charlotte with X-ray eyes, then leaned forward stiffly and lowered his voice. 'It's a German plot,' he said. 'The Pentagon. Those blue-blooded Americans are actually Prussians.'

Charlotte raised her eyebrows and glanced at Scott, but her friend was evidently used to Stanfield's theories and was ordering food for the three of them, but the analyst kept up his soliloquy. 'Look at the names on every door in that hallowed building, Charlotte. They're all the Kaiser's men.' He spoke rapidly and with a crooked smile twitching at the sides of his mouth. 'The Hun don't behave like rampaging militaristic nuts any more. They just keep making damned fine cars. But the Krauts who crave the Blitzkrieg have moved here, and they've taken over the Pentagon. Entry-ism. *Very* clever, Charlotte. Very. Clever. People. And I should know. I worked with 'em.'

Charlotte nodded thoughtfully. 'They're infiltrating banking in Britain in the same way. Everyone assumes the long-established merchant bankers in London are Jews, and some of them are, but that's not the point. Rothschilds came from Frankfurt, Barings from Bremen, Hambros from Hanover, Schoeders came from Hamburg, and so did Warburgs. All from Germany.'

'Excellent, Charlotte. Excellent. This is a good woman, Scott,' Ed said in his precise, android manner. His eyes swivelled to the American journalist. 'Let's get wrecked.'

Plates of spicy shrimp, blackened red fish, and other peppery Cajun delights appeared, and Ed continued his rant on the military industrial complex until even he had drunk too much to carry on with any coherence. Scott, more in command of his senses to start with, mentioned that Charlotte might look for a job on the business pages of a paper. Ed straightened out a bit, and made Charlotte give him a potted CV.

'*Wall Street Journal*,' he said without a moment's hesitation. 'I'll introduce you to the big enchilada there.' Then he paused and glared at Scott. 'Charlotte must come to work in New York City, mustn't she?'

Scott nodded, clearly amused by the effect his British friend was having on the Wall Street broker.

'Come on Charlotte, tell me right now. Will you meet the man at the *Wall Street Journal*? Tell me, Charlotte,' Ed chanted. 'Charlotte, I'm going to pick up this food and rub it in my hair, right this minute if you don't tell me.' He dug his fingers into the plate of garlic shrimp in front of him.

'Yes, yes, yes,' she chanted in return. 'I'll see the man at the *Wall Street Journal*.'

'Good,' said the broker, and went off to wash his hands.

When they had filled their gills they trooped into the sweltering night, and the shock of emerging from the restaurant air conditioning hit them like hammers to the temple.

'Right,' said Ed authoritatively when they climbed into a cab. Then he peered at the driver's identification papers which were displayed at the front of the car. 'Mr Baddelli,' he said. The driver jerked his head around.

'Mr Baddelli,' Ed began again. 'This is Charlotte Carter, an important member of the British press. We must show her our great capital. We'd like a tour please, avoiding the black neighbourhoods where they rip us white folks from our cars and nail us to the telephone poles, if you don't mind. Then we'll go to the Phoenix Hotel, sir.'

He settled back in his seat, and Charlotte thought he had become peaceful and sleepy. But the minute they got near the downtown area, he was leaning over her, pointing out of the windows at national monuments. Both he and Scott were talking at the same time, indicating different tourist attractions and Government buildings.

'That's our equivalent of your Natural History Museum, Charlotte,' Ed explained as the cab swung around a corner at a speed which made Charlotte wonder if the driver was a worried man.

'There's a big tank of fish in there. Fish from all over America. *American* fish,' Ed said, his voice getting louder and angrier. 'And do you know, there isn't enough fish food for those fish in there? Mr Baddelli – did you know that? The Government is running out of fish food!' He was yelling now. 'It's a NATIONAL DISGRACE!'

Mr Baddelli put his foot flat on the floor. Neither did he hang around for a tip when his passengers clambered out at the hotel.

'Nice guy,' nodded Ed as they watched the taxi squeal around a corner and roar off into the distance.

Charlotte was nursing a throbbing head the next morning when she switched on the TV for the business news. She ordered breakfast in her room, but only the coffee made it past her lips. When she emerged from the shower, wrapped in giant American towels, she brushed her teeth a second time. Garlic and alcohol festered in every pore of her body. She glared in the mirror and examined the facial damage, but a string of words from the TV intruded on her audit of physical destruction. She raced into the bedroom, hangover forgotten.

> *'. . . The bid for the British company came in a dawn raid when the London stock market opened four hours ago. The CEO of Martindale, Sir Terence Purves, has vowed he'll fight the move by Mount Laurel, New Jersey-based GT, which he called "a wholly unwelcome and aggressive act". GT shares show every sign of rallying on the news when Wall Street opens . . .'*

Charlotte rang Global Technologies' headquarters; then she phoned Bob at NNN in London.

'Get Maurice to book me a satellite,' she instructed her boss. 'I've got an interview with Max Clark and Dick Zander at GT at eleven a.m., my time. You can get it on the bulletin if you turn it round fast.'

As she pulled on her clothes she was trying to figure out how quickly she could get herself and the TV crew up to Mount Laurel, New Jersey – wherever the hell that was.

Sir Terence Purves was still choking with rage when his Daimler deposited him at Hogarths, his new merchant bank, that same Tuesday afternoon. He stood on the pavement of London Wall and glared up at the canyon of uniformly shabby buildings. These financial cathedrals had glittered like pyramids of glass, steel and piping when they had been new in the 1980s; now they were as pollution-stained and worn as the cement tower blocks a mile to the east, in impoverished Bethnal Green. The prospect of poncing in and out of here over the next couple of months, sitting in meetings with a bunch of toffee-nosed merchant bankers, made Purves despair.

The men from Hogarths listened patiently as Sir Terence outlined his plan to fight GT, calling on British shareholders to back a British company. But the Managing Director was the only person from either the bank or Martindale who believed that such a campaign would provoke more than a snigger from the City and the press. The bankers preferred a strategy of feigned outrage that GT had offered so little for their client's firm. That meant more to the Square Mile than flag-waving. Hogarths knew the institutions would sell out to Fidel Castro if he offered enough cash.

Then Purves played his 'appeal to my friends in Government' card. Again the brokers listened, keeping their eyes firmly on their notepads. There was silence when the businessman finished, and the lead Hogarth man on the team, who looked like a camel, seemed embarrassed. He struggled for the right words to explain to Purves that his contributions to Party funds might have been enough to merit a knighthood, but were insufficient to bring about a U-turn in free market ideology. Nevertheless, Camel urged the businessman to conduct his high-level discussions, by all means. It was a way of keeping the Managing Director busy.

As the financial alchemists at Hogarths were running Purves through the limited options available to Martindale, his discomfort was causing a party atmosphere 200 yards down the road. The dealing room of Brodie McClean was gripped by a carnival mood. Gary Smith was happy. More to the point Gary's client, the Dr Crippen of fund management, was delirious with joy. Having reluctantly been lumbered with a surfeit of Martindale, he was now looking at a massive profit.

The moment that the GT bid had been announced, the beleaguered Martindale price had roared up as men in dark glasses across the Square Mile filled their boots. It was like packing your suitcases for a summer holiday. Everyone wanted a bit of Martindale, just to make sure they were in on the action. The Brodie McClean clients who had muttered and cursed when they had reluctantly held on to Martindale were now toasting the day that they had accepted the extra stock. Some punters were grateful to sell immediately and take the profit while it stared them in the face. Others would hang on, believing that another company, possibly a European one, would step in to bid for Martindale, and that the ensuing war would push the shares even higher. Happy days were here again.

For James Malpas it had been a morning of supreme triumph; the Chairman had come down to the salesroom to watch the dawn raid at nine o'clock sharp. Then Sir Anthony had congratulated James on his brilliant coup, and even his enemies were admitting that the bid had been a master stroke. Malpas had rescued himself and his department from the mess of Martindale, and had confounded his critics. They were not to know that James had been the invisible hand behind the recent collapse of the Martindale price. Nor that he had used his offshore nominee accounts, Marlborough and Cleopatra, to buy as much Martindale stock as possible in the last few days. Now the share price was roaring ahead, and James was already looking at a ninety-pence profit on each share. Corporate Finance would be turning in fantastic results this year. And the election for a new Chairman took place next week.

David Stone was eating a very small carrot for breakfast when he found out about the GT bid. 'Baby vegetables' were being grown on his farm because their novelty guaranteed a higher margin than the adult equivalent. More for less, so to speak. None of them had any taste whatsoever but they looked most attractive; they were of uniform length and colour. He had imagined that they would be tender and sweet, but in reality they were completely bland. It seemed that food scientists developed strains of vegetables in their own image.

David sat at his desk, chewing the diminutive root, and pondering the madness of producing toy food for jaded palates. And the arrogance of supermarkets that rejected tons of carrots because they were half a centimetre too long, while children died of starvation in unspeakable faraway countries.

'You'd better read this now, David.' Sheila held out the shiny curling pages of the fax from James Malpas, and David registered the worried expression on his secretary's face as he took them from her.

'Oh, bloody hell,' he grumbled, when he had scanned the first paragraph. He glanced up at Sheila, hoping she might break the spell, but her lower lip was trembling and she had turned away, pretending to examine the cyclamen on his windowsill. You were right, Charlotte, he thought as he leaned back in his chair and stared blankly at the ceiling, wherever you may be. His gloomy contemplation was interrupted by a call from Nick Durridge.

'These Americans aren't going to give a damn about styrene monomers,' his friend assured him. 'Anyway, they'll have their plate full with Martindale and won't notice us slipping Verdi out the back door. And forget any appeals to your institutional investors, old love,' Nick advised. 'They're a bunch of cunts. Greedy, short-sighted little cunts. Just concentrate on Verdi.'

But David was not so easily pacified. How many times had he regretted telling that analyst from Brodie McClean about Verdi? In all likelihood the young man had forgotten all about it, but maybe he hadn't. David tried to put it out of his mind: he already had enough reasons to loathe Paul Roberts. Then he wondered how he would break the news of the bid to his father . . . It was enough to give the autocratic old man a second stroke.

'What a bunch of turkeys!' Scott Burns laughed as he switched off the TV. He and Charlotte were sitting in his office at ABC, sipping beers and watching the other networks' attempts to explain the GT bid. The American business commentators knew everything about GT there was to know. What was foxing them was the English victim. No one on this side of the Atlantic had ever heard of Martindale.

Scott Burns was a political journalist, so GT wasn't his story, but he was in the happy position of having 'an expert' on hand when the news broke. His boss had dragged Charlotte on to every business bulletin from early afternoon, when she had returned from Mount Laurel, until the main evening news.

The five-hour time-zone difference worked against the other American stations. Everyone in the Square Mile was going home by the time the US business correspondents had dug out their press cuttings on foreign firms, and started calling around the British broking houses to find a coherent defence analyst to interview. Consequently, only ABC understood the business story of the week. It was a victory that meant nothing to the viewers, but everything to the journalists involved. They would congratulate themselves for days to come, revelling in the misery and embarrassment suffered by the other channels.

'Hey, you know you're damned good,' Burns told her as they headed out of the building. They were going to Scott's house where they would join his wife for a drink, then all go out to dinner. 'My boss thought you were absolutely great, a first-class broadcaster. She said so.'

They stood on the sidewalk outside ABC, enjoying the warm evening breeze and waiting for a cab. 'I really had fun today,' Charlotte smiled then paused, wondering if it was right to mention the possibility of a career move again. 'I was just thinking how much I like this country.'

Scott grinned. 'I don't think there'll be much problem finding you something. Just be patient.' Then he turned towards her and saw that she was studying him with narrowed eyes. 'Look, Charlotte,' he teased, 'the problem is your accent.'

She raised an eyebrow. 'I don't *have* an accent,' she said snootily.

'Don't be crazy, of course you do,' Scott laughed. 'You have an English accent, and that's a problem if you're broadcasting on American television.'

'But it's you lot that have the accents,' she persisted, but her friend cut her off.

'We *all* have accents – everybody in the world. There's no one single unaccented way of speaking, is there? Everyone has a different accent. It doesn't make my way of talking wrong and yours right,' he continued in his good-natured way.

All of her life, Charlotte had believed that Oxford-BBC English was how God created man. She sank down in her seat in the cab feeling rather stupid.

'Listen,' he continued, 'there's something going on at the network – but I can't promise you anything, 'cause I don't make the decisions.'

'Yet,' she added, and he saw that her eyes were sparkling again.

It wasn't until the following morning that Charlotte found out about the other half of the GT bid: all the US media's attention had been focused on the multi-million-dollar offer for Martindale, and there had been no mention of William Stone & Son. Charlotte learned the full truth when she called NNN from her hotel room to get her instructions for the day, and Bob told her to discover why the American giant was interested in a comparatively tiny firm.

When the call was over, Charlotte sat on her bed, pulsing with anger: Paul's fingerprints were all over this. Perhaps he had suggested that the Americans take a job lot? Then she imagined David's reaction, and wanted to call him immediately. But she remembered Maurice's advice: don't weaken, ignore him, forget him, get on with your life. She steeled herself with a bit of symbolic fist-clenching, and went to meet her crew.

A hundred and fifty miles north of Washington Dick Zander was suffering no such reticence. He picked up the phone and began with an apology to David for not calling sooner. 'We were kind of busy here, and I asked Brodie McClean to keep you informed. It's an impersonal way of doing things, I'm afraid,' the American said meekly, 'and it's not an ideal start to a relationship.'

David was perfectly aware that GT could buy him a hundred times over from petty cash, so he dispensed with the pretence that he was going to fight a glorious battle for independence. 'I'll be blunt so we don't waste time,' he responded, with as much civility as he could muster. 'If you can offer me a deal that saves my employees then I won't put up a fight.'

'Oh.' Zander seemed surprised.

David paused and considered taking a gamble. 'You see,' he explained, 'I'm in the process of starting another business, so I just want to sort out the question of my workforce.' It was a preposterous charade to imagine GT cared one way or another if he accepted their offer, but he had to give it a try.

'What kind of arrangement did you envisage?' Zander asked him without missing a beat.

'How many will you make redundant?' David began with a heavy heart.

The American sounded baffled. 'Mr Stone, we've had a look at your, figures – well, as good a look as you can take from a distance – and we reckon your finances and operations are pretty sound.' He could have added that Stone's accounts were a delight to behold compared with Purves's maze of confusion and bribery hidden in 'entertainment' funds.

'Oh.' David was puzzled by this news. He looked out of his office window, across the fields. A heron lifted itself slowly out of the wheat and into the air like a ponderous dinosaur. He listened for the prehistoric squawk that usually accompanied its takeoff.

'If you want us to guarantee a certain level of employment then we can start talking right now,' the American said.

David watched the heron climb upwards, then wheel around and circle the field. Ask for the impossible, and cave in thereafter, he thought.

'Well, I have about two hundred employees here. Given natural wastage, and an offer of early retirement by your company, I'd like you to keep a hundred and fifty of them for the next three years.' David winced as his words travelled across the Atlantic.

'OK,' came the laconic reply. 'A hundred and fifty for the next three years. Fine. And a generous offer of early retirement.'

They agreed that David would issue a press release recommending that his shareholders take the GT offer. That was how easy it was to get rid of the work of generations, he thought morosely.

'Oh, I know – there's something else, Mr Zander,' David remembered before they finished their phone conversation. 'I own a few shares in my company, so I suppose I'll soon be taking your shares in return. How's your price reacted to the news of the bid for Martindale?'

'Well, funny you should ask that,' the GT man chuckled. 'They're going up because Wall Street's been waiting for us to make a move for a helluva time. And we've been helped by an English journalist who's over here at the moment. She's been on TV non-stop telling everyone that GT is getting Martindale at bargain-basement level. Investors like to hear that. Shares are up seven dollars at ninety-two bucks apiece. OK?'

'OK,' said David. He reached for his pocket calculator, and stuck the information about the TV reporter at the back of his frazzled brain. That's it, thought David as he hung up. It's over. The figures on the calculator face glowed up at him. At least he wouldn't be reduced to selling off his Renaissance paintings.

He felt restless and angry with himself, so he left his office and went for a walk around the William Stone & Son site, hands deep in pockets, eyes on the ground in front of him. How many of his employees would thank him for having floated the bloody company on the Stock Exchange in the first place, he wondered as he paced along the gravel drive. What about the women on the production line who had known him since he was a little boy? How could he explain that there was a new boss, one who would never know their name, and who might sell them on to someone else within a year?

When David reached the end of the site he leaned on the wooden fence and stared out across the wheatfields to the horizon. Despite himself he yawned and hoped the whole wretched takeover would soon be concluded. There was a peculiar sense of detachment from events, and he wondered if his lack of emotional involvement was a bit like having a leg amputated. Did the patient stop regarding it as his own flesh and blood before the operation as a way of preparing for its removal?

Then he recalled his reaction when the doctor had told him that Billy was dying. It had been impossible to distance himself, or to put up a protective wall. But with his company? He was under no illusion that his major shareholders would pledge him their loyalty while they could gobble up more money from GT. It wasn't worth fighting for.

He turned around and headed back to the office, aware that he had to drive to St Albans that afternoon to sort out the financing for Verdi. As he set out in his Volvo with a CD of Mozart's Requiem blasting away, his mood improved, as if a burden had been cast off. But as he hit the M11 he realised that he'd failed to ask Zander the most obvious question of all: why did GT want his company?

As David drove to St Albans, Dick Zander was taking a seat opposite Max Clark in the CEO's office at Mount Laurel. The Financial Officer seemed rather pleased with himself as he relayed the substance of his conversation with Stone.

'So should we be asking some questions about this new company he's setting up?' asked Clark, never one to look on the bright side of things for too long.

'Of course I'll check that out,' Zander responded smoothly. 'But he doesn't have the slightest suspicion what we're after. He's probably going to open up an art gallery – you know how his CV reads.'

Clark shrugged his meaty shoulders in disinterest. Zander got up to go, then remembered he was meeting with NNN later that morning.

'Anyway, I'm giving another interview to the British TV station we talked to yesterday, so I'll make sure they understand we're after Stone for the quality of its products. "Global expansion into niche areas" – all the usual stuff,' Zander said as he registered the brooding annoyance in Clark's eyes. 'But I'll check out the research position, and Stone's new company,' he continued, 'and if we reckon something's going on then we'll neutralise his technological capability as you suggested, although I think that's a bit drastic. This guy's just not keen enough to defend his honour, if you ask me.'

Clark shrugged again and muttered, 'We'll see.'

Zander nodded with an appropriate look of concern and respect.

At Nick Durridge's office they were discussing how much money David would put into the business when they were interrupted by an urgent call from Sheila. She could handle virtually any crisis using her irresistible combination of bullying and bossing, so David was worried by the intrusion.

Sheila handed over the phone to his research boffin, Sarah. She was apologetic about bothering him, but something had just happened in the lab that David had to know about – immediately, she said. She sounded near to despair and her words came out in a panic-stricken jumble.

'Just stop talking, Sarah,' David said gently. 'Wait ten seconds, think carefully what you're trying to say, and have another go.'

The young woman sighed dramatically, and David feared she was about to cry. She had been measuring the ability of the Verdi material to maintain heat. The hamburger box, or more accurately, Grandson of Hamburger Box, had been undergoing protracted torture for several days now. Despite all the other demands on his time, David had kept up with her progress: now he was hearing the result.

'I knew you were seeing Mr Durridge about Verdi today,' Sarah said, miserable and agitated. 'That's why I thought you should know . . . It caught fire. Then it melted. I don't reckon it's going to work.'

Chapter Twelve

When Charlotte had the smooth, but never terribly forthcoming Dick Zander in the can, she drove back to Washington for her interview with Colonel Vagg, the Pentagon procurement bigwig whom Ed Stanfield had arranged for her to see. To the British reporter, the Pentagon was a legend in concrete; a fortress, the biggest office block in the world, with several unseen floors deep under ground. At the bottom was the Operations Room, so effectively buried that it could withstand a direct nuking, according to urban mythology.

Thousands of people worked inside the Pentagon, yet with all their expensive resources they hadn't managed to produce a decent large-scale map of Grenada for their troops when they had invaded it. Odd, thought Charlotte. She could have bought them one any day, at Stanford's map shop in Covent Garden, London.

As she strode towards the entrance she felt a childish excitement from being at the command centre of the greatest military machine in the world. The thrill didn't last long. The lobby area was as dingy and bare as a British National Health Service waiting room. On either side of the antiquated X-ray equipment stood a couple of military security guards. They chewed their wads of gum like cows, and had an equally bovine light of intelligence in their eyes. When Charlotte offered her pre-arranged pass for inspection they looked through it as if they couldn't read, which was probably the case, and waved her by without even a cursory inspection of her camera gear. Yet if the crew had been visiting the Ministry of Defence in Whitehall, they would probably be in cubicles with spoons up their rectums by this point.

Charlotte had imagined that the security here would be tougher still, but in less than thirty seconds they were in the endless corridor that skirted around the Pentagon. Rows of tatty hard chairs stood against the walls, and noticeboards announced the dates of basketball team practice.

Charlotte and the crew roamed through the bowels of the building, looking as out-of-place as a group of tourists in Alma-Ata, but no one stopped them or challenged their right to be there. Was it really as easy as it seemed, to waltz into the 'Strategic Airborne Interceptor Planning Office' and pass the time of day with USAF Captain Dwayne Shicklegrubber? If so, why weren't there bands of Shining Path commandos armed to the teeth, stalking the corridors? Charlotte had been given a harder time walking into department stores in London.

Neither did Colonel Vagg match her image of the steel-hard cold warrior. He was about five foot eight and balding, with the fleshy type of face that might bruise like a peach. Charlotte guessed that he was in his fifties, and she tried to work out where he had collected his stars: too young for Korea, too old for Kuwait. That meant Vietnam. Yet Colonel Vagg did not look like the type who would rampage around villages setting fire to old ladies and spraying napalm in children's eyes. He had a bookish air and a dry wit that Charlotte found charming. Out of military garb, she would have assumed that he was a librarian.

Despite some caustic remarks about gravy trains, Vagg gave her a favourable picture of Global Technologies, and he was particularly interested by Charlotte's special knowledge of Martindale. They agreed that GT would use the British company as a base to attack the European and Middle Eastern markets. So long as his friends in Mount Laurel didn't offer exclusive Pentagon products to the North Koreans, everything would be OK as far as Vagg was concerned. However, the Colonel couldn't help Charlotte figure out why GT wanted a company that made measurement equipment. When she had explained the other Stone activities, Colonel Vagg mused that Max Clark might have decided to become a gentleman farmer in his latter years.

While the crew packed their gear Vagg asked who else she was interviewing, and when she mentioned Senator Marc Sandal, who was her next appointment, the soldier's face darkened ever so slightly. Then his lip curled and he warned the reporter that Sandal's ambition was not matched by his intellect, and that she must be careful about his wilder conspiracy theories. 'Just ask yourself whose interest Marc Sandal is really representing,' he concluded, 'and you'll find that it's neither his electors' nor the public's, in most cases. He doesn't believe in anything but self-promotion.'

When Charlotte was on her way back to the main entrance and its vacant-eyed guardians, Vagg placed a call to GT. Dick Zander was less than happy that the same young British journalist who had interviewed him twice in the last couple of days was going to be calling on Senator Sandal. Nor was he pleased that she apparently remained unconvinced by his justification of GT's bid for William Stone & Son.

'Let's monitor the situation,' Vagg suggested.

Zander was conscious that although his customer was speaking calmly and without anger, he was giving his supplier an unmistakable message: control this, and don't let it become a problem.

'Fine,' he responded in an equally unruffled manner. 'I'm sure there won't be any difficulties.' Then he concluded with a reassuring smile in his voice: 'My people will liaise with your people.'

Marc Sandal shook Charlotte's hand in the firm North American way that causes the British pain and embarrassment. His eyes sought hers and held them in an unnatural, deliberate way learned from *How To Make A Good Impression On First Meeting* books for salesmen. The perfect white teeth represented a small fortune in dental fees; they were a statement, in the same manner that North African men display their wealth in the form of gold bangles on their wives' ankles.

The Senator's carefully clipped JFK hair was cut like a topiary; he had a strong chin and flat features. In short, Sandal was a typical Democratic Senator with his sights on higher things: handsome, radical, and destined to fail. Only the odds-on chance that he would self-destruct through some personal scandal or failure of judgement stood between him and the White House.

The crew set up their equipment in his book-lined room at the Old Executive Office Building, and Charlotte explained the purpose of their interview. But at the mention of GT there was a strange twinkling in the Senator's eyes. In Britain he would be the type to chain himself to the railings outside Downing Street demanding a written constitution, or proportional representation.

The Senator sat forward in his leather-upholstered chair with a puzzled expression on his face. Then he hesitated, as if he was struggling between his responsibility to stay quiet, and his desire for publicity. Charlotte could hazard a guess which side would win. 'GT's developed a new nerve gas called Dermitron,' he began deliberately, 'and the Administration isn't too keen on that right now. They're in the middle of arms negotiations with the Russian Republic, and this could really screw it.' He nodded as if he was in full agreement with himself.

Charlotte's eyebrows arched in surprise. 'Let's go, please,' she muttered over her shoulder to the cameraman. 'Running up,' came the reply. She asked Sandal for his opinion of Global Technologies. His eyes glazed over, and the automatic answering system switched on.

'GT's been producing nerve gas and chemical weapons over the past thirty years,' the Senator began. 'Napalm and herbicides made it a rich corporation in the sixties. Now they're using the same fundamental technology to make fertilisers and pesticides, but there's concern that GT's still really in the same business. People've left GT because they found the research work so disturbing. And the Russians aren't too keen on it either.' He paused dramatically. 'My buddies and I didn't go to Vietnam and fight for this country, just to have a bunch of businessmen foul up the chance for a lasting peace.'

Charlotte suppressed a squeal of delight: she had a new angle on the GT takeover bid, a story no other UK hack would find unless they came here and started digging around. She thanked Sandal profusely for his time, and as she prepared to go he scribbled a name and number on a piece of paper and handed it to her.

'Talk to this guy. Here, use the phone if you like,' the Senator suggested casually. 'He'll tell you about GT. He was a research chemist there. Knows defoliants like the back of his hand.'

The research chemist was reluctant to talk, despite heavy dropping of Sandal's name. But when she guaranteed that the interview wouldn't be used on American TV he relented, and twenty minutes later Charlotte was sitting in his dilapidated apartment. It was like a student activist's bedsit: piles of publications stacked in corners, posters on the walls, discarded coffee cups festering on shelves.

The Senator's source looked quite mad, and as pale as the Undead. He had a straggly beard and frizzy short hair at the sides of his head; the top was balding and yet unpleasantly furry. He was too young to be retired, and she wondered why he wasn't at work. Had he been fired from GT? Would his story be sour grapes?

His eyes darted about the room, which Charlotte took to be a sign of dishonesty, or perhaps more charitably, fear. Once she got him talking he calmed down a bit. She asked him about the nerve-gas work at GT, and he described the development of the chemical Dermitron.

'Who is Dermitron being developed for?' she asked. 'The Pentagon?'

'I don't know. I just did the basic research, and it wasn't at the production stage when I left.'

'Why did you leave?' Charlotte tried again.

'God told me to.'

'Ah,' said Charlotte with a tense smile.

'My life was barren before. Now I'm devoting myself to work that really matters,' he said, becoming rather more animated now they were off chemical weapons.

'Oh, I see.'

'I'm working with Jesus to stop the slaughter of millions of innocent lives every year,' he said in a matter-of-fact way. Charlotte sat forward, hoping they had returned to Dermitron. 'People talk about Hitler and Saddam Hussein, but the holocaust is happening right here in America, every day of every year. Tiny souls are being murdered in abortion clinics.'

His voice was intense and shaky, and it rose as he catalogued the sins of the flesh, as opposed to the burning of it, which Charlotte was more interested in. He was so absorbed in his speech that she wondered if he would notice if she pulled a face at him, or punched him smartly on the nose. Finally she interrupted him, but he wasn't taken aback by her rudeness. It was as if it happened to him all the time, which it probably did.

'Why would GT want to buy a small English company that makes measurement equipment?' she demanded. He shrugged. 'And a bit of farming, with some defence sales,' she continued.

'No chemicals work? No gases? Nothing unusual?' the man asked.

Charlotte shook her head. Then she remembered Verdi, the straw product that David was so touchy about. What the hell, she thought, David's company is screwed anyway.

'They've got a substitute for polystyrene, using straw,' she said slowly. 'You sort of mush it up and make it into a polystyrene alternative that keeps things hot, only it doesn't destroy the environment.'

The man was rubbing his bearded chin with a pudgy pale hand. 'It replaces styrene monomers?' Charlotte shrugged feebly. 'Then that's it! GT need styrene monomers for Dermitron. It makes it stick to the surfaces on which it's sprayed. It wouldn't work otherwise, because people could just rub it off when it landed on them. Remember in the Lebanon? They used phosphorus bombs and the stuff stuck to people's skin, and it kept on burning them even after they were dead. That's styrene-monomer technology.'

Charlotte's stomach turned over. 'So why does GT want an alternative to styrene monomers, if it's the styrene monomers they need?' she asked. 'The straw stuff won't be any good to them, will it?'

'They don't want an alternative to styrene monomers. They want to stop it reaching the market,' the man said in an alert, analytical and almost normal way. 'You say it's still in development?' When Charlotte nodded, he rubbed his bearded chin once more. 'Then the reason GT wants the company is so they can stop the research. If there's an alternative around, there's nothing to prevent a world ban on styrene monomers. The green lobby has been campaigning for it for years, and it's even reached the UN, but the problem's been finding a replacement.'

Charlotte groped her way towards an unpleasant conclusion. 'No styrene monomers, no Dermitron?' The man nodded and pulled his beard triumphantly.

They left him to his quest for global salvation and headed for a public telephone that took credit cards. Charlotte called Dick Zander at GT to ask if she could interview him about Dermitron. He said he'd be delighted to discuss GT's agricultural chemicals, but perhaps she would prefer to speak to the Vice President in charge of the Fertiliser and Pesticides Division.

Charlotte gripped the receiver and gritted her teeth as his good-natured words drifted down the line. When she suggested that Dermitron was actually nerve gas, the humour left his voice and he told her she was being ridiculous. He sounded even less smug when she revealed that she had two people on film who were contradicting him. It was her turn to smirk as she replaced the phone in its cradle.

Charlotte stood with her head in the bubble of the phone booth, wondering what to do next, then she dropped a quarter in the slot and made a local call to Senator Marc Sandal. He devoured this new information like a starving man. Charlotte repeated her request for radio silence until Stone's straw product was launched, and she promised that he would be the first to know when it was public – then he could score as many political points as he wanted. Sandal asked if she was free for dinner, but Charlotte declined the invitation as gracefully as possible. Then he warned her to be careful – a melodramatic touch that smacked of her chum Scott's warnings about him – and she got off the phone.

Regardless of Maurice's advice to forget David, Charlotte had to alert him to GT's real intentions. Within a minute she was speaking to the William Stone & Son answering machine. She left both her ABC number and that of her hotel, then, video tapes in hand, she hailed a cab to ABC for a mammoth editing session. Twenty minutes later she was settling down in front of the screens in the VT suite with a pack of tortilla chips and a diet cola, blissfully unaware of the flurry of activity that her inquiries had caused.

'I want to help with your crusade,' the woman at his front door explained. 'They said you were the one to talk to.' She spoke quietly, and shifted her weight from one leg to the other as if she was uncomfortable and impatient. She made him nervous, but he unchained the door and let her in. He needed every bit of help he could get for leafleting, picketing and collecting signatures on Right To Life petitions, so he wasn't going to turn away a like-minded person, even if it was after nine at night.

She was in her late thirties, about five foot eight, with mousy straight hair in a pony tail, and no make-up on her heavy face. She wore a light summer raincoat and carried a canvas tote bag in one hand, he noticed when they were standing awkwardly in his cramped hall. But he was more interested by the v-shape of skin where her shirt was buttoned at the neck, and the outline of her large breasts. A silver cross nestled there like a temptation, pulling his eyes to it.

The woman followed him into the sitting room where he kept the campaign material. He would tell her about the next picket they were organising at the abortion clinic, but it occurred to him dimly that he should offer her a cup of coffee or something first. He wasn't used to entertaining. This was the second intrusion on his privacy today; first the British reporter, now this.

The woman said yes, she'd like a cup of coffee and asked if she could use his bathroom. He went into the kitchen to rinse out a couple of mugs and put on the kettle.

'Oh, excuse me,' she called out from down the hall. 'Could you come here, please? Could you help me?'

He felt his pulse race, and finding the bathroom door open

slightly, was unsure what to do. 'I'm sorry to bother you,' the woman said from inside, 'but I've got a problem. Could you come here?'

He pushed the door open but the bathroom appeared empty. He stepped inside, wondering where his unexpected guest had gone, but before he could look around she had the crook of her arm around his throat and had pushed him towards the tub so fast he had no time to react. He lost balance and tried to reach up, but she grabbed one of his arms in an iron grip. The other one she squashed against the wall as she shoved him to the end of the bath, winding him in the process.

Then with one deft movement she had him doubled up and hanging over the tub, struggling for breath. He felt the blade of the knife under his ear and tried to pull away, but she had a lock on him like a professional wrestler, her knee pushing hard into his leg like a sharp stick, causing him to slump forward. All he could think about was how the blade stung like lemon juice as it sliced its way across his throat from ear to ear. On the second journey it opened his windpipe, and he yelped as the drowning began.

She let the knife fall into the bathtub which was already splattered by a drizzle of crimson. Then a vial was held under his nose and a sickly vapour wafted into his nasal passages. His heart started to thump in response to the chemical stimulus, and the blood coursed through his veins. The more he gulped in air, the worse the bubbling of blood in his windpipe became.

Still he struggled against her but he was dizzy and breathless, and she was leaning her full weight against him. His face was by now so awash with blood trickling through his beard and into his eyes that he could hardly see. His heart raced, and the pounding in his veins accompanied the tap-tap of blood dropping into the bath. Every gasp for breath became a popping, spluttering noise. He knew that if only he could stand up straight somehow he could stop the gushing, and pull this woman off, but she had him in a lock. His temples throbbed, and a purple veil descended in front of his eyes. The last image in his mind was of a pig in a slaughterhouse, having its throat cut over a stinking drain. Five minutes later he was lying in the bathtub looking like Che Guevara on his deathbed, the knife nestling in his limp fingers.

Charlotte left the ABC offices close to midnight. Her editing was almost complete, and she had also made the arrangements for the following day's filming in New York, which included a long and entertaining phone call to Ed Stanfield whom she would be interviewing for an analyst's view of GT.

When she reached her hotel room she set her alarm for five o'clock so she could catch an early shuttle. She had just pulled on her long white night-shirt and slipped between the sheets when she was startled by the phone. Then her eyes narrowed with irritation: something had gone wrong at NNN, and they didn't want her GT profile after all. As she picked up the receiver she was bracing herself for Bob's dulcet tones. Then she realised that it was six in the morning at home. Too early for her podgy editor to be at work.

'Charlotte? It's David Stone.'

Her stomach somersaulted, and she fought an impulse to put down the phone. Here was the ultimate test of her resolve to purge him from her soul.

'Thanks for returning my call,' she replied, precise, formal and as distant as possible. 'I'm sorry to bother you,' she paused but there was silence at the other end, 'but I've come across an unpleasant bit of information here that you should know about. GT's after your styrene-monomer replacement. I know you want it kept secret, but listen, this is important.' She babbled like a rabbit on speed, telling him everything that she had learned, not leaving him a second to butt in. When she had finished she expected him to scoff at her melodramatic message.

'Charlotte, GT isn't going to get its hands on Verdi. Not that it's worth having, by the way,' he added. 'I'm putting it into a separate company – you know, like the Crown Jewels lock-up that you told me about. As long as it stays secret, it's OK.'

'Oh,' said the reporter, taken aback by this news. Then she felt a chill of concern that she had yattered to both Marc Sandal and his loony friend about David's product.

'Thank you for calling me though,' he continued, and her heart lurched, hoping that he would say the things she longed to hear. But his words trailed off, and Charlotte thought he sounded dejected and tired. Her never-very-firm resolve was about to crack. She was going to say something hackneyed about missing him; or she would put the phone down. One or the other, she knew not which.

'Right,' she blurted out cheerily. 'Well, I'd better get on. Goodbye.' She replaced the receiver and cursed herself for almost weakening just then. She shut off the bedside lamp and wriggled down into the bed, thinking how unwise it would have been to give in. Maurice was right.

David stood up and walked over to his office window. The early morning sunshine turned the wheatfields into a golden sea shimmering in the breeze. He rubbed his eyes, dark-ringed from hours spent plotting with Nick yesterday afternoon; a night ploughing through the mountains of neglected work; an inability to sleep from worry about Verdi Mark Two – and, of course, the elusive Charlotte. He went to the coffee machine in Sheila's office and when he had poured himself a cup he stood lost in thought. 'Damn,' he mumbled.

Charlotte started just as nervously when the phone rang a second time, although she was nowhere near sleep. She fumbled about in the dark for the receiver and answered it even more suspiciously than before.

'I just remembered something,' he said by way of greeting. 'I want to be with you right now . . . are you in bed?'

'Yes,' she croaked through a throat as dry as the Sahara.

'That's where I wish I was.' He shut his eyes, expecting her to hang up again, or to tell him to go to hell. But there was silence at the Washington end. 'I'll tell you what I'd be doing if I was with you, but you have to do as I say.' Still no reply. 'Put your hand between your legs and stroke yourself. Do it, Charlotte.'

'OK,' she breathed timidly.

'Good,' he said slowly, like a man planning some form of torture for his victim. 'You do that and listen to me. My fingers are running up the calves of your legs . . . I'm tracing my way across your body

. . . then my fingers are travelling across your hip-bones, up your stomach, across your breasts to your shoulders. Can you feel me?'

'Yes,' she murmured into the dark, the movement of her right hand becoming more urgent.

'Right. I'm nuzzling your neck, your shoulders . . . now I've reached nipples . . . first my fingers . . . now my tongue.'

Involuntarily Charlotte's hips worked against her hand. She felt a burning heat throughout her body as she began to fall down the long tunnel of pleasure.

'OK,' he said in a voice both shaking and hoarse. 'I'm back between your legs and my kisses are everywhere except where you need them . . .'

Charlotte was breathing in quick little spurts as her fingers slipped in the dampness around her vagina. She was hovering, quivering, trembling when he said, 'Now you feel the heat of my tongue right on you . . .'

As Charlotte came in a rush of bottled-up tension, David heard her gasp. She lay shuddering and dizzy, trying to catch her breath. 'Oh God, David. That was . . .' She pulled herself up on one elbow. 'What about you?'

'No.' he said tremulously. 'Wait till you're back here. You'll owe me two then. Right now I've got work to do.' He hung up. Then he took a sip of coffee and allowed himself a glimmer of a smile, the first to crack his worried features in days.

When the phone rang for a third time Charlotte answered it with a grin on her face.

'David?' she said. 'Are you there?' But there was only silence after her warm greeting, and Charlotte realised that the echo of the international line was gone.

'Hello, can I help you?' she asked in an irritated voice. 'Hello?'

'Ms Carter?'

'Yes!' she replied sharply. 'Who is this?'

'It would be a good idea if you went back to England.'

'Who is this?' Charlotte repeated, and pulled herself upright in bed.

'You're wasting your time interviewing paranoid politicians and crazies. Just drop the whole thing and go home, if you know what's good for you.'

'Are you threatening me?' Charlotte spat in fury. 'If GT thinks I'm going to drop a story just because some loony rings me up in the middle of the night, then you can piss off. Go back to Dick Zander and tell him to screw himself,' she declared, and slammed down the phone.

She lay back in the bed, shut her eyes and listened to her heart pounding with anger. Then she sat up again and phoned the front desk. 'Don't put through any phone calls, please,' she instructed. What a bloody nerve, she thought as she switched off the light. What a silly cow. Then for the first time she was conscious that her caller had been a woman.

Chapter Thirteen

When Paul Roberts arrived at his desk on Thursday morning he found a typically terse note from his boss, summoning him.

'Dick Zander called me at home last night, about ten-thirty,' James began when the young man stuck his head around the door. Malpas was not one for wasting time with banalities like, 'Good morning.' 'He wants us to tie up Stone as soon as possible. Now David Stone's accepted we should be able to get a move on.'

Paul resented the implied suggestion that he had been dragging his feet and he said rather defensively: 'Stone's shareholders will get the offer documents in the post today.'

'Yes, yes, yes.' Malpas waved his hand, as if he was swishing away a wasp. 'The point is, I want you to lean on the lawyers to put the GT shares into Stone's back pocket fast. We don't foresee any problem getting the Stone investors to accept, do we?'

'What if there's a counter bid?' Paul said meekly.

Malpas ignored the question. 'Some journalist's irritating Zander no end.' The Corporate Financier looked up at Paul who was standing helplessly by the door. 'A peace campaigner, Zander thinks. Anti-arms sales,' James explained sourly. 'What I don't like is that it's the same bloody woman who was breathing down Terry Purves's neck a few weeks ago.' James didn't add that he knew perfectly well who Charlotte Carter was, and that she had been useful to him in the past, although she would never know it.

'Have I mentioned her before?' Malpas asked his junior, who felt a rush of blood to his cheeks. 'Anyway, this girl from NNN thinks GT has some sinister reason for going for Stone.' Malpas laughed, but his mouth remained in scowling mode. 'Still, it'd be tiresome if we had a media campaign against the GT takeover. You know, Labour MPs bleating on à la Westland helicopters.'

Paul was feeling increasingly uncomfortable as his boss kicked his feet up on the edge of his desk and leant back in his chair. 'Why would they object to the Stone takeover, and not the Martindale bit, if it's defence they're worked up about?' the analyst remarked innocently.

'I hadn't thought of that,' Malpas admitted in a rare moment of frankness. 'Zander said this reporter inferred that the fertiliser division was making chemical weapons!'

'It is,' Paul replied simply. Malpas's chair catapulted him back to his normal ramrod upright position, and the smirk disappeared from his face as he listened to Paul's matter-of-fact explanation. 'It was a core part of the GT business until the chemical weapons ban was signed. Now the emphasis has shifted to industrial and agricultural chemicals, but the know-how is there, and so is the market.'

Malpas frowned. 'So this reporter thinks GT will use Stone to make its chemical weapons in Britain, is that it?'

'I don't know what she thinks,' the younger man said flatly. He wondered if Malpas knew about his connection with Charlotte, and was trying to trap him.

'Paul,' Malpas began, and waved his hand at a chair. For the first time since the analyst had appeared in his office, his boss indicated that he should take a seat. 'Why does GT really want Stone?'

Paul slumped into the chair on the opposite side of the desk, relieved to be off the touchy subject of Charlotte Carter. 'While I was running through the details with their people at Mount Laurel they kept asking me about Stone's research. I got the feeling they were interested in this new technology he's developing.'

'What new technology?' Malpas sounded rattled.

'David Stone wants it kept secret until he's got it in production.'

'Well, what the hell is this bloody thing?'

Paul looked bemused. 'That's what's so strange. It's no big deal. It's called Verdi, and it's an alternative form of packaging made with straw. It would replace polystyrene. It's nothing to do with defence.'

'And why would anyone want to replace polystyrene?' Malpas said impatiently. 'Is this straw stuff cheaper?'

'Yes, and the problem with polystyrene is that the basic ingredients are styrene monomers,' Paul began, 'and they destroy the ozone layer. They're thought to be carcinogenic, too. So David Stone's people have found a way of creating a heat-retaining packaging material that uses straw and doesn't damage the environment.'

'That's all very nice,' James sneered, 'but why on earth should Dick Zander and Max Clark give a damn about the environment?'

'You're quite right. It's a mystery,' Paul agreed, hoping to smooth Malpas's ruffled feathers. His boss looked thoughtful, and jotted a few words on the pad of paper on his desk.

'Paul, why don't you talk to this reporter at NNN? Take her out to dinner or something, you know how good you are with these journalists. Tell her she's got the wrong end of the stick, OK?' He paused and ground his teeth. 'Zander was rattled last night. Furious. So we've got to stop this woman making a stink about the Stone bid. Now what the hell was her name?' Paul went rather pale and noticed Malpas's gaze upon him. 'Charlotte something,' James said with a disingenuous vagueness. 'Ask at NNN.'

'OK,' Paul said without enthusiasm. 'I'll call her this morning.' His heart turned to lead as he imagined the kind of reception he would get. He went back to his desk wondering how on earth he would make her see that she must leave this little story alone. No chance, he thought as he dialled NNN.

When James was alone again he called Sir Anthony Brook's secretary to ask if he might have a very brief word with the Chairman. Over the telephone would do, he said obligingly. Within thirty seconds the conscientious Corporate Financier was giving his superior a 'report' on how well the GT bid was going, and how soon Brodie McClean would be able to announce that their new American clients had been successful in winning control of Martindale.

'This is wonderful news for the bank,' the Chairman remarked, like a headmaster presiding over prize-giving at the school sports day. 'The business pages think we've managed this rather cleverly.

You must pass on my congratulations to your team,' he said, his voice creamy with pleasure. 'Should I meet Paul Roberts, your new whizzkid? It sounds as if he's quite a find.'

'Oh no,' James responded quickly. 'Paul seems to have focused attention on his own role, which is unfair to the others. It's been a team effort all the way through.' James paused significantly. 'Paul has his weak spots, to be honest.'

'I see,' the Chairman replied, as if he quite understood the situation. 'Well, congratulations to the team, James. You've done a marvellous job.'

Charlotte's cab threaded its way through the Canal Street area of Manhattan, dodging the waves of young men and women in the regulation battledress of tailored suits and gym shoes, who poured out of the subway. They walked purposefully through the crowds on their way to work, but they had the look of people who knew that right now someone was designing a computer that might make their job unnecessary next year. Charlotte couldn't share their edginess or gloom this morning: the prospect of seeing David when she returned home put a grin on her face. It would not remain there long.

The ABC crew she was borrowing was waiting at Doughty McMurchy, a tinted-glass monolith wedged in between the other angular shards of crystal around Wall Street. They squeezed into Ed Stanfield's office which was already crowded with models of cruise missiles and Sea Slug torpedoes. On the wall were pictures of Ed in uniform. Scott had told her, in jest she presumed, that Ed had been a military adviser in Central America in the early eighties. The analyst himself was barking wisecracks into his telephone when Charlotte took a seat opposite him, and pinned the microphone on to her silk blouse. He looked quite as frenzied at ten to eight in the morning as he did with a gizzardful of tequila at midnight, and he twitched in his chair like a man with St Vitus's dance.

'Such a vision in my humble office,' he said when he was off the phone. 'I am honoured.'

She smiled, aware that he flustered her in a delicious way. When the tape was rolling he produced a crisp sound-bite with the skill of someone accustomed to providing 'expert opinion'. To Charlotte the man pulsed weirdness, but she doubted that it would be evident to the viewers. They would find his bright red tie more diverting, particularly as it matched his hair.

'What about GT's agricultural division?' Charlotte asked. 'Are they still making nerve gas and defoliants?'

'You shouldn't pay attention to Senator Sandal's accusations,' he said with distaste and held up the *Washington Post* by one corner.

'Stop the tape, please,' Charlotte muttered over her shoulder. Stanfield handed her the paper and pointed to a story on the third page. As she read it, she felt her throat tighten.

Sandal had called on the Administration to back the UN move to ban styrene monomers. He claimed that a British company had discovered an alternative that would make styrene monomers obsolete. Now there was no excuse not to outlaw these environmentally damaging and carcinogenic substances, he proclaimed, particularly as the US had signed the all-embracing chemical weapons ban, and everyone knew styrene monomers were used in chemical weapons. He pointed out that it was ironic that an American manufacturer of napalm in years gone by should now be bidding for the British company. The Senator went on to deny that he was accusing the Pentagon of buying chemical weapons. The public were left to read between the lines.

'Oh no,' Charlotte moaned as she put the paper back on Stanfield's desk. Then she recalled those warnings about the publicity-seeking Senator, and it made her even more angry with herself. Round Two of her friendship with David might have drawn to a premature close. Charlotte looked back down at the article and blinked away the tears that had just sprung to her eyes.

'This guy's nuts if he thinks the Pentagon's buying chemical weapons,' Ed Stanfield was saying. 'Just ignore ninety per cent of what Sandal says. He'll do anything to project himself into candidate name recognition territory.' Charlotte felt the heavy hand of dread pushing down on her shoulders as Stanfield went on. 'He's got himself confused about their fertiliser work. Christ only knows whether GT're making chemical weapons, but I can tell you it isn't for the Pentagon.'

'How can you be so sure?' she asked him.

Stanfield lifted his hands aloft as if he was appealing to God for help. 'Charlotte, stitching things up with the Ruskies is far too important for this Administration. They're hardly going to piss it away for a few squirts of chemical. They can't afford to have the talks go wrong. There's no money to fund another arms race.'

She looked at him doubtfully. 'Can you say for certain that they're not making this stuff?'

He held up his index finger in warning. 'I never said that they weren't making it. Remember, GT is the company that worked with the CIA to find a drug that would make Fidel Castro's beard fall out. Their problem was getting close enough to inject him. Really, this company is capable of anything. What I do know is that the Pentagon isn't buying it.'

'So who is?' Charlotte shot back. 'The US Government must know what GT's up to, and they must have given tacit approval to GT to export it.'

Ed sat back in his chair and sighed. 'Oh, come on Charlotte, let's get real. South Korea, Thailand, Indonesia, Pakistan, Turkey – any of these guys have carte blanche to buy whatever they like from Uncle Sam. They're on our side, for Christ's sake. China too. And the Khmer Rouge.'

'But they're both Communists,' Charlotte objected and set her pretty mouth in a sulky frown.

Ed shook his head. 'There are Communists and Communists, my dear. China and the Khmer Rouge are anti-Vietnam, and you know how the old saying goes – "my enemy's enemy is my friend". Anyway, the British Government does its best to kiss Chinese ass, and you've been training the Khmer Rouge for years. Am I right, or am I right?' Then Charlotte saw him glance at his watch. 'Have you got enough?' he asked apologetically. 'I'm due somewhere now. Sorry.' She thanked him, but as the crew was packing up Stanfield warned her about the voluble Senator again.

'You know the kind of people who are obsessed by who shot

JFK?' he said, standing up and putting on his jacket. '"They" are behind everything, some dark force, some faceless group of power-brokers on whom we can blame anything awkward or impenetrable. Through history it's people like Sandal who end up holding the Jews responsible for unpalatable national problems.'

'OK,' Charlotte said tersely. 'I get the message.'

Stanfield hovered in front of her, gripping his document case to his chest like a shield. As he registered the annoyance in her voice he frowned.

'Here's a better theory,' he stated. 'Stalin was actually Lord Kitchener. You look at pictures of them. Lord Kitchener's boat was sunk about the time old Iosif Dzhugashvili appeared on the scene. Really.'

Charlotte smiled despite herself. The red-haired analyst was twitching with nervous electricity again. 'And Tito. Everyone knows Tito was actually a woman,' he said with urgency. 'Remember, we're going to have a tête à tête about you working here in New York City. So when are we going to get together?' he asked as they followed the film crew down a corridor towards the Doughty McMurchy reception.

'I'm getting a flight back to London tonight,' she replied.

'Why go back?' he asked with outstretched arms. 'What's the hurry? There's a great Cubism retrospective at Moma.'

'I'm sorry. I was looking forward to it, but when my boss tells me to get back, I can't really argue,' she said apologetically.

'What about lunch today?' he said as the lift glided down twenty floors to the street.

'I have to get this edited and sent home,' she explained.

'Resign. Tell these limey bastards to go to hell,' he suggested while Charlotte's crew were looking around for a taxi to take them uptown to ABC. She stood on the sidewalk's edge while the ruddy-faced analyst assaulted her with persuasive arguments. 'Come on. Why do you have to go back to England?' he said, and she glanced away to avoid the question.

Her eyes settled on a woman who was standing on the other side of the street, waiting in a doorway. The woman seemed to be watching Charlotte, and the reporter wondered why she was so familiar. She looked like any other Wall Street woman, in a dark skirt suit, and a silk blouse with a big floppy bow. Probably thirty-five years old, Charlotte guessed, plain, and chunkily built. So where had she seen her before?

'Are you going back to some man?' Ed suggested. 'Is that it?'

'No,' Charlotte answered quite truthfully. There probably wouldn't be any man waiting for her, not after he'd seen Verdi being discussed in the pages of the *Washington Post*.

She glanced back at the woman, who was still watching her. Then she noticed the handbag, a Burberry one in that check that Charlotte loathed. It had registered on her, albeit unconsciously, earlier today, because at the time she had wondered idly if whisky, mackintoshes and jumpers were all that Britain could export these days. When had that fleeting thought occurred? On the plane to Newark? At the airport in Washington . . . ?

'Keep in touch, OK?' Ed persisted, and she snapped her attention back to him. 'I'll call you,' she promised as she got into the taxi beside the cameraman. 'I'm sure I'll be back soon.' She paused and grinned at him. 'I just have to find a newspaper to hire me.'

As her cab pulled out into the uptown traffic Stanfield waved at her weakly, like someone in a trance. But Charlotte had craned her neck around to look at the doorway on the opposite side of the street. The woman was gone.

Scott Burns had arranged for her to borrow editing facilities from ABC, and when she arrived she went straight into a suite. She had to slot Ed's comments on GT on to the end of the work she had done yesterday, then send it to London, but she gave the piece the once-over first. When it came to the clip from the interview with the ex-GT research scientist, the VT editor suddenly froze the tape.

'Shit!' he exclaimed. 'How'd you get this guy?' The technician was transfixed by the image in front of him. 'Christ, do they know you have this?' he asked in amazement. 'Better call upstairs.' He summoned the news editor down to their suite.

'This guy was found in a bathtub of blood this morning, in DC,' the technician explained. 'Killed himself. Left a note saying it was an anti-abortion protest. We're doing a big package on fundamentalists and whackos, you know, how violent and militant they're getting, then this happens, so we're leading on it.'

'Are you sure it's the same man?' Charlotte asked, trying to keep the panic out of her voice. The VT editor nodded and slotted another tape in his machine.

'These're the rushes,' he commented as the screen came to life with views of the interior of the same apartment in Washington that Charlotte had visited the previous day. She sat on the edge of her chair, clenching her fists, too incredulous to comment.

The camera panned across the anti-abortion posters, then it tracked out of the sitting room and into the bathroom. Charlotte braced herself for what was to come. The rushes from any human disaster were gruesome, since cameramen were instructed to shoot everything the police would let them get. Editors liked to see the lot, and make their own decisions about how much to put on air. Charlotte had seen rushes from plane crashes, with charred bodies being carried out of fuselages, burnt into their seated positions like carbonised statues, their last moments of agony forever preserved. It had destroyed any illusion she might have had that death in an air disaster was painless.

This record of events was equally clinical. There was a long shot of the man's body, slumped in the tub, and close-ups of his blood-stained shirt; the glazed expression in his half-open eyes; the blood-covered knife at his side. Charlotte thought she was doing quite a good job of not vomiting on the spot when the news editor of ABC, a willowy ash-blonde with a sharp face, breezed in and shook her hand affably.

They watched the rushes of Charlotte's interview with the dead man only twenty-four hours before, and the editor whooped with joy when the research chemist did the bit about quitting his job because God told him to. 'Brilliant,' she kept muttering as the tape rolled.

'Are you sure he killed himself?' Charlotte asked while a dub was being made.

The news editor nodded her blonde head vigorously and tapped the points off on her manicured fingers. 'Suicide note typed on his own typewriter, fingerprints on the knife, no signs of a struggle, and we've got acquaintances saying he was a crank, fired from his job, totally obsessed with his cause. This is great timing for us, Charlotte. Thanks a lot.' She got up and was about to bounce out of the room when she turned at the door. 'Come and have a look at the piece. Suite 3, OK?'

Charlotte smiled weakly, and noticed that her hands had become stone cold and clammy. She slurped at a can of root beer to wash the sickness out of her throat, and got to her feet. Maybe if she saw the network's piece it would convince her that her scientist *had* committed suicide.

All was chaos in Suite 3, but Charlotte got a chance to see what they had pulled together so far. There was the standard police stuff, followed by an interview with a former GT colleague who said the dead man was 'fixated' by abortion, and that he had been a strange, withdrawn person to work with. A GT human resources factotum implied that he had been fired for his unreliability. Then the report went on to the main meat, which was the increasing violence of the pro-life versus pro-choice debate.

Charlotte noted down the name of the former colleague at GT, one Bruce Carretta, just on a hunch. Then she had to face her own problems. She couldn't use her dead expert, so she needed someone to make the link between styrene monomers and Dermitron. She called Columbia University and tracked down a pointy head who would do the job for her, if she could get a crew there immediately. Naturally there was no chance that this academic could make the further essential link to GT, or even say that Dermitron was a chemical weapon rather than a fertiliser. But he would have to do in the limited time before she had to feed to London.

Charlotte bundled herself, and a two-man crew into a cab, still pondering that stumbling block.

Chapter Fourteen

The fax machine in James Malpas's office rang a couple of times, then began its mating ritual and hummed into life. The photocopy of the article from the *Washington Post* was accompanied by a handwritten note from Dick Zander who wanted Malpas to call him as soon as he had read the clipping. The Corporate Financier looked through it twice but he failed to see its relevance so he summoned Paul Roberts.

The analyst sucked noisily through his teeth as he scanned the fax. 'Now we know why GT was so interested in David Stone's research work,' he remarked.

'What do you mean?' James asked when Paul had settled into a chair on the other side of the desk.

'This Senator's talking about GT,' the younger man explained. 'He knows they're manufacturing chemical weapons, I suppose . . . but I haven't got a clue how an American politician would have found out about David Stone's straw product.'

'I still don't see why Dick Zander and Max Clark give a damn about straw alternative to styrofoam,' Malpas sighed.

'They'll care very much if styrene monomers are banned by the UN,' Paul retorted.

'You mean Stone's product'll earn big profits for whoever owns it?'

Paul looked puzzled by his boss's question. 'I wasn't thinking of that,' he said, 'but yes, you're right – enormous profits. No, I meant GT is buying Stone to *stop* Verdi. The UN can't vote to ban polystyrene if there is no alternative on the market.'

A cloud passed over Malpas's face. 'You'll have to explain yourself more clearly,' he snapped.

'GT needs styrene monomers to make their chemical weapons work. That's what the article says. This Senator is firing a shot across GT's bows, but he isn't openly accusing them. What Sandal is getting at is that GT wants to stop Stone's straw product before it leads to a ban on styrene monomers.'

Malpas began to nod his head vigorously as if it had been obvious to him all along, and now he was impatient with the long-winded explanation.

'Can we check it out, Paul? This must be where that NNN woman got her stuff. Have you been on to her yet?'

'She's in the States,' Paul replied coldly. 'Her office expects her back tomorrow.'

'Well, you must talk to her. Zander's going wild about this.' Malpas looked at the article again. 'What do you think he'll want?'

Paul looked distracted. 'Oh, Zander's worried that someone knows what they're up to. This newspaper thing's pretty heavy.'

Malpas chewed the end of his pen for a moment. 'Find out from some scientist or something if there's any truth to this, would you, and tell me immediately. I've got to call Zander now.' He shooed Paul out of his office with a wave of the hand.

The analyst returned to his desk, appalled by Malpas's ignorant categorisation of everyone from rocket technicians to daffodil breeders as 'scientists'. It was to be expected from such a man, he thought as he flicked through his address book, and he realised how much he disliked his boss. He wished he'd never come to work in Corporate Finance. It was nice earning lots of money, but it might have been fun to spend some of it too.

He put his grumbles to one side and rang the tutor who had taught him at Cambridge. After a brief but jolly exchange about the latest departmental backstabbing, the tutor gave Paul the name of a lecturer who could help him. Five minutes later he had established why chemical weapons needed styrene monomers – but the lecturer had wanted to know precisely who Paul was, and why he was calling. After Paul had explained about the newspaper article, the academic became even more unforthcoming.

Finding his employer on the phone to Zander, Paul wrote on a piece of paper: '*styrene monomers make napalm type weapons stick to skin and plants*'. Then he put it in front of Malpas who read it and screwed the note into a ball. Paul returned to his room, wondering how he could persuade Charlotte to see him.

Zander was unusually rattled, and his jumpiness was infectious because an unhappy client meant problems for James. The American was concerned about British public opinion, and more specifically how much Charlotte Carter would stir things up.

'Is there going to be a big reaction over there when people realise a US defence company is buying their pioneering environmental technology?' Zander asked.

Malpas was genuinely surprised. 'No one will see the piece, let alone understand it.'

'But it says it's a British company, right here in the article,' Zander insisted. 'Won't journalists start asking questions? And what if another company reads this and puts in a bid for Stone? It's damned big money potentially, this styrofoam replacement.'

At that point Malpas realised that his client was continuing the pretence that GT wanted the product for its own sake.

'And what about the environmental lobby?' Zander fretted. 'They won't be very happy about this getting into the hands of a former chemical weapons maker.'

'If it was something to do with torturing bunnies the entire nation would be in uproar,' Malpas quipped cheerfully. 'But the recession has put global warming out of the collective public mind.'

Zander expressed disbelief so the Corporate Financier went on to relate what he had been told a few weeks ago by the man who ran Morton's ethical investment funds at the drinks party in Knightsbridge, although he did not mention his source. 'People only switch if the environment-friendly option is cheaper,' he explained.

Zander was not greatly pacified by this explanation of British shopping habits, and he urged Malpas to make sure the woman from NNN stopped spreading 'garbage' about GT. The financier was quick to assure him that the matter was in hand.

'No, James,' Zander interjected, 'it is *not* in hand because she's still here in the US, interviewing radical shit-disturbers like Senator Sandal.'

'Well, I can promise you that there's been nothing on the news here, or in the papers,' James said haughtily. 'We can put her straight in due course.'

When his client was off the phone James sat back in his chair, shaken by the passion in Zander's voice. He had dealt with some grim and paranoid characters in his time, but never one who became so agitated about an idle press report. Did all Americans talk as if they were participating in B-movies, or was there some substance behind his words?

Then his mind returned to his beleaguered acquaintance at Morton's ethical fund. Perhaps he knew about David Stone's packaging material. James dug out the man's card and called him. Fortuitously the fund manager was well up on straw-based products, but he said Verdi wasn't a replacement for polystyrene, just an alternative packaging material. The new company was looking for support right now, and Nick Durridge of GreenBack Investments was the man putting together the start-up.

When Malpas was off the phone he stood by the window in a contemplative trance, admiring the beauty of David Stone's manoeuvre. James was not fooled by the bluff about 'simple packaging', but it was a shrewd move, what with GT breathing down Stone's neck. The financier knew he should call Dick Zander immediately, but that could put the bid in peril. It would look appalling for Brodie McClean if GT backed out, and it would damage James at this stage of the chairmanship race.

Instead, he called his wife's broker in Bristol and asked him to contact Nick Durridge's investment group immediately.

Two hours later, Nick Durridge bounced into David's office with a smile on his cherubic face. 'Great news!' he announced like a town crier as he took a seat. 'We've found a home for the last five per cent.'

David nodded absentmindedly, finding it difficult to share his friend's buoyant mood this afternoon. Before Nick had arrived in his office David had been visited by his miserable straw boffin: Paul Roberts from Brodie McClean had been asking questions about styrene monomers at Sarah's Cambridge college.

David's whole strategy had depended on the slim chance that Paul Roberts had forgotten Verdi. But the analyst's phone call to the university meant that Brodie McClean knew precisely what David was up to. He was bracing himself for the carpet-bombing mission from GT any minute now. Of course, he could tell Zander that the polystyrene replacement material didn't work any more, but he realised that it wouldn't sound very plausible.

Nick had assured him that eco-investors were a cut above the fund managers whom David had encountered. Even if the polystyrene buster had died prematurely, Nick's people were still prepared to back the new, rather more modest idea. It was still environment-friendly, and that was the main point, his old schoolchum told him in a rallying manner. David had nodded grimly and kept his reservations to himself.

'This woman's going to take the final five per cent,' Nick repeated, hoping his friend might react with a bit more gratitude since the placing closed tomorrow. 'Her name is Fiona Carmichael and I got a call from her financial adviser just after lunch. Well, actually it's her husband who takes the interest in eco-things: it's done in her name for tax reasons,' he added, but he saw that David was distracted once more. The name Carmichael had rung a bell; he couldn't recall if he had met the woman or read about her.

'Anyway, the chap got on to his client immediately,' Nick said in a louder voice, trying to penetrate David's wall of preoccupation. Stone muttered an encouraging, 'Oh, yes?' although he was still struggling with the woman's name. 'And she's agreed to put up the money without even seeing the details. Pretty keen, eh?'

'Oh, bloody hell,' David groaned as he rifled through his desk drawers.

'What on earth is it?' Nick peered at him.

'Fiona Carmichael,' David muttered. 'Now I remember where I've come across her before.'

'What in God's name are you on about, David?' Nick's perpetually bloodshot eyes flashed. 'I've just given you excellent news. Christ, I've saved you an extra quarter of a million pounds out of your own pocket,' he complained, but David took no notice. He was searching through his desk like a gerbil digging through straw. 'This woman of yours is addling your brain,' his friend added pointedly.

David shushed him and glanced anxiously towards his secretary's office, hoping that Sheila was out of earshot. He resented having his personal problems aired.

'Here it is,' he announced as he dragged the latest share register on to his desk. Nick looked on impassively as David turned over page after page. When he stopped he chewed thoughtfully on his lower lip. 'Carmichael . . . She knows what she's doing, Nick. She bought my shares just before the bid.'

'Aaaah.' Nick sounded like a patient in an ear, nose and throat clinic. He repeated the noise when David told him about Brodie McClean's call to the Cambridge college.

'How would you like to bet Fiona Carmichael works for that bloody merchant bank?' David asked angrily.

'I doubt it,' Nick sniffed. He shifted his bulk in the chair, and peered across the desk at the register. 'Very dodgy business, such blatant insider trading.'

'How'd she know about GT and Verdi?'

'But that's it.' Nick rapped on the desk. 'Whoever this woman is, she thinks she's investing in the original hamburger box. That's what the analyst was asking about, yes?'

David nodded, and looked doubtfully at the share register. 'So who is she, this woman and her husband, who are so confident about Verdi that they don't even want the detailed prospectus before they sign up?'

'Could it be the Brodie McClean analyst, the one who knows about Verdi? Maybe he's got his wife or girlfriend to do the purchase,' Nick suggested.

'No,' came the unusually cool reply.

'It's very odd,' Nick mused, but David was silent. He had put his head down on his arms which were folded on the desk to make a pillow. Nick watched him, wondering if he had nodded off. 'Do you want me to tell this Fiona Carmichael that we have enough funding?'

'Perhaps it's someone else's wife, someone with the inside track on GT and us.' David raised his head and looked at Nick with bleary eyes. 'I wonder if it's James Malpas? He's the one who runs the show at Brodie McClean.'

He was up again, and on his way to Sheila's office. The company had kept a complete London directory since British Telecom had started charging out-of-towners a fee for telling them metropolitan phone numbers. It was a provincial penalty that BT had awarded the rest of the nation as a punishment for not being Londoners, and thus lacking their directories.

There weren't many Malpases, even fewer J. Malpases. David ran his finger down the list, looking at the addresses, and wondering where to begin. Then he saw one J. Malpas who lived in Marlborough Road in Richmond and it provoked a quizshow buzzer in his memory. He returned with the directory and examined the share register again.

'Look at this, Nick! "Marlborough" took an enormous stake in us just before the bid. This is the mystery investor, you know – the one Charlotte was interested in. She told me to issue a 212 Notice to find out who the real owner was, but I haven't had a reply yet.'

'Looks like it's James Malpas,' Nick said mournfully, and studied the directory.

David sighed. 'There's only one way to find out.' He sat down behind the desk, dialled and exchanged worried looks with Nick. 'Hello, may I speak to Fiona Carmichael, please?'

'Yes, can I help you?' she replied in her gentle Lowland Scots accent.

'I hope you can,' David began. 'It's about Cleopatra.' There was a moment's silence, and David wondered if his rather wild gamble had backfired. He winced at his chum opposite him.

'Oh, of course,' said the woman, as if she had just realised who was ringing. 'I'm sorry to sound so vague, but it's really more James's interest than mine. Perhaps I could give you the number of the people who run the stables, or can James call you back?'

David took the stable number and got off the line. 'Sheila,' he called when he had hung up. Nick raised his eyebrows in anticipation of a report of the conversation, but David's mind had moved on. 'Could you please find out if anybody in the factories has a copy of today's *Sporting Life*?' His secretary clicked her tongue in mild disapproval and went off for a perambulation about the site.

'What is Cleopatra?' Nick asked as his friend darted next door. 'And what are you doing?'

He struggled to his feet and followed him to the Xerox machine. David copied the relevant page from the London directory and drew an arrow to J. Malpas of Marlborough Road, Richmond. Then he did the same with the shareholder list and circled Carmichael, Cleopatra and Marlborough. Nick watched David as if his friend were performing some peculiar Fenland ritual.

David had just written '*Mrs Fiona Malpas, née Carmichael*' on one of the photocopies when Sheila returned with a newspaper that listed the day's race meetings. David split the pages between the three of them and asked them to look for any mention of a horse called Cleopatra. Then they sat in frenzied silence, searching the fine print of the paper.

'Here it is,' Sheila announced after two minutes. 'Cleopatra – running in the three-fifteen at Sandown.' When she looked up at David her brow was wrinkled. 'I refuse to believe that a horse has taken a stake in your company,' she remarked.

'Look at the name of the owner, and this.' David pushed the photocopy of the phone book in front of her. She studied the address. Nick craned his neck to see the racing paper on her lap.

'The common denominator is James Malpas,' she announced triumphantly.

'Brodie McClean,' David added. 'He's been using funny accounts to buy our shares. And he's got one in his wife's name too.'

'So she can carry the can for him?' asked Sheila. 'Nice man.'

'A paragon of virtue,' David muttered as he photocopied the *Sporting Life*, and then drew a circle around Cleopatra's name and owner. 'But if he's prepared to put a quarter of a million pounds into Verdi, who am I to stand in his way?' He shrugged. 'Could you please fax these to Charlotte Carter at NNN, with the usual covering note.'

'Oh, *very* romantic,' remarked his friend. 'Who says that the age of poetry and flowers is dead when we have a Casanova like Stone here?' Nick looked to the bewildered Sheila for support, but she pretended to be busy at her desk.

'Nick – shut up,' David said sharply. He turned on his heel and returned to his office. 'Come on, we have work to do,' he called over his shoulder.

The name 'Fiona' had also taken on significance to Paul Roberts that afternoon. He had used Fiona backwards 'ANOIF' to hack into his boss's files. The most obvious password in the world for the unsophisticated terminal user, Paul thought with disdain. He had reached the stage now where he doubted everything the wily banker told him. The only way to find out about GT and Stone was to search his personal files; and now was his chance because his boss had just left the office.

Once he had hacked in he could see nothing enlightening, but what he did find was rather more disturbing. This morning Malpas had received an internal memo sent through the bank's electronic mail system from the head of Personnel. It discussed levels of staff cuts that had been agreed at board level. Personnel was working on the assumption that the same principle would be used throughout the bank – last in, first out. Below, said the memo, were the seven people most recently taken on by Malpas. Paul's name was second from the top. He read on. Had James any changes or objections to the list below?

Paul found the response in Malpas's Memos Sent file. The Head of Corporate Finance had simply duplicated the Personnel memo into this file and typed '*agreed*' at the bottom of it. The memo had been sent through the system at ten o'clock that morning.

Paul did a circuit of the balcony around the atrium, hands deep in pockets, and his head in a fever of anger. He had so much dirt on Malpas: that would change his mind about making Paul redundant. He turned and marched back around the corridor. Then he realised that his boss had rather more evidence of insider dealing against Paul. Malpas could point any Fraud Squad Inspector straight at Mrs Irene Roberts's dealing account.

It was a pretty pickle he'd got himself into, as his father would quip with glee. He pressed his burning forehead against the glass of the corridor and tried to hold back the tears. Finally he returned to his desk, shaking and exhausted. He looked at the notes he had scribbled earlier that afternoon when he'd been on the phone to his former tutor. So much for the cash and glory; he would have been happier if he'd stayed at Cambridge.

Then he recalled that his tutor had mentioned that the college was advertising a part-time teaching vacancy. Perhaps Paul could carry on with his PhD, and lecture in his spare time? He would write to the college authorities immediately. They were bound to see his experience at the sharp end as an added bonus, and jump at taking him back. He reached for an envelope, feeling altogether happier.

When James called his bank after lunch, the Corporate Financier was amazed to be told that the manager would *not* see him at seven o'clock the following morning. Nor at eight, the secretary said haughtily, as if James had suggested that they perform some foul and unnatural act together. Then he tried a wild idea – four o'clock today? – just for ten minutes. James had clearly ground her down with astonishing notions, for she agreed, and made it sound as if she had magnanimously granted an audience with the Pope.

James had to consult his bank manager before Fiona could write a cheque for a quarter of a million pounds for Verdi. They had a joint account, but only the name Fiona Carmichael appeared on her cheques. It was a precaution James took to make sure that shares purchased in her name could never be traced to him. If this particular cheque went crashing through their account unannounced, it could cause problems. He understood the minds of minor bureaucrats well enough to know that they had to be kept in the picture, or else they panicked in an unseemly manner.

When James was seated in the stuffy, overcrowded office, the bank manager had assumed that his client's visit was about the joint Malpas-Carmichael overdraft. James tried to correct him, but the narrow-faced man peered down his nose at the file, and made tut-tutting noises about Cleopatra's stabling costs. James sat rigid and hot on the opposite side of the man's desk, wishing the bank manager would shut up and let him get to the point of his visit.

'I was never happy about this second mortgage on your house,' the man commented, and stroked the manila folder in an oddly sensual manner.

James cleared his throat and tried to stop himself from barking at the man. 'I think you'll find that my salary is large enough to ensure that repayment isn't going to be a problem.'

The bank manager, a long-limbed man in his fifties, looked up at James for a second, comparing his client's expression with the patronising tone of his voice.

'As far as I can see, Mr Malpas, you're using a large percentage of your income just to cover the interest charges. And your expenditure has been rising steadily in the last year.' He spoke as if he were reading a list of concentration camps.

'My salary will be going up significantly soon,' James said reassuringly. 'I'm not being too optimistic if I tell you I'll soon be Chairman of the bank I work for – but please keep that to yourself,' he added with a smirk.

Then James reflected that maybe this fellow was over-awed by his hugely successful client. James would make an effort to soften him up a bit. However, the heat in the gloomy broom-cupboard made James bad-tempered, and the plain grey walls had a strangely depressing effect on him. There were no pictures, save for a nasty calendar, and the glass in the window was frosted, to stop anyone's mind wandering beyond the limits of their work.

'Well, I'll have to impose a limit on this overdraft, Mr Malpas,' the manager said at length. He noticed James's eyebrows arch in surprise. 'You're earning a great deal, but you're also spending a great deal, if I may say so.' He gave a censorious twist of his thin-lipped mouth. 'What I have to concern myself with is the relationship between the two, not the bald sums. And I think we must call a halt to this particular overdraft where it is, right now.'

The bank manager registered his client's fury, but he seemed unimpressed. James leaned forward and fixed the man with his oft-employed, gimlet-eyed stare.

'I fully understand your concerns, of course,' he began politely. 'But I think you must appreciate that I'm hardly a high risk case.' He tried to ease a bit of humour into his voice. 'Every day I have to make the same decisions that face you,' James added chummily. 'Do I lend a few million here to these people, or do I back this start-up venture?' He smiled at the bank manager, but there was no reaction. Like bombing yoghurt, James thought as he left the bank. Not a wave or a ripple.

James kept his temper until he was outside; then he could have broken the neck of the first person he saw. How could Fiona write a cheque for £250,000 if the J. P. Morgan of Richmond wasn't even going to let them buy a few dozen bottles of champagne? Then he recalled Fiona's account at Coutts – the one into which her father paid her allowance. Coutts might be more easily persuaded to give her such a loan . . .

When he reached his car he found a parking ticket tucked under the windscreen wiper. He checked his watch and saw that he had been inside the bank for half an hour. He tore the ticket up, plastic envelope and all, and threw it into the gutter. Little people everywhere were conspiring to get in his way today, deliberately trying to stop the inexorable rise of James Malpas.

As he drove home he wondered what he could tell his wife. A version of the truth, perhaps: that the bank was not going to give them the money to pay for the farmhouse, and they would need to find a quarter of a million loan somewhere else. This solution cheered him, as did the thought of dinner. He and Fiona were going to the home of Sir Anthony and Lady Brook this evening.

Chapter Fifteen

'We really loved your tape of the guy,' the ash-blonde news editor of ABC gushed when Charlotte arrived in her office in New York City. 'And our Washington bureau is delirious. We're the only channel in town to have any angle on him,' she added with a generous smile.

'Oh, good,' the English reporter replied and glanced surreptitiously at her watch. She had very little time to get her opus edited and on the satellite to NNN in London. But the moment she had returned to ABC from Columbia University she had been dragged in to see this extremely Big Bagel. Since Charlotte was borrowing both crew and facilities from the woman she could hardly tell her to poke off.

'So I never got a chance to ask you why you were interviewing him in the first place,' the Big Bagel asked in a manner that invited Charlotte to sit down, have a cup of coffee and shoot the shit for half an hour. The reporter smiled thinly and hovered by the window. It was already three-thirty in the afternoon in England, and Bob would go berserk if she didn't feed her edited piece before five.

But no response from Charlotte was necessary because the television executive was still revelling in victory. When a phone call interrupted the monologue the English reporter gazed out of the window, wondering how she could escape. Down on Forty-Second Street, a taxi had just drawn up at the kerb, and a woman got out and looked up at the ABC building. None of it registered on the preoccupied Charlotte until she saw the handbag: Madam Burberry, complete with floppy-bowed blouse.

Charlotte's throat constricted as she watched the woman cross the street and approach the ABC entrance. When she was out of sight the reporter turned her eyes, but not her attention back to the Big Bagel, who was off the phone once more, and describing her network's push into global business news broadcasting. New York had been caught out too often by news breaking in Tokyo or Frankfurt, she said. The financial community had to be aware of Japanese index moves, Euro-currency fluctuations, German industrial output, Saudi ministers' ruminations. Charlotte nodded her agreement, and wondered several different things at once about La Burberry. Why here? On behalf of whom? What for? Am I imagining this? Is this simply coincidence?

The Big Bagel had moved on to the problems of putting together a business news show across different time zones, and the need to find journalists with a broad-enough expert knowledge. Charlotte felt the seconds slipping away, but she put her head slightly to one side to indicate her profound interest.

'I really liked the stuff you did on GT the other day,' the Bagel began again after a sip of coffee. The mention of the company grabbed the distracted reporter's attention once more. 'You were great, you know. People here were saying how well you handled it all.'

'Thanks very much,' Charlotte replied with as much warmth as possible, and fought an impulse to stuff a handkerchief in the woman's mouth. 'In fact I'm just cutting a piece on GT for NNN right now, er, so I suppose—'

'Oh, shit!' the Bagel exclaimed and sat upright in her chair. 'I'm gabbing away here and you've got work to do! Go ahead, please.'

This time Charlotte's smile was genuine. Once in the corridor she broke into a run, but when she reached her assigned editing suite she and the VT editor couldn't find the tapes. They scrambled around on the floor, looked under discarded take-out food cartons, and scrutinised labels on tapes piled in the corner. But none of them were Charlotte's.

They checked the other editing suites in case some harried reporter had taken theirs by mistake. Nothing. The rushes of

Colonel Vagg, Senator Sandal, Ed Stanfield, and the now-deceased research chemist were gone. So were the shots of the GT building, and the edited piece she had put together in Washington the previous evening. All she had was her tape of the Columbia nerd linking styrene monomers and napalm: not the makings of a full-scale profile on a giant defence corporation. The copy of Charlotte's interview with the ex-GT research chemist had already been wiped and sent out on another shoot.

She sank into a chair and contemplated the abyss. Her heart was racing, and it seemed like a gang of Siberian miners had taken residence in her cranium. Once more a hail of paranoid questions descended on her, and she clenched the arms of the chair in an effort to drive out the Marc Sandal-style conspiracy theories that were lining up for admission. Then reality in the form of her monthly pay cheque took over, and she dialled NNN in London.

'Bob, I've had a problem,' she began casually, and waited for the thermo-nuclear meltdown at the other end of the phone. 'The tapes have disappeared and one of my interviewees killed himself yesterday. I have nothing to put into the package on GT.' Silence. More silence. 'I can do something for tomorrow—' Charlotte chipped in, but he cut her short.

'Tomorrow this is a dead story. Nobody'll give a damn about GT – not while there are rumours of a big bid in the brewery sector.'

'But this isn't just a profile of a company, Bob, this is sensational stuff,' she gabbled. 'GT are making a new nerve gas called Dermitron and I have reason to believe they're selling it to the Pentagon. Anyway, they want to buy William Stone and Son to stop them marketing their polystyrene-replacement product which would lead to a UN ban on styrene monomers. You see, styrene monomers are used in nerve gas and chemical weapons to make the stuff stick to people's skin.' She paused to catch her breath.

'Hang on, hang on,' her boss interjected. 'If you seriously think I'm running that you're out of your fucking mind, sunshine. I asked you for a bloody profile of this company, and the only reason I'm interested in them is because they've bid for Martindale which employs thousands of our viewers. I don't give a toss about some crazy rumour you've picked up. And NNN is not about to start accusing an outfit like GT of making bombs, or whatever the hell you're talking about.'

'But this is all true,' she said with an intensity exaggerated by fatigue and worry. 'And it *does* affect Britain because it's about to win William Stone and Son.'

She heard Bob groan. 'How many times do I have to tell you to drop it? Get on the next bloody plane back here right now, because I've got work for you to do. Understand? *Now!*'

'But what about this package on the US defence industry you wanted?' Charlotte whimpered.

'Nah,' came the blasé response. 'Can't let you loose on heavy stuff like defence. You're producing crap. Stick to the lighter industrial stories in future. I'll find a defence reporter to do it.'

Working for Bob had taught her that dramatic displays of emotion had no impact, so she gripped the phone as if she were squeezing his balls. 'I'm really worried about you,' he was saying in a manner that betrayed no concern whatsoever. 'I can't have a business reporter who doesn't know loony tunes from good stories. You'd better pull yourself together, Charlotte. Just think about it on your way home. And I want you in here tomorrow morning, OK? Or else you can start looking for another job.'

Charlotte got off the phone and sat with her head in her hands, trying to impose some order on the day: the *Washington Post* article, the disappeared tapes, the Burberry woman, her so-called career in jeopardy. And the Siberian miners were still there, drilling into her temples. But there was something else competing for attention in her overcrowded brain – the death of that research chemist. Maybe he *had* been bonkers; there were lots of people in political parties and single-issue groups just like him – social rejects and misfits for whom activism was a sex substitute. But they didn't kill themselves. The man had struck her as someone with a lot to live for, a sense of mission, whether one agreed with him or not. It was odd to protest the murder of the unborn with a sacrifice of life.

She flicked through her notebook and reached for the phone. 'Bruce Carretta, please,' she said when she reached GT's headquarters in Mount Laurel. 'Hi, I saw you on ABC's report about the guy you used to work with . . . yeah, that's right. I wondered if you'd be prepared to tell me a bit more about him, because I interviewed him just yesterday on an important subject to do with GT, and I've got some questions you might be able to help me with. I'd be grateful for any background you could give me about what he was working on, and why he left GT.' She hoped that by pressing on she would put Carretta at ease. There was a long pause.

'I don't know,' he said in a barely audible voice. 'I'm not sure I should say anything. It's . . . it's really difficult.'

'Look, I understand that, Bruce,' Charlotte said soothingly, 'and I don't want to cause you problems, but I think your former colleague was in some kind of trouble, and I also don't think he killed himself. I just need to talk to someone who knew him the way you did.'

Silence, and presumably the biting of fingernails and scuffing of shoes. The more reticence Charlotte detected, the more certain she was that she was on to something. Finally Carretta sighed. 'I don't think I should do this. I mean, I have my job to think of,' he concluded lamely.

As the reporter listened she grimaced. Her lead was slipping away from her. 'I know about Dermitron,' she threw in, since she had nothing to lose. 'He told me about it. And I also know why your employers are buying a small company in England at the moment.'

'This is very difficult for me—' Carretta began, but Charlotte cut him off.

'—And it's rather difficult for lots of other people if this Dermitron thing goes ahead. That's what I'm worried about.'

'Yeah, I know,' was the humble reply. 'Look, I can't see you till nine 'cos I'm attending a departmental quality review, and I'd be missed.'

He gave her the address of a bar in Mount Laurel, and told her that if he wasn't inside, it would be because he had spotted GT people there. If that was the case he would be in the parking lot in a red Lumina. In turn she told Carretta what she looked like, and said she would be renting a car in Philadelphia.

Feeling the adrenalin of investigative journalism pumping through her veins once more, she skipped upstairs to the Big Bagel's office, and thanked her for her kindness. They had another half hour on the challenges of global broadcasting, and Charlotte's career to date, and then she was on her way. It was only as she took her seat on the Amtrack train that Charlotte realised that the Big Bagel had been interviewing her.

David was being pursued by faceless enemies; he was running blindly into the dark, too tired to go on, and too terrified to stop. Suddenly he heard a siren behind him, and knew they were coming to get him. The siren got louder and nearer, until David emerged from sleep and realised that the noise was real.

When he got to the offices, the fire brigade were just turning their powerful floodlights on, and spraying water into the laboratory.

'What the hell have you got inside that barn?' the fireman in charge shouted at him above the gushing of water and roaring of fire. 'It's burning like it's made of matches.'

'It's a lab,' David bellowed back. Then he stood helplessly to one side, and surveyed the twisted beams, blackened walls, and the sheets of flame licking around the remains of the door.

'Anything in there likely to explode?' the fireman bawled.

David nodded. 'Chemicals and preservatives.' He paused. 'Boxes of straw. D'you know how this might've started?'

'Faulty wiring? Or did someone leave some substance around that they shouldn't have?' The fireman shrugged. 'Or maybe someone started it. Can't tell yet.' Then he moved away to supervise his colleagues who were trying to stop the flames spreading to adjacent buildings. David stepped back, away from the wall of heat, and watched his beautiful lab disappear into the night sky like a coffin up a crematorium chimney.

'Hey, pretty woman. You waiting for me?'

Charlotte turned around and gave her questioner a withering smile. 'No, I'm not. I'm meeting someone here,' she said, and scanned the crowded bar for Bruce Carretta, the man she had seen interviewed on the ABC package. There were no single white men sitting about eager to catch her eyes. There were no white men at all. And the more Charlotte thought about it, the stranger it was that Carretta had asked to meet her in a steamy dive full of macho young black men drinking beer and listening to rap on an amazingly loud sound system. Charlotte found rap about as stimulating as making conversation with a hairdresser, and she could feel her irritation grow.

'Come on, lady, what you doing here?' the six-foot-four hunk of muscle-bound ebony inquired, not entirely without reason. 'I'm Gareth. Who're you? You from out of town?'

'Honestly, I am supposed to be meeting someone, only I can't really remember what he looks like.' Charlotte looked around the bar once more. 'Don't take it personally.' Then she wondered why a black man from New Jersey would have a name more fitting to a Welsh rugby player.

'Yeah? Well, I do take it personally,' Gareth responded with a hard edge to his voice. 'Do you have a problem with African American men, or do you come here to stare at us?'

Charlotte sighed and looked at Gareth for the first time. 'I have no problem with African American men, please,' she said impatiently, and could have added that she would have had no problem with someone as handsome as he was if she wasn't worried about missing her contact. Then she noticed that a cloud of anger had passed over the smooth regular features of her unwelcome inquisitor.

'Well fuck you, bitch,' he snarled and pushed past her. She didn't much like his tone of voice, and as she watched him rejoin his friends at the bar she rather hoped he wasn't going to find assistance in taking out his anger on this representative of political incorrectness. However, she was too concerned about the location of Bruce Carretta to think about being gangbanged. Her entire Dermitron story hung on his willingness to point her in the right direction. If he couldn't assist her then it would be back to unreliable Senator Sandal.

After one more walk through the bar Charlotte wandered uncertainly into the parking lot at the back of the building. It took her eyes a moment to adjust to the darkness, and she stopped in her tracks. There was a bit of light from Mount Laurel's six-lane main drag, but not much else. A more desolate and unpleasant urban wasteland she could not have hoped for. Surely, highly paid research chemists didn't knock around places like this?

Then she saw the red Lumina. It wasn't hard to spot because it was the only shining new car among the forty or so rust-buckets parked around it. She walked slowly, picking her way between pot-holes, until she was about twenty feet away, and could see the silhouette of the driver sitting behind the wheel. The headlights flashed at her once, briefly. Then the parking lot was dark again, and as Charlotte's eyes readjusted she heard the crunch of gravel behind her.

'Get into his car,' said Madam Burberry, a mere ten feet away. No tell-tale handbag this time; she was wearing a crumpled-up waterproof mac that wouldn't make it across the threshold of Burberry's emporium. Charlotte bolted like a greyhound released from a trap, heading towards the corner of the parking lot where she had left her rental car. The woman was clearly surprised by this spirited attempt to escape but didn't tear after her, and when Charlotte reached her car she saw why. The tyres had been slashed and both the windscreen and side windows had been smashed in. A brick lay on the ground in a glittering pool of glass.

Charlotte came to a halt, clenching the car keys pointlessly in her hand. Then she realised she had run into a corner of the parking lot and her shoulders heaved in despair. The sound of footsteps made her swivel around, but this time she wasn't fast enough to spring out of the way. The impact of Carretta's body against hers threw her on to the bonnet, and he sprawled across her with his hands around her neck. She plunged the car keys into his face, and he jerked away, but his grip remained firm.

Then suddenly he was being prised off her, like a tortoise lifted up by his shell, with his arms and legs paddling the air.

'Nice guys you socialise with, huh?' Gareth remarked. 'You would have had a better time with me.' He jerked Carretta's head back. 'This the guy you were waiting for?'

Charlotte climbed off the bonnet of the car and slumped to the ground like a limp piece of cloth. When she looked up at her saviour he was hugging the bewildered man close to him to prevent him from wiggling away.

'Thank you,' she panted and shook her head in a daze. 'I didn't expect him to greet me like that.' But just as she managed a grateful smile, Gareth's neck exploded in a mush of red as a bullet ripped through him and into Carretta's back. The two men slumped forward on to the car. Charlotte rolled out of the way as they slithered to the ground, groaning and struggling against each other. When she looked up, La Burberry was standing about five feet away with a gun in her hand.

The reporter fumbled for the brick at her feet as Burberry stepped closer and raised the gun. Charlotte's fingers closed around the brick as the woman levelled the weapon at her target's head, and her eyes narrowed to take aim. Charlotte hurled the brick with all her might, and it caught Burberry off-balance, making her stumble, just long enough for Charlotte to spring forward and knock the gun out of her hand. She reached down and grabbed the brick once more, then she whacked it against the woman's head, and Burberry pitched forward on to the ground.

Charlotte looked down at her, stunned by what her wits had achieved in a matter of seconds without the help of her brain. Then she saw the streak of blood down the side of the car and heard Gareth's last gurglings as his shattered throat belched out blood. The man beneath him was silent.

Her ears might have been ringing from the noise of the explosion, but her head was suddenly clear. She bent down beside the woman and gripped a handful of the hair on the back of her head. Then she ground the woman's face into the pool of cut glass, ignoring the incoherent moans. Once again the brick came in useful as she delivered a parting blow to both Carretta and Burberry.

Her hands were shaking as she dropped it and turned to her saviour. Gareth was still and silent, and judging from the shiny, sticky pool around him it seemed unlikely that he had survived the massive haemorrhaging of blood. She grabbed his wrist and felt for a pulse but there was nothing. Since he was dead she had no intention of calling an ambulance for the White People from Hell.

She stood up on shaky legs and surveyed her handiwork with disbelieving eyes. The parking lot was empty: on either side were industrial buildings, their windows in darkness. Evidently the sound of gunshot was so familiar in this part of town that it had not roused the rappers in the bar, or anyone else in the neighbourhood. She was alone with one corpse and two more possibilities. Now seemed like the appropriate time to panic.

She pulled her suitcase out of the boot of the rented car, and retrieved her handbag from the ground by Carretta's Lumina. Her brain was numb and muddled, but she knew she could hardly wander out on to the main drag and thumb a lift. Nobody would walk around this area after dark, and her presence would be both noticeable and memorable to anyone driving by.

Her hands were jittering so badly she could hardly turn the keys in the steering column of the Lumina. When the engine sprang into life she fumbled impatiently with the indicators and other irritating switches trying to find the headlights. To make matters worse, the engine roared like a hungry dinosaur when she tapped the toe of her shoe against the gas pedal. Surely dozens of people would be watching this performance and reaching for their phones to alert the police. She had to leave immediately, so she eased the car forward, all the time trying buttons and dials, but none of them illuminated the headlights. As she reached the exit of the parking lot, she located the ridiculous but correct little dial and they came on. She whimpered with relief and pulled out on to the main drag.

Then suddenly she was just another car cruising along past the pizza restaurants and discount furniture warehouses. Behind her was a wrecked rental car that had been registered in her name, and a bar full of men who had seen her talking to their mate Gareth before he was killed. Running was hardly the smartest thing to do, but what alternative did she have? As she made an effort to drive cautiously and within the speed limit, Charlotte wondered how Philip Marlowe would have behaved. He would probably have gone to a bar and ordered a gimlet, whatever one of those was.

Nevertheless Charlotte marvelled at the fact that she had acted like a hero in a cartoon. What alien voice had told her to hurl the brick at Madam Burberry? What instinct had made her grab it just before Burberry's bullet started its journey towards her? What secret and unfamiliar part of her had taken control at the right moment? All of a sudden her well-ordered life had shifted from real and normal to surreal, and the new décor didn't much appeal to her.

She was still trembling ten minutes later, but driving the car had a slightly calming effect. At the intersection ahead there were signs to Philadelphia, and Charlotte followed them for no particular reason. Now what, she kept asking herself. Go to the police in a stolen car? Explain her fantastic tale that began with Dermitron, went via an obscure company in rural England, and ended with three bodies in a parking lot in New Jersey? Probably a one-way ticket to Death Row.

Or should she go back to ABC in New York and tell them the whole thing, without a shred of evidence? No one would run with such a house of cards. Bob had been right about this improbable story, and the anger pounded inside her once more.

Scott Burns would give her somewhere to hide, she thought suddenly. He could talk to ABC, persuade the police to look again at the research chemist's suicide. Senator Sandal would back her up, and David could explain the relevance of his product to the world. She would drive to Philadelphia, and then down the turnpike to Washington. This sudden resolution eased the frenzy in her mind, and she turned on the radio to block out the stampede of negative possibilities.

Twenty minutes later, the station took a break for a news summary: the President's initiative to fund a drug-crop destruction operation in narcotic-producing countries had passed both Houses of Congress; a hurricane was threatening Florida; five more Democratic senators had been caught with their fingers in the till; there would be a schoolteacher strike in New Jersey next week. But, thank the Lord, there were no reports of a multiple killing in Mount Laurel. Charlotte drove on.

By eleven-thirty she was south of Baltimore, and Tamla Motown had given way to hip hop, so she searched for a public service station that catered for news junkies.

'Among the Democratic Senators mentioned today is Marc Sandal, whose name was added to the list of suspected bribe-takers just hours ago when fresh evidence of Mr Sandal's private affairs came to light. The junior Senator from Illinois is the only one of the five who denies all suggestions that he was secretly taking money from a leading cigarette manufacturer. Sandal's office said he was being framed, and that he will contest the accusations . . . Teachers throughout the state . . .'

Charlotte snapped off the radio and pulled the car on to the hard shoulder. A fat lot of good Marc Sandal would be as a witness for the defence now. She sat back in the unfamiliar driving seat and shut her eyes in concentration. It was crazy to go to Washington, and selfish to drag her friend Scott into this mess. The people who were after her did not appear to want a dialogue; they intended to kill her, and presumably anyone else who was in the way, like the treacherous Bruce Carretta at GT. La Burberry's employers would send another android after Charlotte, or possibly Scarface herself, if she was still alive.

Since her hasty departure from Mount Laurel, Charlotte had been blocking these unhelpful thoughts from her gibbering mind. But now they came into sharp focus. How could she keep on running like a fugitive in a country where she knew almost nobody, where she couldn't even name all the states of the union, let alone navigate without a map.

As she sat on the hard shoulder listening to cars whoosh down the turnpike and on into the night, she had the feeling that she had just woken up and confronted reality for the first time in days: now she saw the evening in its true ghastliness, and she began to cry. How much she wished she was an anonymous person driving along this road, unconnected with Charlotte Carter, the TV reporter and murderer. How she would love to be an ordinary woman, driving home to a 'regular guy' who lived in a nice town somewhere along this road; to have never heard about GT or Dermitron or David

Stone's wretched product; to settle down on the sofa with some tortilla chips and a beer and watch an old repeat of *Cheers*.

As the tears of self-pity stung her cheeks she realised that there would be no more grand gestures in defence of investigative journalism today, and no more bravery. She was going home before every airport in the country had her photograph peeling off their fax machines. When would the first flight leave New York? She searched around for a map and found a dog-eared atlas in the glove compartment. It might be wise to avoid Philadelphia and the Mount Laurel section of the New Jersey turnpike in case the police were out searching for Carretta's car. But how? By swinging west in a big circle into Pennsylvania? York? Harrisburg? Then Allentown and on to Newark? It looked like miles, but then again she had nothing better to do for the rest of the night. She could hardly check into a hotel, so she might as well explore the American north-east.

Bolstered by this new determination, she drove to the next gas station intending to fill the tank. But as she opened the car door the internal light came on, and she noticed that her blouse was splattered with blood and dirt. When she checked her face in the rearview mirror there was more blood – Gareth's blood, she presumed – on her cheek. A handkerchief and some spit dealt with it, but it made her feel sick. A more dispassionate observer might have comforted herself with the knowledge that Gareth was statistically quite likely to have been killed by his friends or the police by the time he was thirty anyway. But Charlotte was full of remorse for this casualty of her search for truth and justice.

She pulled a jumper over her blouse, and clambered out of the car, gulping back another wave of tears as she did so. Then with a full tank, some candy bars and a diet cola to sustain her, she got back on the highway and turned north.

Chapter Sixteen

'Zander's been on to me already today,' James explained to his apprentice, whom he had summoned into his presence.

Paul quickly calculated that it was only seven in the morning in New Jersey, and braced himself for the melodramatic report of some catastrophe or other.

'It's about this business reporter from NNN who's out there, asking stupid questions,' James explained, and fixed Paul with a bad-tempered glare.

On the other side of the conference table the young man wriggled inside his dark-grey suit. 'I've left hundreds of messages for her at NNN,' he shot back, uncowed by his boss's irritation. 'How am I supposed to contact her if they won't give me her number in the States?' His bluntness made James feel uncomfortable. 'The newsroom people I spoke to were expecting her back in the office this morning, but she hasn't shown up – and she's not at her flat either. It seems she's still in America – so why doesn't Dick Zander talk to her?' he concluded with a belligerence that Malpas didn't much like.

'Because he's paying us to deal with these things,' James said flatly, then planted his eyes on Paul in a manner that left no more room for discussion. 'Look, Zander is obsessed by this bloody woman at NNN. He's absolutely positive she's going to start pumping out wild stories about GT's military sales.'

'But there hasn't been a single thing on the TV or in the papers about it,' Paul interjected. 'He knows that, doesn't he?'

Malpas sighed and shook his head in irritation. 'Of course I've told him, but he's the bloody client, and if he's worried about his company's image in this country, then we have to respond. This is where GT wants to set up the base for their European and Middle-Eastern operations, so I have to take his concerns seriously.'

'It's so irrational—' Paul began, but he stopped in surprise as Malpas brought his fist down on the desk.

'Damn it, Paul, listen to what I'm telling you! Zander is talking about pulling out of the whole Martindale deal if this Carter woman keeps bleating on,' he snarled. 'He thinks she's on her way back here with some fantastic load of nonsense about some defoliant programme or something – I don't know, but the point is he wants *you* to shut her up.'

Paul shrugged his shoulders and laughed without humour. 'It's ridiculous. I can't tell a journalist not to run a story, no matter how many expensive lunches I buy her.'

'I want you to understand something, Paul, just between us,' said his boss in the manner of a schoolmaster reprimanding an errant pupil. 'Dick Zander is used to getting what he wants. We aren't going to mess him around.'

Paul's brow furrowed. 'What are you talking about?' he asked, raising his voice for the first time in Malpas's presence. 'Should I lock her in a cupboard until the bid is over?' he sneered.

Malpas was shaking his head again. Then he stood up, and closed the door. When he came back he sat on the edge of the desk, right in front of Paul, and leaned towards him.

'I just told you something important, you stupid little wanker,' he said, quietly and concisely. 'Defence manufacturing is not a substitute for charity work. Zander and Clark are ruthless people in a cut-throat world, and they don't expect to have their wishes disobeyed. You are never going to make it in this business if you don't grasp some realities, like, for instance, if your client wants you to stick your cock in a vice, then you bloody well do it.'

Malpas stopped and watched as Paul looked away and shrugged once more. 'Read this, laddie,' he said, and handed him a hard copy from the wires terminal. 'There was a fire last night at David Stone's factory. Think about it – then you might treat Dick Zander's requests with the respect that they deserve.'

The nonchalant defiance evaporated, and the younger man's eyes narrowed as he read the fax. 'What happened?' he asked, and realised that his boss was genuinely afraid, almost shaking.

'You'd better find out where that bitch Charlotte Carter is, and persuade her that she's barking up the wrong tree. You can do it if you put your mind to it,' James replied bluntly, and returned to his side of the desk with an air of finality.

Paul got to his feet slowly, as if he was debating some last remark, but he was too curious about the fire in Ely to hang about, and he went down to the salesroom to look at the Reuters terminal.

Ten minutes later James left the office and walked down Moorgate towards Finsbury Circus, where he had an appointment for a routine examination for his health insurance. As he skirted the neat bowling green in the centre of Finsbury Circus he reflected that Paul had become a terrible pain, a real let-down, insufficiently motivated – even a liability. Thankfully he would soon receive his redundancy notice, but in the meantime he was proving exceptionally dim.

On a happier note James was still savouring Sir Anthony Brook's message to him at dinner in Chelsea the previous evening. While they had been enjoying brandy and cigars at one end of the long Regency sitting room, and their wives had discussed gardening at the other end, Sir Anthony had spoken as clearly as he knew how.

'I've been a bit unhappy about your bold-as-brass approach – well, I expect you know that,' Brook had giggled, 'but I reckon you're best equipped to take us through the cut and thrust of the next few years. This business has become a nightmare, really,' he added with a baffled look on his patrician features.

That was one way of excusing his incompetence, thought James privately, assuming the air of a disciple at the knee of the Prophet. Brook might as well have said: 'The day for gentlemen is over, and we have to make way for tykes like you.' The message was not lost on James, but the old fool's prejudices were irrelevant. His blessing was another matter, however. James reckoned it would be enough to sway the lily-livered waverers his way, when the board voted next week on who would be the new Chairman of Brodie McClean.

The other reason for the spring in his step was the forthcoming launch of Verdi, and his success in getting Fiona to arrange the financing for what she assumed was the purchase of the farmhouse. He would find some way out of that little lie when he had time to address his mind to it.

In the meantime he was more diverted by the thought of increasing his net worth as the value of his Verdi shareholding increased. Nick Durridge had faxed all Verdi investors that morning, assuring them that the product launch would go ahead, despite the fire at the Stone lab. The recipe for the miracle compound was kept on a floppy disk in David Stone's office, so although the prototypes had been destroyed, more examples would be ready by next week. It did not surprise James that David Stone was maintaining the bluff that his material was only a cheap ecological packaging material. By now he probably appreciated Zander's resolve to get hold of the polystyrene replacement. Once it had been publicly launched at a press conference, GT could do nothing to destroy it. Still, the fire had been a rather drastic form of business negotiation, and it had sent James's bowels into a watery quiver.

He crossed the road to the other side of Finsbury Circus, then slowed his pace and glanced at the nameplates on the buildings to his left. He saw the one he was looking for – Dr Adams – and entered the pompous Victorian doorway. Inside he climbed the stairs to the doctor's office, leaping them two at a time. He was still on track for the top.

The William Stone & Son site was still in chaos that Friday afternoon. David had just left a message at NNN for Charlotte to call him – yet another unanswered message – and now even they didn't know where she was. They said she had been due in on an overnight flight from New York. He scowled at the phone and then realised that Sheila was hovering at his door with a thin, frozen smile on her face.

'David, the police would like a word with you,' she said in her official voice which David found ridiculous and amusing at the same time. 'This is Superintendent Farrow, and he'd like to see you now.'

The officer walked past her, making it clear that he wasn't asking for an appointment. 'Mind if I close the door?' he asked David when they had shaken hands. As soon as he had sat down he began his questions. 'Mr Stone, what were you doing last night between about ten o'clock and the time the fire brigade were called by that passing motorist?'

David ran his fingers through his hair absentmindedly as he tried to get his exhausted mind around the policeman's question. 'I, er, I was working in my study at the Hall, then at about eleven I went to bed.'

'Can anyone verify that, Mr Stone?'

David pulled a face, and shrugged. 'No, I live alone.'

The Superintendent rubbed the end of his pencil along the Kirk Douglas ridge in the centre of his chin. 'Then we've only your word for it, is that correct?'

'What are you getting at?' David said with an undiplomatic glare.

'Do you think you could come down to the station to answer a few more questions, Mr Stone? Now?' And Superintendent Farrow gave the briefest of perfunctory smiles.

The earthbound part of Charlotte's odyssey ended at Kennedy Airport at eight o'clock on Friday morning. Earlier on she had phoned a recorded information tape that told her there was an American Airlines flight at 9.30 a.m. from Kennedy getting into London at 9.30 p.m. She caught a bus there from the Port Authority bus station in Manhattan, having dumped the Lumina in a parking lot in the Ninth Avenue-Forty-Second Street area. The keys were in the ignition, so it was only a matter of hours until it was stolen. Now she had to pray that the Mount Laurel police had not been able to reach anyone from the car rental company yet to find out who had ditched their car close to the scene of the crime. If the police knew she was British they might be watching the airports for her. Otherwise she had only GT to worry about as she tried to leave the country.

During her nocturnal journey through New Jersey, Philadelphia and New York, Charlotte had had little else to think about. The rest of the time she had looked out at a hundred towns that seemed familiar the way everything in America seemed familiar: the fast-food places with their huge roadside signs, the muffler replacement workshops, the streets of identical low-level 195Os bungalows. What was curious, was how often these places parodied themselves. Then her mind slipped from such banalities back to reliving those horrible moments in the parking lot.

When she reached Kennedy she bought a ticket, checked her bag, went through Passport Control and retreated to the lavatory to clean herself up. In a just and decent world she would deserve some breakfast after her Illiad, but she wasn't hungry – just sick, exhausted, and paranoid. Not a good recipe for a healthy appetite.

But she did have phone calls to make so she found a credit-card booth and rang Bob at NNN. When she explained that she was still in the States he sucked in his breath thoughtfully, and then he sacked her. It happened so rapidly that Charlotte later wondered if it had been premeditated. More likely, her stubborn disobedience had simply been the final straw. There was little point in attempting to justify her absence or to explain her ordeal. He had obviously written her off, and her no-show in London that morning had confirmed his judgement.

The funny thing was that the end of her career at NNN didn't come as a surprise. Luck alone had taken her this far as a TV reporter, she reckoned, so she was far from devastated by the news. Being sacked was rather an anticlimax after the last twenty-four hours, anyway. She had no space left in her mind to worry about how she was going to pay for the car rental, or the flight home. Survival came first. She glanced around her to make sure she was not about to be pounced on by a lunatic, and picked up the receiver once more.

On a whim she called the car rental company in Philadelphia, wondering if she could give them some cock-and-bull story which would delay them putting her name and description on the police wires. To her surprise it was they who were apologising to her for the 'inconvenience' she had suffered with the car. The 'problem' had apparently been reported late last night, by whom it wasn't clear. Charlotte, cross-eyed with tiredness, accepted this new development and bade them farewell.

Before she could ponder this peculiar turn of events, she called David Stone's office in Cambridgeshire, where it was about one-thirty in the afternoon. Sheila explained that her boss was out, and she was unable to say when he would be back. Charlotte debated whether to leave a message for David to 'be careful'. It would sound melodramatic, and scarcely credible to anyone who hadn't been awake and frothing at the mouth for the past thirty hours, but she took the plunge. To her surprise Sheila was unfazed, and promised to pass her message on.

'Yes,' she had commented wearily. 'He does need to be careful. Things are looking awful for him.'

The feeling of dread returned. 'What's wrong?' Charlotte shot back.

'Haven't you heard yet? Last night a fire destroyed the lab,' Sheila said, and then paused, overcome with emotion. 'Well, I know I can tell you this, off the record or whatever, because of all the help you've given us,' she went on shakily, 'but David's being questioned by the police. They seem to think someone set the fire deliberately.'

'Is that where he is now?' asked Charlotte as she closed her eyes to concentrate on Sheila's voice.

'His solicitor's there too. I made sure he knew immediately, but it's all so terrible. I can't believe it's happening,' Sheila said mournfully. 'Why can't they just accept that it was an accident? There's a horrible streak in this country, you know. People are always wanting to find someone to blame.'

'Are you sure it was an accident?' Charlotte asked doggedly. 'No one was seen messing around the factories or anything?'

'Good grief no.' Sheila sounded shocked at the very idea. 'I'll tell David you called,' she concluded curtly.

Charlotte dragged herself to a bench and slumped down like a boxer who has been stunned by a sharp left-hook to the head. Another coincidence? she wondered. What was she running back to? Should she stay here? It would be easier to disappear in England, though, where at least she knew her way around. Maybe she could convince the police that evil forces were at work, setting fires. Here it seemed less likely that the law would give her a sympathetic hearing, since she had her own bodies to account for. She rubbed her eyes and glanced about at busy people rushing for early flights. No one seemed to be wielding a machete or an Uzi. She suppressed the urge to weep and returned to the loo where she hid and waited for her flight to be called.

In London, the phone in her Gloucester Road flat was ringing.

'Charlotte, it's Paul calling again on Friday afternoon, around three-thirty. I've left you several messages to call me, but this is important.' He paused, thinking how ridiculous he sounded. *'Please call me as soon as you get this.'*

Paul put down the phone on Charlotte's answering machine, hoping to God that she would take him seriously, then got up and wandered into Malpas's office to make sure that his boss was not about, because he didn't want him to overhear the next call he made.

Then he returned to his desk and studied the latest Associated Press news report that he had printed off the wires terminal in the salesroom. It was a regional wrap-up of obscure events in the Eastern Counties area, including a car crash in Norwich and a bank robbery in Peterborough. The final paragraph was of more interest to Paul. At two-thirty the Cambridgeshire Police had confirmed that they were questioning David Stone, Managing Director of William Stone & Son, regarding a fire at his factories the previous evening.

Within five minutes Paul was speaking to Superintendent Farrow. He explained that he knew all about David Stone and his company, and that the last thing the man would have done would be to destroy his own research facilities. While the police officer was absorbing this information, Paul strained his ears to make sure that James was not about. He could hear nothing next door, so he continued.

'It's most likely that an American company called GT had a hand in causing the fire because they want to destroy Stone's product,' he said quietly. Then he explained the link between polystyrene and chemical weapons, hoping that the policeman was taking all this down. He expected to have to explain the chemistry again, but he was wrong-footed by Superintendent Farrow's response.

'Well, all this is very interesting, but the product that was being made in the lab was just a simple kind of cardboard, as far as I can make out. There's nothing to do with hamburger boxes or the ozone layer, Mr, er, Roberts.'

Paul's eyebrows rose into arches of consternation. 'Are you sure?' he asked. There was a sigh at the other end.

'Straw-based cardboard is what Mr Stone calls it,' the officer replied, obviously bored. 'However, I'll bear in mind what you've said,' he responded politely before getting his caller off the line.

Paul drummed out the rhythm from 'Message in a Bottle' on the desk with his pen, then flicked through the *FT* to find the television listings for this evening, He was damned if he was working late for James Malpas any more.

Dick Zander had been planning on leaving Mount Laurel early on Friday afternoon, but Max Clark insisted on a powwow at close of play. The Chief Financial Officer wondered if his boss's timing was a deliberate ploy to stop him from getting to Oyster Bay before sunset. Now he'd be lucky to be back with his wife and children before they went to bed. But Zander knew better than to let his irritation show. Max didn't appreciate that some men wanted to be with their families at the weekend. Clark's wife could have made a living as a stand-in for Leonid Brezhnev's spouse, and the CEO of GT was never in a hurry to get home. It was hard for Zander to know which of them he pitied more.

He took a seat opposite his boss, and his eyes were drawn to the fax on the desk between them. Morton's merchant bank in London had sent it to Zander earlier on, and he had passed to Clark. It was about the fire at William Stone & Son, and it included a copy of Nick Durridge's message to Verdi investors.

'So, what's this about simple packaging material?' Clark began, as if they were already in the middle of a conversation. 'Is Stone bluffing, or what? I thought we'd rubbed the fucking stuff.'

Zander felt the muscles in his neck tighten as he contemplated the time it would take to convince Clark that everything was all right. 'I'm sure we've got nothing to worry about, Max,' he started brightly. 'This is just a pretence to keep his investors with him.'

Clark screwed up his face in irritation. 'So why are we still bidding for the company? It's a waste of our goddamned time, isn't it?'

Zander smiled benignly. 'If we withdraw, it'll cause suspicion. Stone really isn't costing us much, and we've got to stick with it or someone might start asking questions, Max.'

The CEO cleaned the dirt from under his nails with a letter-opener, and grimaced. 'OK. Just so long as we get hold of this fucking stuff.'

'We will,' Zander responded with a soothing nod of the head. Then he froze as he saw Clark's shoulders begin to shake with laughter.

'Terrible what these niggers get up to in downtown Mount Laurel, by the way, huh?' he remarked with a mischievous grin. 'All we have to do is stand back and let 'em kill each other. So how's our boy doing?'

'Bruce'll be OK. It wasn't too serious. Didn't hit anything essential, although he'll have quite a distinguished scar for the rest of his life.'

Clark was still concentrating on his fingernails, but the amusement had left his face. 'Well, let's make sure there isn't another fuck-up like that.'

'It's under control,' Zander assured him rather too emphatically. 'Our people are on to it right now, and the situation will be stabilised shortly.' He tried not to notice the contemptuous curl of Max Clark's lip.

When David Stone was finally allowed to go home it was nearly eleven o'clock. His solicitor gave him a lift back to Westhorpe Hall but refused the offer of a drink, much to his client's silent relief. David felt he deserved to be left alone, and when he opened the front door he went straight to the kitchen for the wine bottle. He wandered around the echoing rooms, sipping generous swigs from his glass, attempting to blot out the grimness of the police station.

His inquisitors clearly suspected him of setting the fire for the insurance, but they lacked the proof, and they had been unable to charge him. To hell with them. He gulped down a second glass of wine and went to bed, too nauseated to eat, too miserable and exhausted to stay awake.

Charlotte was virtually sleepwalking by the time she reached her flat on Gloucester Road that night. She had been awake all but five hours in the last seventy. Finding it impossible to snooze on the plane back to London she had dumbly watched the in-flight film, and wondered at the physical beauty of Harrison Ford.

But by the time she had disembarked, collected her suitcase and struggled into London, she was so tired and dazed that she was beyond fear. As she climbed out of the Tube station and walked towards her flat she didn't even bother to look behind her. Sod it all, she thought, heaving her case up the stairs to her flat. If they're going to get me, they're going to get me. This is not bravery, she reflected as she pushed the front door open: this is the acceptance of defeat. No job, no one to believe me, and nowhere to hide. Might as well surrender and be done with the whole bloody mess, she cursed through clenched teeth.

She flicked the light on and stood for a moment in the doorway, studying the curious normality of her sitting room. It was just as she had left it – a Marks & Spencer Chargecard bill on the coffee table, and her 'Eagles' Greatest Hits' CD, waiting to be put back in its case. Alfred the Rabbit was lying on the floor of her bedroom where she had left him, looking reproachfully at the ceiling. None of the lunacy of the past few days had made any impression on this more permanent part of her life, and she wondered for a moment if she had dreamed it all.

She ran a bath and poured in a generous slug of scented oil, thinking that no one in Britain deserved that little luxury as much as she did tonight. But before she peeled off her over-familiar clothes, she sat down by the answering machine to put its blinking light out of its misery. The first message was from Paul, and it made her cringe in embarrassment. The second was from Scott at ABC, and she jolted to attention as he told her that the Big Bagel in New York wanted to arrange a formal interview for the job of presenter of the new international business news programme.

'This is fan-fucking-tastic, Charlotte,' her friend raved. *'I told you they liked you. Anyway, can you do an interview on Monday? I know it's short notice, so just spend the weekend resting, and tell NNN that you have to go to New York 'cos you left your purse there by mistake, OK? I was talking to Ed Stanfield who's very excited about you moving to Manhattan for ABC, and he wants you to call him so you two can get together on Monday or whatever. What kind of spell did you cast on him, honey? And I have to pass on a message that was left with the switchboard at ABC. Can you ring this number: 215 229 2999 extension 543? No name or message. Anyway, call Bagel as soon as you can to confirm Monday. Sally sends her love and says why don't you come stay with us for a couple days till you get the result of the interview. Good idea, huh? Give us a call. Bye.'*

Charlotte's brow wrinkled as she stared at the machine. She reached out an arm as heavy as lead and stopped the tape. Back to New York? Well, that would certainly confuse whoever was following her. She rewound the tape and wrote down the relevant phone numbers. Then she yawned: the bath and bed awaited her – and right now, that was all she cared about.

Chapter Seventeen

'Hold still and it won't hurt,' he commanded. He grabbed her and pushed her down with one deft movement. Now she lay beneath him in the grass, immobilised as he hovered over her with the knife. She peered up at him fearfully, breathing in short terrified spurts. He saw her eyes widen as he eased himself down on top of her. Then he took hold of her front right-hand hoof and began to cut away the excess toenail.

'There, that wasn't so bad, was it?' David commented as the angora goat frisked away, her regular hoof-trimming session finished. She returned a moment later, and leapt up on him to get the carrot he had pulled out of his pocket.

He wandered back to the house recalling how his son had shrieked for joy when together they had clipped the goat's wool each spring. Billy would hang on to the horns while David gripped her between his knees and sheared her with the electric clipper. Then his son would roar with laughter as the startled goat emerged naked and bewildered.

Not a day goes by when I don't think of him, he reflected sadly. He struggled to keep the reminiscence pleasant, to hold a picture in his mind of a healthy-looking little boy playing with a goat. What was burnt into his memory, however, was the thin, world-weary waif with the brave smile, lying in bed patiently waiting to die, never complaining.

David looked into the refrigerator and studied the shelves of food, but he felt sick, a familiar reaction recently. His stomach was churning at the thought of Billy, and he poured a glass of wine: not a very wise move, since even though it was a Saturday, it wasn't even excusably near lunchtime. Then he wandered into the sunroom, sat in a wicker chair and gazed out at the garden. It was beautiful, of course, but he had no one to share it with, and felt selfish keeping it to himself. The place needed to have a happy family running around it.

What was the point of staying here? He would make Verdi a success, but that would hardly absorb one hundred per cent of his life. What would he do with the rest of it?

David had sent Charlotte a letter after their memorable transatlantic phone conversation, but she hadn't responded. Nor had she used the information about James Malpas that he had faxed her. Who could blame her for losing interest in him – dull, provincial, approaching middle age. Why would she want to get tangled up with a boring farmer whose idea of fun was spending two hours in a second-hand bookshop?

In what he now realised was a pathetic gesture, he had sent her a copy of *Pride and Prejudice* explaining in his letter that it was an example of lovers being driven apart by misunderstandings. Would she heave at his sentimentality and throw it in the bin with a shrug of contempt? It seemed that he had blown it. He sipped his wine, bewildered by his own incompetence.

Charlotte arrived at NNN at about noon on Saturday. She wanted to clear out her desk at a time when she wouldn't bump into Bob, or her former colleagues. Thankfully the newsroom was deserted so her humiliation was a private one.

In her pile of mail was David's fax and its impersonal covering note. She bit her lip and studied the photocopies of the *Sporting Life* and London phone book, then grinned widely. 'Gotcha Malpas, you scumbag,' she said to herself, but the smile evaporated as she realised that she couldn't get the story on air. She thought for a moment, then reached for an envelope. Why not use the time-honoured method – the anonymous leak? But who would run with this and make it stick? She pulled a face, and wrote Jonathan Slope's name and the address of BBC Television Centre on the envelope. Then she put it in the out-tray. Greater love hath no woman than that she should give a bloody good scoop to the wretched Slope.

She sifted through her other post, seeing nothing of interest until she found a thick manila envelope postmarked Ely. Out fell *Pride and Prejudice* and David's letter. She tried not to squeal as she read it, but her heart thumped its enthusiastic applause. This is all very well, she thought as she tucked it in her handbag, but I'm on my way to America for a job interview. And some unfriendly people have been trying to kill me recently. Neither of these developments made her an ideal girlfriend, and to be practical and unromantic about it, she had other things on her mind just at the moment.

So far there was no evidence that she had been followed from Mount Laurel, or that her pursuers were in England. After a good night's sleep her more rational mind wondered if the fire at David's lab could have been a simple coincidence. Perhaps by now her enemies had realised that no one was going to believe Charlotte's story, and that she was no threat. Maybe they would leave her alone, as long as she stayed quiet.

She was happy to oblige. She wasn't a daring modern heroine struggling against the forces of evil; she was frail and frightened Charlotte Carter who had stumbled on to something that was far too big for her. Perhaps Ed Stanfield was right: who cared about yet another chemical weapon? There were already several varieties on the market, and if GT didn't supply them to unspeakable dictators around the globe, someone else surely would.

Having struggled with that moral dilemma Charlotte logged into the NNN terminal for the last time and wrote a farewell note to Maurice, telling him about the showdown with Bob, in the unlikely event that he hadn't already heard, and explaining that she was going to New York City for the job interview with ABC on Monday morning, thanks to Scott Burns. Then she put lots of X's and O's, and logged out.

Her final act at NNN's expense was to call the mystery number that had been left at the ABC switchboard. 'Global Technologies. Good morning, how may I direct your call?' Charlotte raised her eyebrows and recited the extension number she had been given. In three seconds she was listening to the voice mail of someone called Don Redman. 'I'm returning your call on Saturday morning,' she said simply, 'and I'll call again on Monday, when I presume you'll be at work.'

What the hell was all that about, she asked herself as she walked down to the car? How much odder could life become? The possibility of a job at ABC; the reappearance of David Stone in her life; phone calls from GT employees she had never heard of – what next? A Serbian politician who told the truth?

As she pulled out of the NNN car park she remembered too late that she had meant to call Paul Roberts. She sat at the traffic lights, wondering what to do. If she phoned him or went to see him, he would pull the 'let's be friends again' act, and it would be cringe-making. It was hard to believe he had anything important to tell her, anyway. When the lights changed she pointed the VW in the direction of Gloucester Road.

Twenty minutes later she had her shopping bags of NNN mementos in hand, and was struggling up the stairs to her flat. She stopped on the landing to push her hair out of her eyes, and fumbled for the front door keys. Then she grasped her load again and started up the final flight of stairs.

Her front door was ajar. The lock had been forced, and the paint around it was chipped away. Charlotte put down her bags and took a step backwards, down the stairs. She strained her ears, but could hear nothing from within. Should she run away, or carry on? Run away where, she wondered, and threw herself at the door. It swung open to reveal a sitting room that looked like Sarajevo. Every drawer had been pulled out; each book had been taken from the shelves, torn in half and tossed on to the floor; the sofa had been sliced open; the television was lying on its face, the back prised open and wires spilling out.

Her bedroom was the same: clothes on the floor, the contents of drawers strewn about, a genuine medieval sacking. Then she saw him, and an iron claw gripped her heart: Alfred the Rabbit, decapitated and cut open. She picked up his pieces and held them gently in her hands, the tears burning in her eyes. Suddenly the frightened, bewildered Charlotte was gone.

'Right, you bastards,' she murmured. 'I'm going to get you for this.'

It was a muggy New York City evening and the sky was still light when Charlotte checked into the Barbizon Hotel the next day. She showered away the remnants of the long Polish Airlines flight, and tumbled into the big soft bed with a groan of pleasure. She was far too tired to even consider the possibility that someone was about to burst into the room and axe her to death. Just like an escaped convict, she had been on the run and deprived of sleep for so long that she had lost the meaning of the freedom that she had cherished so much.

Charlotte had flown from London to Warsaw on Saturday afternoon, and then from Warsaw to New York on a flight that left the Polish capital on Sunday morning. No one would expect her to come back to the USA so soon, or to get there via Warsaw. Even if a GT agent of death had seen her check in at a British Airways 'all destinations' desk at Heathrow, he wouldn't know where she was headed. If his friends had been waiting for her to get off a BA flight in New York or Washington they would have been disappointed. No one would be checking LOT arrivals the following day.

The pity of it was that there had been so little time to enjoy Warsaw's carefully restored beauty, although the memory of the lemon vodka, smoked salmon and wild boar filet lived on. Also, the best steak tartare she had ever consumed in her life, in Warsaw airport cafeteria, where she had eaten breakfast many hours ago. Fee Fi Fo Fum: a new personal first in gross breakfasts for C. Carter.

Before she had left London she had bought 2000 dollars on a credit card, allowing her to use cash and false names in hotels. Her as-yet uncancelled company credit card had come in handy when paying for the air tickets to Warsaw and New York. To hell with NNN. She snuggled into the pillows, concentrated on her favourite David fantasy, and plummeted into a deep sleep.

* * *

When David Stone arrived at his desk on Monday morning, he found among the usual nonsense from soliciting management consultants an unopened letter postmarked *Hounslow* with *Personal* written on it. He ripped it open and flipped to the bottom of the last page where he found Charlotte's signature. He sat forward, tense and alert, and began to read:

Dear David, I'm writing this on the Tube on the way to Heathrow. Thank you for your letter which made me very happy, and the Jane Austen which I will try to read on the plane. Where to begin with this explanation? First of all I'm writing to you because I have to put down all that I know in case something happens to me.

Second, I have to warn you to be careful, to watch out. I've already told you that GT is after your polystyrene-buster product because a world ban on styrene monomers would stop them making a chemical weapon called Dermitron, which GT says is just a fertiliser. I don't know if you really believed me at the time, but I hope you do now. I interviewed a former GT researcher who had worked on Dermitron but he died the following day. The circumstances were peculiar, and I refuse to believe it was suicide. Then my tapes of the interview disappeared. I went to see one of his colleagues, and I was ambushed in a parking lot near the GT headquarters, and one, possibly three people, ended up dead. I escaped and returned to England on Friday night. Also a Senator who publicly pointed the finger at GT has suddenly been charged with fraud, so he no longer appears credible. This morning I found that my flat had been trashed by an intruder. I leave you to draw your own conclusions about the fire at your lab.

I have no option but to go to New York now because I've been contacted by someone at GT, and I must get a lead if I'm going to get to the bottom of this. I've lost my job at NNN, and I'm sure no other news organisation will carry my story because

I have no proof. What I don't fully understand is what's so important about Dermitron. If I can sort this out then I'll come back home, but I don't really know what's going to happen. Hopefully, one day we'll see each other again. Love, Charlotte.

David laid the sheets of paper on his desk and sat back in his chair. The colour had drained from his face, and he felt confused, as if he had stumbled into someone else's nightmare. The postmark said 6 p.m. on Saturday evening, so she must have been in the States for over twenty-four hours, and maybe the worst had already happened. He pushed that dreadful scenario from his mind, and tried to work out what he could do to help her. Then he lifted the phone, dialled NNN, and asked to speak to anyone who worked with Charlotte.

'If you think I'm interested in talking to you, then you're mad,' an old man snarled when David explained who he was. 'As a matter of fact I do know where she is and what she's doing there, but I'm not going to tell you. I've heard all about your shenanigans. Now leave her alone, and go to hell,' Maurice concluded concisely, and slammed down the phone.

David frowned at the receiver for a moment, then called his secretary in from her office next door. 'Sheila, I've got myself in a bit of a mess,' he began when she had taken a seat opposite him. She glanced up from her notepad and feigned great surprise. 'This is serious. I need your help.' He paused and chewed his lower lip, debating how much to tell her. 'I've got to get to America today, to find a woman.'

'Any woman in particular? Someone you saw on *Oprah*, or are you going to take pot luck?'

David smiled weakly. 'Charlotte Carter, the reporter at NNN,' he said, feeling himself blush. 'I won't burden you with the details, which are bizarre as you'd expect, but she's in trouble. All I know is she's gone to New York, and I've got to find her as soon as possible.'

'I knew it was her,' said Sheila as she tapped her pen on her notepad. She sounded as if she had just solved a crossword clue. 'I had a feeling it was Charlotte all along.' Then, seeing David's expression, she giggled. 'Cradle-snatching, aren't you? Right,' she said, getting a grip on herself, 'we need a plan of action.' She glanced at her watch and frowned. 'You know the police won't be too pleased if you disappear. Anyway, you go back to the Hall for your passport, then start out for London immediately. While you're on your way to Heathrow I'll book you a seat on the flight you're most likely to catch. And I'll talk to the people at NNN. They're bound to know where she is and what she's doing. Then if you call me when you arrive at the airport I'll be able to pass on what I've learned, and tell you which plane you're getting.'

'Brilliant, but there's one flaw,' David said with a shake of the head. 'She's been fired from NNN, and on the strength of the conversation I've just had with one of her former colleagues, I didn't get the impression they'd be very co-operative.'

'Nonsense!' Sheila exclaimed. 'I know – you turn up there and sweettalk someone sympathetic. You can be quite convincing when you try.'

David clicked his tongue and listened to her sniggering. Then she groaned abruptly. 'What's wrong?' he asked.

'You aren't going to have much time to find her, are you?' she said seriously. Then seeing his confusion she added, 'Whatever you do, you've got to be back in London tomorrow morning at eleven. Remember? Your love-life is one thing, David, but our collective future matters too.' She saw him struggle to follow her line of thought. 'Verdi – the press launch!'

'Oh my God,' he wailed as he punched his knee in frustration. 'This is impossible.'

'No, it isn't. You'll work out a way to find her,' Sheila said positively, with a toss of her head. 'Stop hitting yourself like some penitent Opus Dei member, and start thinking.'

From the window of her hotel room Charlotte had a perfect view of the Manhattan skyline. As she lay in bed she had only to raise her eyes to see the gargoyles of the Chrysler Building glinting in the first rays of the sun. The busy noises of a new day drifted up from

Lexington Avenue, fifteen floors below. Under different circumstances it would have made her feel happy to be back in New York.

Her bewildered internal time clock had woken her at four-thirty, and although she knew she needed more rest, her attempts to snooze were futile. Charlotte had two speeds only: completely asleep, or full throttle. Once her eyes were open in the morning her antennae would emerge and scan about to find out what was going on. Then her brain would click on and wonder what was on the day's agenda, and what was for breakfast. There was no going back to sleep, even when she was still tired.

So it had been this morning at four-thirty: she sat up in bed with a pad of paper on her knee, and started to map out her day. It was a more complicated exercise than usual because she was attempting to live two parallel lives; she was the journalist who was running and hiding and digging into the truth about some poxy nerve gas; and she was also the out-of-work reporter who needed to convince the massively important people at ABC to employ her.

The problem with organising her time was that she had no idea how things would turn out in her new nomadic-style life. Little distractions kept cropping up: disappearing video tape, murdered interviewees and wrecked apartments. The only way to dispel such negative thoughts was to ring room service and order a stack of pancakes with maple syrup. Sure enough, they revived her spirits, although she got rather sticky in the process.

Then she worked her way through the morning papers so she could be up to speed on anything the ABC people asked her about. When she had demolished the *Wall Street Journal* and the *New York Times* she surrendered to Jane Austen. She had started the book on the plane, expecting to find it so boring and difficult that she would abandon it, along with the sick bag in the magazine flap in front of her. Much to her surprise this intimidating intellectual masterpiece turned out to be a romance about five silly sisters and their young men. So, David read slushy stories about women in long dresses . . . It was a revelation.

She left Georgian England for a moment and stood by the

window, lost in thought. Down on Lexington Avenue the occasional limousine whooshed past, taking Power People to Power Breakfasts across the city. There weren't many pedestrians at this hour though, just a few dog-walkers and joggers. The glow from a delicatessen window shone in square-shaped patches of light out on to the sidewalk like an Edward Hopper painting, but otherwise the shops were closed and securely locked with metal grilles.

What was David doing now, she wondered. Had he got her letter yet? Had he read it and thought she was mad? Who would want to be dragged into this craziness? The tears sprang to her eyes, and she blinked fiercely to get rid of them. She sat down on the bed and tried to stop herself blubbing. Then she thought of the wretched God Squad man who had paid for talking about Dermitron. Would he have died if she hadn't poked her journalistic nose into other people's business? Was it enough to justify everything in the search for truth? Or was she just another reporter who cared more about boosting her reputation than exposing evil or corruption?

She dried her eyes and stared out of the window, wondering who could be so determined that they could mobilise a web of arsonists and murderers to protect a nerve gas that was hardly novel or special. Was it Global Technologies alone? Or had she upset a nest of Third World Dermitron customers – beacons of democracy, freedom and human rights – the paragons of decency that Ed Stanfield had told her about, poised to spray their neighbours with nerve gas. Not to mention dismembering people's toy rabbits, she thought mournfully. At that moment the defeated, miserable little girl was gone, and a new wave of anger kick-started Charlotte's resolve once more.

David reached the NNN studios at noon, and dumped the Volvo as close to the entrance as possible. The telephone kiosk on the road that led up to Paddington Station smelled like a *pissoir*, and its walls were a mosaic of sticky labels advertising unlikely services, but David was in too great a hurry for aesthetic objections.

'Sheila, please send a fax to Dick Zander at GT immediately,' he babbled. 'OK, as follows: "*I'm pleased to report progress in finalising arrangements. Perhaps a delegation of your engineers and management would like to visit our plant in Ely to see our current projects, meet their opposite numbers here, and gain a better understanding of our company. For your interest I enclose a press release that will be sent out on Tuesday a.m. regarding my new company that will be making a straw-based packaging material that will provide a cheap and ecologically sound equivalent to cardboard. Our original plans to find a polystyrene substitute failed. Your research personnel are welcome to visit us. Look forward to hearing from you. Blah, blah, blah, David Stone.*" That's it, Sheila. Got to run. I'll call from the airport.'

As he jogged down the street to the NNN entrance he wondered if he was entirely wise to confront Zander with the ex-polystyrene buster, since it was equal to telling the man he knew GT was up to no good. It was a risk, but if there was a chance that he could persuade Zander that Verdi was no threat to his Dermitron, then he might call his dogs off Charlotte. The other possibility was that GT wanted her silenced because of what she knew, regardless of the truth. Maybe they had already done the job.

'Could you please call the old man in the newsroom and ask him to come down to see me. My name is David Stone,' he puffed breathlessly when he arrived at the NNN reception. A minute later he heard a familiar malevolent voice behind him.

'Let me guess why you're here,' A thin, wiry man with a lined face stood beside him. 'I'll see this gentleman out,' he said to the receptionist who glanced at them nervously.

'Don't give up, do you?' Maurice remarked tartly. He grasped David firmly by the elbow and steered him to the door, keeping up his monologue as he guided him out. David deserved castration with a rusty tin can. Charlotte had the sense to steer clear of him, so why didn't he leave her alone? The lecture continued until they were standing in the NNN car park. It had begun to rain quite heavily and they were soon wet, but the old man had clearly been saving up this speech.

'I need your help,' David interrupted when Maurice paused for breath. 'I'm going to Heathrow now to get a plane to New York to find Charlotte.' As David spoke he saw the surprise register on his audience's face. 'She's in terrible trouble.'

Maurice grunted and took a step away from him. 'You're the terrible trouble in her life. Find someone else for your help.'

David watched him walking back to the front door of the studio. He knew that time was running out, and his only hope of finding Charlotte was disappearing before him. The last feeble strings of self-control snapped. He caught up with the old man and swung him around more violently than he had intended.

'Read this. *Now!*' he demanded, and released the old man's shoulder.

Maurice looked shaken but he took the letter and stood in the shelter of the NNN entrance to keep the rain off the pages. After a minute he glanced up at David with a look of disbelief. The pale flesh on his lined face hung down in a mournful exhausted frown, and David saw that he was struggling to keep his composure. Then he motioned David to follow him, and they went up to the newsroom.

'There's a job interview at ABC this morning,' Maurice said as he wrote out what he knew on a piece of paper. 'She's got a friend who works for ABC in Washington, Scott Burns. He might know what she's doing. That's his number there. Let's call him now,' he added after a doubtful look at his watch. David hovered impatiently by his desk as he dialled.

'They're expecting him in soon,' Maurice reported after his brief conversation with the ABC switchboard operator. 'Call him before you get your plane,' he instructed. Then he sat back and rubbed his grey-whiskered chin. 'Look, have you told the police about this?'

'They already think I set fire to my lab,' David said with exasperation, and a pointed glance at his watch. Then he recalled the scepticism of the Ely police. 'Anyway I think she's into something far too complicated for them to understand.'

Maurice nodded wisely. 'Yeah? Well just be glad you're not Irish. Anyway, the police are too busy hassling the middle classes for driving at seventy-five miles an hour on motorways.' He looked up at the clock on the office wall. 'You'd better get going, hadn't you?'

Chapter Eighteen

The rumour started in the Press Office that morning and had percolated through Brodie McClean to Charles Ravenscroft's ears by lunchtime. Apparently a BBC reporter had asked the bank for a comment on an insider-dealing story that involved the Corporate Finance Department.

As Charles waited for the glass lift he gazed out at the atrium and fantasised about Fraud Squad officers leading James Malpas away in handcuffs. Secretaries would line the balconies and hurl abuse down at the hated head of Corporate Finance as he was marched out past the fountain by the Boys in Blue. Charles toyed with this image as he was hoisted to the top floor, and walked along the plushly-carpeted corridor to the Chairman's office. It was Charles's last remaining hope before tomorrow's board meeting. He clenched his teeth and knocked on Sir Anthony Brook's door.

'You're overreacting, you know,' his Chairman said with a pained expression on his face. In the last five minutes Charles had outlined his concerns calmly and without rancour, but the older man looked tired of the discussion before it had begun. 'I shall never understand your vendetta against James. He's the most capable Corporate Financier in the Square Mile.' Brook took a sip of his tea. 'And he's pulled off an extraordinary coup in getting those Americans to bid for Martindale. A stroke of genius, Charles. It might not be your style or indeed mine, but it was an act of brilliance.'

Charles shifted uneasily in his chair and wondered how he could shake the Grandee out of his complacency. The bank was about to be handed over to a cut-throat bandit, all because Brook was too dotty and naïve to smell corruption when it was right beneath his nose. But did Charles have a shred of evidence to offer the old man? No, just rumours that the BBC was about to embarrass the bank.

'I've already spoken to James about this,' the Chairman continued. 'In fact, he came to see me first thing this morning. It seems the BBC hasn't got more than a whiff of gossip. Just bored journalists looking for a story.'

'And you're going to accept that?' Charles asked with lips as tight and white as a mountain-climber's. Brook looked vacant. 'Why are the BBC bothering to sniff around the bank if they're not on to something?'

'What on earth are you saying?' asked Brook, screwing up his eyes intimidatingly.

Charles ignored the glare and pressed on. 'There were rumours at the time of the bid, you know. People within the bank reckoned James had accumulated far too much Stone and Martindale stock with no effort at all.'

'Oh, for goodness' sake, Charles!' Sir Anthony exclaimed. 'What are you getting at, man?'

'I'm saying that James Malpas has been salting away shares in his wretched overseas accounts, then pulling them out of the hat when he needs them. It's called insider trading.'

'Charles, you are warped by jealousy,' Brook said quietly as he set aside his sherry glass. For a moment he looked down his nose in distaste. 'I don't relish saying this, but I can't imagine what's happened to you in the past few weeks. Perhaps you can't take the pace.' The older man studied the correspondence on his desk. 'Now, if you don't mind, I've got some work to get on with.'

When he had been dismissed, Charles Ravenscroft went back to his office, burning with indignation. He was almost choking with rage, and had to drink two glasses of mineral water before he could even breathe properly. Then he sat down and ran his hands through his hair to rearrange the blond mane. When his heart had stopped pounding he went back out to the corridor and called the lift. This time he went down to the basement, to see his colleague in charge of the Press Office.

'Sorry to bother you,' he said quietly when he poked his head into the man's office, 'but have you got the name of the BBC chap who rang this morning?'

Just after 8 a.m. Charlotte called her mystery man at GT. 'Something tells me I shouldn't be talking to you,' she said by way of introduction, 'but curiosity is getting the better of me.'

'I tried to warn you about Carretta,' he said defensively. 'I rang all the car rental companies to leave a message for you not to come that night. But no one had any record of your reservation. I couldn't think of any other way to contact you. I didn't know who you were flying with, so I couldn't stop you at the airport.'

'I came on the train,' Charlotte said bluntly, and in a tone that let the man know she didn't believe a word he was saying.

'Oh,' he said, surprised. 'I was trying the car rental places at the airport. You see, I realised what Carretta was doing – meeting you, I mean. I heard him discussing it with people here. And I did try to warn you.' He sounded anxious – *too* anxious, Charlotte thought.

'So that wasn't you I had the pleasure of seeing at Mount Laurel's equivalent of The Polo Lounge?' she asked as she lay back on the hotel bed and shut her eyes.

'I overheard Carretta on the phone to you, and I knew why you were talking to him, because I knew the guy you interviewed in Washington. I used to work with him, too,' he added. 'He wasn't the first member of my team to die, incidentally.'

'Well, you've certainly grabbed my attention, but perhaps I should begin by asking you who else is listening. Dick Zander, perhaps?' Charlotte asked with a malicious laugh. 'So who are you, and what do you want? Why did you call?' she continued impatiently.

'I'm Don Redman. I work here on the project you're interested in. I work with Carretta, and I'm *not* trying to set you up. You've got to believe me,' he stressed. 'Look, you're on to something.'

'You don't say? Has Dick Zander promised you a bonus if you snare me?'

She heard him sigh. 'OK, I understand how you must feel. I don't know what happened that night because no one here discusses things openly, not since Raul Gutierez died a few weeks ago. We've been told that Carretta's had an accident and he's still in hospital.' He hesitated. 'These people have a lot to protect, and they're determined this project'll go ahead.' He paused again. 'Two of my friends are dead, so maybe it's time someone caused a stink. That's why I called you. Can you come here? Where are you now?'

Charlotte laughed. 'Do you really believe I'm going to tell you where I am, or even more incredible, that I'm coming within a hundred miles of Mount Laurel?'

'There are things about this project you should know. I can't give you an interview, but I can tell you the truth. No one in GT can go on the record. But if you know the facts—'

'Well, if you're so keen to tell me then you can do the running around. Meet me this afternoon, in New York City, or we don't meet at all. And it's got to be somewhere crowded and public so your chums can't turn up with their violin cases.'

'I can't just walk out of here,' he countered in a panicky whisper.

'Think of an excuse – you know, like bad period cramps or PMT. That usually works,' she shot back, and rolled over on to her side so she could write on her pad of paper.

'You're making this really difficult for me,' he whimpered.

'Yes, I'm nasty like that, Mr Redman,' she said pleasantly. 'How about we meet at three o'clock, at Rockefeller Plaza, on one of those benches in front of the RCA Building, at the edge of the sunken bit? You know, where they have the ice rink in winter. I'll be the one with the bullet-proof vest and the blue UN helmet.'

'I know what you look like,' he said in a pained voice. 'I saw you on TV when the bid for the British company was announced. Christ knows how I'm going to get there, but you have to promise me you won't be wired. Don't tape-record me with a hidden mike.'

'I promise I won't be wired,' Charlotte replied and made a note on her pad of paper. 'The trains from Philadelphia are regular and fast, incidentally. I'll look forward to meeting you, but perhaps you can let me know what *you* look like.'

'I'm quite tall, and my wife says I'm skinny. I have sort of light-brown hair.'

And you'll be sporting a bull's-eye target, thought Charlotte as she put down the phone. She lay back again and looked vacantly at the Chrysler Building glinting like a sacred monument to an Art Deco god. This was surely one of the most stupid things she had ever done. She was walking into a trap so obvious that it had flashing neon lights. Why did she believe Don Redman was sincere? Because he sounded like a nerd? No, she realised: it was because she needed someone to explain why there was such a fuss about Dermitron. Someone who could point her at concrete proof – at some way to make her story believable. Otherwise the running would *never* end . . .

That was too horrible to contemplate so she called Ed Stanfield at his Doughty McMurchy office on Wall Street. She had promised she would ring, and she felt like speaking to a real person for a change. He sounded very pleased to hear from her.

'Dinner tonight?' he asked immediately. 'Let me introduce you to the greatest margarita in Manhattan. Or would you prefer something more subtle, like pretentious New American cooking?'

'I'm not sure I can make dinner, Ed, much as I'd love to. I'm going to Washington later to stay with Scott and Sally.'

'A drink before you go?' he countered. 'When's your interview at ABC? Good luck, by the way. You'll slay 'em, I know it. When is it?'

'This morning. But I have something important on this afternoon, and I'm not sure I'll be able to make it for a drink.'

'What is so important that you can't see me for a drink?' he said, as if his pride had been wounded. 'This is a blow, Charlotte. I thought you were starting a new life in America, and I was going to be part of it.'

She wasn't sure if he was serious, or just fooling around. Either way it was enjoyable to be pursued by an admirer, as opposed to an assassin, for a change. Not that she would have dreamed of returning his lust: David was still firmly wedged in her libido and her heart.

Ed made her promise that she would call him if she could get away from her second appointment in time. She hung up and realised that she had felt almost normal for five minutes. Then it was back to her preparations: she flicked through the *Yellow Pages* and called the first high-tech private investigation firm she came across to confirm that they had the equipment she needed.

Five minutes later she caught a cab outside the hotel, and headed for the less salubrious lower west side of the island. Up a rickety flight of stairs to a dusty, badly-lit corridor she found the company she was searching for. Once inside, the comparisons with a Philip Marlowe story ceased and she was confronted by a spartan white office, computer screens and modern Swedish furniture.

An immaculate young man with blow-dried blond hair, memorable aftershave and a precise manner of speaking talked her through the options available for remote high-quality surveillance and monitoring. Charlotte chose the most accurate and expensive equipment available. For her money she got the use of a cameraman and his recorder, and a directional microphone that could record outdoor conversations from a distance of seventy-five feet.

The young man agreed that Rockefeller Plaza would provide ample opportunities to record a good quality, even broadcastable conversation without being observed in the process. He showed her how to stake out the best place to sit once she got there, and how to position herself in line of view for the cameraman. 'Just keep your subject's attention, if you can, so he doesn't scan the crowd. We'll do our best to be inconspicuous,' he said comfortingly.

She defied the local aversion to walking by wandering across Manhattan back to the Barbizon Hotel. On the way she bought a pack of large strong envelopes, and some stamps, then indulged in a bit of window-shopping on Fifth Avenue to divert her attention from GT. The Gap might have been more her financial level, but she couldn't resist a bit of glitz and sleaze, and she hardly expected to be gunned down in Gucci on a Monday morning. No one knew where she was, so she could enjoy the euphoria of being an anonymous person in a vast city.

Back at the hotel she spent ten minutes on her make-up, hoping to disguise the jet-lag puffiness around her eyes. Then she changed into her best natural silk skirt-suit and cream-coloured silk blouse, and purged her mind of everything but global business facts and figures. In her handbag she put her passport, envelopes, stamps, and the video tape of her interview with the Columbia nerd – all that remained of her previous attempt at a package on GT. Recent experience had taught her to be ready to run at all times, so she carried the essentials around with her. Then she left her suitcase at the front desk and checked out. She could postpone any decisions on the rest of the day until after she had seen the Big Bagel at ABC, and her visitor from Mount Laurel.

Who knew what other delights lay ahead in the increasingly interesting life of Charlotte Carter, she thought as she hailed a cab on Fourth Avenue.

Chapter Nineteen

It was ten to two when David reached Heathrow and skidded around the short-term car park, his heart thumping like the rotor blade of a helicopter. He had driven across London as if he was auditioning for a *Mad Max* film, ever conscious of the minutes slipping away until the plane departed without him. The car shuddered to a halt, and with passport, wallet and a Trollope in hand, he ran towards Terminal Four, praying he had switched off the radio and locked the door.

At the check-in area he had to lean on the desk, panting and coughing before he had enough breath to speak. The British Airways operative's nervous eyes never left him as he perspired and puffed in front of her. Finally he managed to gasp out his name, and the woman's frozen glare melted a degree or two.

'Your secretary warned us,' she said as she handed him his ticket and boarding card for the 2.15 to Kennedy. 'You've no bags, is that right?' she asked suspiciously, as if remarking on his leprosy. He shook his head and looked about for a telephone. 'You must go directly to the gate,' the woman said sternly. 'Right now.'

The list of instructions at the international credit-card phone box ran right down the side of the kiosk, but David was too impatient to read the thirteen-point guide so he simply rammed his card in and dialled Scott Burns's number. As he waited for an ABC switchboard operator to locate the political reporter, he glanced up at the display board and saw that his flight was closing. He skipped about like a boxer until the mellow North American voice on the other end told him Scott was at a White House press briefing. In due course he spoke to a reporter who consulted Scott's desk diary. 'It says here *Charlotte p.m.* Is that it?'

Once he reached the departure lounge he had a free run to the gate, and he pounded along the corridors clutching his book, ticket, money and passport to his chest like a baby. As he tore past clutches of fellow travellers he imagined arriving at the door of the airplane just as it was locked in his face, and could see himself banging on it, and having a heart attack and dying.

It was only later, when David caught sight of himself in the plane's lavatory mirror, that he appreciated why the ground staff had stood way back to let him through on to the plane. His eyes were bulging out of a grey face, like vulpine orbs on stalks. His hair had not recovered from its earlier soaking, and all he lacked was a thin river of blood dribbling down his chin from each incisor.

Once safely on board, David had sunk into his seat, closed his eyes and panted gratefully for five minutes. He was so happy that he nearly wept, but the passengers on either side of him were already uneasy enough about his dramatic last-minute arrival, so instead he opened *A Small House at Allington* and anticipated the drinks trolley.

At two o'clock Charlotte was politely declining the offer of yet another dry martini and saying she really ought to let everybody get back to the newsroom. 'To hell with that,' said the Big Bagel with feeling, and raised her perfectly-manicured hand to summon the waiter for another round. The interviewing panel from the commanding heights of ABC had adjourned to the restaurant at twelve-fifteen, having decided that it was a nicer place to discuss international oil prices.

Since then Charlotte had been listening to them gossip across the white linen and bone china about salary rises, and the contemptible figures on offer in other TV news organisations. They included Charlotte in every conversation, as if they were passing on information essential for her survival at ABC. She asked pertinent questions, told a few jokes about print journalists which went down well, and drank her dry martinis. It was only when Bagel finally motioned for the bill that she mentioned the job. 'When can you begin?' she asked simply.

At a quarter past two they returned to the ABC offices in Forty-Second Street to 'sort out a few details'. As they waited for the elevator Charlotte noticed a young man in sunglasses watching her. He was slouched in one corner of the reception hall, and looked as if he were demonstrating bad posture on an orthopaedic poster. To make matters worse, he was chewing gum. This vision of youthful insolence made no attempt to hide his interest in Charlotte, even when she glared back at him.

She followed her new associates into the elevator and back to Bagel's office, wondering if her jet-lagged and over-active imagination was getting the better of her. By a quarter to three she had said her last chummy goodbyes to her future employer, and was wandering around the bowels of the building, looking for a rear exit so that she could avoid the international nerve-gas salesmen.

Eventually she found a delivery bay with a ramp that led up on to Forty-First Street, and as she emerged at street level she stayed close to the building and looked around, feeling astonishingly foolish. There was no unprepossessing creature in shades lurking with intent, but Charlotte wasn't about to start taking risks. She craned her neck over the crowds of pedestrians and spotted a cab slowly lumbering along, hunting for a fare. She hovered by the building, like a runner poised on the starting blocks, until it was almost parallel to her. Then she lunged forward and threw herself in the back seat.

In between urging the driver to please hurry up, and scanning the streets of Manhattan through the back window, Charlotte had time to pull two envelopes out of her handbag and address them. Then she stuck on the stamps she had bought earlier and returned the envelopes to her bag. Her heart was pounding by the time she clambered out at Rockefeller Plaza and began her search for the GT mystery man. She hadn't given Don Redman a second thought since they had spoken this morning: it was better not to contemplate an appointment with Death if you knew about it in advance, she reasoned as she crossed the Plaza to the front of the RCA Building.

Most of the people on the benches around the sunken plaza were woman with small children eating ice creams, or tourists consulting maps. The lunch crowd had long since returned to their offices. Charlotte glanced about for a tall thin man with light-brown hair, but found no one matching Redman's description. It was two minutes past three, and there was no sign of any other GT heavies. She chose a bench that was positioned as the private eye agency had instructed, and sat down.

Five minutes later she was still shivering with nerves, but at least she had found her cameraman. He was standing on the opposite side of Rockefeller Plaza, well-obscured by pedestrians. Charlotte ducked her head in case Redman was watching her. By a quarter past three she was convinced he had chickened out, or had been stopped before he could get beyond the GT compound. She studied what was left of her appalling fingernails, and asked herself penetrating questions about her sanity.

'Charlotte?' She jerked her head around and found a gangling stick insect of a man, about her own age, standing beside her. She smiled a tense, polite little smile, and gestured for him to sit down. He folded himself into an uncomfortable bent-up shape on the bench and crossed his long, denim-clad legs as if adopting a protective position against imminent attack.

'Thank you for coming,' she began. 'I'm sorry I gave you a rough time on the phone, but my previous encounter with GT personnel wasn't particularly fun.' She smiled again at his sharp, worried face, hoping to assure him that she wasn't terrified too. 'Any problem getting away?' she asked for something to say.

'I told them I was going to check something in the library in Philadelphia. I do that often enough for it to be credible,' he explained, but he looked less than convinced by his own excuse.

'OK, well, we probably ought to get to the point,' said Charlotte with another frenzied smile.

Redman nodded half-heartedly. 'I've been working on Dermitron for a year now,' he told her. 'There was a team of seven to start with. Now we've had one accidental death, one suicide, and Bruce is in hospital, as you know.' He stopped abruptly and looked up at Charlotte. 'Are you wired?' he asked.

She opened her handbag and let him examine the contents, then she leaned back and began to undo the buttons at the part of her blouse that tucked into her skirt. Once she had shown him a couple of inches of suntanned belly he looked away, apparently convinced that she was not taping him.

'Had to check,' he muttered apologetically.

'So, what's special about Dermitron?' Charlotte asked when she had modestly rearranged her clothing. 'Why are so many people tetchy about it? I don't understand: lots of countries are making chemical weapons.'

'It's not just a chemical weapon. It started out as a fertiliser,' he said after taking a deep breath, 'and the reason GT is so protective of it is because of the President's initiative.'

Charlotte made 'slow down' motions with her hands. 'I've no idea what you're talking about.'

'Well, the President has announced this new war on drugs,' he began. 'The Administration is going to sponsor the destruction of drug plantations in Central and South America. They're going to tear up the coca, and plant food crops in their place. The farmers won't have to do a thing, and the US Government will even provide the seeds. So you'll have armies of local people who'd otherwise be unemployed, going through the countryside, destroying drugs and giving the farmers a new livelihood. The idea is to stop the flood of drugs into the States. You're from England so you probably don't appreciate what a big problem drugs are here.'

Charlotte smiled patiently, wondering what the hell this gawky young man was talking about. Had she found herself another obsessed lunatic like the God Squad fellow? 'So?' she prompted him politely.

'So Dermitron is a fertiliser with a difference. You do aerial spraying on your crop of coca, and not only does it add phosphate to the ground and make the plants grow like hell, but if you touch it or get too close, the Dermitron will act like nerve gas: it'll burn your eyes and throat and skin, and of course your nerves too. Two days after it's been released it can still make your eyes water so much you can't see properly for hours. Takes about a week to lose its potency.' Redman paused as he watched the colour drain from Charlotte's cheeks. She sat forward, watching his lips move as if he was speaking in Munchkin.

'Damages your brain anyway, but not the plants,' he continued. 'After three days it burns your skin to the touch. You aerial spray your crops when you know the anti-drug brigade are on their way. They won't come back in a hurry, and they won't get much further than ripping up one or two plants. They haven't got mechanised reaping in these countries so it's all done by hand.'

Charlotte fiddled nervously with the fastening of her earring as she listened. 'So there are no military implications, then?' she croaked through a dry throat.

'The point about Dermitron is it can be used as a straight nerve gas that won't kill plants. Remember what Agent Orange and those low-tech sprays did in Vietnam? This can also be used for crowd control in hostile civil unrest situations. Works very fast, and depending on how you dilute it you can vary the damage you do: instant death or prolonged burning of the skin and brain damage,' Redman explained. 'Doesn't ruin the land around it either, just the people and animals.'

'And what happens to the drug crops themselves? Will they be poisoned by Dermitron?' she asked, her forehead wrinkling in disbelief.

'No. It took us so long to develop this because it fertilises coca. It's very sophisticated. That's why GT's into it – you can charge a huge amount of money for a small quantity. The idea is that the rain'll eventually wash it off before it's harvested. The farmers'll be OK if they wear protective gear in the meantime.'

'And when it's processed?' she asked with a wince.

'A bit sticks to the leaves, and in a small number of cases it could be dangerous to the consumer. Small risk, however. Kill maybe one per cent of users.'

'Oh, only one per cent!' Charlotte snorted sarcastically. 'Well then, that's all right! By the way, when we say farmers, we're talking about the drug barons doing the spraying, yes?' She wasn't sure she believed a word of it: life was slipping into surreal mode once more.

Redman nodded and recrossed his legs carefully. 'They're the customers for Dermitron,' he said with a nervous scratch at an earlobe. 'They won't have to use too much of this stuff before word gets around that taking money from the Americans to destroy drug crops is a dumb idea. These are uncomplicated peasant societies we're talking about. You won't be able to drag the locals back on to that land for all the cash in the world.' Charlotte looked incredulous. 'Remember when Pablo Escobar was killed?' he continued rhetorically. 'The ordinary Columbians mourned him because he'd spent so much money financing urban renewal projects. Drug barons aren't demons there; they provide work. That's why they'd be reluctant to go around shooting the peasants who do the harvesting. Too unsubtle. This stuff'll be seen as a curse from God.'

'But this is like a declaration of war on the United States,' Charlotte exclaimed with a bewildered shrug. 'It *can't* succeed.'

Redman was unmoved. 'There's a hell of a lot of money in it for GT. And there're enough people here and in the drug-producing countries who want to keep up the flow of narcotics – politicians, the armed services, and the CIA of course. And as far as they're concerned, the farmers are just using a new agricultural chemical. It's an enormous business we're talking about.'

'Wait, this is crazy,' she said in exasperation. 'Doesn't the Pentagon know what GT's up to? And why is the CIA into it?'

'Why should the Pentagon be interested in agricultural chemicals?' Redman responded with an edgy, hollow laugh. 'GT stopped making nerve gas five or six years ago. And as for the CIA, in 1990 their operatives were caught bringing a ton of cocaine into the US from Venezuela "by mistake".' He clicked his tongue and sighed. 'That's just one occasion when they were found out. Imagine what goes on most of the time.'

'What if the President sends in American troops or the Drug Enforcement Agency? American men will die if they try to destroy the crops that've been sprayed.' But she stopped as she saw Redman shake his head quickly.

'The point about the President's war against drugs is that he's using the Third World aid budget to pay local people to do the work. That's why the whole programme is acceptable to the countries concerned: they get something out of it, and the US isn't seen as an imperialist power bossing everyone else around.'

Charlotte sat back on the bench and studied Redman's earnest expression. Perhaps GT had given up trying to silence her, and were going to get her to run with a tale that discredited her. Yet Redman didn't look like the other GT stooges, and he was as nervous as hell. If he was genuine then he was risking quite a lot to tell her this.

'It seems very unlikely to me,' she said bluntly. Her new acquaintance pursed his lips and shrugged.

'Not when you think of the cranky, ridiculous things GT's done in the past,' he countered. 'Exploding cigars to kill Castro, mind-drug tests on unsuspecting civilians – the works.'

'What do you think I should do about this?' she asked him simply.

'A sensible person would forget he or she had ever heard this, and would go back to wherever they came from. But since you're a reporter, I guess that isn't likely,' he said with the first touch of humour since they had met. 'Why don't you get a British TV company to run the story? Or a Canadian one. Maybe a Mexican paper, or something. Then the American press can pick up on it.'

'Why is Marc Sandal in trouble? Was it the piece in the *Washington Post*?' she persisted, but she could see she had lost Redman. He glanced at his watch and made as if he was going to get up.

'I've got to go now,' he said with a nervous blink. 'Please don't drop me in the shit.'

'OK,' Charlotte answered as she got to her feet. 'Thank you for coming to see me. I'll do my best to make a proper story out of this, but it'll be hard without witnesses.'

'I know,' he said sheepishly. 'Bye.'

She sat down again and watched him disappear into the crowd. The rational part of her brain told her to reject the entire fable, but her instinct said he was on the level. Then she remembered the cameraman, and looked for him across the Plaza. When she gave a slight wave, he dropped the camera from his shoulder. A moment later he was by her side and had handed her the tape.

'Nice clean sound,' he announced with the pride of a skilled artist. 'Not many people around so I got a fairly uninterrupted line. He had his face covered with his hands a bit too much – you know, scratching his nose or whatever – but you can still see it's him.'

Charlotte thanked the cameraman and watched as he too walked away. Then she wrote *Int. Don Redman. GT.* on the tape label and put it in an envelope with a note instructing that a block be superimposed on his face and that his voice be disguised. But why would anyone believe him, when even she was unconvinced? Then she felt a wave of terror; the jet-lag had worn down her internal grit, and she felt young and frightened and exposed to danger once more. Where to run, where to hide, who to believe? Then she thought of the one person who knew GT inside out.

'Where are you?' asked Ed Stanfield. 'I'll come and get you.'

'No, it's OK,' she said, glancing about as if she expected a monster to plant a scaly hand on her shoulder. 'But I really need a drink.'

'Come to my office at five. Is that OK? What the hell's happened? You sound awful.'

'I've just interviewed someone who's told me a terrifying story, and I don't know what to do.'

'You did a TV interview? What about? Who for?'

'I'm trying to pull a story together, something I mentioned to you before,' she said cryptically. 'I haven't got enough meat to take it to a station yet, but what I'm hearing is creepy, and I don't know if I'm being set up.'

'Come here and we'll talk. Now, you take care, OK?' he added with a concern that Charlotte appreciated under the circumstances.

When she hung up she glanced at her watch. Four-fifteen. By the time she had negotiated the traffic down to Wall Street, it'd probably be near five anyway. She grasped her handbag close to her body and walked towards Sixth Avenue.

At exactly five she stepped out of the lift and into the Doughty McMurchy reception and asked for Ed. He appeared almost immediately and rushed towards her with his arms held out. 'Sounds like you've been through hell,' he murmured as he gave her a hug. 'Let's go get a drink.' She nodded, lost for words.

'It's so good to see you again,' he told her as they threaded their way through the bustle of commuters who were heading for the subway home. 'I thought you might have forgotten me.' He gave her a crooked smile and caught her hand for a quick squeeze, only a second, but a gesture invested with feeling. She couldn't help but grin, and a bit of the terror wore off. When she was alone she doubted her own sanity, questioned her every reaction. Now that she had a human shield she could let her guard down, and try to keep events in proportion.

Ed led her to the South Street Seaport, a pier that had housed Fulton fish-market before it was yuppified in the eighties. Now the wrought-iron building was stiff with cappuccino bars, restaurants and boutiques.

'Can we sit out here for a minute, Ed? I feel a bit faint,' Charlotte said pointing to a bench at the end of the pier overlooking the East River. He seemed surprised, but followed her. She perched on the edge of the bench, and glanced at his attentive face. 'Please don't think I'm crazy, Ed, but this is what I've been told about Dermitron, the GT thing.' She saw his eyebrows twitch with doubt, so she rushed on. 'I know you told me it was rubbish when we talked about it before. But listen first.'

'OK,' he said, keeping any note of judgement from his voice.

'I've been told Dermitron is a fertiliser for drug crops in Central and South America, and it's going to be sprayed on them to warn away the drug-task forces that are part of the President's initiative. You know what I'm talking about?' She turned and saw him nod thoughtfully. 'The point is, Dermitron will do serious damage to the locals, if not kill them.' She hesitated and searched his impassive face for reaction. 'That's what I was told,' she added feebly, thinking it sounded ridiculous, and wondering why she had believed a word of it in the first place. She fiddled with her dangling silver earrings, and waited for Ed to tell her she'd been taken for a ride.

He sat back and scrutinised the warehouses on the Brooklyn side of the river, and he seemed to be choosing his words with care. 'OK, Charlotte, it's time for some facts of life. And I'm not going to bullshit you.' He spoke in a firm, if patronising manner. 'Yes, this *is* more than a fertiliser. Sure, it'll protect the interests of drug barons in poor, lawless, disgusting countries thousands of miles from here. OK,' he repeated, his hands spread out as if he were admitting guilt. Then he paused and looked back over his shoulder at the pier behind them.

'What is it?' Charlotte asked.

'Nothing. Listen, the reality is there's no serious money in military equipment. or even nerve gas these days. There's too much cheap, ex-Soviet crap floating around the world market. GT'll go out of business if it tries to compete, so it's got to find other avenues to survive – and to keep thousands of Americans employed and paying taxes. Did you know that a million people have lost their jobs in the defence industry since the end of the Cold War? A *million*,' he emphasised. She tossed her head, as if she took the remark as a personal sting.

'Charlotte,' he persisted kindly, but relentlessly, 'the real money is in drugs; seventeen billion dollars' worth a year in the US alone. And if you think that you're going to get at the root of the problem just by digging up a few plants, then you're as idealistic as the President.' He reached across for her hand, but she drew it on to her lap and kept it knotted angrily in a fist as he continued.

'The problem of drugs is not supply, but demand: simple highschool economics. If any Government wants to wage war on drugs, it'll stop these young airheads becoming addicts in the first place. But you know what's been happening in cities across this country? Drug rehab clinics are turning away people because they don't have the resources to treat them. They're saying to junkies who are begging to be cured, "Sorry, guys. Come back in six months when we can afford to see you".

'Charlotte,' he said again, and tried to wrest her gaze from the Brooklyn Bridge, 'that's the real politics.' He sounded exasperated as he registered her silent defiance. Then he shifted around to face her so he was sitting sideways on the bench, still trying to make eye contact.

'And I'll tell you the other financial reality, and that's the people getting big bucks from drug interests: politicians, businessmen, respected members of the community, the CIA, the FBI, and naturally the Pentagon. Why do you think that George Bush personally insisted that Noriega was on the CIA's pay roll, and doubled his remuneration? How do you imagine so much crack finds its way into the country every day? Do you really believe the coastguards are well-manned and given all the resources they need to fight the drug trade? You reckon they can cover every entry point into the US? How did Miami get so rich, if it wasn't by laundering drug money?'

She shook her head, and shut her eyes wilfully, as if she could make his words stop.

'The drugs will keep flowing in because so many people have been bought off, here and in the producer countries. Even Fidel fucking Castro is a drug-runner. So are the M-l9 guerrillas in Columbia. This is the biggest money around,' he said with irritation. 'Military sales are just chicken-shit in comparison.'

'But the President won't stand by as drug barons spray Dermitron on these peasants,' Charlotte retorted, like a six-year-old having a temper tantrum.

'Drug barons? Charlotte, we're talking about countries where Marxists terrorise the population all the time, with kidnappings and assassinations, setting off bombs to make their cranky political statements, while the so-called governments in these places can't even maintain order beyond the suburbs of their own capital cities. It'll be obvious to anyone who's interested, that the guerrillas are to blame. Maybe rival drug barons,' he explained slowly, as if he was a man of infinite patience.

'And if you seriously think the Pentagon will go along with some form of military intervention in these hell-holes, then you should get a fuller understanding about the way this country is run. No President will sanction a foreign invasion to clean out a drug ring. You know that more drugs have flowed in from Panama since Noriega was captured, don't you? The Panama invasion had everything to do with Bush's poll rating and Noriega's bloody-minded independence, and nothing to do with drugs. Now, after that lecture I hope you realise you're into something brutal, and these people are not going to leave you alone until they know they can trust you to be silent.'

'Oh come on, Ed. They want me dead, wouldn't you say?' she said, turning to look at him with eyes that burned with anger.

'I'll tell you what they want: they want to know you'll never blather about Dermitron. Simple. Just shut up and give them that tape you made today, and everything will be OK,' he said in a fatherly manner.

'How do you know this?' she asked. Then she sat back and looked at him as if he had changed appearance in front of her. 'What makes you so sure?'

He sighed. 'OK. The truth. Give me the tape, and I'll give it to them. You don't want to know why, or how, but I'll set things straight.'

'So, once you've worked for the CIA you never stop – is that it, Ed?' she asked, incredulous and angry. 'Did you let them know about my interview at ABC this morning? Is that why they were there?'

Ed clicked his tongue in disgust. 'Don't be ridiculous – I'm on your side. I thought you realised that,' he added more gently. 'The CIA isn't after you: it's GT's clients. I don't know who they are, but let's just say I have contacts, and I can assure you that if you give me that tape you'll be OK. I'll take care of everything, right now, this afternoon. No more being hunted across the world,' he said sympathetically as he saw how his words had hit home.

Charlotte hung her head in her hands and sobbed. 'I can't take it,' she whimpered, her shoulders shaking. When she looked up her cheeks were wet with tears. 'What on earth am I supposed to do, Ed? I know I can't make this story stand up, and I've run out of places to hide.'

'Oh honey,' said Ed, putting his arm around her shoulder and hugging her close to him. 'Stop that crying. It's going to be OK. But I've got to have that tape you made. That's the price they'll want,' he added with a squeeze of her shoulders.

She nodded, and reached into her handbag for a tissue to dry away the tears. Then she took a deep breath and tried to stop the outpouring of emotion as he talked on, soothingly, reassuringly, quietly.

'I understand what you've been through, but it doesn't have to carry on. Now, you give me the tape, I'll make a phone call or two, and it'll be all right. Then you can get on with living your life, and incidentally, paying more attention to me.' He smiled, and looked at her encouragingly. 'You know, I'd make a pretty good bodyguard.'

'You win,' said Charlotte with a sigh, and a final miserable shake of her head. 'Here it is.' She opened her handbag once more and he glanced into its messy but commodious interior. 'It's in the envelope.'

Ed retrieved the package, and felt it carefully for a moment as if checking that it was indeed a video tape. Charlotte had addressed it to herself in London. 'Good,' he muttered, as much to himself as to her. Then he looked back over his shoulder at the pier.

'What's wrong?' asked Charlotte.

'Shall we go and have that drink?' he responded. 'Or do you want me to get on the line to Mount Laurel?'

They stood up, and Charlotte ran her fingers through her hair in an attempt to bring some order to her jetlagged appearance. 'Both,' she said wearily. 'You call, then I deserve a drink.'

They walked side by side along the pier towards the wrought-iron market building.

'Just a moment,' he said and stopped in his tracks.

She turned back to look at him. 'What's wrong?' she asked, but her words had failed to penetrate his barrier of preoccupation. Then for a split second his eyes shifted slightly to the right, to an area over her shoulder, in the distance. She swung around in time to see two men, perhaps a hundred feet away, jogging towards them.

When she pivoted back, Ed's eyes had gone a cold, clear, empty blue, like shards of ice. Just as he put his arm out to grab her, she threw herself into battering-ram mode and plunged past him. With her handbag gripped across her chest like a machine gun she headed for the opposite side of the market building, and what she prayed would be the street end of the pier. However, when she turned a corner, she found herself in a cul de sac with a restaurant at the end of it. To her left was a florist's shop, so she darted quickly inside, looking around frantically. Taking the spiral staircase to the upper level of the shopping mall would be a dumb idea, so she raced across the humid, congested floor, brushing past a jungle of people and ferns to the exit on the other side.

She turned right to where the pier joined land at the foot of Fulton Street, and started running, her chest heaving and her knee muscles complaining. Dozens of office workers were sitting at outdoor cafés: more were pouring off Fulton Street, heading for the pier and its attractions. As Charlotte picked her way between them it was like swimming against a tide. She stopped and swivelled around once, scanning the sea of bobbing heads for Ed's red mop. Instead she saw the sunglasses from ABC. He was fifty feet away, and closing fast.

She pushed forward once more, knocking into people as she went, and getting a few elbows in the ribs for her trouble. When she reached the street with its intersection of three roads she hovered on the kerb, trying to decide which one to choose. Then she saw it: a little yellow light, a free cab, straight ahead on Fulton Street, maybe a block and a half away. She bobbed forward into the road, and heard a horn blare. It sounded as if it was right under her nose, and she leapt backwards to let the car pass. It had happened too fast to scare her, and she threw herself forward again into the middle of the busy road, hugging the central line and waiting for a break in the traffic.

She checked over her shoulder and saw Sunglasses leap off the kerb after her. She hurled herself into the path of a car that stood on its brakes, and made it to the other side on a serenade of horns and yells of abuse. Then she had a free run along the gutter of Fulton Street ahead of her. When the cab was half a block away she raised her arm and started to wave. Then she saw it indicate and turn out of her line of fire, disappearing into a side street.

She dashed across the street and around the corner, praying that it wouldn't speed away. It was there again, and going slow enough that she might reach it, if only she could run faster; if only the cab didn't sail through the green light ahead. The sound of heels behind her echoed on the brick buildings to either side, and as she ran she unzipped her handbag, stuck her hand in, and felt for her trusty penknife. But instead her fingers found a can of hair mousse.

Up ahead the light turned red, and the taxi's brake-lights came on. She caught up to it, and fumbled with the door-handle. Sunglasses was only ten feet away when she catapulted herself on to the back seat and wrenched the door closed behind her.

'Go! Go now! Please!' she screamed at the driver, but he was craning his neck to have a look at what had arrived in the back seat. 'Lock the doors!' she wheezed between breaths. The driver's face was still blank as the Shaded One drew up alongside and yanked open the door.

'Please go! NOW!' Charlotte squealed, her voice deserting its usual register and rising into new territory.

The cab driver took note of the alien presence that had grabbed on to Charlotte's arm, and put the car in gear as she was sinking her teeth into Shade's paw. Then as the cab jolted forward she ripped his glasses off, took aim and squirted a sea of Marks & Spencer's hair mousse foam in his eyes. It was enough to loosen his grip for a second, and with another surge of acceleration he fell out on to the road. Charlotte scrambled across to shut and lock the door, then sank back on to the seat.

'OK, lady? We're outta here,' the driver yelled. 'Where we going to, lady? Where?' he implored.

Charlotte looked behind her at the crumpled figure in the road. Around the corner appeared Ed and his other chum.

'La Guardia airport, please!' she yelled back. 'The satellite terminal for Washington.' But her eyes were glued to her pursuers. They became smaller and smaller as the taxi sped forward, rocking up and down over the bumpy road.

'You OK?' asked the driver as they paused on the corner before turning left towards the Brooklyn Bridge.

'I think so,' she gulped, but then she saw Ed, no more than a stick man now, hailing a taxi.

The minute David emerged from Kennedy Airport's Customs and Immigration, he called Scott Burns at the Washington ABC office. Maurice had warned the American reporter, so he knew why David was calling, but he regretted that he couldn't give him much help. He was expecting Charlotte this evening, but didn't know when. All he was certain of was that his friend would be catching a shuttle from La Guardia. It was at this point that David learned that planes went to the capital from all three airports – Newark, JFK and La Guardia. And that the one he wanted was a twelve-mile cab-ride away. David took down Scott's home number just in case and thanked him hurriedly.

Seven hours after he had run through Heathrow, he was running around JFK. At twenty past five he scrambled into a taxi, and blurted out his destination, adding that it would be worth a great deal to him if the driver went as fast as possible. As he sat by the window letting the warm afternoon air of the Van Wyke Expressway blow against his face, he considered the chances of finding Charlotte before she left for Washington. They were pretty slim, he decided. She could be getting on a shuttle at this moment. He would hang about the terminal, hoping to catch her, then drag her back on the evening flight from JFK to London which left at nine. He had to be on that plane: Verdi's future depended on it, and he could not let down his employees or his investors.

When they pulled up at the La Guardia taxi bay David gratefully stuffed fifty dollars into the mitt of the driver, and sprinted into the terminal building. When he got to the Washington shuttle gate he found a line of people, but Charlotte wasn't one of them. He hovered in front of the airline operatives' desk, and urged them to please, please tell him if Charlotte Carter was on the flight now boarding. It was terribly important, and he had just flown all the way from London to give her a message. This incredible story caused raised eyebrows, but there was no crack in their officious reluctance to divulge the names of passengers.

David found a seat with a good view of comings and goings, and began his vigil, sweeping his eyes across the terminal every few moments. She might arrive late for this flight, he thought, or she might be aiming to get the next one in an hour's time. Either way, he would intercept her on her irrational trip to Washington. What on earth was she trying to achieve, he wondered. Was she crazy enough to confront Zander? Did she expect to bully him into confessing his sins? Didn't she realise the danger? And wasn't going to Washington the silliest of all options?

David surveyed the steady stream of travellers, and became rather annoyed with Charlotte for the stupidity of her mission. Why couldn't she have called him days ago and trusted him, instead of walking into this wasps' nest, he fretted. Then he realised that hiding out at Westhorpe Hall would make her a sitting target, too. He could hardly take her back there.

What, indeed, was going to happen now? he asked himself. Would she return to London with him? Perhaps they could fly to Italy and wait for the storm to blow over. David knew enough obscure corners of Tuscany in which they could go to ground – *after* he had launched the wretched Verdi company tomorrow morning. Was it all feasible? How long could he afford to wait here for her? When would he have to abandon her and return to JFK? When should he call Washington to check if she had arrived there?

His head throbbed with the appallingness of her predicament, which was now his, as he contemplated the mass of humanity in La Guardia airport. The six o'clock flight had gone, and there was still no sign of Charlotte.

'How far now?' Charlotte asked the driver. He jerked his head back to get a good look at his passenger in the rearview mirror. She deserved closer examination, he reckoned, even if she was scared to death, and running away from a very angry man.

‘ ’Bout two miles. They still trailing us?’ he asked in an even, calm Brooklyn voice. He’d seen it all before, and he had half a mind to tell the pretty young woman to just relax and get a decent divorce lawyer.

Charlotte twisted around in the seat and studied the road behind them, but the freeway was too busy for her to see beyond the first few waves of cars to their rear. She gave up and flopped back in the seat.

What now, she wondered as she watched block after block of Queens fly past. Her belongings were still in the hotel’s left luggage, she was headed to La Guardia, and chances were she was being chased. Should she go to Washington where she would be on unfamiliar territory? And put Scott and his wife at great risk?

She knew New York City better, and it was big and easy to disappear into. Perhaps she should trick Ed and his chums into thinking she was catching a plane, then jump into another cab and head back into Manhattan. She could go back to the hotel, hide beneath the blankets, then what? To England? Then where – Finland? How long could she run? How long would it take before GT and its customers became bored with chasing The Outlaw Charlotte Carter, or realised that no one was going to use her story anyway?

She had been praying that Ed would tell her that the Dermitron-drug axis was a set up. Instead he had confirmed Don Redman’s story. How long had Ed been the good ex-operative, passing on what he knew about her and her movements? She fought off the tears, and then the self-pity gave way to pure anger. What a tart he was, she thought as she ground her teeth: all those pretty words and declarations of lust. How she would look forward to getting a big, long, rusty spike and hammering it into his red-haired testicles.

‘Almost there,’ the taxi driver announced, ‘so you wanna get your money ready so you can hit the ground running, huh lady?’

‘Good idea,’ she replied with manic cheerfulness, and smoothed the ten-dollar bills on her knee. What was she going to do? It was decision time: catch the first flight to Galveston, Salt Lake City, or Des Moines, Iowa – or back into Manhattan after a trot around the terminal.

'Good luck!' the driver called after her as she tore into the entrance. But just as he was tucking the bills into his change bag he heard a squeal of brakes and saw three men, one of them with very red eyes, climbing out of a cab that had drawn up behind him. These divorce cases could be murder, he ruminated, and eased his cab out into the traffic.

At first Charlotte was just a blur in the corner of his eye. Then David registered that it was her, and that she was running very fast. He waved, but she kept on going in the opposite direction from the Washington shuttle check-in. He started to run after her, but was quickly overtaken by three men. He began to trail after them, then stopped in his tracks and jogged the other way.

His stay at La Guardia had given him a reasonable idea of the shape of the place, and he reckoned Charlotte was running in a circle – not that she or her pursuers realised it. He went from jogging to running, and headed back to the Washington shuttle check-in, then around one desk further where a crowd was gathering for Boston. He grabbed a luggage trolley, and obscured himself behind a pillar.

A moment later Charlotte ran past him, her face pale, and with terror in her eyes like a fox with a pack of hounds on her scent. He gripped the luggage trolley steering handle, and waited for the footsteps to get closer. Timing would be everything: David tried to imagine he was about to catch an awkward goat, rather than three hard-faced loonies. He thought of goats and threw himself and the trolley into their path.

The metal bars at the front of the cart caught two of the men on the shins, and they crumpled like bowling pins. The one with red hair saw him coming and veered out of the way just in time. David abandoned the trolley and pounded after him. With a lunge that owed its origins to the rugby field of his adolescence, David brought him down with a tackle to the lower legs. They both crashed to the ground, and David scrambled up the man's prostrate body and sat on his back.

'Get a policeman!' he bellowed at the brain-dead airline employee who looked on in horrified stupidity from her check-in desk. 'This man has a gun!' He didn't know if it was true, but assumed it would generate some action. Out of thin air, two large, musclebound security guards appeared and took charge of David's prey. 'There are two more there,' he gasped, pointing at the men who were sitting on the floor rubbing their legs. A third security guard arrived and drew his gun with one hand and got on his walkie-talkie for back-up with the other.

With the three stooges now under supervision, and a considerable crowd spectating, David glanced around. Charlotte was standing by the Washington departure gate, rigid and expressionless like a dummy. He jogged over to her, all smiles and open arms, but she registered only the vaguest hint of recognition. He took her hand, cold as a block of ice, and pressed it to his hot, sweaty cheek. For a moment he wondered if she had forgotten who he was, or had been brainwashed. Or if she was about to faint.

Then she sobbed and threw her arms around his neck, and he felt the full weight of her body sag towards him, like a puppet with its strings cut.

'It's OK. You're going to be all right,' he promised as he squeezed her tight. 'I've got you now, and I'm never going to let you go.' She held him as if she was hanging on for dear life, and whispered his name again and again.

'Come on,' he said as he walked her to the taxi rank outside. 'Let's get out of here before they start asking questions. Have you got your passport? We've a plane to catch.'

Chapter Twenty

James Malpas arrived at Brodie McClean at his usual early hour on Tuesday morning, his high-octane metabolism humming with expectation. The board meeting was scheduled for eleven o'clock, but he had several projects to keep himself busy until then. He began by writing a fax note to Dick Zander, confirming that Martindale acceptances were pouring in.

Then he visited the bank's Press Officer, bearing a coffee and a Danish pastry for the fellow. After a tediously matey conversation James believed he had succeeded in stiffening the bewildered man's resolve that the BBC's inquiries were to be ignored. James did not add that the reporter who was digging around probably wouldn't have the faintest idea how an offshore nominee account worked, so no proof would ever be found.

By eight-thirty Malpas was back in his office, and finding it hard to keep still. He paced back and forth by the window, running through a mental checklist of board members for the umpteenth time and wondering if the vote would be too close to call. He pulled the original list out of his pocket, and as he counted the declared supporters he tried to relax. The chairmanship was his; even if three of his backers were lying, James still had enough solid support around the table to win the vote. This would be a marvellous morning, he told himself.

As if his boardroom coup wasn't enough for one day, James was expecting a report from the Verdi news conference. An embargoed press release was due on the wire services soon. This morning's *FT* had an ill-informed piece on 'processing straw into practical packaging materials'. The article wittered on about excess straw production; no mention of the potential UN ban on polystyrene. The *FT* had missed the point entirely, he sneered inwardly. Or perhaps Stone was misleading everyone until the last moment. The *FT* would have to eat its words when the City realised that the man had a virtual licence to print money . . . And James Malpas had a share of it. He grinned at the thought, and tried to concentrate on more mundane matters.

Fiona Malpas was startled by the knock at the front door, and glanced at her watch. A quarter to ten. The officers from the Fraud Squad, a man and a woman who looked equally uneasy, introduced themselves and said they would be grateful for a word with her. Fiona led them into the sitting room, and having offered them coffee which they politely refused, she perched on the edge of the sofa.

'We're looking into the circumstances surrounding a bid for two companies, William Stone and Son, and Martindale, by an American firm.' The woman read from a spiral-bound notebook. Her words were received with glacial blankness from Fiona Malpas. 'Stock Exchange trading records show you took a stake in both companies just before they were bid for.' The woman paused and watched Fiona's smooth, ivory brow wrinkle. 'We've crosschecked the Stock Exchange files with both companies' records. Now, obviously as your husband was involved in both bids—'

'Then why aren't you speaking to him?' Fiona interrupted gently, and with a gesture that was only half-executed. Her hand settled back in her lap and tightened into a tense little fist. 'I'm afraid I really don't understand a word you've been saying. I haven't bought any shares.'

The Fraud Squad officers tried not to exchange glances. 'But the Stock Market transactions show very clearly that Fiona Carmichael bought shares in both companies. Fiona Carmichael is your maiden name, isn't it?' the woman asked with an arched eyebrow.

'Yes, but I didn't buy any shares.'

The woman flicked through her notebook. 'You have a dealing account with a stockbroker in Bristol, Mrs Malpas, and it appears that hardly a week goes by when you don't trade options or shares.'

Fiona examined the white knuckles in her lap for a moment. When she glanced up at the woman officer the polite smile looked as if it might dissolve into a scream. 'My husband opened that account eight or nine years ago,' she said in a tight, precise voice. 'He suggested that I use it to apply for share allocations when the big utilities were privatised. Which I did – BT and British Gas, I think. But I haven't touched the facility since.'

'So you have no records, and no knowledge of this?' the woman said, peering into her interviewee's eyes. Fiona blinked as if she had just dismissed an idea, then stood up.

'Why don't we have a look through my husband's desk? I think he keeps his share-dealing records there, and you might find what you're searching for.'

Five minutes later, when the police had left with the files, she went to the telephone. An unpleasant possibility had just occurred to her. Something far more important to her than James Malpas.

At twenty-five to eleven Tessa announced that she was putting through a call from James's wife. This both surprised and worried him since Fiona never rang him at work. He wondered somewhat tetchily if there was a domestic crisis that he would be expected to sort out. His suspicion was correct; her voice was shaking with emotion, as if she had suffered a terrible shock and was struggling to hold herself together.

'I've just called the estate agent—' she said in a hysterical rush, but her husband cut her off.

'We'll talk about this later,' he barked, in a tone that left her in no doubt that he was livid with her. 'I've got the board meeting now, and I can't have this on my mind.'

'I don't give a damn about your board meeting,' she interrupted. 'Where is my money? Where is the loan I arranged?' Her voice was wild, harsh. 'Have you used it to pay off one of your little boys? Or is this more insider trading in my name? The police have just been here, James, and I'm ringing my solicitor now. Then I'm going to put this place on the market, and buy that farmhouse. And you won't be able to do a thing about it.'

Malpas slammed down the phone and buried his head in shaking, perspiring hands. It seemed utterly impossible that Fiona could have yelled those obscenities at him; malleable, docile Fiona. He clenched every muscle in his body, willing his self-control to return. His mind must clear of all else but the board meeting. This had to be the performance of his life.

He paced around the office trying to quieten his fevered brain. Had the police linked him with those offshore nominee accounts? How could they, without issuing a 212 Notice? Or had Fiona denied buying the shares that he had purchased in her name? He would break her neck when he got home, the fucking disloyal bitch – except that she probably wouldn't be there . . .

Tears of fury had filled his eyes when the words '*Verdi embargoed*' appeared in the corner of his terminal and flashed at him. He called the full text on to his screen and began to read it. He was wading through the rubbish about the environment when his telephone rang. Tessa eventually picked it up in the outer office, and James glanced at his watch. He would have to read the details later, after the board meeting. He slipped on his jacket, his eyes still skimming over the press release on his screen.

'James!' bellowed Tessa. 'Telephone.'

'No!' he snapped as he re-read the paragraph about cardboard boxes. 'Tell them to call back after the board meeting.' What on earth was meant by 'a straw-based substitute for cardboard', he wondered. There was still no reference to the UN or polystyrene or hamburger boxes, and he was already threequarters of the way through the blurb.

'James, pick up the telephone. It's important,' his secretary sang out again.

'What do they mean about cardboard?' Malpas muttered to himself. He stood up straight and glared down at the terminal. Not a single mention of styrene monomers, nor the multi-million-dollar takeaway food-packaging market. 'What the fuck do they mean about *cardboard made from straw*?' he growled out loud. He opened his desk drawer and fished around for the prospectus and offer papers that Nick Durridge's company had circulated. James never had time to read this kind of bumph, not when he already knew what he was doing. 'What is this FUCKING CARDBOARD?' he said again, as he leafed frantically through the prospectus.

'James, for God's sake!' Tessa yelled. 'It's your doctor, and he says he must talk to you. He wants to fix an appointment to see you as soon as possible.'

'I haven't got a bloody doctor,' he screamed through the open door. His eyes blazed when he found the product description paragraph in the prospectus. There it was: 'Cardboard made from straw', just as David Stone had been saying all along. He turned back to the screen where the same words appeared throughout the press release. 'I didn't take out a quarter of a million pound loan just to invest in bleedin' cardboard,' he barked, his accent slipping like unelasticated socks.

In the outer office, Tessa was busy explaining that Mr Malpas had an important meeting in a minute, and could the doctor tell her why it was so important that he should come to the phone at that moment. James remained riveted to the spot, clenching his fists as if he was about to destroy the terminal, ignoring his secretary's well-bred voice completely.

'James, you have to pick up the phone,' Tessa insisted. 'This is the doctor who did the medical insurance check-up last week. He's got to see you as soon as possible to discuss something he's found in the course of your blood test. 'Now please pick up the phone!' she shrieked, losing patience. 'You have to go round there to the surgery today.'

James turned away from the news terminal, red in the face and shaking. 'What?!' he shouted. Then in a fresh rush of anger he snatched up the telephone, ready to tell the bloody doctor to go to hell.

'Mr Malpas, this is Dr Adams,' the rather strained voice began. James rolled his eyes impatiently, wishing that the fool would get on with it. 'I must see you about something that's come up in your blood test.'

At that moment the Malpas temper boiled over and he told the doctor abruptly: 'I'm due to address a very important meeting right now, so I'm afraid we'll have to talk later.'

'Mr Malpas, this is more important,' the doctor replied, stressing each word carefully. 'I'd like you to come to my office immediately. This is very serious—'

'I'm sorry to contradict you, Doc—,' James interrupted with a furious snort, but this time it was Adams who had been pushed beyond the limits of civility. Then James listened, and he recalled that ill-judged moment of sensual abandon in The Mineshaft in New York. At the end of the conversation he slumped into his chair, like a dangling corpse that had been cut down from a scaffold.

When Dick Zander reached his office in New Jersey at seven-thirty, he found two fax messages from London waiting on his desk. The first one was from James Malpas, and he skimmed over its contents without interest. The second was from the Head of Corporate Finance at Morton's merchant bank. It consisted of one paragraph – a quote from the Verdi press release – and it brought a broad grin to Zander's face. He did a quick calculation and worked out that it would be eleven-thirty p.m. in England. He picked up the phone and dialled.

'It's a relief to know it wasn't a Trojan Horse after all,' the American said when he got through to the banker, and sighed as if an enormous weight had been lifted from his shoulders. 'I had a nagging suspicion at the back of my mind that David Stone was bluffing, you know. And when you told me about Malpas putting his own money in I was sure he was really on to something.' He kicked his heels up on his desk, relishing the prospect of James Malpas's discomfort.

'I imagine he'll be rather disappointed this morning,' the Englishman laughed. 'A Trojan Box rather than a Trojan Horse, I think.'

Zander glanced at the fax that had been sent to New Jersey earlier this morning. 'It looks like Brodie McClean are pretty near to wrapping up Martindale,' he told the banker, 'so let's get down to business.' He flicked through his desk diary with his free hand. 'When can your people come over here to run through the break-up options? Next week any good to you?'

The Director from Morton's made unctuous noises about how keen his team were to present their ideas on the wholesale dismemberment of both Martindale, and William Stone & Son. They could be in Mount Laurel next Monday morning, he assured Zander.

'It'll be a regular garage sale, won't it?' the American mused, and stroked the leather armrest of his chair. 'I want everything ready and in place for the moment we complete the purchase of Martindale.' He hesitated as if he was deliberately tormenting the Englishman. 'Then we'll announce that we're dropping Brodie McClean and switching to you guys,' he added.

The Corporate Financier made more ingratiating remarks about how pleased Morton's were, to be allowed the opportunity to work with so esteemed a business as GT. 'I'm grateful to you and Mr Clark for giving us this chance to—'

'But I'm grateful to *you* for letting me know what Malpas was up to,' Zander interrupted gently. 'We would never have found out if it hadn't been for the diligence of your people, the Manager of your Ethical Fund in particular, of course. You will pass on my sincere thanks, won't you?' Zander paused and rubbed his recently-shaved chin, thinking how plausible his disingenuous innocence had sounded. 'Amazing that Malpas threw so much of his own cash into this Verdi thing.'

'I can't imagine what he was up to,' the man at Morton's sniffed.

Zander had no such trouble identifying Malpas's motivation. 'He's just another greedy banker,' he would have loved to say to his new adviser, but he remained his usual polite self, and said he was looking forward to meeting the Morton team on Monday.

When he had finished the conversation, Zander leaned back as far as he could and shut his eyes with satisfaction. Out of his encyclopaedic music memory came Ella Fitzgerald singing 'It's Only A Paper Moon' and he toyed with the melody for a moment. Then he remembered that there was someone else who would be relieved to hear about Verdi. He glanced at his watch and sat up straight at his desk. No one from the Pentagon got to work this early, so he looked out Vagg's home number.

'Well, Colonel,' he began affably when he got through to Vagg's Virginia condo, 'that English product is nothing more dangerous than cardboard made from straw. David Stone was on the level all the time. It's OK. No styrene-monomer ban.'

'Thank Christ for that,' the rough, nicotine-tortured voice remarked. 'Trust that sonofabitch Sandal to get it wrong. Mind you, little bastard had me worried for a while. What about that English reporter?'

'*Niente*. She's back in England – a foul-up at the airport, I'm afraid,' Zander explained. 'The tape we got from her was nothing to fret about, by the way. She interviewed a nerd at Columbia who gave her some basic chemistry. God knows why she wanted it so badly. We lost her when she left ABC, and picked her up later on with one of our operatives. She told him quite a tale about the person she'd interviewed, but none of it was on the tape. Anyway, we'll take care of it,' he added wearily.

'Better do that,' Vagg commented and paused. Zander heard his client take a puff at his cigarette, then laugh. 'You *will* deal with it, won't you Dick? We can't let this drag on.'

'Yeah, don't worry,' said Zander calmly, with what he hoped sounded like cool authority. 'The situation is under control. Anyway, Dermitron lives to fight another day.'

'Great,' the Colonel said, savouring the good news. 'When can you start deliveries?'

Paul Roberts received a phone call from his Cambridge tutor at about the time that the Brodie McClean board meeting was due to begin. He hadn't expected such a quick response to his letter about the part-time teaching post, and he assumed the college authorities wanted to set up an interview as soon as possible. His tutor sounded rather uncomfortable as they made small talk about the test match, however, and Paul wondered if he had been deputed to raise the awkward subject of remuneration with Paul. The college was probably terrified that their alumnus would expect the same astronomical salary he had been earning in the City. They would be pleasantly surprised by his humility, he thought.

'I gather you've written to the bigwigs about coming back here,' his tutor said, finally biting the bullet.

'Yes,' Paul responded with a smile in his voice. 'I know I'm turning down a lot here, but money isn't everything,' he laughed.

'No,' the tutor replied at length, and Paul realised his hunch about the salary had been right. 'It's a matter of vacancies, really,' the man continued in his halting voice. 'There, er, aren't any. Except a part-time teaching post.'

'Yes, that's what I was interested in,' Paul confirmed.

'Well, the thing is, we've been inundated by applications from blokes like yourself, in the City, you know, analysts who're bored, or who've been made redundant. There's more supply than demand,' he chuckled nervously.

'Oh.' Paul wasn't quite sure if he had understood.

'That's why I'm calling,' the man continued, 'just so you won't be disappointed, Paul. We can't offer you anything. It's strange, you know. First we lost everyone to the Square Mile in the eighties; now the tide's turned and they want to come back. Anyway, sorry, Paul. You're best staying where you are, I think.'

'Thanks,' the analyst replied bravely. 'I'm sure you're right. I was just considering it anyway.' He paused and tried to sound blasé. 'It was just an idea, really.'

Epilogue

Five days later, Jonathan Slope was in an editing suite in the Spur at BBC Television Centre putting the final touches to his piece on the downfall of James Malpas, when a messenger from the newsroom darted in and handed him a package.

Jonathan glanced at the envelope without interest, only vaguely registering the American stamps. Then he noticed the handwriting. He had seen it once before, on the anonymous envelope that had so kindly brought him the Brodie McClean offshore account scam. He held up his hand and indicated that the messenger was to hang on for a second while he opened the package.

Inside was a tape with *Int. Don Redman. GT.* written on the label. A piece of paper gave instructions to disguise Redman's voice and face. Slope handed it to the VT editor at his side. 'Can we look at this now?'

The VT editor turned it over in his hand and frowned. 'We'll have to have it transposed first,' he remarked doubtfully. 'It's on American VT. Doesn't work on this gear.'

While the messenger was dispatched to find the right machine, Jonathan turned back to the screens in front of him. He was viewing the rushes of a press conference this morning, at which Fraud Squad officers had announced that Malpas was facing prosecution for insider-dealing prior to GT's bid for William Stone & Son, and Martindale. And on sundry other counts: Slope's great exposé, and a true moment of glory.

The BBC reporter had been planning to include an interview with David Stone in his Malpas piece, a sort of 'serves the bastard right' pay-off at the end. But that was not to be. Jonathan fingered the sheet of paper that he had printed off the wire terminal's business news before he had left the newsroom earlier, and ran his eyes over the catch-line; BRITISH BUSINESSMAN KILLED IN ITALY.

The report went on, '*David Stone, 38, of Ely, Cambridgeshire died in a motor-accident in Tuscany on Sunday morning. Italian police say Stone's car plunged off a rural hillside road and into a valley near Siena. Initial investigations reveal possible brake failure. Stone was Managing Director of William Stone & Son plc, recently the target of a bid from American company Global Technologies. Stone had also completed the private financing and launch of Verdi Packaging last week. Police say he died instantly. Also involved was another Briton, Charlotte Carter, 28, of London, who was a passenger in the car, and who died some hours later in hospital. Colleagues say Stone and Carter had planned to marry, and were on the third day of a two-week holiday in Italy. Ends.*'

Jonathan would have to record his own pay-off instead, and stick it after the clip of the new Brodie McClean Chairman. Charles Ravenscroft had rapidly distanced himself and the bank from Malpas, and promised a clean sweep of the Corporate Finance Department.

Jonathan was jotting down a couple of lines of script when his producer bustled into the editing suite. 'You've got to hurry it along,' she babbled. 'South Africa's missed its satellite so you're lead. Are you nearly finished?'

The reporter's eyes narrowed testily. 'I'm going up on the roof to record a pay-off,' he began, but the producer shook her head angrily.

'No time to put your ugly face on it. Just do a voice-over some film of Malpas or something.'

Slope glared at her as she phoned the editor; he hated missing a chance to show the viewers who had created his masterpieces. He'd never be a household name if he couldn't stick his face on the screen. The producer had just hung up when the messenger returned with the transposed mystery video.

'What's this?' the producer asked in disbelief. Jonathan slotted the video into the player and waved impatiently at the VT editor to start the tape. 'What are you doing, Jonathan? We've got to get this piece done now!'

Then she noticed the reporter sit up and stare at the screen as he recognised Charlotte Carter on a bench talking to a tall man. 'No,' he said as if he was in a trance. 'This is important.'

'Try again. "*Mi scusi, signora, dov'è la cattedrale, Per favore*?".'

'*Tosca La Bohème Rigoletto*?' she began, and broke into giggles. 'This is pathetic! I'm never going to get the hang of this language.'

'But you have to, *cara mia*, or you'll never be able to order the simplest thing in a shop or find your way around.'

She frowned prettily, and then turned her face into the full glare of the sun. 'Oh, let's have another drink, then get some lunch.'

'Say it.'

'You beast. OK, *ancora due vino bianco per favore, e prendare mangiare subito*.'

'Truly *terribile!* But lunch is an excellent idea. I'll see if Gianni'd like to join us. He might have heard something.'

'I'm sure he'd let us know if some Americans were ringing him up and asking for coroner's reports,' she said, and stretched out her brown legs with a sigh of satisfaction. 'God, it's tough hiding out at a Tuscan farmhouse with its own pool and vineyards.'

'Just thank Gianni,' he commented after another sip of Gavi di Gavi.

'Yesss,' she drawled. 'Tell me, do you keep in touch with all your former students from Florence, or just the sons of the local chief of police? Now I understand how Italy functions.'

'Don't knock it, *Bella Bambina*. With a few connections you can achieve anything here. I think I'll call Gianni.'

'And I'll ponder more important matters: *pomodori e mozzarella ed avocado con oregano ed olio*.'

'Why is it that you have a perfect command of all Italian words that describe food, yet you're absolutely hopeless at asking where the ethnological museum is?'

'I can't imagine. Now, where was I? *Funghi sott'olio, fettuccine alla marinara*—'

'What a uniquely greedy young woman. And how lucky I am to have found her,' he said as he got to his feet, and kissed her tanned forehead. 'But one enduring question remains: how does she stay slim?'

'Ah, well, it must be all the bonking.'

'Perhaps I'll ask Gianni to join us for dinner this evening instead,' he said as he paused in the doorway of the farmhouse. 'How about a little *antipasto* right now?'